The Key in the Lock

'Dark, clever and utterly enthralling, this is historical fiction – and storytelling – at its absolute best' Elizabeth Macneal

'A masterclass in atmosphere . . . haunting, vivid and urgent, like *The Witchfinder's Sister*, *The Key in the Lock* demands to be devoured whole' Stacey Halls

'Underdown's latest is a gothic mystery of the highest order. Chilling, sad, beautiful and so elegantly conjured, it's a story that summons Du Maurier but retains ghosts all its own. I raced through it, my heart in my mouth. Superb' Emma Stonex

'A Cornish landscape evocative of Daphne du Maurier . . . brilliantly plotted' Louise Hare

'I was captivated by the characters, the story and the sinuous, seamless plotting' Sarah Hilary

'I was completely enthralled by this poetic, beautifully conceived and executed mystery full of secrets and subtlety' Imogen Robertson

'Deliciously intriguing from the very first sentence, with shades of Du Maurier and Dunmore. I was hooked by this exquisitely written tale of secrets and lies' Sara Collins

'Reads as if a classic. Eerie, immersive and compelling. This is a book to savour' Essie Fox

'Engrossing . . . conveys emotion and excitement so elegantly' Adèle Geras

'Its eerie, claustrophobic atmosphere is reminiscent of Du Maurier . . . there's a poignancy to the writing that's so beautiful' Emma Carroll

'Atmospheric, dark and compelling: an exquisitely crafted mystery' Tammy Cohen

'Marve

LONDO D0026393 3

Praise for Beth Underdown's haunting debut,
The Witchfinder's Sister

'A compelling debut from a gifted storyteller' Sarah Perry

'Beth Underdown grips us from the outset . . . at once a feminist parable and an old-fashioned, check-twice-under-the-bed thriller' Patrick Gale

'A richly told and utterly compelling tale, with shades of Hilary Mantel' Kate Hamer

'Atmospheric and filled with foreboding, it's a novel that draws you under its spell' *Stylist*

The Key in the Lock

BETH UNDERDOWN

PENGUIN BOOKS

PENGUIN BOOKS

UK | USA | Canada | Ireland | Australia
India | New Zealand | South Africa

Penguin Books is part of the Penguin Random House group of companies
whose addresses can be found at global.penguinrandomhouse.com.

First published by Viking 2022
Published in Penguin Books 2023
001

Copyright © Beth Underdown, 2022

The moral right of the author has been asserted

Typeset by Jouve (UK), Milton Keynes
Printed and bound in Great Britain by Clays Ltd, Elcograf S.p.A.

The authorized representative in the EEA is Penguin Random House Ireland,
Morrison Chambers, 32 Nassau Street, Dublin D02 YH68

A CIP catalogue record for this book is available from the British Library

ISBN: 978–0–241–99173–2

www.greenpenguin.co.uk

MIX
Paper from
responsible sources
FSC® C018179

Penguin Random House is committed to a
sustainable future for our business, our readers
and our planet. This book is made from Forest
Stewardship Council® certified paper.

For Chris

I still dream, every night, of Polneath on fire. Smoke unravelling from an upper window, and the terrace bathed in a hectic orange light. And every morning I wake, convinced that Tim is under my bed.

Thirty years have elapsed, since the business at Polneath. I have married Richard, given birth to Tim, mothered him and watched him grow, but I see now that the decision I made at Polneath was the only decision of my life. Everything marred in that one dark minute.

I have got as far as I can, now, with writing it down, but the dream will not shift, and the feeling of Tim beneath the bed every morning grows, if anything, more distinct. I suspect it is because the Polneath business is not finished, still. Not yet.

I cannot say where it will end.

But I know perfectly well where it began: with the stopped mills amongst the damp trees, the silent house, and the death of a child. Somebody else's son. The kitchen clock in my father's house, ticking on past midnight. Tea on the table, well stewed, and the coals in the grate subsiding comfortably. And a woman – a girl, really – nineteen years of age, with her three good frocks and her habit of biting her index finger. Myself, as the flames licked upwards a mile away, looking at the clock, and waiting.

I.

1918

Our son Tim was killed in February. Ten months ago, now. This is the first Christmas, and in that sense alone was always bound to be difficult.

Today is the 23rd, and only this afternoon did I make the customary garlands for the dining room fireplace. Jake brought in the greenery and deposited it on the floor of the study, with a nervous glance at me. I suppose he is still wary, after the trouble I have caused these last weeks. At any rate, he brought in his armful of ivy and mistletoe and willow, as I'd asked him to, without a word, as though he were any other servant.

Making the belated decorations, I found a spider's egg sac frozen amongst the foliage, which turned to a kind of dust as I touched it, making me shudder, leaving me sad at its ruined hopes. I finished the garlands quickly, and had Mrs Fossett pin them up, though of course I eat alone these days – breakfast, luncheon, dinner, the chair opposite quite empty. Nobody to enjoy the garlands but me. I do not think the Fossetts care much about garlands, but still I am glad I made them, if only so that something, anything, might be as usual.

Now my painful hands are leaving green marks on the page.

It is dreadful, of course, not to have Tim here, though in fact this will be the third year I have missed seeing his face on Christmas Day: 1915, that was the last time. Tim's training was finished, and in the January, he would be going over. He always liked marzipan on Christmas cake, smooth and thick as a counterpane, but I hadn't been able to get the sugar for it. The afternoon he came home I was still fussing with the cake, how to make it look less bare, while Jake went to the station to collect him. After his previous visit home, I was resolved, this time, to keep an irreproachable grip upon my emotions.

I tried to tell myself I was reconciled to Tim's going. I had held out against his joining up. Then they had come in the summer to make lists of all the men. Only that, only lists, but it suddenly seemed inevitable. Tim had turned nineteen, in any case, and volunteered. Then, a week before his visit, the list makers had come again to the house. I'd told them the truth. That Fossett was over the age; Jake not quite, but that one of his legs was two inches shorter than the other, and he cannot run without pain. I answered the men's questions, Fossett hovering nervously at my back, and told them that they already had our boy. Our only boy.

When Tim arrived he was in uniform, a dreadful, stiff thing; he looked older. He kissed me tenderly and gave me one or two wry looks, while Mrs Fossett brought tea and Richard began to deliver what he considered to be the men's news: smuggling convictions in the district; a mare sold as pregnant who turned out only to have a tumour inside her the size of a grapefruit; disputed fence boundaries. He was thinking of reviewing the rents for the top fields. The drainage needed repair by the bottom road.

I sat, picking the bits of peel out of my cake, and tried to admire Richard's assiduousness, his attention to detail. His ability to be ordinary, even in the face of this. But the dull green-brown of Tim's uniform insisted upon itself, and I looked at Richard, I looked at my own husband, and I thought: he doesn't care. Our son is going to *that*, and he doesn't care.

So I took myself off, as soon as Mrs Fossett put her head in for the plates. I went outside, to the freezing but sunny bench, and tilted my face upward, and felt the light on my closed eyelids, and listened to the voices of the men through the dining room window. There are winter days, in our part of Cornwall, which make a pale, cruel imitation of summer.

After a quarter or half an hour, Tim came out, and sat himself down, and asked how things were faring at my end. Then, more softly, 'How have you been, Mother?' A little touch, on the back of my hand. 'Really, I mean.'

'Oh! Well enough,' I said. And then, 'I've missed you.'

He moved his arm, kindly, dismissively. 'It's no different than when I went up to Oxford, surely.'

I looked at him – of course it was different – and he dipped his head in acceptance.

'In any case,' I said, 'Oxford, you know, I can *imagine* that.'

He accepted this, too, but I instantly regretted having said it, because suddenly it was clear to me, utterly clear, as it can be only to a mother. That despite his loud brave voice and his bright new buttons, he was frightened.

Besides, I had determined not to argue with him any more. I wanted instead to say something to him, something that would make him just get *through* it, would prevent him from being brave. But I did not know what that thing would be. In silence, we watched a blackbird prospecting the lawn, and then he said something about the training having not been so bad.

Then I asked, 'But you don't know where you'll be stationed?'

'They don't tell us. I rather like it.' He was moving his feet around, scuffing his boots, and I almost said a sharp word to him: but of course he was still getting used to them. Perhaps they were painful. I held back from asking about blisters, but I did press his hand, where it rested on the bench. Ridiculous in its solidity, it seems now. So very warm.

'You mustn't worry,' Tim said, and when I didn't answer, shaded his eyes and turned to me. 'I'll write.'

I looked away into the garden and Tim looked, too.

I said, 'Did I tell you? Theo Stainforth's mother says he's getting married.'

Tim shifted on the bench. 'Do pass on my congratulations,' he said, lightly. 'Good old Theo.'

Then Tim went away, and the waiting began. But I was born for that. My great-uncle was a gunpowder maker. St Rumon's is tucked into a fold of land, deep woods stretching up to the open fields and below to the reed beds of the estuary, but though the water is salt there is no sight of the sea. No fishing, here: the village men are employed on the Earl of Falmouth's estate or on the farms. The same families handing down the job of gamekeeper or dairyman, father to son. Or, until the Polneath mills closed, there was powder making – coarse powder for blasting, fine powder for shooting.

Powder makers do little but wait. The incorporators especially, crouching outside their pairs of mills, listening, listening for that catch in the workings which might mean a piece of grit, a spark, disaster. The mill hands could not smoke their tobacco – nor chew, in case it should drown out the sound of the millstones – and so they simply held the stuff, silently, in either cheek. The mark of a St Rumon's man is still a quiet manner, a ghastly brown smile.

At any rate, I waited. I found it easier after Tim left to avoid the news, though Richard read the paper from cover to cover, calm, implacable. And then, of course, most days there were telegrams. They had always been common enough, in our household, with Richard's work, and until Tim went away he had treated them with nonchalance. Fossett would come into the dining room and lay down the little salver, and Richard would thoroughly wipe his lips, place his napkin to one side, and open the message, using his letter knife with precisely his usual exactitude, while Fossett went to ask Jake to bring the car round. But it was different, once Tim was away. The doorbell would ring, and I would jump; and if it was a telegram, Richard would open it quickly, fumblingly, while I looked on.

The day Tim's came, it was as though Richard knew. There was a letter opener at his elbow, but in haste he tore the message with his thumb instead, leaving that cloudy ragged edge on the paper, the exact shape of which I would come to know so well. His lips moved, and he looked up. I let out a small sound, the kind one can't always keep in when the doctor has to do something painful.

KILLED.

Just that.

I didn't understand, about the phrasing, not then. I think perhaps that Richard didn't, either. Men don't pick over these things amongst themselves, the way women do.

*

For some days, I lay face down on my bed. Richard was out a great deal, and I imagined him striding into his club in Falmouth, handing his hat over to be hung up, being greeted by all the other gentlemen whose sons had fallen, as though they had tripped and skinned their knees at rugger.

I imagined them all, condoling, congratulating, while I lay in bed, imagining *how*. Father having been a doctor, I had heard plenty of talk of the powder accidents of past years, which were my nearest comparison. And perhaps it was that association which led me to find myself, in those first days of my grief, thinking of Polneath again. Thinking of Edward Tremain; and then, appalled that I could be thinking at such a time of anything but Tim, tormenting myself all the more with what might have happened to him. Shards of wood bedded deep in the stomach, the bruised organs of a man blown clear. All kinds of seeping, gasping pain.

I pushed Polneath, pushed Edward, out of my mind, and concentrated on fretting and fretting that Tim's death had been slow. It never occurred to me that it might have been shameful; until, a few weeks later, my friend Edith came. It was the first time she had been back to St Rumon's since her father had retired from the parish and moved to join her in London. Her boots were too nice for our late winter dirt, but she was kind. She did not tell me what to be grateful for, nor produce stories of other people and other people's griefs.

She wouldn't have pried, except that she picked up a small blue glass horse she had given me many years before, which had been weighting the telegram to the table. Then she saw it, and looked at me in enquiry, and I nodded, and I watched her read it. The years have scarcely touched Edith, her hair hardly faded, her face the same lovely oval. Altered, as she read, with a frown.

She supplied – reluctantly, after some pressing – that the frown was at the simplicity of it. 'Killed in action', you see, one knew what that meant, and 'died of wounds', too. But 'killed' – well.

Go on, I said.

But she retreated quickly, and replied that it was only that she hadn't seen that form of words before.

A few days later, I failed in my resolve to put Edith's comment out of my mind, and asked the vicar's wife, when she came to return a pudding dish she had borrowed months before. She frowned, just as Edith had, and turned the cut-crystal dish nervously about in her hands. 'Killed in action', she said, meant in the course of duty: quick. 'Died of wounds' was next best: that meant the man had not lingered long, but passed away at a clearing station, or at a hospital just behind the lines. But 'killed': killed meant something unusual, something amiss. More than that, she could not say.

It was easy not to resume the slot in the church flower rota, which I had abandoned when news of Tim had first arrived. Easy, too, to refuse the vicar's wife's kind invitations, and those few others that came from ladies in the district. Easy to shut myself away and fret, until, a week after Easter, another visitor came to give shape to my fretting: Theo Stainforth. Richard had known Theo's father, who had some sort of mining interest. Theo had gone from Truro Grammar up to Oxford the year before Tim, though they had drifted since. But I had continued to correspond occasionally with his mother, and not long after Tim died, I'd learned that Theo had been wounded. He ought to come and see you, his mother had written – only that, he ought to come and see you. And so of course, I had replied. Of course he must come and see us.

I didn't tell Richard until the morning of his visit. When Richard pointed out that I hadn't mentioned it, I said he needn't sit with us, then.

Having avoided visitors for so long, I had to remind myself to look in the mirror before going downstairs, for I was still lying down a great deal during the day. I studied my reflection as the bell rang in the hall, trying to make my hair less of a fright.

I remembered Theo as a kind boy. Rather dim. Solid and sporting, so it was a shock to come downstairs and see a young man, rake thin and missing an arm. Or the lower part at least. Whatever was left below the elbow was tucked, coddled into a sling, as though it might be comforted.

I received him at the front door, Fossett trying to get out of the way, Richard lurking in the hall at my back and Mrs Fossett behind him, come out of the kitchen for a look at this boy who had known Tim.

'It's terribly good of you,' I said, meeting the boy's eyes very pointedly; not looking, not at all, at the arm.

'I'm sorry it's taken me so long,' he said. He moved the sling. 'I got this soon after Tim – but of course, they kept me in hospital a good while . . .'

'How's your wife?' I said.

He smiled, uncertainly. 'She's expecting a child in June.' He saw Richard looking at the arm, and he moved it again, and said, 'Shrapnel. Four days before they could get us back.' With his good hand, he was digging in his watch pocket, and he produced a hard, sharp scrap of something, as big as a shilling. 'Septic,' the boy said.

Richard reached to take the piece of metal. I felt a wave of frustration, waiting there as he examined it, silently handed it back.

'They had to amputate, of course,' the boy said.

'Let's go through,' I said. 'Mrs Fossett will bring us something.'

Theo followed me to the conservatory. Richard stood in the doorway a few moments, but then of course he came in, and sat. Theo's jacket kept trying to fall off his shoulder, where it was draped in an almost coquettish way. It made me think of managing a stole one is not used to, over a gown, at some formal occasion. At any rate, his face contorted briefly in impotent rage as he pulled his jacket straight for the fifth time, before settling again into worried politeness.

First, we gave him tea, while I asked a great many questions about the child. Whether they had a cradle yet, whether they had thought about names. Mrs Fossett had made a simnel cake, which was disastrously crumbly and, I quickly saw, impossible to manage without another hand to hold the plate. The only possibility was not to see the crumbs that the boy was obliged to drop all over himself. Richard did not eat a bite, but only watched him.

When the cake was done with, I said, 'And so, you were stationed near Tim?'

Theo nodded. 'My unit was sent up next to his.' The boy said that they had been days in the line; a strange, quiet, tense part of it that saw little action but frayed the nerves, the Germans being rather close. As it happened, that morning a German patrol had been shot from our trenches, having failed to get back to their lines before dawn broke, so the feeling was worse than usual, of something coming, of something about to break.

'And you were there,' I said. 'When he –'

'Not on the spot,' Theo said, shifting in his seat. 'Is that what Mother –? No.' He looked at me. Said, reluctantly, 'But I did see.'

I looked at Richard, then back at the boy. 'You saw what happened?'

'Yes,' Stainforth said. He looked uncertain now.

I found suddenly that perhaps I did not want to know, after all, that perhaps it was better not to know. But it was too late now.

'It was . . . I'm not sure. Late afternoon,' he continued. Looked down again. 'The sun was setting. I wouldn't have known anything of it, except I had rather a useless fellow on watch, and I went up to check on him.'

'And then?' I said.

Richard was looking at his hands.

'Tim was –' The boy broke off.

'Shot?' Richard said.

'Yes, sir.'

'But how?' I said. 'How, if he was in the trench, safe in the trench?'

Theo paused. 'I suppose he . . . I suppose it rather appeared to me that he . . . stood up.'

'Suppose?' said Richard.

I glanced at Richard. 'You mean, above the –?' I moved my hand, unsure of the word.

Theo looked away, as though there was something worrying him outside the window. 'Yes. His head was over the parapet. I'm afraid I saw him simply stand up, and . . .' The boy stopped, seemed unsure whether to say more. He looked at us, one to the other. There was a long silence. 'The fact is, you're crouched double like that, all the time, and it drives you –'

'Yes, quite,' Richard said.

But I was leaning forward. 'You said the sun was setting. Perhaps he thought he couldn't be seen.'

Theo swallowed miserably. 'It wasn't dark yet.' He looked at me. 'There were no orders to attack.' He stopped, and then murmured, 'There isn't one of us who hasn't felt the urge, you know.'

'To attack?' I said.

But Theo didn't answer. He looked at Richard.

'I was one of the first along,' the boy said, and then he began on how it had been too late, already, by the time he reached Tim; that his mother had thought I might be comforted by that.

Somehow, we all managed to pretend that Theo had not said what he had said, that he had not implied what he had implied, while the car was brought round. I was thinking of the bullet, swift, we knew that now, to the face. Cheekbone, or forehead, or his temple where that little pulse had used to beat, when he was an infant. He had simply stood up. Quick, then, after all. Quick.

At last, Mrs Fossett put her head in.

'Jake will take you back to the station,' I said.

Richard and I both went to the front door, and I raised a hand to the car as it swung round by the hedge, and Theo Stainforth raised his own good hand in reply. That could have been Tim, I thought. A kind wound like that.

The crocuses which Jake had planted were still showing raggedly mauve and blue. It was the first day upon which it was not quite painful to stand in the fresh air. Perhaps that was why I did not shut the front door straight away. Instead, I stood on the step to breathe for a moment, and Richard lingered beside me. The Fossetts, as though they knew what was coming, had made themselves scarce.

Without looking at Richard, I said, quietly, 'What ought we to tell people?'

'About what?'

'Well. What he saw –'

'What he thought he saw,' Richard said, calmly.

I turned. 'You suppose he was mistaken?'

'A great deal has happened to the boy, clearly –' He had stepped back in, gone into his study.

I closed the front door to follow him, halting on the threshold.

'I mean, who knows what went on there.' He gestured to his arm.

'You don't *wish* to know what happened,' I said.

He leaned on the desk with both palms. 'What good would it do?'

Coldly, I said, 'Or you already did know.'

'What on earth are you driving at?'

'You kept it from me. About the telegram. What it means. Mrs Benson told me, that simply "killed" means something queer. You needn't lie –'

'Why on *earth* would I lie?'

'I don't mean lie. I don't mean that.'

He had taken his hands from the desk and stood straight now, facing me.

I looked away from him. 'But we ought at least now to write to some of the officers in Tim's unit . . .' I paused. 'To be certain.'

'We'll do nothing of the kind.'

'See? You *don't* wish to know.'

'You can't ask a man to do his duty,' he said, 'to fight for his country, and then rake over it –'

He was calm again, explaining, as though to a child, and for a moment, I hated him.

'You were the one,' I said, 'who wanted him to serve.'

He had unscrewed his pen, to refill it, but now he stopped in that operation, and stared at me.

'I was trying to make him wait for the call-up,' I said. 'Every day he was in this house I tried to persuade him, and you did nothing.'

Still he kept his calm, laid the halves of the pen down. 'They were conscripting soon after. We don't know that it would have gone any differently. It might have turned out worse.'

'But we could have kept him clear of it. Another week, another month –'

'He wanted to serve with his friends.'

'And you wanted to look well in front of yours,' I said.

He moved then, quick as a coiled spring, and I backed a step into the doorway, frightened, though even now as he spoke, he mastered himself, his voice cold.

'You were the one,' he said, 'who asked what we ought to tell people.'

He pushed the door into my face, gently but firmly, and I was out alone on the cold tiles of the hall, the clock ticking on decorously at the foot of the stairs.

I went upstairs, and lay face down on my bed, eyes shut and leaking. My blouse grew warm and damp and crushed. Not for the first time, I thought that if I could only stay still for long enough, I too might die. All that it would require would be persistence.

But as the light faded in the window, there came a tap at the door. I said nothing, and it opened. I felt Richard sit on the side of the bed, a careful foot away.

'My dear,' he said. 'My dear, come down for some dinner.'

'I'm not hungry,' I replied.

Richard hated losing his temper. That was why he had come up: to make amends for a momentary failure of calm. It maddened me, knowing that, even as I lay there – as did the knowledge that if I came down, if I ate my dinner, Richard would think that order had been restored. That everything was alright.

But my body was betraying me. My stomach growled, and to disguise it I sat up, swung my legs over the side of the bed. He watched me brush myself down.

Then he said, 'I wish Stainforth had never come.'

Downstairs, there was a piece of fish, and potatoes and spring cabbage. The fish was overdone. I suppose Mrs Fossett was upset: she has always been an inveterate listener at doors. I made my way through the fish regardless, soothed by the methodical penitence of picking out the bones. Fossett lurked about, nervously, his large red hands rattling the silver as he fetched and cleared. I knew better than to say anything more then. Richard never liked to speak in front of the servants.

After Fossett went away, we sat for a moment, each with an inch of wine remaining. Ordinarily, this is when one or other of us would have briskly excused ourselves, but that day we did not. Perhaps we both felt that there was nowhere to excuse ourselves to. Richard looked pink-faced and tired.

I thought about saying nothing.

But I said, 'The trouble is, it's my fault.'

Richard raised his head. 'How can it possibly be your fault?'

'I mean, it's my comeuppance. Isn't it? Well. Or ours.'

He wouldn't look at me. I could feel that I was flushed, excited.

Mrs Fossett came in with a tray. Her eyes were swollen. 'Oh, forgive me,' she said.

'Never mind, we're getting up now,' Richard said. He put down his napkin as he rose.

His clothes were as pressed and perfect as they had been that morning, while I was conscious of being horribly creased, my hair all anyhow.

Coolly, Richard said, 'You might sweep around the wicker chair in the conservatory, Mrs Fossett, when you have a moment.'

'Of course, sir,' she replied.

I followed him out into the hall, thinking he would go into the drawing room, where Fossett had laid another profligate blaze. But Richard paused on the shining tiles, muttered something about going to bed, then walked slowly, heavily up the stairs.

It was the last time I ever saw him do so.

That was the night the dream came for the first time. Polneath. Licking orange. Somewhere the crash of a beam falling. The feeling of being out of doors, insufficiently clothed.

I had moved into Tim's room after the telegram, feeling that there was no longer any point in pretending. His had been the small room at the front, leaving three larger for guests who rarely came. He seemed to prefer the smaller room, I suppose because it felt friendly. No dark corners, no ominous cupboards.

I woke from the dream, morning light creeping between the drapes. It took me a moment to understand that I could not truly smell smoke. The narrowness of his bed had prevented me somewhat from thrashing about, but still I was drenched in sweat. I lay listening, certain someone was there. That Tim had come back. It was the absolute feeling of him, just exactly his suppressed way of being still. He was under the bed. I was afraid to look, and ashamed to be afraid.

I hauled myself to the edge of the bed and, holding my breath, looked.

Nothing.

I lay back, and breathed. Why was I dreaming of Polneath? But I knew very well why.

Comeuppance. The bill sent in, after thirty years.

The previous day rushed in upon me. Theo's visit. What had his mother meant by sending him? It was hard not to feel that she had been gloating. Look, here is my son, and almost whole. And then Richard, Richard of all people, asking what good it would do, to enquire. But I knew that there would be no rest without knowing for certain that it was as I suspected, that the fault of Tim's death lay with me. Without knowing whether what Theo Stainforth had implied was true.

I resolved to defy Richard. I would write to some of Tim's fellow officers, I thought, as I summoned Mrs Fossett to ask for bathwater.

Richard wasn't up yet, she told me, as she arranged the soap and towel, the small pitcher for rinsing my hair. She said she hoped that the master wouldn't be troubled with more visitors that day.

I replied that I was sure he would not be; that he might appreciate his coffee in bed.

I waited until she was gone, before I took off my nightgown. I stepped into the water. It was too hot, but I kept my foot where it was, bearing the heat until I should grow used to it.

I heard Mrs Fossett come back up, her steps careful with the loaded tray.

The creak of his bedroom door.

And then came a crash, and a cry of panic, and running feet on the stairs.

2.

1888

The inquest would estimate the date and time of William Tremain's death as the 23rd of December 1888, in the small hours of the morning. As he died, I sat oblivious in my kitchen, drinking my tea, watching the clock. Father was late, but it was not the first time that I had listened to midnight strike, alone, waiting. Everyone always seemed to save their emergencies for when Father might most hope to be at home in bed, or at least with his feet pushed up close to the grate. Almost Christmas, and yesterday there had been a carthorse down in its traces, which kicked the man trying to get it up; then, the parish constable with a nasty fall – bruises and a badly sprained wrist – as well as the usual colds and rheumatisms. Father had hardly paused all week, in fact, so that as it got dark and the foreman of the powder mills came to say his wife's waters had gone, I had sorely considered speaking sternly to Father and insisting he call in someone from Truro. But Father had gone himself, hours ago, and I had finished my tasks, sent Mrs Humphrey home, and settled down to wait. Though the parlour was all decked out for Christmas, I had chosen to wait in the kitchen, where the fire was in, and the only sign of the season a large ham sitting cooling near the stove.

At least the foreman lived in the village. The weather had just that day turned dry after weeks of freezing rain, but the wind had not abated, and the roads were dreadful. I had been trying to persuade Father to get a gig, but he liked his old horse Tess, though she made his journeys around the parish no swifter than they would have been on foot.

I stood, and paced about, and peered into the glass over the mantelpiece. The truth of it was that I was oppressed by the thought of festivity. My ordinary blue eyes looked back at me, dark in the dim kitchen; I poked at my hair, more brown now than gold. I missed my friend Edith, who had married that autumn. She would be at her new house, in London, putting together gifts for her new neighbours. Going to hear concerts. I knew, looking into the glass, that I would never leave St Rumon's, never be free of my duties of helping Father with his patients, of fruitlessly tending the chest complaints of the powder makers, of answering the door while Father was over at the Polneath mills to look at a crushed thumb, a lower back suddenly in spasm.

There came a creak, and I glanced away from the glass, but no. Every rush of wind in the bare tree branches, I thought it was Father coming in. I'd never liked birth, how dreadfully and suddenly it could turn, and each one a reminder of all the others that have gone before. The happy ones – ones the child survived, and the woman did – and then the ones by which both were taken, as my mother and brother had been, when I was twelve years old. The wind throbbed in the chimney and made the fire back and smoke, and I stepped away to save my petticoat, which was clean on that day. The night seemed to collect and merge in the darkness with all those other nights. How Mother would fret, when Father was out at a birth.

And yet: births, illnesses, accidents, that was life, and there had been nothing dreadful lately. Father had been managing, had been getting, on the whole, seven hours' sleep and three meals per day. Seeing to that had always been my occupation – my sole occupation, now, since Edith had gone away. I stood, warming my legs at the hearth, pinching my cheeks. I had overheard a woman in church say that nineteen was no age to be married. But for myself, I felt ancient. I licked a finger, and smoothed first one brow, then the other. Edith's sister had asked me to make up a party for charades on the 27th, and I supposed I would go, even though Rose and her friends were two years younger, and it would hardly be the same. There would be men there, though likely none I had not already met, already discounted. Though I had been finding all other men more agreeable since Father had found more frequent cause to mention Mr Boscawen, the district coroner, who had the big white house on the top road.

As for Edward Tremain, he wouldn't go to the party. He couldn't, even if he wished to: by my calculation, he was not quite out of mourning for his wife.

I wondered if the frock I had worn for Edith's wedding breakfast would do.

But here, now, Father came – the sound of the front door loud and distinct, after all, as it knocked into the coat stand. I poured out his tea, overstewed, and put the kettle back on its stand, to rescue it. He came in, looking like a cloth that had been thoroughly wrung out. But cheerful.

I got up, and took his bag from him. 'Is everybody well?'

He nodded. 'A boy.'

He sat down, and I passed him his cup.

'Name yet?'

'Noel.' He set his cup back down in the saucer – rather a cheap set, for I had finally put away Mother's wedding service. The cup rattled as he tried to extricate his finger from the handle.

We both smiled. We had been doing that for months: he shaking, myself pretending not to see.

I set the bag on the table, and nodded at his plate of bread and jam. 'That's the last of the gooseberry,' I said, and sat down opposite.

I felt drowsy suddenly – quite contented. I had loved these moments, ever since Mother had died and the task of sitting up had fallen to me. Father and I would have our 'midnight feasts', scratch meals of which Mrs Humphrey would discover the crumbs the next morning, and only be able to scold when it was too late. I could relish the excitement of a difficult birth, or some other emergency. Once it was over.

'Edith has written,' I said.

Father had jam at the side of his whiskers; but I would wait, and tell him when he had finished.

'Oh yes? What does she say?'

'I don't know. I'm saving it for Christmas Day. Since there won't be another before then.'

He nodded. The jam glistened.

'I wonder if they've fixed any dates for Paris,' I said.

She could chaperone me, now. That was the only silver lining. It was different than when we had dreamed of it together, before, knowing that there would be no point in so much as asking permission; now, our going would be unimpeachably proper. Her husband was a sensible fellow, a surveyor for the railways.

Father had put down his slice, and detected the stray jam. He engaged in some careful licking, and then said, 'My dear, Edith might not – now that she's married, she might not –'

The clock struck one, and it was then that the hammering came.

I hesitated a moment, before I moved to the door. I would, I really would insist they sent to Truro, or waited till morning. But it was Boscawen, the coroner. Was he ill himself? He did not look ill. But he had been running.

'Fire,' he said. 'At Polneath.'

My stomach dropped unpleasantly. The powder mills. Everyone in St Rumon's feared fire.

'At this time of night?' Father said. He had stooped to tie his boots again, and craned his neck to look up at Boscawen. 'How many hurt?'

Boscawen was unpleasantly out of breath, his cheeks red. 'Not the mills. The big house.'

'Is it out?' I said. I was attending to Father's bag. I had unloaded a variety of bloodied rags on to the scrubbed kitchen table, and now I was holding the morphia bottle up to the light. At Boscawen's approving look, I put the bottle down.

'They were making sure when I left. It didn't spread beyond the north wing. Tremain's office on the ground floor, and above, one of the bedrooms used by the female servants,' he said, in a rush. 'The maid lost her head rather. Her skirt caught fire, and she ended up in the pond. She was insensible, but breathing. The cook has turned her ankle, and Tremain looked a little singed to me, but –' He tried to catch his breath. 'The maid caught the worst of it, I think.'

'And Mr Edward?'

Boscawen looked at me. 'He seemed alright.'

Father reached for his bag. 'I trust she is being kept warm –'

I had taken off my apron, and balled it up in my hand. He raised his eyebrows, as I fastened my coat.

'I'm coming, too,' I said, firmly.

'I'm on foot –' Boscawen said.

I asked Father whether I should tack up Tess, but he protested that he had only just rubbed her down, it would take longer than it was worth, that he could perfectly well walk. I didn't protest, only put the guard over the fire, and followed them out.

I tried to tell myself my nerves were rattled from fretting about the birth. Smoke inhalation, I thought. A chill, minor burns. Salve, bed rest, a little steam. It comforted me to rehearse the diagnoses and the remedies. Mr Edward was well, I told myself. But something already felt dreadfully wrong.

We took the short way, the lane skirting the foot of the Polneath woods, which extended a mile or more on every side of the mills, and through which Old Tremain, Mr Edward's father, was known to hunt. I had glimpsed Old Tremain more than once, through the trees, his shotgun draped over his arm, and ducked out of sight behind the wall, counted to a hundred as he passed on. Occasionally, he would nail a badger kit to the posts of the mill gates, as though the little corpses diminishing in the wind would teach others to keep away. But tonight the gateposts were empty, the gates open, as we turned up the track through the mills. Father walked in the middle, and we had to keep shortening our strides for him. I walked close to him, trying to shield him from the wind which was thrashing in the oaks whose boughs almost joined overhead.

Men poached in the Polneath woods. The walls around them were high, but there were trees which grew close enough to help scale them. A less agile man could creep in during the day, and lie waiting for dark. Tremain grudged what he spent on lead shot; for hares and rabbits he'd lay little delicate snares. The gun, it was said, he reserved for birds and men. Mrs Humphrey had always told me to keep out of the Polneath woods, and I had certainly never been in them alone, and never been in them at night. Some said

Tremain was not so bad, only a little gruff, but even had he and the poachers not frightened me, there had always been foolish talk of a ghost in those woods: a yellow ghost, a child, though nobody could say whose child, or where the story had sprung from.

We walked without lights, there being enough to see our way, just, from the moon between the racing clouds, which picked out the paler track from the darker woods. I had last been up to the mills in the spring, after an owl had got into one of the incorporating mills – Tremain had not been attending to the rooves, one of the hands had said, and now look. The owl must have got grit into the workings, for a pair of the mills had gone up. We had heard the blast at home, but there was no one badly hurt, only a stray fragment of stone to remove from the foreman's cheek. 'Lucky,' Father had said, as the foreman perched on a stool, and Father steadied his tweezers.

It had not been like the other time, when I was little. I could still summon the noise of that. Mother saying it was fortunate that her uncle had retired from his position there. That explosion had moved rocks which now the moss grew over, and the intestines of one of the incorporators had been found festooned in a tree a clear mile away. It had put out the windows in the lodge keeper's house – almost a half-mile distant – but it had not touched the big house, huddled behind its great blast wall.

I had not seen Edward Tremain, when the owl got in, in the spring. Only his father, raising his voice to the works carpenter. Old Tremain was the sort of man who wished to think himself cheated; who, if a thing did not work the first time, kicked it, to see if that would make it go. He also liked to think himself clever, but he drank his money and so, as the years had gone on, had become penny-pinching, too.

His son was as different from him as day from night. He really *was* clever, and generous, and liked in the village; people had been hoping for years that he would settle to the mills, bring in new ways of doing things, though no one had imagined it to be the loss of his young wife, not quite a year earlier, which would bring him back to Polneath at last. All year I had only seen him in church, where he had looked light, starved, gentle; the little boy,

William, sturdy and watchful. A lovely child, and Edward as doting a father as Old Tremain had been a harsh one.

We passed the mill buildings, the wind buffeting the bare trees planted to keep the air moist and cushion the shock of any accidental blast. The rushing sound of branches drowned out the trickle of the filigree network of waterways, falls and runnels which turned the mill wheels and dampened the air. My teeth were chattering, and it was not only with the cold. I had long been foolish about Edward Tremain. Only a few days ago, I had prayed, let something, let anything happen to bring me into a room with Edward Tremain. And now look.

But nobody badly hurt, I reminded myself. I would not think about him any more.

Father slowed for breath, and Boscawen and I held up, too. Now that we might hear each other, Boscawen said, 'I hope the maid's alright. That fellow fished her out, I think he's the gardener –'

'Jake,' I said. 'Jake Feltham.'

Father looked at me. 'Yes, I should think it was Feltham.'

'What of the little boy?' I asked Boscawen.

'Mr Edward was looking for him.'

'William's been missed?' Father said.

Boscawen moved his hand, dismissive. 'He'll have got frightened. Run off somewhere. It was only the servants' wing, as I said. The cook and the maid are both out.'

He started on again, and we followed him. There was the blast wall, grown up with young trees and moss, and the little fold in it where one could get through.

We emerged beside the pond; the house four-square in the darkness, lights burning in one of the downstairs rooms. Over by the north wing there were more lights, men moving about and calling to one another. As we approached, I recognized Boscawen's man, and the lodge keeper behind him. Both grey-faced.

'It's all out, thank God,' the lodge keeper said. 'The master's office is a sorry mess.' He lowered his voice. 'Looks as though it spread upstairs, but started in there. Can't tell how.'

Old Tremain appeared then, from the gaping door of the north wing, and threw down an empty bucket. Boscawen's man nodded and started back down to the pond, ready to make his slow progress back with another full one. I saw Jake appear at the north wing door, and take the bucket from him, as Tremain shambled towards us. He was wearing a coat, thrown over a nightshirt, his legs bare above his boots, and I looked away from him, the hint of grey hair at his throat. He was not like himself. Usually he was such a square, swaggering bully. Now he looked white in the face – old – but when he spoke it was in his usual hectoring tone.

'Cardew. Come for Mrs Bly's foot?'

'Mr Boscawen says you've a burn I ought to look at, sir,' Father said. 'And that one of the maids is in a sorry state.'

Perhaps Boscawen *was* worried, for now he asked Tremain, 'Has the boy turned up?'

Tremain's lips moved, and he glanced away. 'We're still looking.' Abruptly he turned, nodded at us to follow. 'The women are in the dining room.'

We shadowed him around the pond, towards the large French doors of the terrace, and I could smell it now, the fire. Like the charcoal-burning huts near the mill gate, when they stood cold afterwards.

I followed Father in. The dining room seemed cavernous, and filled with a red, hectic light. Somebody had roused a banked fire with fistfuls of kindling, far too many logs at once, so that the flames leapt high. No sign of Edward, but there was the cook, Mrs Bly, seated at the table as though she was about to be served something, coughing and rocking slightly with each cough, a tablecloth clutched about her to preserve her modesty and those present from the sight of her nightgown.

The maid was laid out on the sofa nearest the blaze. Father moved swiftly to her, and knelt by her side. Unlike Mrs Bly, she was dressed, though all soaked through. Her eyes were closed, and her chest moved shallowly, a bad catch in every breath.

'What about a change of clothes?' said Father, as he felt for her pulse. But nobody moved. 'What's her name?'

'Agnes,' Mrs Bly said, and coughed.

'Draper,' Old Tremain said, to Boscawen, over Father's head where he knelt on the rug.

Boscawen nodded, frowned; Tremain moved to the hearth and lurked there. There came a noise at the French doors, and we all looked up.

Edward Tremain came in.

Like his father, he wore a nightshirt, but trousers too, and a coat thrown over it all. 'Has he come back?' he said. He was flushed, a shake in his voice.

'Get hold of yourself,' his father snapped, vicious suddenly.

It was almost reassuring, so peculiar had it felt to behold him flat and white.

Edward turned in frustration, looking out across the pond. 'Where's he *got* to?' he said, resting his forehead on the cold of the glass.

'Her pulse is steady enough,' Father said, and that recalled me to my duty. 'Let's have the salts, Ivy.'

The maid, Agnes, lay still, her eyelids beginning to flicker, her colour returning.

He put the bottle under her nose, and almost at once Agnes opened her eyes. She looked at us, at Edward.

'He's in –' she took a rasping, shuddering breath – 'my room.'

The inquest would record what Agnes Draper said, but not the expressions of those present, after she said it. Nor how Edward Tremain sprinted to the door; nor how Old Tremain spent another moment taking it in, and went after him; nor how Father, Boscawen and I followed, stumbling, no pausing for manners or to hold the door for one another. Round the pond, in at the north wing door, with Jake gaping, up the stairs with the burned smell strong suddenly, acrid in my nostrils. I saw Edward go in at the door of the maid's bedroom, which was swinging blackly open, and Tremain after him. By the time I was in the room, Edward had fallen to his knees.

Someone had thrown open the windows, but the smoke had still not cleared. The only furniture was a bed and a chest of drawers, both licked black, and Edward was making a terrible sound, as though all the air had gone out of him. Tremain was silent. It was horribly warm. For a moment, I didn't understand; and then Boscawen stepped forward and, gently manoeuvring around Edward, knelt, cheek to the floorboards, and looked under the bed.

I crouched, too. There, looking back at me, curled tight but with his eyes quite open, was William Tremain.

I scrambled backwards, out of the way.

Jake had come in, and began gently to pull the boy out from under the bed. William looked even smaller than I remembered him, his pale little face dirty, eyes open. He was in his nightshirt, lace at the throat and cuffs, stained with dust and soot. His feet were bare.

Father bent down, in case there should be a pulse, but I knew there was not going to be a pulse, and I, who had seen deaths before, who had seen children's deaths before, felt my joints begin to shake. I put my hand to the floor rather suddenly, and found it inches from Edward Tremain's. He looked at me, and I placed my hand over his own.

I was not thinking clearly.

'He's not dead, though, is he?' Edward said.

'I'm terribly sorry,' Father said.

'God have mercy,' Boscawen said.

I remembered myself, and moved my hand.

'I didn't look in,' Edward said. 'I didn't say goodnight to him –' Falling silent, he looked past me, to the doorway, where Tremain was standing, unmoving.

Then Tremain put out a hand for the door frame, and with the other he covered his mouth. 'She did this,' he said. 'That bitch did this.'

We all thought of Agnes, alone downstairs. *He's in my room.*

'Sir,' Boscawen said, looking at me, and then, 'Dr Cardew, can you take Mr Tremain to his room?'

Old Tremain looked white, sick.

Now Boscawen turned to Jake. 'Feltham, perhaps you can help Mr Edward to his?'

'I don't need taking,' Tremain spat. But he swayed a little, on the spot, and he went with Father, who out of long habit had run upstairs holding his bag.

'After, come back up here, and help me,' Boscawen said to Jake in a low voice.

Edward was stumbling, as if he couldn't see, even though the smoke was almost clear. Jake took his arm.

'What can I do?' I said. I kept my eyes on Boscawen, his collar and his neatly cut hair. I couldn't look at the floor.

Boscawen sighed, and rubbed his face. By the door, the lodge keeper stamped at an imaginary spark. Boscawen said to him, 'If you'll give us a moment. I'll call you, when I'd like help carrying him down.'

I touched my face, and was surprised to find it wet.

Boscawen looked at me, evenly. 'What do you think, Miss Cardew?'

'What do you mean?'

His eyebrows lifted slightly, and he gestured about him. 'I mean, what do you think?' He spoke not unkindly, but firmly, as though he might next shake me for my own good.

I reminded myself that, as coroner, it was his job to be without feeling. No doubt he was thinking how efficient, how convenient it was that he happened to live nearby, to be present at William's very discovery. How much easier it would make the paperwork.

There was a smell coming from him, a pleasant smell of cologne, but I took a step backwards which I could not help.

Boscawen was looking about him. The room was a bare one, as servants' rooms must often be. The fire had taken the curtains. He moved to the chest of drawers, and boldly opened the top drawer, then the middle. Nothing. He looked at me, and then at what sat just behind me, at my feet. Just by the door. A carpet bag, blackened and charred.

'If I may,' he said.

I moved out of the way.

He opened the bag. It was full of clothes, all spoiled. He looked at me, stood up, looked down at William, and then at the open door. 'It would have taken – what? Ten minutes, at the least, for the fire to spread up here from the office?' Then he stooped, and looked past William, at the dark space beneath the bed. 'There'd have been less smoke, at floor height.'

For a moment, I thought I might be sick. But I governed myself, and it passed. My ears seemed to clear, and I could hear the men calling to one another, outside.

'But what was he doing here?' I said to Boscawen. 'Why didn't he try to escape?'

He looked at me. 'Those, Miss Cardew,' he said, 'are some of the questions.'

Boscawen sent me down then, to see to Agnes, who was sitting up, coughing, when I entered the dining room. Somehow, she had acquired Mrs Bly's tablecloth, but Mrs Bly herself was nowhere to be seen. Agnes's sodden clothes had already begun to turn the tablecloth translucent. Her white apron was stained with pond-weed, and her skirt had a great rent in it, where it had caught fire. Her face was dirty, but here and there tears had tracked their white courses through the dirt. Her hair, drenched dark, was more usually reddish-brown – I had noticed it, envied it, in church, more than once.

She wasn't liked at church. Mrs Mason from the King's Arms said she gave herself an air. Agnes was older than me, by perhaps two years or three. She wouldn't gossip, and she wasn't from St Rumon's: she was from Falmouth, from the foundling hospital there. A charity case. Tremain had taken in unfortunates over the years, provided, as Mrs Mason noted, that they were willing to work.

Agnes was shuddering, and trying to control it. For a strange moment, it reminded me of Father.

'I couldn't get to him,' she said. She spoke so bleakly, it was as though it was she who was the little child, dying alone and in the dark. 'I couldn't even get to the door.'

I crouched at her side. 'It's alright,' I said, and felt foolish, even as it dawned on me what her words meant.

She took one unsteady breath, and that set her off coughing. 'It's my fault,' she said, when she recovered. She smelled of burned feathers.

I left a beat. 'What do you mean?'

But Agnes didn't answer. Her eyes were wandering. Shock, that was.

'Agnes. You weren't in your bedroom, were you? You weren't with William –'

She shook her head. 'I didn't know he'd come down.'

I paused. 'Then where were you?'

She looked at me and, for the first time, seemed to see me. Midnight, and she, a servant, had been fully dressed, out of her bedroom. Her bag of clothes packed and ready.

'I didn't light it, I didn't start it – whatever he says. Is that what he says?'

'What who says?'

But she avoided my eye. 'I tried to get to Will,' Agnes said. 'I was looking for him, and then it came to me, where he must be. I had to crawl. The smoke –'

'But where had you been?'

I was about to say, where were you going – when the door creaked, and Father came in. I stood up, and joined him, leaving Agnes by the fire, staring at the muddied carpet. I had to concentrate, to attend to what Father was saying.

'Mr Edward's had a draught,' Father said. 'Tremain's gone back out, to send the men off to get some sleep. He seems to be over the first shock.'

We looked together out of the French doors, to see Tremain lumbering around the side of the pond towards the lodge keeper and the others.

'Mrs Bly will mend,' Father went on, 'and of course there's nothing can be done for the boy. Boscawen has put him in the gun room for now.'

'What about her? She sounds bad,' I said softly, nodding at Agnes.

'She oughtn't to be moved tonight.'

'She won't say where she was,' I said.

Our eyes met. He looked so tired.

'Where she was?'

'Well, she's not in her nightgown. And surely if she'd been in her room, she'd have saved William . . .' I paused. 'She said she tried to fetch him out.' I found I couldn't tell him, what else she had said. *It's my fault.*

Father hesitated, looking at Agnes. 'Let Boscawen take you home, Ivy.'

'What about you? What about her? With what Tremain said, you know –'

Father looked uncomfortable. 'I've asked Mrs Bly to warm a bed for the girl. Shock can do queer things. I must stay.' He touched my arm. 'But you must go home. You might be needed, tomorrow.'

'Mr Boscawen has a lot to do,' I said. 'I'll ask Jake to take me.'

'As you like,' Father said.

I crossed the room back to Agnes, and Father moved to put the fire guard around the hearth. The flames were leaping too high.

'I'm going home now, Agnes,' I said. 'Have you anything else to wear?' I thought of her ruined bag.

'There might be something in the wash.' Agnes's mouth quivered, and she bit her lips together. Suddenly, her eyes were full. 'Could – could I come with you?'

'Come with me?' I replied.

Father came over. 'It's a draught you need now, to help you sleep, not a cold walk through the woods,' he said.

But Agnes's eyes widened. 'I don't want a draught,' she said.

I adopted a reasoning tone. 'But you –'

'Then you shan't have a draught,' Father said, soothingly, and sat at her side, and gently took her hand, upon which was a graze. 'Now then, what's happened here?'

I went to the French doors, and left him to his work. Outside, Jake was collecting discarded buckets from the banks of the pond. 'I'm away home,' I said.

As I'd known he would, he said, 'Let me walk you.'

But now I saw that he was soaked to the skin. Of course. He had rescued Agnes from the pond. 'Nonsense,' I said. 'Get yourself warm.'

He looked dead on his feet, but he did not instantly turn away, only let the bucket he was holding drop a little, rest against his knee. 'Christ,' he said, quietly.

'I know.' I gripped his arm. Then I thought of Father, and I let go. 'She's alright,' I said. 'Agnes. She was lucky there was water near. She was lucky you were near.'

He said, 'The fire was well up, by the time I saw it.'

We stood, our breath going up in clouds, looking at the dark water, at the lights of the house.

'What woke you?'

'Mrs Bly, I think. Shrieking. I looked out of my window, saw the flames.' He nodded up at his own bedroom in the wing opposite, the south wing.

That side had garden stores and so on, in its ground floor, with the men sleeping above. Though only Jake, now. There had been fewer servants at Polneath, of late.

He gestured to the north wing door. 'Mrs Bly came out, with the master. I ran down. And then Agnes came running out . . .' He looked at me. 'You know the church ceiling?'

I nodded. I knew just what he was thinking of – an angel on fire, small, gold, plummeting. From your pew you could see the whites of its eyes.

Carefully, I said, 'What would William have been doing in her room?'

But Jake shook his head. 'He was a one for wandering. He'd go down, if he'd had a bad dream or any such thing.'

'Is she nursery maid?'

Jake looked at me. 'No. All-work. But she taught the little ones, where she grew up, in Falmouth.'

'St Margaret's?'

'That's it . . .' He paused. 'She doted on Will as though he were her own child.'

We looked together at the damage, the north wing door hanging blackened from its hinge.

I bit my lip. 'And what about Agnes? Is she prone to wandering?'

He gave me an odd look. 'You oughtn't to say that, just idle.' He let out a breath. 'I can't believe I didn't see him. I was right there, back and forth with a bucket – do you think he might have been saved?'

Gently, I said, 'The smoke would have taken him already.' I looked at the yawning black of the north wing. 'Wandering or not, she was out of bed. They'll want to know why.'

'God knows.' Jake looked at me.

Perhaps we were both thinking of what Tremain had said, upstairs. *That bitch.*

Then I thought of what Agnes had said. *It's my fault.* But it was clear that Jake thought well of her.

I had stood just there with him, in the spring, after those incorporating mills went up, after the owl had set them off. The foreman told us it had made the workers uneasy – 'That superstitious, some of them' – and uneasier still when Tremain took the mills being stopped as an excuse to come out and shoot an owl, and then, when he couldn't find more, the rooks that nested harmlessly in the oaks. He had nailed the owl up on the mill gates. I thought of its flattened skull, the delicate double handful of it, yellow-cream feathers. A few days after the owl had got in, it was said that a yellow one had been seen, yellow as the brimstone they put in the gunpowder, flitting between the trees.

I didn't want to quarrel with Jake. I wanted to hide with him, from bad luck, from everything.

But then he shivered. Smiled grimly, said, 'You'll be alright, then?' I nodded.

I watched him in, trudging around the pond towards the French doors. Now that there were lights in more of the windows, the house almost looked handsome, like a Christmas card, if one ignored the maimed north wing. When Jake reached the terrace, he lifted his hand. I raised my own in reply. He turned away. For a moment, my hand didn't look real, and I had to shake it, and put it in my pocket. That feeling sometimes did come, after a sudden death.

William Tremain, seven years old.

But children did die. It was terrible, but not infrequent. They were usually littler than William. Slipped away gradually into fevers, their little flushed faces soft and relaxed, and, in the next room, a woman wailing. But this did not usually happen to me – the strange hands. Perhaps it was the suddenness. Just like Mother.

Lingering there by the pond, I remembered the way she had always insisted that Jake had saved my life, once. I was seven. I had been climbing a tree – one of the trees by the Polneath wall. I rather think I wanted to see over. I had been climbing, had got really quite high, and then took fright somehow. I was stuck fast, and I believe I had some notion that Tremain would see me, and come back with his gun. My grip was weakening when Jake happened by with a friend of his. The other boy had run off for Father, but come back with Mother and Mrs Humphrey, Mother already in a dreadful state, though Jake had already talked me backwards, calmly describing the downward climb. But when his friend pointed out to Mrs Humphrey the height of the branch I had reached, Mother embraced me so hard and so long, I thought I wouldn't draw breath again. At last, Mrs Humphrey gently disengaged her grip.

They marched me home, and Father was summoned up from his rounds; he checked me over, while Mother told the story, and Mrs Humphrey interjected that he was a good lad, that Feltham. I had scratches, and a cracked rib, Father said. I met Mrs Humphrey's eyes; said that I must have slipped as I was getting down. But we both knew that I had not slipped. Mother kept quiet, but as I recovered, she was careful to embrace me only extremely gently.

Seven years old.

Turning down the track for the mill gates, my mind would not fasten to it, the idea of the smoke, first the smoke, and then the heat and horrible light of the flames. That William could have died like that, curled into the smallest survivable space, hoping to the last that someone would be coming for him.

As I walked, I saw again his wide blank stare, and my mind swerved it, but there it was again, until the dreadful pity and the dark woods together acted upon my nerves. Though I knew that Tremain would be haunting his smoking, damaged house, still in every shadow I seemed to see him, holding his gun with that horrible poise. Between the dark pillars of the trees I thought I saw a flitting scrap of yellow. With the wind thrashing, I knew I would never hear anything coming up behind – and I ran, I am ashamed to say, I ran ten minutes flat out, and hurt my hand getting in at the back door.

3.

I woke at nine, entirely cramped into myself, portions of me quite cold. I had slept in the kitchen chair. As I stretched, the horrible lowering memory arrived of the night before: of firelight on faces blank with dismay; William Tremain, small and staring; and Edward, that sound he had made as he sank to the floor.

Agnes's blurted words returned – *it's my fault* – and where on earth *had* she been? Why had her clothes been packed? In truth, in the chilly light of that morning, I was thinking, she is guilty. And yet Old Tremain, with his bulk of muscle, his eyes shot with blood, the hum of drink which always hung about him – I had never liked Tremain. The fire had started in his office. Tremain was just the sort of man to accuse someone else, if he himself had left a candle unattended.

Then I sat bolt upright, for there was Father's voice in the parlour, and Boscawen, answering him. No telling what they were saying – their voices at a distance were like bees, trapped in a bottle.

I moved into the hall – quietly, though not quite creeping – and distinctly I heard Father say, 'No, I'm sure she will be willing.'

I paused, for a beat. The parlour door was open a few inches. I cleared my throat, and tapped lightly.

'Ivy.' Father sounded relieved.

The shutters were open, and the room full of plain white daylight. Boscawen, standing by the casement, inclined his head – 'Miss Cardew' – and I smiled what I hoped was briskly.

They must both have been up all the night. Boscawen looked the fresher, his cravat straight, his gloves neatly paired in his left hand; yet so he ought, being twenty years younger than Father. Though for all that, he already had plenty of grey, and a papery look. At church he mostly talked to the old men, about the conveyancing for mining companies which had made him his dull fortune, on top of which his work as coroner he seemed to do only out of duty, or honour, or some other dusty reason. I felt he had no business watching me, always asking what I thought about dull, village matters. How could a man be not thirty-five, and so very grey? And when I walked across a room, he would watch me go. I did it now: went to Father, took his arm.

'You must forgive me,' I said. 'I meant to be up. How do things stand?'

'I'm sending a trap for the body shortly,' Boscawen said. 'The inquest will be tomorrow. No sense delaying it.'

'Do you suppose it's necessary? A horrible accident, surely.'

'Quite, my dear,' Father said, and then began to tell Boscawen about a friend of his who had had factory interests and had mentioned once that, when caught in a blaze, little children would often crawl into a queer tight space like that, nothing unusual in it. 'But very sad of course, very sad.'

'I'm afraid an inquest is necessary,' Boscawen said.

Perhaps it was only because Boscawen was the coroner that I found the idea of an inquest unfeeling, cold somehow, though I glanced, of course, over reports of them in the papers. Whenever a fishing vessel should be lost; when the bodies washed up, and they could not tell who was who. But I had an aversion to the idea of his base, cold attention, to it being turned upon a house in which Edward Tremain lived – even if the purpose were to do things properly for Edward's son.

Boscawen was watching me. 'Apart from anything else, there is the question of how the fire started.'

'Where will you put him?' I said.

Father glanced at me, and blinked.

'The church vestry, for now,' Boscawen replied. 'With the weather so cold.'

The three of us were quiet a moment, Boscawen tapping his gloves against his leg.

Then he said, 'The fact is, I had opportunity to make my own examination of Mr Tremain's office, in daylight. The guard was close around the fire. It looked more as though it had started near the desk. Amongst the papers there, possibly.' He looked at me.

'Tremain, then,' I said.

'Ivy.' Father looked shocked.

'We oughtn't to prejudge it,' Boscawen replied. 'And there is the matter of Miss Draper's whereabouts –'

I looked away. 'Jake Feltham says that she was terribly fond of the boy. She told me she tried to save him –'

Boscawen frowned. 'What else did she tell you?'

'Not much,' I said. 'She wouldn't say where she was, when the fire broke out.'

Boscawen paused, then said, 'I didn't find her very talkative. She would only gasp and cough, and, if I pressed her, turn her face away.'

I looked at Father, and then down at my feet. I thought of Agnes asking whether she could come home with me. Perhaps it was only my stubborn dislike of Boscawen that made me say something then about how shock presents so differently in different subjects – I used those words, 'presents' and 'subjects'.

Boscawen nodded. 'You're right. And as I said, it doesn't do to speculate. I've asked them, at any rate, not to discuss it amongst themselves. At Polneath.'

I looked at Father. 'So Agnes is not to be moved?'

'Well –' Father said.

But Boscawen cut in. 'It's only one night. Mr Edward seems to feel his father might be unduly affected by grief – and that it would look badly to have cast suspicion on her, if it turns out she's clear. She did try to save the boy –' Boscawen looked at me. 'There's no prospect, I suppose, of her successfully absconding.'

It was true. St Rumon's was a small place, and she'd be known at the ferry, or if on foot, she would be easily overtaken on the Truro road. But that was not what I'd been thinking. I'd been thinking of Old Tremain, that quick rage of his; the isolation of Polneath House.

'I don't like the sound of her chest, in any case,' Father said.

Boscawen went on that what he didn't know was what could be done about household help in the meantime, and so close to Christmas. Agnes and Mrs Bly were the only two house servants remaining at Polneath, and only Jake left in the garden. Without

Agnes, the cook would be quite run off her feet. 'But your father will go and watch Agnes,' Boscawen said to me. 'So that frees Mrs Bly of nursing, at any rate.'

'Tremain has a burn on his arm I don't quite like,' Father said. 'And Mrs Bly must be encouraged to stay off that ankle –'

Father was quite in earnest, but I knew what I must say. Half of doctoring was waiting, and most of the time it was not Father who did the waiting, but me; long hours in close, grim-smelling rooms.

'You oughtn't to go, Father,' I said. 'I'll go.'

Father protested for a minute, and then smiled. His hand found the back of the armchair. 'It *would* be a weight off my mind – and I feel you're quite equal to it, my dear.'

Boscawen gave a satisfied nod. 'I ought to see about this trap.' He pointed to the table. 'That there is the summons for the inquest, if you could see that into Mr Edward's hands.'

Father asked me to see Mr Boscawen out; Boscawen kept me rather longer than necessary, buttoning his coat at the door, letting in a draught. Reluctantly, I gave him my hand.

'I know you do not like to leave him,' he said, quietly. He was giving me a measuring look.

I withdrew my hand. 'I have sat with patients before. And as you said, what is one night?'

'Quite.' He looked up at the sky, the cruel white daylight. Conversationally, almost, he said, 'Perhaps Miss Draper will confide in you.'

'I thought you'd asked them not to speak of it.'

'Amongst themselves. But some people will say as much to a doctor as to a priest.'

I looked at him. 'And a doctor keeps no worse confidence.'

He gave me a look which said, *but you're not a doctor, are you?* When he spoke aloud, though, he said, 'You don't think her guilty.'

I looked at my feet. *It's my fault.* 'It's as you said yourself. Nobody ought to decide before the facts are known.'

'You know Old Tremain as well as I. He would smother facts in their cradles, if they were not convenient to him. If you care about the facts, you'll see what you can get from Miss Draper.'

I met his eyes, but said nothing.

He turned away into the lane. By the gate, he stopped, and said, 'She won't be harmed. Tremain knows I'm watching . . .' He paused. 'You and I both saw the bag, Miss Cardew. She was on her way out of that house. And I'd like to know why.'

Back in the parlour, Father was still standing by the fire. My heart was beating hard. Father held out his arm, and I stepped under the wing of it, let him pull me close. I could feel his weariness, feel him almost lean on me. I wanted to say something, but at that time I still thought a woman should show her reluctance in signs rather than words, and Father was not watching the hunch of my shoulders, my pick-picking at the shred of dry skin beside my thumbnail.

'To tell you the truth, her chest isn't as bad as it sounds,' Father said. 'Although she seemed . . . she was shocked, as you said, and chilled, of course, from the pond. But let her have her day in bed. Sometimes women simply need a day . . . She's had a dreadful shock.'

I conjured Agnes's bold, nervy eyes. 'Yes.'

'I'll come first thing,' Father said. 'And check her over, before the inquest.'

I looked up at him again, and then nodded, into his shoulder. She had refused to talk to Boscawen: well, that I could understand. But I couldn't help thinking of a man my father had treated once, in the kitchen of the Polneath lodge. Caught poaching, and shot in the knee – by another poacher, Tremain had said. June, several years ago, those light nights. Mr Edward had been over as usual, with his family, from the Continent. He had come down himself, paid Father quietly, and fixed it so that no charges were pressed. But, while there was a question of the law, everything had seemed to go out of the poacher: guilt had sent him limp, and made him turn his face away, just as Agnes had to Boscawen.

'You'll go to bed, now, Father, won't you?' I said.

'Of course.' Father patted my arm, absently. 'You'll be back before I know it,' he said.

★

Walking to Polneath after a late breakfast, I looked out over the lumps of died-back winter rushes, and the bare mud of the channel, the broken reeds beyond. A flight of curlew made me jump, but after that there were no birds, no sounds except a pair of powder men coming in the other direction, who touched their caps to me, and studied me. One asked if I was going up to the big house. When I said I was, the other paused, and then asked me to tell Mr Edward that he had their prayers.

I walked on, unnerved. The news had got out, then.

I wondered how much had been spoken of. Whether people thought it a pure sad accident, or whether they yet knew about Agnes being out of her room, William curled small beneath her bed, a fire sprung up in the office below and nowhere near the hearth.

The mills would be closed that day, of course. But in the village they would all be asking already when they would open again. They had children to feed, whom they would all hold a little more tightly this evening, and those children would not pause in their hunger. I wondered what the fate of the mills would be.

Boscawen had stated so bluntly the situation at Polneath, a house that would once have needed ten servants. It was well known that Tremain was running out of money, about the groom retired and his duties loaded on to Jake. The butler who had accompanied Tremain on a journey to London the previous year and elected not to return. When Mr Edward had come back to Polneath a widower, it had been expected that Tremain would take on more people again, but he had not – and now there was only a cook, a maid and a gardener. Jake had not said that things were so bad as that, and there was no other way of telling. Those from the village who made deliveries to Mrs Bly did not come into the house; it was Agnes who undertook Polneath's errands, and she did not talk much.

If Tremain was truly in trouble, if the mills closed, it would be the death of St Rumon's. However little Tremain himself was liked, every mine owner in the district had always had reason to treat him well, and he took certain steps to see that he appeared a liberal employer. Every summer, there was a tea given in the mill woods; the late Mrs Tremain had given the tea, and then Tremain had given it himself; and then each June, Edward's wife, Emily, had given it. The workers ate the tea, but they still distrusted Tremain. Nobody would have spoken against him to his face, but the village had ways of making its discomfort felt. They had long wanted Edward to take over the running of the mills, but what if it was too late?

I had pictured fiercely that year, more than once, an accident befalling Tremain, and the prospect of my catching Edward's attention somehow, and becoming mistress of Polneath. It was a foolish wish, with long roots: even at twelve, throwing rice at his wedding, I had felt a pang of spite towards his yellow-haired bride with her London dress. Older, I'd confessed my liking to Edith, who thought it a delicious secret. I had pieced together scraps of knowledge: that Tremain had pulled Edward early from his studies to marry, his degree left incomplete; that his wife had headaches, and did not take to Cornwall. I had watched him become the model of a doting father, and nurtured in myself a calf sort of love, which had nothing to do with bodies. Edward had always been the perfect subject for such a love: his gentle, rather beautiful face, his beautiful manners; hair that was always a fortnight past needing cutting. And never quite present: only in St Rumon's for the month of June. So I wished for him, wished and prayed, and I had thought it didn't matter.

But I knew now, the guilt growing heavier as I walked, that it did. It did matter.

I had known it was wrong, in truth, to think of a married man, a recent widower. But it had been so easy to wish for Edward Tremain, and not least because it meant I did not have to imagine leaving St Rumon's, leaving Father. There were not a handful of men in the district of the right age, and unmarried; even fewer with the means to support Father and me both. St Rumon's was close enough by the daily ferry to Truro and to Falmouth, where the streets were paved and the great ships came and went. But at night, once the ferry stopped, it was a hard hour's ride into Truro, on roads hock-deep in mud and fallen leaves. Even when his hands were bad, Father never wanted to call in men from Truro to help him with his rounds, because the simple fact was they would not come. The effort of the journey did not warrant what they would earn. Father must either give up his position as St Rumon's doctor, or he must keep it up. The possibility of keeping it up seemed by the month to decrease; yet if he did not, how would we live?

Approaching the Polneath gates, I thought of Boscawen. What Father might have meant, when he said to him that he was sure I would be willing.

The gates looked locked, though they weren't, but produced a creak and swing as I opened them. The track led on through thickets of rhododendron, which gave way quite suddenly to thinly spaced trees. Between the trees were the expense magazine, and the stores for the three elements which made up the powder: the brimstone, saltpetre and the charcoal in its airless casks. The buildings for pressing and drying. Over along the stream were the seven pairs of incorporating mills: the newer ones downstream and, higher up, the older ones, two pairs still neatly roofless from the accident in the spring, like soft-boiled eggs with their tops removed. I kept on up towards the blast wall, over which I could just glimpse the roof of the house.

Though the family had been at Polneath for centuries, Old Tremain's father had established the mills. He had rebuilt the house, too, a new classical frame thrown up over the roots of the ancient manor house. But money had run short, even in those days, and the service portions of the house, the north and south wings, were a relic of the old structure – of squat dimensions and old stone. The new main house was loftier, more perfectly square, though once the budget had been spent, savings had been made with the fittings. A grand enough face, I had heard Mrs Mason say, but it was dim and draughty within. It had been hard to tell, last night, in the dark.

I stopped in the shadow of the blast wall, hearing a sound, and then stepped off the path. Boscawen's gig lumbered by. I nodded to the driver. The gig was covered. William's body coming away.

It was cold of Boscawen, leaving Agnes Draper at Polneath another night, even with me to tend her. But then, Boscawen was cold. He had been bred up in St Rumon's as well as I, and knew the powder business. The truth will never out by itself. The quickest way to find the piece of grit in a measure of powder is to grind and grind and grind the three elements, and squat outside the mill, listening carefully for the catch.

4.

1918

I might never have attempted to enquire further into our son Tim's death, had it not been for a memorial notice, which was printed three months ago, in September, just above the casualty lists in the *Times*. I was turning through the newspaper, rather distracted, having woken from the usual dream. Five months of checking the narrow space between mattress and carpet, then brushing the fright out of my hair, dragging myself down to the breakfast table.

Fossett, when he had brought the paper in, had commented that it was a morning for a good brisk walk, and I had taken that to mean that he wished for half an hour away from Mrs Fossett. He looked grey in the face, and I had heard her voice raised in vexation, echoing up from the kitchen as I had poured my coffee. So I had asked Fossett to step round to the vicarage, to say that I would give an hour to the flowers that afternoon, if that would be of use.

He looked at me rather intently, asked if I was quite sure.

I told him I was.

I spread the newspaper flat on the table, telling myself that September was a tricky time of year for the church flowers, the first breath of autumn. Not much in the way of berries yet. The vicar's wife was always so inclined to use the big overblown roses from her garden, so that they might have their last gasp on the altar, but really, they only lasted a day or two before wilting entirely. She ought to accept that the summer was finished, ought to be made to accept it.

All summer I had avoided her, the other St Rumon's ladies. Mourning Tim and Richard's infirmity had furnished my excuses, but it could not go on forever. Perhaps it was time to rejoin the world, to face them.

I glanced over the leading articles. Everything was about the end, towards which we were swiftly moving. I still could not bear the military detail, but I was reading a piece about the proposed expansion of one of the London underground railway lines, when Richard began calling my name from upstairs.

'Ivy!' And a moment later, more weakly, 'Ivy?'

I waited a moment, in guilty silence. I would go up at nine, I always went up at nine; it was now only a quarter to. Out of the dining room window, in the garden, Jake was cutting the grass.

After a few moments, Richard stopped calling.

Besides, I could not go up until I had looked at the casualty lists, so that I might keep an even tone of voice while reading them aloud for him, as he had insisted I do, every morning since he had been confined to his bed.

To work up to the casualties, I always looked at the ordinary death notices; they felt less unnatural, with their ages of sixty-three and seventy-nine, with their mentions of short illnesses, their requests for donations in lieu of flowers.

But then it was that the name caught my eye, and I kept back a gasp. I smoothed the page. I listened, but there was only the ticking of the clock, the shucking of Jake's shears outside, the distant rattle of roof tiles in the wind.

In memory of Archibald Tremain, killed in action.

One year ago that week.

The first thing I felt, strange as it might seem, was a stab of envy. Killed in action. And the next thing, of course, was pity. His son dead a year, and I had known nothing of it.

Correspondence to Mr E. Tremain at his club.

Edward Tremain. It must be him. There could not be many – and that had been his second son's name, Archibald, I was sure of it.

Correspondence at his club; that was queer. But perhaps flowers would upset his wife, as they had me, after Tim died. For I knew Edward had married, as I had; taken his second wife a year or two after the business at Polneath, though never, under-standably, come back to the district. I had heard about it, from

Edith. She had caught and passed on bits and pieces of gossip, over the years, though they were not really acquainted. She'd said that he was something at the War Office.

And now he was childless again.

The club's address was just off the Strand. I was still attempting to decipher my feelings when the front door slammed. That was Fossett back.

Yes, I thought, flowers and black-edged cards would upset his wife: or? Or he no longer had a wife, and spent his days, as London widowers do, in the comfort of his club. I studied the page again.

'Ivy!' came again the shout from upstairs.

I started. My face had turned rather hot. Without thinking, I whisked the page out from between the others, folded the paper and sat on it, just as Fossett came into the room.

'Mrs Benson says that would be extremely welcome, madam,' he said.

'What would?'

'Your help,' he said. 'With the flowers.' He looked confused.

The shout floated down from upstairs again.

Clumsily, I took the rest of the paper, and held it out to Fossett. But I could not stand up, so he had to come right the way around the table to take it from me. But dear Fossett, he only looked sympathetic. He had always been a darling, but since the spring he had been a perfect angel.

'I think tea is wanted,' I said.

Fossett took the paper. 'Are you certain you are quite well, madam?' he said. 'I can offer your apologies to Mrs Benson, if you aren't –'

'I am quite well, Fossett, really,' I said.

He bustled off and I cursed myself, for in taking the memorial notices I had also removed the casualty lists, and Richard would be sure to notice. I shifted my weight in the chair, and pulled out the folded page of newsprint. I kept folding, once, twice, five times, very quickly until it would not fold any longer, only bend. I put the wedge of paper into my pocket. I poured myself a second cup of coffee, which I stirred, particular to not let the spoon clink against the cup. I drank it, looking out on the green jewel of the lawn. Jake would be back in a moment, to pick up the clippings. I could just hear the murmuring of Fossett delivering the tea.

Then the shout came again. 'Ivy!' Insistent, now, aggrieved.

I put my cup down, and began to climb.

The bedroom door was open, and Fossett standing by, his face apologetic.

'Were you calling, my dear?' I felt the first wave of guilt as Richard made to push himself more upright against the pillows.

'The newspaper is missing the casualties.'

Crisp, petulant. You'd never have known there had been anything wrong with his speech. After the haemorrhage, he had formed the habit of talking to himself, when he thought no one could hear, and he was still doing it, even then. Forming his words, very particular, the blur in them no longer detectable, the precision of his vowels and consonants rendering all the crueller the stubbornly useless legs, atop which the newspaper now lay unfolded.

'Missing them?' I paused for a moment, expertly evading his eyes.

'Have a word with the boy, would you?' Richard said. 'Tell him it won't do.'

'I will,' I replied, soothingly, conscious of the wedge of folded paper distending my pocket. I made my voice gentle, offhand. 'Would you like me to read something else?'

'No,' Richard replied. 'I suppose you might go.'

Downstairs, I retreated to the study – what had been his study. I was still getting used to it being mine. Fossett had moved the stack of post to the desk; uppermost, a doctor's bill. I took out the folded page of newspaper, and smoothed it.

Killed in action.

I filled my pen and shook it, and pulled a sheet of paper towards me. I couldn't think what to call him, so I simply began.

I was dreadfully sorry to read about your son. Might I offer you my heartfelt condolences? Forgive me, I hadn't heard – only I saw the

memorial notice. You may be aware that our own boy was killed in
February. Richard has been unwell, since the spring, quite confined
to his bed. Please think of me, if I might be of any service to you, and
consider me,

Yours as ever –

From the moment my pen touched the paper, I knew it was wrong. I was not condoling, or not only condoling. Richard could not be permitted to see this letter. I fetched an envelope, and painstakingly addressed it.

Mr E. Tremain Esq., c/o Timperley's . . .

There, that would do. He could reply, if he wished, and perfectly naturally mention his wife, or else her passing.

I felt disgusted with myself.

I let the letter rest on the desk, and crouched to feed the stolen page of newsprint to the hearth, watched it curl and catch, hoping the boy who brought the paper each morning would avoid a sharp word from Mrs Fossett. I looked at the letter where it lay on the thick stained blotter.

I could hardly say, even now, precisely why I wrote it. Perhaps it was simply the thrill of having an address for him again. I was still aggrieved, of course I was, that Edward had simply *gone*, after what had happened at Polneath.

But.

Over the thirty passing years, I had grown to understand that a young man must make his way. He cannot always follow his heart, any more than a woman can. And we had certainly both been young, though he had not seemed it, at the time. Twenty-eight to my nineteen.

Perhaps I had simply written because I knew that Edward would reply, and that when he did, he would say things, real things, ask questions. He would not seal himself shut, as Richard had always done.

I looked at the letter, laid next to a rather splendid seashell, pearly white and the size of one's palm, which Tim had found on the beach once and given to Richard, and Richard had kept.

Another wave of guilt overtook me. For there was Richard. In sickness and in health. And just as Tim's death was my fault, so was Richard's sickness.

For allowing Theo Stainforth to come.

For saying that, about comeuppance.

Richard had slept a great deal, in the first days after the haemorrhage. The doctor had said it was a matter of waiting, and not to allow any visitors who might have colds, and to be diligent about turning him, to prevent sores. I was familiar, from my father's time, with the sound of a doctor scrabbling about for some small things which one might control, when all that one might do about the larger matter was to pray and wait. On the third or fourth day, when I tried to help him with a bedpan, Richard struggled and made sounds, and then averted his eyes to the ceiling and produced nothing, so I left Mrs Fossett to that side of things. Of course, there wasn't a qualified nurse to be had. But I watched him a good deal, sat with him, all night sometimes. When I put a cool cloth on his head, he would groan, and the small muscle between his eyebrows would let go for a moment. When that happened, he looked terribly like Tim.

It was expected, of course, that he would die: a haemorrhage is usually followed by another, sooner or later.

But, in fact, Richard recovered himself terribly quickly; though the day by day of it felt slow. His speech improved within weeks. Soon there was only a slight thickening, which he rapidly learned to conceal, fixing his eyes upon you when you asked him a question, as if to give you a chance to consider whether the question had been a sensible one, before he began his reply. But his legs did not improve, nor his hands, which remained too weak for writing, too weak for feeding himself.

Summer came, and Jake brought in produce from the garden with a worried air. Marrows, new potatoes. Broad beans, which had always been Tim's favourite. I podded them myself, and fed them to Richard, his mouth opening furiously like that of a baby bird. Though Mrs Fossett put him into fresh pyjamas every day, starched and ironed, he seemed against the backdrop of his pillows to have lost some of his old rigidity. His face paled, and his blue eyes took on a yellow cast. He reminded me of a mushroom, accidentally uprooted. Useless and reproachful.

He could read a newspaper alright, but insisted that I read the casualties aloud. He claimed the print was too small.

Every day began with that torture.

The intimacy of the feeding, the close sickroom and the rumpled sheets reminded me, more than anything, of how in former years at bedtime he would grow rather still, and take longer over the removal of his watch and links, and I'd wait, cheek to linen, looking at the painted wall. Then he'd put out the light. Hold my shoulders, but quite gently, as though determined to spare me all but the essential pain. Very occasionally, he'd brush my hair from my forehead, looking at the pillow above me, where I suppose my hair was spread out, and I would look at some vein or blotch on his face. If he ever caught my eye, he would quickly look away. I suppose the feeding and so on was the closest I had been to Richard in years.

I put up with his impatience, his dark moods, his way of treating his feet like intractable children – and as a terrible indulgence, therefore, my attempts to keep them warm. I put up with his manias: he had been greatly occupied with the question of the repatriation of bodies, earlier in the war, and now went the same way over the question of fitting memorials. He made me take down a letter to the *Times* about it, more than once, then look for it every day, until it was printed.

But he seemed to lose his appetite for the shuffling of paper, which had previously made up the bulk of his days. He soon ceased asking about how a particular farm was faring with their volunteers, or how his derelict mariners' charity got on. I answered the odd personal letter to his dictation, sent out delicately phrased messages to his clients, which hinted at a temporary period of ill health, and I let our agent Murray direct repairs and collect rents on the little handkerchiefs of land we leased.

I walked the fields, looked into ditches and drains, with no idea of what ought to be done about them, then returned to Richard's bedside, and if not there, then to the study, to look at the telegram, and permit myself to think uncharitable thoughts about Theo Stainforth and his mother. Though the months since Stainforth's visit had opened in my mind a margin of merciful doubt: Tim had appeared to stand up, had only *appeared* to put his head above the parapet. Perhaps the boy had been mistaken. Perhaps Tim's death was not my fault, after all.

But still I shunned the village ladies, unable to stand their knowing about the telegram, their gossip and speculation about what Tim might have done.

By August, Richard could lift a spoon, and the doctor said that, while that might be the most we ought to expect, he could live another twenty years, if we were careful. My guilt abated enough to leave Richard with Mrs Fossett occasionally, in the afternoon, and catch the ferry to Falmouth, quite alone, to sit guiltily in the dining room of the Grand with a cup of cold tea, and think of nothing at all.

I wasn't sleeping well. Every night the dream kept on, until each evening I began to anticipate it, and thought more often of Polneath, the disused powder mills and the ruined great house, hardly a mile away. My walks had avoided the place for years, preferring the deep lane down to the village and the fields which lay in the opposite direction. But more and more, as the summer wore on, I found myself climbing the overgrown stile and making for the crumbling wall which bounded the steep woods of the Polneath valley. I would follow the wall, all the way to the bottom lane, cutting home again the village way. I walked and walked the perimeter, but I never went in.

Then came the end of September, and that notice of the memorial service for Edward Tremain's son. I felt envious of his honourable wording. Then sorry. And then I felt something like comfort: because Edward, he would know how I felt. He would want to know. I was like Theo Stainforth with his missing limb, and here was someone similarly afflicted. Richard had only ever wanted to know as much as was useful, but Edward – Edward had always wished to know everything.

And perhaps I felt a flicker of something like the future. The truth was that I had thought of Edward Tremain, at intervals, all the long years of my marriage.

But still there was Richard. In sickness and in health.

I hid my letter to Edward in a drawer. I threw out the over-blown roses I found, as I had known I would, on the church altar, and put in some brisk chrysanthemums. I stopped going to the dining room of the Grand Hotel. I resolved to be even more attentive to Richard, to learn what I needed to learn, about the estate, and to be much stricter with Mrs Fossett about menus. We ought not to be eating nearly so much game.

Everybody said that the war was ending. I must make a start on life again.

That Sunday, the last of September, I stopped Mr Murray out-side church, in the mellow sunshine. He knew I had been handling the correspondence, and obtaining Richard's wobbly signature if one were needed. But that would not do forever, I said, and he agreed.

'It ought to be possible to give you the oversight. He's of sound mind, of course, and you're already his executor,' Murray said, as we stood to the side of the porch.

'I feel I ought to understand the finances better, at any rate –' I stopped. 'You see, it seems to me, Mr Murray, that we have left things rather as though the situation were temporary. And now –'

'Quite so,' Mr Murray replied. 'But –'

'I feel I ought to understand it all as Richard does. I thought a good beginning might be for me to look at everything. Nineteen thirteen, say, and simply look at the bank statements, rent books, everything – and make a list of what I don't understand.'

'Of course,' Mr Murray said, carefully. 'Though if you'd prefer it, I could certainly spare the time to explain things to you myself.'

He wore the same kind of tweed as always, so thick and com-fortable that it makes you think of the word 'encased'. His rather nice brown eyes, unfiltered at that moment by the dreadfully thick spectacles he almost always wore, studied me, worried. He diverted our talk to a smaller matter, a piece of ground upon which the vicar's wife keeps her chickens, upon which the peppercorn rent had lapsed. While the money was, of course, nothing, Murray said it would be untidy were there to be any doubt over the ownership. After a minute or two, he noticed his wife waiting by the gate, looking rather cold.

We strolled down towards her, making our politenesses.

Before we parted, I mentioned the accounts again, and said, 'I shan't trouble you, Murray. Truly. I really feel I ought at least to try to get a grip on it all myself.'

He looked at me again, and touched his hat. 'Just as you like, madam,' he said.

5.

All through October, my behaviour was just what it ought to have been. I only thought fleetingly of my letter to Edward, hidden away in its drawer; when I did think of it, I allowed myself to feel virtuous for not sending it. By the time peace came, however, on the eleventh hour of the eleventh day of November, that had all been blown to pieces. As the distant church bells spoke to the air their confused message of emergency or jubilation, I sat on the back bench, and wept.

I had been there an hour, perhaps, when Jake sat down beside me, nervously patting his knees with those great comforting hands, which he could never quite get clean. He cleared his throat and cleared it again, as he always does when he is not sure how to help.

We were children together, Jake Feltham and I: permitted to play despite the differences in our station. Or perhaps not permitted, but at any rate not prevented. After Mother's death, I took advantage of Father's busy, benign neglect and of Mrs Humphrey's belief that, when it came to children, they could be divided into the good and the bad, and by no other method. Jake she deemed to be a good boy.

Like myself, Jake has stayed in St Rumon's, and lives alone in the village. His little cottage, while in good repair, has taken on that aspect which the houses of solitary men have, as though it might be not a human resident but some clean and complex animal that lives there. It is whitewashed every year, with a monstrous woodpile stacked against the gable wall; one thin washing line, and windows that are clean on the outside but still somehow rather dim. Since Polneath, he has been caretaker for the church, as his father was before him, and latterly, as there has been less to do at the church, he has taken up gardening for us, and looking after the car, and so forth.

We sat side by side on the bench, like a pair of greying jackdaws.

He could see I was making a mess, and his first instinct was to see how he might clean it up. I saw him move for his handkerchief, but then notice how grey his hand was. He sat looking at it.

I said, 'It's fine, Jake.' I blew a sort of bubble as I said it, and pushed my palm across my nose, and he kindly looked away.

'I'm sure he'll pull through, madam,' he said.

The doctor had been again for Richard, the day before.

'I wish you wouldn't call me madam,' I said.

He smiled at that. 'Ah, you see. But I have to get along with Mrs Fossett, as well as with you.'

I smiled back, and looked away. 'It's not that, in any case,' I said, after a moment.

'Ah. Tim, then,' Jake said, in that beautiful way, not quite a question, but an invitation. A nudge, as though he also meant, *but you are not quite simply crying about Tim, are you?* For he must have seen how I had changed towards Richard. Known that there was some form of, as he would put it, 'to-do' going on.

When I didn't answer him, he turned his talk to the war, examining the dirt under his nails. 'Nothing will go on as it did, that's for sure. I heard in the King's Arms that the garden on the Earl of Falmouth's estate, it's just been left, near all the four years. Still forks stuck in the soil and rusted where they left them. Whole place overgrown. It'll be a season's work for whoever does the cutting back.'

We sat quiet a minute, and then I could not help it.

I said, 'I have gone about everything badly.'

'Not everything. You make a lovely blackcurrant jam.'

I laughed, and then the laughter altered, and Jake did reach for his handkerchief this time, which arrived in my grasp slightly grey.

'The post has come,' he said, encouragingly. 'Perhaps there'll be something from Edith. That is, Mrs –'

I smiled, and nodded; blew my nose, while he looked politely away.

Then I said, 'Do you ever think about Polneath, Jake?'

He looked at me then. 'Not really, madam.'

The fact is that Jake *knows*. He was there for much of it. I had often thought he must suspect what Richard had concealed for me; what I had done. There was no need, with him, to use so melodramatic a word as comeuppance.

But his face softened. 'We can only ever act by our own lights,' he said. 'I do know that. That's what you did. That's what Tim will have done.'

Getting to grips with the estate papers had been a serviceable distraction from that last month of the war. After I had spoken to Murray, in between my other tasks I'd gone slowly through deeds, rent books, and found everything in good order. It was the first of November, by the time I got to the accounts. I did as I'd suggested, and dug out everything for 1913, to better understand the recurring costs and income. Richard's filing system was commendable.

It all made a surprising quantity of sense. Most of the standing orders were for housekeeping – the Fossetts' pay, and Jake's, some quarterly invoices from Mr Murray. One or two subscriptions of Richard's, to his learned society. His tailor's bills, a bill paid out to the mechanic for something Jake couldn't fix. Tim's school fees. How ordinary things had been, once. My finger passed on down the page from the petrol bill, and there it was. The 25th of March, the quarter day: £58 12s 4d, to be paid to a Mrs Smith.

Who was Mrs Smith? Curiously enough, we did not know any Smiths. Richard had never mentioned any Smiths. I combed through the rest of the year, but there was nothing more. But there the payment was again in 1914, a little more, and this year almost double. Even this year, a month after Tim's death. I pulled out the accounts for 1912, and there she was. The quarter day, Mrs Smith; and the year before that, and the year before that, and every year since our marriage. The payment had begun at £52 per year, I realized – and increased, in an orderly fashion, with inflation. By the time I had finished my search, I had made a terrible mess, and spent an hour or so in putting it all back.

I knew very well what a regular sum meant, paid from a married man to a woman not his wife. I found myself surprised at what I felt – I did not think there would be any reserves of pain available to me, with Tim already lost. I did not think I would care, given that I would never have married Richard, had I truly had a choice.

But I did. I did care.

I did not speak to Richard about it. Instead, I got the letter from the drawer, the letter to Edward Tremain, my hands shaking rather, and sent Fossett straight to the post, and then to Mr Murray, with a message to call round, when convenient.

While Fossett was out, Mrs Fossett came in, her little tap at the door – which issued from a desire to not be heard, and so to conclude disapprovingly that I was napping – veiling itself well as good manners.

'I thought to make the master's dinner a little earlier from now on, since it takes him that bit longer to feed himself,' she said.

'Right,' I replied.

She stared. 'But that will mean your tea will have to be a little earlier, in turn, madam.'

'Do as you think, Mrs Fossett.' I almost said, *do as you like*, and the next morning, when Richard asked me to read aloud the casualties, I refused.

Armistice Day. That morning, not long before Jake had found me on the bench, there had come the usual plaintive shout, and I had gone up to find Richard sitting up in bed. I was cold with him, as I had been since finding out about Mrs Smith; quite brisk, though he clearly had no notion as to why. Perhaps he thought I was simply tired; at any rate, he was trying to please.

His hair looked sensible and his bed jacket was buttoned correctly to the top. He was pushing himself up against his pillows – both palms downward, that horrible straining. 'Any word on the memorial?' he said.

I looked at him for a moment. 'No.'

I half turned, but he said, 'Stay a minute. Will you look in the top drawer?' He moved his recalcitrant arm. 'On the left there.'

I opened the drawer. Amongst the old medicine bottles sat a small box. I looked at it for a moment, and then brought it to him.

But he said, 'You open it.'

I sat on the stool by the bed. Inside the box was a ring. A silver one, rather a nice one, with a knot design.

'Try it,' he said.

The band slipped easily over my knuckle.

He looked worried. 'Someone told me silver is the thing for twenty-five years.'

'But we're twenty-nine,' I said, carefully. It was a lovely ring. He had always been good about jewellery; always bought the right thing.

'I know. I missed it. I saw this in town, when I was last up. But then Tim wasn't back – and then, I wanted to give it to you when I was better, but –' He stopped. 'I bought it because we have missed too many things. And now, I hoped –' He stopped again, perhaps at my expression.

It was what I had wanted to hear. In February, when we had lost Tim. In April, when we had argued about him. In September, even, when I had governed myself, and put that letter to Edward Tremain away in a drawer. For years, it had been what I had wanted to hear.

But now, it was useless.

I looked at the ring another second or two, then slipped it off my finger, replaced it, snapped the box shut. 'It's rather big,' I said. 'I oughtn't to lose it.'

'No,' Richard said. 'No.' He had the paper spread open on the coverlet, near his legs.

The men had persisted in killing one another, of course, while they waited for the details of the ceasefire to be settled, so there were still plenty of casualties to report. But he didn't ask me to read.

I was standing, staring at the ring box.

'My dear?' he said, gently.

But swiftly I told him that he must excuse me, and I went down to sit on the bench as the bells rang out, and cried.

It was that evening, after the bells had finally fallen silent, that Murray found the time to call. Mrs Fossett showed him into the study. He refused a drink, and we sat.

'Forgive me,' Murray said. 'With things wrapping up, it's been rather all go –'

'Not at all,' I said, bending to his dog. 'Nothing urgent.' I was determined to be calm. There is nothing a man dislikes so much as a woman in pain.

'To tell the truth, it's been rather a queer day at our house,' Murray said. 'The girls are fractious.'

'Yes,' I said. And then, 'All it is, Murray, there are one or two payments I wanted to ask you about.'

Instantly he looked cornered.

'You remember I was going to look at the accounts?' I kept my voice very light.

'Yes –'

'Well, I did so, I looked at nineteen thirteen, and I was able to make them out fairly well, as it happens.' I lowered my voice. I couldn't help it, though there was no one about. 'But there was a payment in the March. And every March before that, in fact. To a Mrs Smith.'

Murray looked at me.

'Beginning at fifty-two pounds, and climbing.'

'Yes,' Murray said. 'I had noticed that, madam. But of course I couldn't –'

'No. Of course you couldn't.'

'I thought it might be one of his charitable causes,' Murray said.

'It's a fairly large sum. And he's never mentioned it.' I fidgeted with my cuff. 'Of course, I could ask him about it, but the doctor has said he mustn't be bothered.' I turned around, and Murray was waiting. 'So I was hoping that you might be able to find out.'

'Find out?'

'At the bank. A full name, I suppose. An address.'

'I can certainly enquire . . .' He left a pause, and then, more quietly, he said, 'Do you really wish to know?'

'I ought,' I said, 'to know if there are any obligations.'

He saw what I meant, of course. He promised directly to notify me, should he discover anything; he would look in at the bank, when next he was in Falmouth. He seemed to think better of saying anything else, and stood up. I stood, too, and touched the bell.

As soon as he had gone, I sat down, to read it again. The post that day had brought, at last, on top of everything else, Edward Tremain's reply.

My dear Ivy,

Yours is the letter I have been most glad to receive, and after so many years. Of course it was dreadful when Archie went. My wife Constance followed a month after him; her heart was quite broken. The only scrap of brightness is that such times can occasion the reappearance of friends whom one thought quite lost. Though not all letters bring the comfort yours has. You cannot imagine how many there have been, all platitudes with black borders. Like a fool, I say that you cannot imagine – but of course you can. I was terribly sorry to hear about your son, and it must be a great trial to suffer your husband's illness in addition.

You ask whether you might be of any service to me, but of course, it would be far more fitting for me to be of service to you. It has been in my thoughts to come and see Polneath again, strange as it might seem. I hope that when I do, I shall also be permitted to visit you.

Forgive the formality of the direction, by the way –

Yours, etc.
E.

Edward. He was coming to St Rumon's again. I would see him again; because why should I not? I asked myself. When Richard, after my summer of watching and waiting, when Richard –

I sat back in my chair, and looked up at the shelves of the study. The fire had burned right down, turning the tooled books of the lower shelves – suitable, unopened books, entirely proper for the collection of a gentleman solicitor, a district coroner – into a wall of gold. Above them sat the rows of buff card files, ranks upon ranks of them, soft with use, his lifetime's work. Hundreds of cases, and the settled facts of them: amongst which, in one particular case, my wrongdoing has concealed itself.

My crime.

Edward had addressed his envelope quite properly, of course, but it must have felt peculiar for him to do so.

Mrs Richard Boscawen.

There it was: my life sentence, in Edward's elegant hand.

6.

1888

When I reached Polneath House, hardly twelve hours after William Tremain's death, all was utterly still. It did not look like a house in mourning, with the drapes hanging vacantly open, but more as though it had been suddenly abandoned: grand, but lonely. None of the houses of Father's usual patients made one wonder whether one ought to ring at the front or the back. I hesitated, then retraced my steps of the night before, crunching around the pond and up to the door of the damaged north wing, which still hung by one teetering hinge.

I stepped in, and almost called out, but the quiet halted me. The lower passage was a mess of discarded buckets. To my right, the stairs disappeared upwards, to what had been the female servants' rooms. They had borne our weight the night before, but now, in daylight, they looked perilous. The door in front of me must be Tremain's office. I peered in, moving quietly. As Boscawen had said, the guard was secure around the fire. There was wet black ash everywhere. A chill little wind blew down the stairs: there must be windows smashed above, or else someone had opened them, to try to get rid of some of the smell.

Looking left down the lower passage, more doors stood open. Quietly, I moved towards them. A laundry, with a big copper and a mangle, which had escaped the flames; then the gun room, with a great scrubbed table, oil and polish and other such items up on high shelves, ten or twelve shotguns mounted on racks. Jars of wax, card boxes of shot. This was where William had been laid out.

His blank eyes came to me again, his curled white hands.

It's my fault.

*

The cook was along in the kitchen, busy with a hot kettle, and I waited until she had put it down before I knocked on the door post.

'Miss Cardew!' she said, wiping her hands. 'Why didn't you ring?' She stepped out into the passage to join me. She was wearing a black armband.

'I'm not here to make work, Mrs Bly,' I replied. 'How are you keeping?'

She glanced down the blackened passage. 'My chest is very tight,' Mrs Bly said. She lifted her foot. 'And this is plaguing me –'

I sat her down at the kitchen table to examine the ankle. 'I couldn't fit my stocking over it,' she said.

The bruising had come up yellow and green. As I palpated it, she winced.

'Mr Edward's in his study,' she went on. 'I took him through some tea an hour ago, he was asleep at his desk, poor lamb. The master's in his room . . .' She paused. 'It's a nasty burn he's got.'

'I believe my father left him some salve.'

Mrs Bly nodded, as though salve did not quite convince her. 'He didn't rest, you know, until every spark was out. If he'd known William was there, he'd have saved him for sure. Though the fire was well up by the time he got to it. It was me that went up to wake him. The smoke woke me. I'm a light sleeper –'

'You roused Mr Tremain?'

'Yes. And he shouted to Mr Edward. Mr Edward's room is just along from the master's . . .' She paused. 'Though it seems like just last week that he had William's room.' Her face had fallen.

'I'm sure it does.' I let the ankle down gently. 'When you do sit down, put it up. I'll help with the house, when I'm not with Miss Draper.'

'Oh, is that –?' Mrs Bly got up. 'Good. I don't like her being up there and nobody keeping an eye.' She folded a dishcloth, thoughtfully. 'And the Lord knows I've no time to be running up and down to her, not with the house to put into mourning.' She wiped her hands on her apron, though they were already clean and dry. 'You're stopping, then?'

'For tonight, yes.'

'Come with me, then, miss. I'll take you to her. Have you been over the house before? We'll go the long way –'

I had never been inside at Polneath, until the previous night. The mill woods, the gardens with Jake once or twice, and last year the terrace, for the works tea, but never inside. Even in daylight, now, I was struck by how dark it was. And large – I supposed Agnes could easily be kept out of Tremain's way, for one night. Mrs Bly brought me through a swing door and out into the hall, lined with pictures like dark postage stamps. The floor of chequered tile had a pale-yellow carpet running along it. Mrs Bly nodded to the open doors, and named them: drawing room, billiard room, library. I glimpsed the dining room, where Agnes's eyes had snapped open the night before, and she had spoken those awful words.

He's in my room.

For a moment, there was only the sound of our skirts, and our heels on the tiles. We emerged into the entrance hall proper, with its high ceiling and the milky glass cupola above. The great dark front door. Stairs led up to left and right, meeting above in a sort of gallery.

As we began to climb, I said, 'I understand that William was very fond of Miss Draper.'

Mrs Bly turned a strange look on me.

Distaste, and something else. Caution.

'She spoiled him, if that's what you mean.'

We gained the gallery, and Mrs Bly paused a moment for breath.

'The master takes it into his head to do a good deed, and now look. Anyone could see it when she came. I thought Mr Boscawen might send the constable to watch her, but there. You'll do, I don't doubt.'

I understood, then, what Mrs Bly thought my purpose was in coming to Polneath. 'How long has she been in the house?'

'Three years.'

A corridor led off to left and right, with grand doors opening to either side – family bedrooms, I thought, and guest bedrooms. Mrs Bly set off to the right, and through a little door at the end of the passage which emerged into a much smaller, cramped stair. It was darker in there.

'And did you have trouble with her? Other than her spoiling William, I mean?'

'Not trouble, no. She was quiet. Sulky.'

'And why was she given charge of him?'

Mrs Bly stopped for breath again. 'Oh,' she said. 'I suppose she was young enough to run after him.'

For a moment, there was only the two of us, close in the dark stairwell, and Mrs Bly's wheezing. The stairs went on and on, up into darkness.

'Do you believe she set the fire, Mrs Bly?'

'I don't see who else would have.'

'But why?'

'She's like all her sort,' Mrs Bly snapped. 'Wants more than she's given.'

'What do you mean?' I said, quickly.

But Mrs Bly moved her head, and set off again. 'How do you expect me to know why she did it? Ask her,' she threw back, over her shoulder. Then she paused. 'I'll say this. She might not have meant to hurt Will. She *was* fond of him, I'll give her that.' Her face was in danger of softening, and now she set it. 'But what does that signify? It doesn't matter what you *mean* to do, does it?'

We emerged on to an upper landing. There were doors to both sides, and a strip of brown baize laid over the bare boards. The skylights above gave a low, grey light.

'It was only the old nursery rooms up here. And storerooms. I'm along there, in an old truckle bed. I've put her into the room she had before she was moved.'

'Moved?' I said.

Mrs Bly looked at me. 'To stop William going crying to her every hour of the night. Didn't work, though, did it?' She bit her lip. 'Didn't stop her mischief.'

I swallowed. 'I'm not here to make her a prisoner, Mrs Bly,' I said, after a moment. 'Only to nurse her.'

Mrs Bly turned away. 'Doesn't matter, does it, so long as you're keeping an eye?' she said, her tone rather colder. She nodded at one of the doors, which had a key in the outside. 'She's in there.' But she opened the next, and allowed me in first. 'You could come in with me,' she said, 'if you'd prefer that. There's nothing else aired or dusted, I'm afraid. And it only being for a night –'

'No, of course,' I replied, using my sweeter voice again. 'Really, Mrs Bly, I don't want to make work.'

But I had guessed whose room this was. Had been.

The air in the room was still, as though he had only stepped out for a moment, and would run back in presently, to fetch his hoop, or a clutched handful of tin soldiers from the box on the mantelpiece. I put down my bag. It was cold.

'I'll bring things up for a fire,' Mrs Bly said. 'Come down when you will, and I'll talk you through the linen cupboard.'

'Thank you,' I replied.

From somewhere below came the sound of a glass shattering, and then a man's cough, which echoed distantly up to us.

Tremain.

Mrs Bly's eyes widened. 'I'd better go and . . .' she said.

'Is there a key?' I said. 'To this one, is there a –?'

But Mrs Bly shook her head. 'The master keeps the keys. Only one, to any door in the house, and no copies made, he won't have it. I've got pantry and wine cellar, and now her room. That's my lot.' She saw my face; perhaps she remembered who my father was, or saw my youth, and softened slightly. 'If you're a wakeful sort, you can put a bit of rag under the door or suchlike. That'll stop it rattling.'

Left alone in the room, I felt strange. There was a little bed, drawers and a wardrobe, a few shelves, a small hard chair. I moved a tiny stationmaster, complete with green flag, along the windowsill. There were battered books in rows, the silk shells of chestnuts curled back on themselves. I remembered Boscawen, opening the chest of drawers in Agnes's room. I swallowed, told myself to be sensible, and noiselessly opened William's. It was full of little shirts and vests, and in the bottom of the wardrobe were a multitude of shoes: small ones, boat shoes and gumboots, sandshoes and fine leather ones with a brown strap. On top of the chest of drawers a snare drum sat, and on the chair was a bear, with one ordinary black eye and one eye of milky white marble.

I shivered. I remembered, just after my mother died, a lady – one of my father's cousins? – taking my hand, and telling me that I must be very grown up, very grown up now indeed.

I opened my bag and draped my spare skirt and blouse over the chair, then moved them, so that the bear could still see. I stepped out into the passage, tapped at Agnes's door. The key felt large, the head a great 'P' entwined with leaves.

I turned it.

Agnes's eyes were closed when I went in. The hand that lay curled on the bolster was chapped and reddened as any servant's, but her face was pale. Her eyes flicked open as I let the door close behind me.

I wished I had something to set down and fuss with, a doctoring bag like my father's. To reassure myself; to make Agnes trust me, and to distract her while I examined the room. Though there was nothing there of hers, of course. Nothing to be told from the bare space. Her eyes really were remarkable: dark and large, and she did not avert them when you met her gaze, as one expected a maid to do. In other houses, where I had been asked to sit with other patients, I had always known just how to be – the soft knock, the sympathetic nod – known just what to do. But now I felt awkward, at sea. I looked at my feet.

'Mrs Bly has put me in William's room. Father sent me to sit with you,' I said. 'We'll try some steam later, if you like.'

There was a small stack of folded linen on the little dresser, a pitcher and beaker, a bottle of the mixture Father had brought, and that was all, apart from a plate of meat and potatoes that hadn't been touched.

I nodded at the plate of food. 'What's that done to you?'

Agnes drew up her legs. 'I can't fancy it,' she said. And then, 'But I am thirsty.'

I poured her some water, and sat down in a gap on the bed where her legs weren't. 'Have you had any of what my father left?'

Agnes shook her head. Her hair was loose in a thick curtain, and I saw that she had made a long and complicated plait near the front of it, imperfectly and from halfway down – not for vanity, but for something to do with her hands perhaps.

'Where's Mr Tremain?' she said, and began to cough. There was a rattle to her chest that was real enough, though it subsided quickly.

When she was quiet, I said, 'Resting, I believe.'

'And Mr Edward?'

'I'm not sure.' I reached for the plate on its tray. 'What've you had, three hours' sleep? Less? It's the mixture or this.' I held out the plate. 'Father won't forgive me if you get weaker.'

She looked at me. 'Give it here, then,' she said.

Agnes began to eat, bolting the food. To avoid watching, I found a little stool near the door, and pulled it closer to the bedside. When she had finished, I took the plate away.

'That looks charming,' I said, nodding at the plait.

Agnes touched it, nervously. 'We learned to do each other's, at school,' she said. 'Some of them went to be ladies' maids.' Her large dark eyes took me in. 'I could do yours, if you like,' she said. 'If you've a comb.'

I hesitated, but reasoned that it might help to calm her. Make her confide. I went for the comb in my bag, and was back in a moment. I sat on the edge of the bed again, felt her pull the pins out of my hair, and loose it down.

'Back in your old room, eh?' I said.

She put the pins down on her little table. 'Yes.' Nothing more.

'There's to be an inquest. Tomorrow.'

'What's an inquest?'

'It's where they look into what happened.'

She was quiet for a moment. I felt the comb catch, and her tease at the snag with finger and thumb, until it dissipated. 'Boscawen decides?'

I almost corrected her: *Mr* Boscawen. And that there was no deciding, of course, only what did or didn't take place. But I simply said, 'A jury. We'll go on the ferry to Falmouth.'

She thought about that for a moment, perhaps wondering whether the women who had brought her up, the women at St

Margaret's, would have heard yet, about William's death. 'I'll be on trial?'

'It's not a trial,' I replied. 'Sometimes a trial follows after.'

She was quiet – combing, thinking.

I said, 'But you mustn't fear. People might be pleasant to Tremain's face, but –' I stopped. 'They know what he's like.'

Agnes said nothing.

'I hope Mr Edward is a better master?'

Cautiously, she replied, 'Mr Edward isn't his father, that's for sure.'

She had separated the hair into sections, and now I could feel her hands relaxing as she twisted the hair together, tight and smooth. This must have been how she had spent hours of her girlhood.

'If you're going about without your hat on,' she murmured, 'you might as well look your best.'

'The inquest will ask why William came to your room,' I said, after a moment.

'I was trying to curb him of it,' she said, a catch in her voice now. 'He was to be sent away to school, after Christmas, I told him he had to learn to soothe himself. But. He was little, so.'

'He was reluctant to go?'

She tugged at a piece of hair. 'Yes.'

'I should have thought he'd have been glad to be away from his grandfather.'

She was quiet for a moment. 'The master – he kept back the worst of himself, around William,' she said.

I nodded, and she straightened my head. 'The inquest will also want to hear about your trying to rescue him. And the fire being too strong. Everything you recall.'

'Going in the water,' Agnes said. She was twisting the plaits up, now, to pin them.

'Jake Feltham saved you,' I said. 'Do you remember that?' I felt her nod. I let that sit, for a moment.

She slid in a pin.

I said, 'In your room, there was a bag of clothes packed.'

Another pin.

'I'd given my notice,' she said.

'When?' I half turned, but she righted my head. 'To whom?'

'Last evening. To Mr Tremain.'

'Why?'

'William was off to school. With him gone, I'd no wish to stay.'

'But no particular reason to leave?' I said.

She didn't answer.

I said, 'So you gave your notice, but you weren't planning to work it?'

Again she did not answer; only said, 'That's done now. There's a little glass in William's room. You can have a look.'

I stood up. 'Well, Boscawen knows about the bag of clothes, too.' I looked at her. 'He'll ask, at the inquest.' I dropped my voice. 'But only I know what you said. When I came down to you, after we found William, you said it was your fault. What did you mean?'

Her lips were pressed together.

I was pushing too hard. I turned away. 'Boscawen will want to know where you were, tomorrow,' I said again, more gently. And then, 'I can help you, but only if you tell me the truth.'

But now she would only look at her hands, her hair falling so that her face was half concealed.

I said, 'We'll try some steam when your food's gone down.' I waited. 'Is there anything else you'd like?'

She raised her head. 'I want to see him.'

For a moment, I thought she meant Boscawen.

Her mouth trembled. 'William.'

I joined my hands. 'I'm terribly sorry,' I said. 'He's gone.'

I explained about the trap that had come for the body, and there was nothing false about the tears that started in Agnes's eyes then. She wept, and refused the draught of Father's that I tried to press on her. She did not seem to want to sleep, but wanted to be left alone. I told her I would come back later.

Outside the door, I stopped. But it felt too peculiar, to lock another person in. I could hardly see the need; as Boscawen had noted, there was nowhere for her to go.

I went into William's room, and looked at my hair in a small smudged glass, the kind a little boy might use to check his neck was clean. By turning and turning my head, I could see what Agnes had done. I touched the plaits. They were perfect. Not showy, but grown up. I had been putting up my hair for a few years, but not like this. I realized I looked rather like Mother.

I remembered what Mrs Bly had said. *Like all her sort. Wants more than she's given.* But Agnes did not seem greedy, or scheming. She seemed rather proud. Watchful, perhaps. I thought about William, coming to her to be comforted. I remembered how my mother had looked, holding other women's babies, when I was eight, nine, ten, and no others of her own had survived. *Wants more than she's given.* Was that what Mrs Bly had meant?

Then I remembered the summons; I ought to give it over. I took the nearer stair, the north stair, thinking to go down and ask Mrs Bly where I might find Edward. I did not like to simply go wandering about the house. As I went down, my hand reaching for the wall in the dimness, it occurred to me that this was the way William would have come. Waking from a bad dream, a lonely progress down through the house. Something made me change my course to match his, turning into the upper passage of the north wing, past Mrs Bly's smoke-damaged room, to Agnes's, where the creeping fingers of the fire had reached.

The passage stank of burning, and there was a cold draught. The quiet had a thickness, as though it possessed its own listening ear, in the very wood and plaster. I stopped at Agnes's old bedroom door, its green paint blistered to oblivion. There was her bag still, charred, packed to go nowhere. I moved it into the wardrobe, and then wiped my hands on the hem of my petticoat.

7.

Mrs Bly told me that Mr Edward was in his study, past the dining room on the left. I spoke to myself sternly, as I made my way up the three short steps, through a swing door and along the dim corridor. I must be ordinary – well, not ordinary, but sympathetic, useful. Edward was in mourning, double-mourning, his wife and now his son. My face should be pale and cool. But it was no good: as soon as he opened the door, and a gentle wave of warmth emerged, I flushed. I couldn't stave off the memory of kneeling on the bare boards, my hand on his.

He stepped back. There were bookshelves over his shoulder, a loaded desk.

'Miss Cardew!'

Instantly I felt I had intruded. 'I don't want to . . .'

'No, please –' He gestured to the chair in front of the desk.

He had changed his shirt and done up his collar, but he still looked rumpled, and as though his lips would taste of salt. He seemed dazed.

'No one could be more welcome.'

He sat, and so did I. On a settle near the fire was a crumpled tartan rug, which made me certain in a flash that he had passed the night there. He looked down, in that diffident way he had, and smoothed his hand over the page that lay on his blotter.

'I have been trying to write a character for Agnes.'

'Oh?'

I saw one or two attempts abandoned. On the latest there was only a letterhead, and then the date in his own hand, but nothing more yet, as though it was that which had made him falter. The date of his son's death, and now there would be all the days after.

'I'm sure there's no hurry,' I said.

I wondered whether he'd begun the character the day before – in response to her giving her notice – but there'd been very little time, and it would have been odd of him to start on it so urgently. Besides, she'd said she had spoken to Tremain. As Edward pressed the character between finger and thumb, I got a sort of feeling that he did not know.

'She started as an all-work maid, but I'm going to put house-maid,' he said. 'It's only fair, she's shouldered a great deal since what's-she-called went away to get married.'

'May I?' I said.

He looked at me, and suddenly seemed to see me, and nodded. I pulled the drafts towards me.

To whom it may concern, I can attest that Agnes Draper has during her time in my employ displayed the utmost . . .

'It's kind of you,' I said. 'Given the circumstances.'

Edward moved his arm. 'Miss Draper was fond of William. Terribly fond. I think Father has been extremely hasty. I don't see how she could possibly have wanted to harm William. Nor damage Father's office – it was only a few ledgers destroyed, the money and deeds and such were all in the safe, and nothing stolen . . . it's ludicrous.' He pushed both hands over his hair.

'You think it an accident, then?'

He nodded.

I touched the character, and pushed it back towards him. 'And yet she won't say where she was.'

I almost mentioned, then, about her giving notice – to see what he'd say about it. Whether he'd be shocked. But he seemed to think as well of Agnes as Jake did, and I wanted somehow to protect that kindness, to shield him in this small effort to fend off utter despair.

Edward sighed, and looked towards the window. Then he said, 'I have always been of the belief that servants are people, Miss Cardew. Their business is their own. It doesn't follow that their business is malicious.'

'I quite agree,' I said, not understanding his meaning.

He raised his red eyes to mine. One of his hands moved over the other. 'You must understand, Miss Cardew, that she doted upon William terribly. And he was without his mother,' he said. 'And I should have been . . . I should have been more with him, but the demands of the mills, and my father –' He stopped. 'And you know, since Emily died –'

There was a scuffling at the door, the handle moving, and Edward got up, but before he could move, Tremain burst in, righted himself. His eyes were small with drink.

I stood.

'Miss Cardew, Father,' Edward said. 'Come to check on us.'

Tremain cleared his throat, and cleared it again. 'Forgive me,' he said, coarsely. He put out a hand for the door frame.

After the night before, I expected anger; but he seemed diminished. His dog appeared at his feet. I had seen it before, the black and white spaniel he kept for shooting.

Savagely, he kicked the dog backwards, then looked at Edward again. 'We must wire to the insurers.'

'I'll come up shortly,' Edward said.

Tremain backed out, shutting the door too hard behind him.

I sat, and Edward did too, lowering himself gently.

He must have seen my face, for he said, 'He swore this morning that no drink would pass his lips, until William is buried.'

I felt my hand move involuntarily. I shifted it from the desk into my lap – said, gently, 'I'm so terribly sorry.'

His lips twitched. 'Thank you.' Already it was the required response, arrived at without thinking.

I wanted to lean across the desk, put my fingertips very gently to his temple, where there was a tiny pulse beating. Instead, I folded my hands.

'He's taken it badly,' Edward said. 'He, too, loved William. Although I'm not sure Will always knew it.'

'Did he beat him?' I asked, in a low voice.

'Rarely.' Edward smiled a bleak smile. 'For myself, I never once laid a hand on him. He never wanted for anything.' His eyes were filling now.

'You all loved him,' I said. And then, 'All of St Rumon's could see the kind of father you were . . .' I paused. 'You were going to say, earlier – since Mrs Tremain died –'

'Oh.' He smiled sadly. 'Only that I have been far too occupied with myself.'

'No, but surely . . .'

'Well. I know it's not a sin you're guilty of, Miss Cardew.' He looked at me, a long look. 'It's been a good while, hasn't it, since we last had the pleasure of speaking?'

Under his scrutiny, I nodded, looked at my hands. 'More than a year.'

'And how is your father at present?'

I looked swiftly up at him. He had guessed, seen it somehow. The way Father worked to conceal his shaking hands.

'Thank you, he's –' I had gone red again, I knew I had. 'He is as well as can be expected. That is, he is holding up.'

Edward met my eyes. But I could delay no longer.

'I ought to give you this.' I pulled out the letter.

Boscawen's confident, perfunctory hand: the black wax seal the size of a thumbprint, with an anchor for the sign. I pushed the letter towards him, and he opened it. I tried not to watch his hands.

He looked up. 'Tomorrow,' he said. 'At nine.'

I nodded. 'At least it gets it over with,' I said, and then felt the clumsiness of my words.

'In St Rumon's,' Edward said, frowning.

'In the village?'

He pushed the letter across to me. The inquest would not be at Falmouth, but at the King's Arms. That was not usually how it was done, not any more. But as coroner, it was at Boscawen's discretion.

'I suppose, with the constable laid up,' I said. 'And the state of the roads – and perhaps it's for the best,' I said.

We looked at one another, thinking of the gossip there would be, the gossip there must be, with a housemaid out of her bed and a fire started with uncertain cause. A little boy dead. Better that the gossip should be confined to the village, for as long as possible. Though it could not be long.

I thought of the letter sitting replicated on two dozen tables around St Rumon's. In warm farmhouse kitchens, the polished dining rooms of tradesmen. Edward smoothed his hand over it. I saw his black coat was quite loose at the shoulder.

He stirred slightly. 'I wonder what on earth one must say.'

I looked up in surprise, almost replied, *well, the truth*. But I stopped myself: he was grieving.

He reached for the letter again, and held it close to his face. 'That is, what will they ask me?'

Gently, I said, 'They'll want you to go over it all. It will be difficult. Mr Boscawen is very particular. You'll have to say what you remember, you know. From the moment you woke.'

He screwed up his face. 'Father was shouting,' he said. 'Out on the landing. He banged on my door. I pulled on trousers, then went up –'

'For William.'

He nodded. I wondered whether he had been told that I had been lodged in William's room. What if he came, to look at Will's things, to mourn? What if he came in the night? The clock on the mantelpiece whirred, and then struck one briskly.

'But he wasn't there,' Edward said.

There was a silence, and after a moment it became clear that he had lost himself in the memory.

I shifted in my chair. 'I should go and see how I can help Mrs Bly. She seems very anxious that the house should be put into mourning.'

He stood up. 'I'll come with you. I ought to talk to her about food.'

I walked just behind him, towards the hall. Somehow it seemed to be already growing dark outside, the day clouding and the glass cupola above the hall becoming like a large grey pupil; the low gaslights picking out the gold of the stair rods and the pink of the columns, which were made to look like marble. In the bend of the stair was a Christmas tree. Somehow I had not noticed it. A splendid one, nine or ten feet high and decked out in baubles and unlit candles, winking palely in the dimness.

Beneath, presents spilled across the chequered tiles.

I stopped behind Edward, but not quickly enough, and my hand touched his elbow. I looked at him, and saw his pain. 'I'll see to that,' I said.

'I'm sure Mrs Bly can –'

'I don't mind,' I said, gently.

He bit his lip, and nodded. 'You might ask Feltham to have the presents sent to the foundlings' hospital, in Falmouth.'

'Are you certain?'

St Margaret's. Where Agnes Draper had grown up.

'Yes, yes. I'm sure that's suitable.'

Mrs Bly seemed surprised to see Edward and me appear together, but his presence meant she put away her sour face from earlier.

'I was going to ask you, sir . . .'

'What, Mrs Bly?'

'Only, I didn't like to bother you.'

'What is it?'

Finally, she came out with it: there was a great deal of Christmas food in the larder. There was a goose, and a quantity of good salmon, several brace of pheasants. Beef, too, of course, and she could stew that, but what about the birds? Of course, she needn't do the garnish.

'Of course you needn't,' Edward replied. 'You must serve what we have, Mrs Bly. It can't be helped. Just do what you think best.'

'My mother always said, at any rate, that grief makes one hungry,' she said, and stepped backwards into the table.

'We'll have something simple after the inquest, I think. We'll eat in our rooms tonight.'

'I'll tell the master, when he comes in,' Mrs Bly said. Added, at Edward's look, 'He's gone out with his gun.'

'Oh Lord,' Edward replied, glancing at me.

'And so, we're not expecting the guests now, sir?'

Edward looked at her.

'It's only that, I could keep back some of the good things, if anyone is still coming.'

'No,' Edward said. 'That is, I suppose one or two might come to condole, but – no. I wired to the Myerses.'

'And Miss Cardew, sir,' Mrs Bly said, glancing at me. 'Will I give her what you and the master have? Or the same as Agnes and myself?'

Edward looked rather stricken.

I said, 'The same as Agnes, Mrs Bly, thank you. You can send it all up on the same tray.'

However much I yearned for the chance to dine with Edward, the prospect of sitting at table with Tremain was not one I could contemplate.

Outside in the passage, Edward stopped. We could hear Mrs Bly again, moving around the kitchen. In the dimness, his face seemed close.

'I'll see to the tree,' I said again.

'Thank you, Miss Cardew,' he replied, softly. 'Boscawen said he would ask you to come, and I'm glad he did.'

'It was Father who asked me,' I said. 'But of course, I'm delighted to, that is . . . I hope I can be of use,' I said.

His gaze had moved away, to a dark corner of the passage. Just discernible, there leaned a hoop and a stick. He dragged his eyes back to my face. 'It's a great solace – I mean, you're –' And now it was his turn to flush. Awkwardly he bowed, and went away.

I listened to his departing steps, then turned back into the kitchen for a bowl of hot water.

8.

Agnes took the steam quietly, coughing an encouraging amount, and then subsiding back on to the pillows. I emptied her chamber pot, took the bowl away, and she agreed to close her eyes while I went about the house fastening the shutters. Those at the front would be sufficient for a chance caller to understand that death had touched Polneath.

With Tremain out of the house, moving through the passages ought to have been gentler upon the nerves, but I found myself treading softly. I told myself it was out of respect for a grieving household; but that did not explain why I also stopped to look over my shoulder every few steps. In the failing light I could hear distant gunshots. Tremain, exercising his feelings upon the rooks.

I began at the top of the house, with the storerooms opposite the rooms occupied by Mrs Bly, Agnes, and now myself, and then moved down to the grander rooms. None of the doors were locked, and unseen draughts shook them in their frames. I thought of what Mrs Bly had said: of Tremain hoarding his bunch of keys, his evident determination that no one should sneeze but that he know about it.

I guessed that Edward's bedroom must overlook the back of the house: the two servants' wings, the pond, and the mills beyond. Tremain's room did – his was the only door that gaped ajar, a cold draught coming from an open window within. I could glimpse a decanter still holding a half-inch of port, sitting on the bedside table. A grand mirror, dusty cut-glass jars catching the light.

The front bedrooms were damp-smelling rooms, too grand to be comfortable; identical four posters draped in a faded peach, the hangings bagged haphazardly, so that surely moth had got in. Spotted mirrors and ornate, cracked chamber pots pushed into corners. Every windowsill was host to a graveyard of dead flies.

The view from these rooms was of the great sweep of gravel at the front of the house, and the rarely used carriage drive climbing away to the top road, where Boscawen lived.

There was a chill to those front rooms. I had rather be in William's, however melancholy.

The last of the grand bedrooms was different. It must have been the one used by Edward's wife, before she died: Emily, William's mother. The room was done in pink. There were small soft slippers beside the bed, and in the wardrobe a host of pale summer dresses and linen, expensive things. Large white hats. She had only ever come for June.

She had been new money, Emily Tremain, though it was not polite to know that. She had been a little thing, fair. People had said that William took after her, although you could not really tell with children what their colouring would go on to be. She had been quiet – Edith had thought her shy, but she had seemed to me aloof, not understanding country things, nor caring to. Her father made cotton in Leeds, while Edward brought the older family, and the southern connection; for it had been made clear to her father, Mrs Humphrey said, that her health meant she oughtn't to settle in the north.

Edward had been so young, when they'd married. Twenty. A year older than I was now, but men were such fools. I could not decide what I would prefer, that he should have loved her, or that he should have been indifferent. He had *seemed* indifferent. Never cruel, but no more than polite; except, the year she was large with William, holding doors for her more carefully, placing a shawl about her shoulders in church.

Some people said there had been unpleasantness, between her father and Tremain; that, while William would have inherited her money, Edward was cut out from doing so. It was not polite to know about that, either. That was why, people said, Tremain had appeared to dote upon his grandson, as he never had upon his son. If it was true, it meant that Edward's money, money that might have been invested in the failing mills, had gone up in smoke, along with his son.

I closed the shutters in Emily Tremain's room, plunging the

scent bottles on the dressing table into darkness. If Edward had not loved her, it was strange that all her things had simply been left like this. He must have, then. He must have loved her.

On the landing, I almost turned my ankle, and then picked up a small spinning top, which had rolled against the edge of the carpet. I thought of the little hands entranced by its smoothness, the delighted counting as it would spin, and I almost thought I heard him – six, seven, eight – and looked around, but there was only the quiet, dim passage, and that air of waiting.

I finished with the shutters on the ground floor. There was a music room, with a harpsichord. The billiard room felt like Tremain's realm: an overflowing ashtray, and a single ugly burn in the green baize of the table. In the library I found the packing for the tree decorations, where Mrs Bly had told me I should find it, pushed under one of the tables. There was thick dust all around. The books were shut up mostly, in glass-fronted cases, and plenty looked as though they had never been touched. I idled along one or two of the titles – temperance and Methodist tracts, which must have belonged to Edward's grandfather.

As the daylight failed entirely, I attended to the tree. Mrs Bly had said Jake would come when I was finished, and take it out. Evidently, it must come down, yet it seemed a shame. Some of the ornaments were exquisite – and old, too. There was a porcelain Holy Family: father, mother, little son. There was an alabaster dove, and a lovely little drummer boy, perfect in every detail.

I began with the presents beneath the tree, packing them into a crate Mrs Bly had given me. As I touched each one, I could not help feeling for what was inside. One was soft. Another felt like a little set of cricket stumps, or skittles perhaps. None had a name on, Will having been the only child in the house, and it occurred to me that this was fortunate, since the presents would now be going to other boys, and then chastised myself for the cold practicality of the thought.

The presents done, I moved on to the tree; the heavier things, and then the baubles. Usually I would enjoy the feel of the ornaments, the peculiar bend of my reflection in the blown glass. But there was no joy in the task. Some of the tissue was almost disintegrating, and I was tired, I realized, more tired than I had thought. After Mother died, when I would decorate the tree, Father would cry. I had got into the habit of bringing the ornaments down from the attic myself, dusty-handed, and decking the tree while he was out on his rounds. A surprise for him, I would say to Mrs Humphrey.

Now I took down the Holy Family, but I must have mishandled it somehow, for the child came away from the manger, snapped off at the root like a tooth. I looked around me, at the dim and quiet hall. The break was a clean one, perhaps it could be mended; I dithered like that, for a minute. I ought to put the ornament aside, and give it to Mrs Bly, or to Edward. Instead, I wrapped it in tissue, with clumsy hands, and put it away with the rest, telling myself they had other things to think of.

The mistake made me anxious to see Jake. Keen, as well as nervous.

It had been nagging at the edge of my thoughts, what Edward had said about servants. That their business is their own. That it did not follow that their business must be malicious – I had not been able to avoid veering towards what Edward might have meant. Avoid proposing to myself the reasons a maid might have, for being out of her bedroom at night, that were *not* malicious. *Their business is their own.* Could she have been meeting a sweetheart? And there was but one manservant at Polneath, and that was Jake . . . but it was impossible. I was running too far. Jake would never be so underhand – and now I was eager for nothing more than to see him, to have the solid reassurance of him.

When the front door opened, I leapt to my feet. But it was Tremain: he gripped the door frame, dropped his hat. Over his arm was a half-dismantled gun.

'Have I missed dinner?' he said.

'It's not yet five, sir,' I replied.

He looked at me, properly. Weak but dangerous, as a beast when it is wounded.

'Good evening,' I added. I was thinking, Edward, come out of your study. Jake, come in for the tree.

'Didn't you get married?' Tremain said, reaching for his hat.

I looked down. 'My friend Edith was married, sir. In the autumn. The vicar's daughter . . .' I paused.

'Ah *yes*,' Tremain said.

I looked up in time to see the unpleasant expression which had overtaken his face.

'And you're here to check on us.'

'I'm helping Mrs Bly,' I said.

And at that, Jake appeared behind him. Tremain dropped his hat again, lurched for it, and almost lost his balance. Jake stooped to help him, taking the gun with a murmured, 'Allow me, sir.'

Tremain made for the stairs, using the bannister to haul himself up, step by arduous step.

'I'm almost finished,' I said to Jake, when Tremain was out of earshot.

We stood and looked at the tree, a strange, sentient scrap of the outside.

'They burn nice. Do you remember my father would make a bonfire of ours?'

'I do,' I said. And then, 'Mr Edward said, would you see the presents sent to St Margaret's in Falmouth.' I gestured to the crate.

Jake nodded. 'It's sad.'

He looked thinner, suddenly. Weary. I remembered him wet through. Was it only the night before? I looked up the stairs after Tremain. 'He thought I was Edith.'

'You're nothing alike,' Jake said.

I looked back at the tree. 'Inquest tomorrow.'

'Mm. And then you'll go home.' He was fidgeting with the gun. 'Your father oughtn't to have sent you,' he said, suddenly.

'Whyever not?'

He didn't answer.

'Jake?' I stopped, dropped my voice. 'Jake, do you suppose Agnes was happy here?'

He still said nothing.

I whispered, 'She said she'd given Tremain her notice.'

Jake looked at me. 'Did she?' His gaze moved back to the gun. 'Does Mr Edward know?'

'I don't think so,' I replied. 'I didn't want to burden him with it . . .'

Jake had fallen quiet again.

'Jake?' I said. And then, 'Do you like Agnes?'

This time he did not look at me, only balanced the gun across the useless presents, hefted the crate. When he had a grip on it, he said, 'You shouldn't be here. You should go home.'

'It's only a night. The inquest is tomorrow.'

He looked at me. 'You're not a servant,' he said. 'I know you're in and out of houses – that you help people, because of your father. But there are things you don't understand.'

'For instance?' I said, more coldly now.

He looked at me for a long moment, but then only gave a resentful kind of shrug, and went off with the crate.

When he had gone, I lingered in the hall, gathering the few stray scraps of tissue to put in the fire. I thought Jake might come back for the tree, and then I might sweep the needles, but he didn't appear again.

Nor did Edward. The house was quiet, and I was alone.

Mrs Bly had lit the gas mantle in the stairwell when I went down, and she thanked me, curtly, for the shutters and the tree. There was a stew ready, and some roast beef for the gentlemen. I waited while she finished the plates. Mrs Bly told me she would take the master's, and Mr Edward's, so I carried two bowls up the stairs for Agnes and myself. My knees ached. I knew I must press her, about the packed bag, about where she had been. I knew I ought to ask her about Jake. I left one bowl in William's room for myself, set it on the little chest of drawers, and took the other in to Agnes.

Her eyes were closed as I went in, but she quickly opened them, and then calmed as she saw who it was.

'Manage any sleep?' I said.

She nodded. 'A bit.'

I stood by with the stew as she struggled upright against the pillows. She was just reaching for the bowl, when her eyes flicked over my shoulder.

I had never seen the colour drain so fast from a face. From pink to white to grey in half a moment, and her mouth fell open and a sound came out.

'What?' I said. I whirled about to put down the stew. I thought she was having some kind of turn. 'What is it?'

'Did you put it there?' Agnes nodded at the door.

And then I looked.

Hanging upon the door across the two hooks was a grubby, yellow garment.

Though I didn't recognize it, I felt suddenly cold. 'No. What –?'

I looked at Agnes, and understood. It was a child's nightshirt. Small, spoiled with dirt, and stained now a bright, sick yellow. There was mangled lace at the throat and cuffs. It was William's nightshirt. Dyed? In the dim light of the bedroom it seemed almost to glow.

'How did –' I looked at it again. 'You didn't hear anyone come in?'

Agnes was pale. 'The noise of the key would have woken me.'

I looked at the shirt again. Hanging, like a rag for scaring birds. Brimstone, that was the colour. Like they put in the powder. My hands, my arms had gone almost numb, and I realized my breath was quick. Aware of Agnes's eyes on me, I worked to be calm, and made myself touch it. The cloth was fine, and almost imperceptibly damp.

I thought of the child in the woods, the yellow ghost.

I made myself fold the shirt.

'I didn't lock you in,' I said. 'I didn't like to.'

It took several minutes to calm Agnes down, and even then she would not accept the stew. She insisted that she felt sick, but took a little of the draught my father had left, after I'd promised to lock the door.

As Agnes's eyelids began to look heavy, I told her that I would be just through the wall, a cough or a sneeze and I would hear her. I thought she looked comforted. I held the nightshirt bundled behind my back, and nodded at the now empty hooks on the back of her door.

'Do you suppose it was Mrs Bly?' I stepped closer. 'Is she cruel to you, Agnes? Is that why you wished to leave?'

But Agnes was already half asleep, in spite of herself. She only said, 'When you turn the key, you'll take it with you?'

I did as she asked. Locked her in, and took the key, put it on the little table near William's bedside, leaving the nightshirt draped at the end of the bed. I ate my own cold stew quickly, trying to think.

Tremain had accused Agnes. Mrs Bly would not hear a word against him. Had woken to the fire, and turned not along the passage to Agnes's room, but up the stairs to wake Tremain. I picked up the yellow nightshirt, and rolled it up, tucked it into my apron, and went down.

I set my empty bowl down rather hard on the kitchen table, and Mrs Bly jumped.

'Everything alright with the stew, Miss Cardew?'

'Where is William's nightshirt?'

She turned from her work. 'His –?'

'His nightshirt. The one he was wearing when he died.'

Mrs Bly's face was a careful blank. 'In the wash, I suppose. I put him in a new one, and wiped his face and hands –'

'Why did you do that?' I said, and when it was clear she didn't take my meaning, I added, 'The nightshirt is evidence, Mrs Bly. Mr Boscawen will want to be able to examine it. Along with any marks on William's person.'

She looked scared at that, and began to bluster that she would find it, she was sure she could lay hold of it.

I could hardly tell whether she was honest, she had such a flinching, averted way about her. At last, I held up the nightshirt. Clutched in one fist, it looked like a grubby yellow rag. 'Is this the one?'

'Is – what's the matter with it?' she said. 'Why is it –?'

But I could not make out what was behind her eyes. Was it guilt? Or fear?

'I don't know,' I said. 'Nor how it got to Agnes's room.'

'To where?'

'To Agnes's room.'

Mrs Bly swallowed. That blankness returned. 'I suppose she did it herself,' Mrs Bly said. 'No doubt she wished to trifle with you.'

★

In William's room, I put the bundled nightshirt on the floor by the door, and paced. I could not settle. Ought I to go to Edward? But he had so much with which to contend, and the memory of his heavy head and red eyes earlier was enough to stop me. Besides, what would I tell him? That a nightshirt had gone astray – turned yellow – it almost sounded ridiculous, and hardly described the feeling of seeing it hanging there, the sick glow of it, and realizing to whom it belonged. What was more, I hardly knew what to think. Agnes's fear had seemed real. But what if she *had* put the nightshirt there? She might have. After all, I hadn't locked her in. Suddenly I felt that I did not understand her at all. As though I had waded beyond my depth.

I felt resentful, suddenly, of the task Boscawen had set for me, the manner in which he had pulled me in. Who was he, to ask this? And yet at the same time I felt grateful, that the inquest was tomorrow, and that I could hand it all to him. Never think of it again.

To calm myself, I dug out the spinning top I had found earlier, and set it on the bookshelf, beside a mysterious felt bag, the contents of which I recognized the moment I lifted it. I tipped the marbles out gently on to the coverlet, nudged them to and fro. There was one that was clear, with a swirl of green smoke. Another that was blue.

Edith and I had been given marbles as little girls, although I hadn't liked to play the games where one could win or lose them. I had been fiercely attached to each of mine, knew their colours and depths. Once, Father had caught me holding one on my tongue – it was summer, and they were so cool, like sweets – and had made me spit it out, and then shaken me quite roughly, the only time he had ever laid an unkind hand on me. I could remember the shock of it. I thought of Father, now. Wondered whether Mrs Humphrey had gone for the night; whether he was missing me.

Once, when we were already too old, no doubt, for the marbles, I had insisted that Edith and I each choose our favourites and exchange them, as a token of friendship. She chose a sea-green one, and I parted with a blue. That would have been the year after Mother died – I know, because it was the first year that

Father allowed me to attend the works tea with Edith and her sisters, notionally supervised by her mother, who fell asleep within half an hour beneath a tree. We roamed through the woods, keeping away from the mill buildings, as we'd been told. It wasn't frightening, as it seemed on other days, for from all around came the shouts of other children, Jake amongst them. Edith devised a game, a version of hide and seek, though she called it 'Yellow Ghost'. We played for hours, shrieking deliciously when we were caught, until I lost her. I searched for ages. When I found her, it was in a hollow at the foot of a tree with Jake Feltham, sitting close together and in earnest conversation.

As very little girls, even our parents had mistaken Edith and me for one another, but by that summer it was impossible. I had thickened and grown, Edith remaining small and neat; my own hair had darkened, while Edith's remained fair. She had better teeth than I, though she took no care of them, and I watched them that day, flashing white in the dappled sun as she laughed at something Jake had said. For weeks, I had been carrying around with me her sea-green marble. I did not disturb them – I was unequal to it – but I took out the marble, and dropped it purposely in the grass. I was cold with her for days after that, and would not tell her why; with Jake, I was entirely ordinary. It was she I blamed.

I put back the bag of marbles, and picked up William's books in turn, flipped through them. School books were to the right of the shelf. The Latin was a primer, familiar enough. In a book on the Ancient Romans, on page forty-nine, I found a rude drawing of a man. Turning back to the front of the text, however, I found five or six boys' names written on the flyleaf in various hands, and the one which made the sketch belonged to neither of the last two names: Edward Tremain, elegant, and then, at the bottom, neat, careful, William Tremain.

There was *The Pilgrim's Progress*. There were adventure tales, cautionary tales, and there was *Alice*, well thumbed. I pulled out the copy. Something fluttered out of the book and fell to the floor. I got up off the bed. It was a drawing, simple but careful. 'Papa', it said, in a childish hand, and the figure was rather good, he had caught something of Edward's grace. But the face he had attempted too many times. It had ended up blurred. Perhaps that was why he had not given it to Edward. I folded the drawing, and shut it into the volume again, replaced the book upon the shelf. Alice. A child who has to make sense of strange large beings, I thought, with their own reasons, and their own ways of going on.

If only, I thought – if only I could see what William had seen, that night. Hear what William had heard.

I remembered again how Boscawen had been, in Agnes's room – how cold, how businesslike. I opened the wardrobe. The wires in the drum rattled, and made my heart beat faster for a moment. I laid out each of William's pairs of shoes on the rug. Then I brought out each item of clothing in turn, into the light. The small blue sailor suit. The crisp little white shirt. I brought out the new school blazer, dark blue with black piping. It was rather larger than the rest of the things.

I was about to put the blazer back when I noticed that the lining had a weight and a swing, and I felt it: the unmistakable shape. The places where the stitches of the hem had been broken to accommodate it. Another moment, and I had it out. A key. It was a Polneath one – that same ornate, overblown 'P' at the head.

One key for each door, Mrs Bly had said, and no copies.

I got up from the bed, and tried the key in William's door, but it wouldn't go. Not this room, then. He had hidden it, or someone had, in a place where nobody would look. Or, I corrected myself, where no man would look.

I put the key under my bolster, so that it wouldn't be confused with the one for Agnes's room. The nightshirt I hid in the bottom of the wardrobe. I could not bear the glow of it in the dim light. I used one of William's shoes to wedge the door of the room in place, took out the pins and undid the plaits that Agnes had made. The roots of my hair felt sore.

I changed into my own nightgown, and lay down. I could not tell Edward about the nightshirt. Not when he already had so much to distress him. Tomorrow I would see Father, and then Boscawen. It made me uneasy; how little I wished to burden Father with Agnes and Mrs Bly, with the nightshirt and now this key. Boscawen, then – but he would not simply want the facts. He would want what I made of them. And the truth was, I was groping in the dark. Even if Agnes had started the fire, I did not see why she could have wished to hurt William. And, when he heard and smelled the blaze, why had William not fled? It was all very well, what Father had said about children tending to hide from fire, but William was not so small. He must have understood his danger.

Some unseen current of air rattled the wires of the snare drum again. At length I got up and shut the drum in the wardrobe, too. Lying awake, I thought of a small boy creeping down a dark stair, his hand following the wall like a line of print.

At some point sleep arrived, like a snuffed candle. I dreamed of a yellow shape amongst the trees. I dreamed of William's nightshirt, that it had somehow got over my face. I woke, and heard the creak of floorboards in Agnes's room – she must have been using the chamber pot – and then, dreaming again, the sound of a key turning, and Old Tremain in the doorway saying, 'Ivy.'

That woke me properly. But my door was as I had left it. The house was still. Through the wall, I heard the creak of Agnes turning over.

9.

Never before that Christmas Eve had I woken to silence. No sound of Father trying to keep his boots quiet on the stairs, or Mrs Humphrey singing, but a silence that had a texture in the ears. It was still half dark. I slipped out of William Tremain's little bed into the freezing room, into the renewed sadness of his toys and little bookshelf.

The mirror was so small and dim that I opened the drapes to use the window instead, backed by the slowly lightening sky. Jake was already out, taking the damaged door to the north wing off its hinges. I saw Agnes's key on the table, checked under my bolster for the one I had found in William's blazer. Still there. I hadn't dreamed any of it. Something made me slip the key into my pocket.

My hair was unruly, from what Agnes had done. I managed to tidy it, and perhaps it was for the best that I looked plainer than I had yesterday. Today's business was a sober one. I put my things into my bag. Jake could fetch it, after the inquest, or perhaps I could find a reason to come back myself, and see Edward. I wondered whether he had finished Agnes's character.

Today Tremain would claim, before dozens, that Agnes had lit the fire which had killed William. But what would the jury say? What would Boscawen? He would ask me, and I could not answer. There was Tremain, a drinker, and the blaze begun in his office. To whom Agnes had given her notice, about which he'd mentioned nothing. There were Edward and Jake, who seemed to think well of Agnes – Jake, perhaps, *too* well. There was the nightshirt, and Mrs Bly, who took no pains to conceal her dislike of Agnes, her blame. And there was Agnes herself, packed for a hasty departure which was never made; out of her room at midnight, and still I had been able to extract no explanation. Last, there was William, another enigma. Hiding under a servant's bed.

Tonight, I would be sleeping in my own bed. I wondered where Agnes would be sent, after the inquest was done.

When I went down to fetch Agnes's breakfast, Mrs Bly was sitting at the kitchen table, Father kneeling to prod at her ankle.

'Father,' I said, and he stood up, dusting his hands. I took both of them. 'Her chest is much better, I think you'll find she's fit enough to go.'

'Hello, my dear,' he said, and, 'it's doing just nicely,' to Mrs Bly, whose face had soured.

'Thank you, Doctor,' she said, and nodded at a tray with two covered bowls.

I picked up the tray, and Father followed me out.

Subtly, I studied him. When Father hadn't slept enough, he trotted out more frequently his little reassurances – *doing nicely, wholly to be expected* – but in a tone which sounded distracted, rather thin. Now, he dropped behind me as we climbed the stairs.

'She still won't say where she was,' I said, but he didn't answer. At the top of the stairs, I let him pass ahead of me to open the door. 'And what have you been doing?'

He stood back. 'Examining William.'

'Was it as you thought?' I prompted. 'Asphyxiation?'

He looked away, down the passage. 'I – pardon? Yes, my dear.'

'Are you quite well, Father?' I said, in a low voice.

He frowned distractedly. 'Of course. I'd better –'

I showed him Agnes's door, saw him lift his eyebrows as I unlocked it, leaving the key in the door. But I didn't want to explain to him: about the nightshirt, about her asking me to lock her in. Agnes could tell him if she liked, but I suspected she would not. Better that he should just declare Agnes fit to testify, and be done. I would take it all to Boscawen.

Agnes was dressed when I put my head around her door. She seemed calm, but refused the porridge – 'I couldn't,' she said – and when Father asked how the draught had suited her, she looked at him, simply and sadly. 'When I woke this morning, I'd forgotten he was dead.'

Father nodded at me, and so I took the porridge back to

William's room, and ate my own, and Agnes's as well. Then I went down to the hall. Jake must have been for the tree. I waited, stooping to pick up stray pine needles with my fingernails, until I heard feet on the stairs. It was Agnes, and Father behind, holding tight to the bannister as he descended. He looked, in the clear white light of the hall, greyer in the face than before.

From behind me, Edward appeared. 'Dr Cardew, it's kind of you to come out so early.'

At that, Father seemed to rouse himself, and came down to take Edward's hand, and condole with him properly. Mrs Bly came from the direction of the kitchen, wearing a rather prim hat, and Agnes made a nervous movement with her hands, and looked away at the open front door.

'I came in Mr Boscawen's gig,' Father was saying, 'but, ah, we may not all fit –'

Last of all was Tremain, who paused at the top of the stairs, as though to ready himself. He looked as though he had been scrubbed with wire wool. Edward gave the smallest flinch at the sight of him, but Agnes's countenance remained carefully blank. Tremain looked at her, one look, and then began to stump down the stairs, with a rough, 'Are we going?'

The gig was outside on the gravel sweep, Jake rubbing the horse's nose. Edward helped Mrs Bly up. Agnes went next, not taking the hand he proffered; the effort of climbing produced a fit of coughing, which she tried to suppress as Tremain laboured up the step to sit beside Mrs Bly. Agnes crammed herself as far away from Tremain as she could get and looked resolutely away. Edward helped Father up next, and insisted that he himself could perfectly well walk, that it would do him good.

Then he turned to me and said, 'I suspect you'd welcome a walk, too, Miss Cardew?'

The gig outstripped us quickly, Father's pale face bobbing further and further ahead. As they slipped out of sight, we were passing the stables. Most of the upper doors were shut.

'One of the economies,' Edward said, nodding at the buildings. 'It's only William's pony, now. He'd almost outgrown her – Father was planning to sell her.'

At our voices, the creature put out her head, and we went over. Edward scratched the space between the pony's ears, murmured to her. 'Oh, Floss,' he said.

'William loved her,' I said. I was thinking of the day of the summer tea, the year before; the last one hosted by Edward's wife, the first to which I had been invited as a young lady. 'He was so particular, that time – do you remember? Him showing me how to feed her?'

Edward looked at me. 'I remember,' he said.

We set off, the gravel crunching under our feet. The cold was enough to make one sick, but the fresh air was a relief. The gig would go by the top road, but we walked round and past the walled gardens, through the side gate and around the blast wall, and started down through the mills.

'Father seemed sober at least,' Edward said. And then, 'I suppose there will be a lot of people.'

'It's at Boscawen's discretion,' I replied, but there would, there would be at least the thirteen jurymen – the dozen required by law, and the spare – who would all have been chosen from St Rumon's and around, along with anyone else who cared to hear the proceedings. An inquest, I had heard Boscawen say, ought always to be open. He might, if he liked, admit as many as would fit in the room. Had the thing been done in Falmouth, there might have been a little more remove, but since he had decided to do it the old way, and hold it at the King's Arms, I suspected it would feel as though the village had turned out to adjudicate.

Edward blew out air, and turned away. 'I should think every man with a stake in the works will be there,' he said. He looked at me. 'I was only keeping on with it for William. It was his future.'

I looked at him. 'It's the village's future, too.'

Lightly, Edward kicked a pine cone. 'I know. Father put a great deal into making fuses, this year, but it hasn't quite . . . and I blame myself for that. I encouraged him.'

I was quiet for a moment. 'And now William's money is gone.'

He looked at me. 'You know about that.'

He looked so despairing that I put a hand on his arm, and he stopped. Our breath clouded the air.

'I keep going over,' he said. 'All the places. All the places I looked, and I didn't stop and *think* –'

He was weeping, a little, and angrily, as men will. I offered him my handkerchief, and he shook his head kindly and took out his own, and turned away.

'My God,' he said. And then, 'Forgive me, Miss Cardew.'

'Not at all.'

When he had composed himself, he offered me his elbow, and I took it. For a minute we might have been any couple, walking together in the woods. The trees were bright and dripping, and I could not help it, my heart lifted, and I felt despicable for it lifting.

'It's all hopeless, now, in any case,' he said. 'You've seen what Father's like. Perhaps it's for the best that the mills should close.'

I pressed his arm. 'You certainly oughtn't to have to think of it today.' I wanted to say, *you could leave him, now*. But Edward only just had a grip on himself, I felt. It was clear, too, that Agnes Draper and her fate was the very last thing he was thinking of. Better that I should speak to Boscawen.

Soon we were passing the churchyard, with its climbable, hummocked wall.

I said, 'I threw rice, from just that spot, on your wedding day.'

He paused, and smiled. 'You didn't.' He glanced at me. 'And what were you? Nine?'

'Older than that.'

He let out a breath. 'At least she didn't live to see this.'

I remembered them, coming out of church. The small, fair bride, the rather chilly way she had turned her cheek to his kiss. A wife with a dead husband would still be in deep mourning, but it was different for men. A year was more than respectable, I thought: then felt despicable again.

He glanced back once more at the churchyard wall. 'I suppose you've never left here, have you?' he said. 'Not for school . . .'

'I haven't. Though I'd like to.' I spoke decisively, and without thinking.

Now Edward looked at me. 'I thought, with your father –'

'Well. To travel a little, at least, perhaps,' I said. I could feel my face reddening, uncertain suddenly of what we were speaking. 'My friend Edith, you remember her? The pretty one – she's just back from Venice and Rome.'

Edward sighed, and smiled. 'Sometimes I dream of it. Those great columns. And all of the most beautiful stone, pale as butter.' He looked at me. 'And the heat,' he said.

'You were happy there.'

'Will loved it. But you know, I first went there before I took my degree. When I was quite a boy. Younger than you are now.'

'I've always wanted to go . . . well. Anywhere, to tell the truth.'

Edward smiled. 'I'm terribly glad,' he said. 'That just now, you're here.'

We lapsed into silence. When we were in sight of the King's Arms, I relinquished his elbow.

There was Mrs Mason at the door, and when she saw us she squawked, and came running out to meet us. 'Come in, sir, come in,' she said. 'What can I bring you? Tea? Of course, there's port wine, but –'

About the door, there were several labourers from the mills, each folding his cap in his hands, their faces at once grave and searching. I knew each of them.

Cauldwell said, 'Our condolences, sir.'

To him Edward replied, 'Thank you, thank you,' rather vaguely. To Mrs Mason he said, 'Tea will do very well.'

I saw then how the villagers must seem to Edward: a little sea of faces, that earnest accent, the same twelve surnames replicated again and again. The pent-up curiosity.

I followed him past the landlady into the back room of the inn. The tables had been pushed back against a wall, and a dozen or so wooden chairs set in two rows for the jurymen. There were three upholstered chairs near the hearth, and Tremain was sitting in one of them. Edward dutifully went to him, leaving me alone at the door. Tremain stood up, and put a hand on Edward's shoulder. Agnes had taken a seat on a bench by the window. Mrs Bly occupied the other end, Jake next to her, with a careful space between himself and Agnes. Father must have stepped home for a moment.

Then Boscawen appeared, at the door which led out to the inn yard at the back; he must have been to the convenience. Now he said, 'Miss Cardew?' quite loudly.

I was obliged to cross the crowded room and go out into the yard with him, while people whispered behind me. In the yard, it was damp and quiet. Boscawen led me a few feet from the door, to be sure we weren't overheard.

He turned to me, and I took a step back.

'Well?' he said.

I glanced at the windows, where one or two men were looking curiously out at us. I ducked my face away from the stares. 'I don't have much,' I said. 'She did tell me she'd given her notice to Tremain. That with William going off to school, she had no more wish to stay at Polneath. But she'd given her notice only that evening, and she wouldn't say why her bag was packed. Nor where she was at midnight.'

Boscawen glanced at the windows too, then gave a quick nod. 'Very well. Anything else?'

I hesitated. 'There was his nightshirt.'

Boscawen looked at me. 'Nightshirt?'

'William's. It was hanging in Agnes's bedroom, when I went up to her last evening. But it was yellow. Bright yellow, like brimstone – it gave her rather a turn.'

'Indeed,' Boscawen said.

I felt he could tell: that it had not only been Agnes who was frightened.

'I rather think Mrs Bly put it there,' I said.

'She dislikes the girl?'

'Yes, and –' I stopped, then met his eyes. 'I don't know what happened. I haven't fathomed that. All I can say is that it seems to me as though everyone at Polneath was fond of William. That no one intended to harm him. I cannot say that Miss Draper did *not* light the fire, but there was nothing taken. So concealing a theft could not have been her motive.'

'No,' Boscawen said, more slowly now. He was looking at the sky, as though trying to judge the chance of snow.

My opportunity to mention Edward's hint – my filigree suspicion of Jake – came and then passed.

Then Boscawen looked at me. 'We'd better go in,' he said – and then, just at the door, in a lower voice, 'I ought to warn you – your father has turned up something of his own, which sheds rather a different light on things.'

And with that, we were in amongst the noise of the back room, Boscawen striding away to his chair at the front.

I moved to the bench. Agnes shifted along, and I sat between her and Jake. Not touching, but close enough to sense the bulk of him.

'Alright?' he said.

I nodded. But I was nervous now.

Jurymen were arriving, singly and in twos. Stamping gently and cursing the cold, they congregated, hailing their fellows: 'Come and see me, will you, about that heifer?'

All were known to me, in one way or another; farmers, but also the land agent to the Earl of Falmouth, his gamekeeper, and one of the vergers from St Rumon's. I knew from the papers that more would be summoned than were needed, in case some did not appear, but they had all turned out, and on Christmas Eve. Each of them held a pint of porter, except the land agent, who had a glass of wine.

Minutes passed, then half an hour. What had Father turned up? And where was he?

The Reverend Green came in, and various Falmouth men I had seen before. Tremain sat up straighter at the sight of them; investors in the mills. The constable arrived, still recovering from his fall, his hand cradled in a sling.

The jury quietened, and now began to take their seats, Boscawen marking their names off on a list produced from somewhere in his pile. He excused two of them, from the most outlying farms. Then he collected the room, and began to swear the jury. I hated what an age it took, Boscawen's quiet, precise voice droning on; as the men spoke their oaths, I dug with my thumbnail into the bench. As Boscawen swore the last juryman, Father came in. He stood near the door, still pale, but steadier. I wondered whether he had taken something for his nerves. I wished I could go to him, and tried to make him look at me, but he avoided my eyes.

When the jury were all sworn, Boscawen cleared his throat, and planted his hands on his square knees. 'We are here to enquire into the death of William Tremain, on the twenty-third instant, in the small hours of the morning at Polneath House,' Boscawen said. 'Now, our first matter is that myself and the jury should view the body . . .' Boscawen cleared his throat. 'For you are all required to swear that the boy is, in fact, deceased.'

I turned cold. I had forgotten that this would come first. Father had told me about it once, a piece of procedure, but now, to be faced with it – I wanted to go to Edward, to go up and touch his sleeve. I could see the side of him, and his hand, moving nervously on the arm of his chair.

Boscawen signed to Mr Mason, and a moment later the landlord was pulling something out of the storeroom at the back: oh God, a trolley table on castors, and on it I could see two small, bare feet.

Then William was there, hardly four foot of him. His small, white face. His eyes were closed now, his arms tucked under the covering sheet, but you could see the press of his thumbs into the cotton. I felt Jake let out a breath, as Agnes stiffened on my other side. A hush came over the jury, into which one man coughed sharply, and smothered himself.

William's face was like a saint's face in a window – smooth, absent, his lips slightly parted, as though a scroll of Latin text would be drawn in next. The gap between his lips was very dark, and his face had that yellowish pallor of stained glass.

For a strange moment, I was tempted to grope for Agnes's hand. But I did not.

Then, 'Thank you, Mr Mason,' Boscawen said, and Mason pushed the trolley back into the store, shut the door on it. 'Very well, then,' Boscawen murmured. His voice in the room sounded loud and coarse. 'Now that we have viewed the body, we must – forgive me, it is for form's sake – we must have someone swear that the body viewed is, in fact, William Tremain. So, ah, Mr Edward Tremain, if you would be so kind?'

'That is my son, of course,' Edward replied, quietly.

Tremain had a handkerchief out, and was mopping his face showily, but Edward was very still, his jaw set, braced as though for someone to hit him. At his elbow sat a cup of tea, cooling.

Boscawen asked him first to relate what he knew of the circumstances of William's death, and Edward spoke briefly and to the point, about how the fire had started in the north wing of the house, in his father's office after everyone was abed, and had spread upstairs to the maid Agnes's room, where his son was very sadly caught in it, and had died –

Here Boscawen interjected, to inform the jury that nothing firm could be established about how exactly the fire had started. It had been around the desk, 'Either on purpose,' Boscawen said blandly, 'or through some negligence, perhaps.'

At that, Tremain shuffled in his seat.

Boscawen returned to questioning Edward, asked why William might have been in Agnes's room at all, and Edward related what I already knew: that William had been in the habit of going to Agnes, should he get frightened in the night; that this had been happening more of late.

'What I can't think,' Edward said, shakily, 'was why he hid. Why he did not run away from the flames. But Dr Cardew has given me to understand that little children are known to act strangely in such circumstances.'

Boscawen was quiet through Edward's account, giving the occasional nod, and making assiduous notes, and the jury, too, listened attentively. Tremain kept looking at Edward, and made a noise of disdain at the suggestion that William might have been afraid to go away to school.

Across the room, Father was listening, too. He looked from Edward to Boscawen and back again, his eyes large. Why had Boscawen not begun with Father? If what he had to say could alter matters so materially?

But Boscawen turned next to Mrs Bly, one of the jury saying, 'And you first detected the fire, madam?'

Yes: she had heard a rushing sound, and smelled the smoke. She had gone up for the master, thinking Mr Edward would be able to then go most easily for William. The juror asked one or two more questions about the plan of the house, and Mrs Bly explained how the two service wings were built at the back – the north wing had the kitchen and such downstairs, and Agnes's bedroom above, as well as her own. But the ceilings being higher, in the grand part of the house, you had still to climb two flights of the north stair between her own room and the gentlemen's.

The juror glanced at Boscawen, then said to Mrs Bly, 'And so you went for Mr Tremain first – not Miss Draper?'

But Mrs Bly met his eyes. 'To put it blunt, sir, the smoke was already that bad, and I could see flames – I yelled, and got no answer, and I thought, she's dead or she's out. And she was out. So.'

Boscawen nodded, and allowed her to relate how Tremain had helped her downstairs in the thickening smoke, how she was unscathed but for a turned ankle from a missed step near the bottom, and then thanked her.

Then, 'Might I ask you to stand up, my dear?' he said, awkwardly, to Agnes.

Tremain was rubbing his thighs, angry or nervous.

Agnes stood up, and took one large step forward, keeping her hands folded like an assiduous child, and raised her eyes to Boscawen.

'You put yourself in great danger, I understand, searching for William.'

Agnes looked at her feet. 'Anyone would, if they'd caught on to where he was.'

Boscawen nodded. 'Everyone is very exercised,' he said then, 'to know where you were, my dear. Before you went to try to save him.'

I turned to look at Agnes.

But she had lowered her gaze. 'I can't say.'

'Ask Jake Feltham,' Mrs Bly said then, loudly from the end of the bench. 'He was quick enough into the pond after her.'

A heavy feeling settled in my stomach, as a new murmuring spread amongst the jury. Tremain and Edward had turned to look. People were asking one another who was Feltham, and there was some pointing, as the murmur increased, and Jake grew tense next to me. He did not turn to look at Mrs Bly, but one of his hands crept to hold the other. Agnes was very still.

'Mr Edward Tremain has related Feltham's heroics already, Mrs Bly,' Boscawen said. 'I would ask you to keep your counsel. You'll be called upon, if you're required again.'

But now Tremain was struggling to his feet.

Boscawen's face clouded.

'The plain fact is, I'd given her notice,' Tremain said. 'Because of,' he gestured to Mrs Bly, 'that matter. And very clearly the girl set the fire. For revenge, you see.'

'Mr Thomas Tremain,' Boscawen said, and appeared to write his name down, though everyone on the jury knew well who he was. Then he looked up. 'That is a serious accusation, sir,' he said, calmly.

'I stand by it,' Tremain replied.

Edward had his head in his hands.

'I am not accustomed,' Boscawen replied, 'to allow an inquest to proceed in this manner. Witnesses will be called in turn. And I believe it might be pertinent, before we proceed further, to turn to the medical evidence.' Boscawen turned to Father. 'Dr Cardew was the physician present at the body's recovery, and has conducted an external examination.' Boscawen nodded to Father.

Father cleared his throat, and shuffled rather on the spot. He had cut himself, I noticed now, just under the ear. He had been doing that more, of late. I missed him suddenly, with an ache that could have made me cross the room.

Boscawen asked him very easy questions, yeses and nos, that conveyed to those assembled that what had killed the boy was asphyxiation by the inhalation of smoke.

'But you made another observation, I think,' Boscawen said, 'during your examination.'

Father's eyes moved to Edward. 'Paint,' he said, gently. 'Under the boy's fingernails. From the door, I think. The door is green, is it not? Bruising to the hands, too.'

At this, a particular silence fell.

'The door was not difficult to open,' Boscawen said. 'And the handle perfectly within the boy's reach. Had it been hot, he had a nightshirt to protect himself. Mr Feltham, when he went up later to extinguish the flames, along with two or three others, stated that the door was found standing open. So I think we must be forced to conclude that at some point that night the door was locked.'

Boscawen looked at Edward, too.

'Locked?' said Edward. 'But why –'

'And unlocked again,' Boscawen said. 'By a person or persons unknown.'

Father was swallowing and swallowing, and Edward had lurched to his feet. Paint. I thought of William, battering and clawing at the door. Yelling, and nobody hearing. I could see Edward thinking it, too. The wind had been loud in the trees that night. Only when escape had become hopeless had William retreated as far away from the smoke and flames as he could. Until they had claimed him.

I could feel Agnes on one side of me, trembling very slightly, and Jake on the other. He was shaking his head. She'd said she had given notice, but now Tremain said she'd been served with it. But to start a fire – to lock a child, a child she loved – and in *revenge*. When she'd have known she would be blamed . . .

But as the jury muttered amongst themselves, Tremain was feeling in the inside pocket of his coat, and now drew out a bunch of keys, searching through them with trembling fingers. Then he stood up.

'This here is the only set of keys for Polneath. The key to Miss Draper's room is missing,' he said, loud with triumph. 'And if you look with an ounce of diligence amongst her things, I'll wager you'll find it. William was never as fond of her as she pretends. She sought to draw him to her, make him loyal to her. Perhaps the better to steal from me. And when he would not – or else when he stumbled, innocent, across her sordid practices – no doubt she dosed him with something, and locked him in –'

Boscawen was up. '*That's enough*,' he barked.

Tremain's mouth fell open in shock.

Boscawen half turned to the jury, as though it would save face to pretend his reprimand had been only for them. He took a breath, calming himself, as the jurymen looked at one another.

I was thinking of the key I had found in William's blazer, hidden where no man would look. The key in my pocket. Realized, suddenly, where it might belong. Could Agnes have used it? Hidden it there?

Boscawen had mastered himself, and when he spoke to Tremain again his usual tone of politeness had returned. 'Why,' he asked, 'would Miss Draper have harmed William? At such great risk to herself? And then attempted to save him?'

'A sudden change of heart. She's mad,' Tremain said, as though the question were a stupid one. 'Mrs Bly will tell you.' He waved his arm at the cook.

'Mad,' Boscawen said, doubtfully.

Mrs Bly hauled herself up, and took a step away from Agnes. 'She made off with one of his nightshirts,' she said, looking at the floor. 'Last evening, and dyed it with brimstone, and hung it up in her room, as though it were a spook.' She glanced at Tremain and Edward. 'It gave Miss Cardew there a turn.'

Now the noise reached a new pitch. Edward was sitting in exactly the same position he had been before Father said about the paint. I could see his hands gripping the arms of his chair, as though the room were turning, as though the chair were the only steady thing. Could it be true? Agnes, vengeful at being sent packing; mad enough to attempt harm upon the only person Tremain seemed to hold dear?

'Is that so, Miss Cardew?' one of the jurymen said.

I stood up. 'I saw the nightshirt. Though not who put it there.'

'Gentlemen,' Boscawen said, briskly. 'Perhaps we ought to adjourn –' he moved his hands, to quell objection – 'to allow me to make some search at Polneath. And to allow Miss Draper to be assessed by Dr Cardew for any disturbance of the mind.'

The jury started to rustle, as though to depart.

'A moment, sirs, there is one thing more,' Boscawen said, levelly. 'Given the specific nature of Mr Tremain's accusation towards Miss Draper, I am minded to order a full post-mortem to be completed on William Tremain's body.'

Silence fell.

Boscawen was gazing coolly at Tremain. Tremain did not flinch.

Edward's hands moved. 'But surely –' Edward began, when Boscawen broke in, in his most even voice.

'I will appoint Graves from Falmouth, he is a good man. Now, if that concludes our business –'

'No,' Tremain said then. He was looking at me. 'Let Cardew do it. Cardew ought to do it, if someone has to.' He twisted in his seat to look at Father. 'It shouldn't be an incomer.'

I shifted, half rose, sat again.

Boscawen hesitated. 'Mr Tremain, it is for the coroner to appoint any requisite medical experts, and I don't believe –'

Then the verger piped up. He had always abased himself before Tremain. 'Mr Boscawen, is it not so, that we the jury can propose the appointment of an alternative medical expert?'

Boscawen sat back, frowning. 'That is the case.'

'Then the family ought to have who they like. And Cardew is our man. We propose Cardew.'

I had to concentrate, in order not to leave my seat, to shout, to halt this somehow. To make them spare Father, without telling them how he dissembled and fudged now to do even his ordinary duties.

'So be it.' Boscawen, looking rattled, began to put away his notes. 'I will send for Graves – there must always be a second present in any case. And we will adjourn, for the moment. Three days, I think. The twenty-seventh.' He stood up, bowed shortly to the room, and went out, avoiding my eyes.

Edward remained in his seat, stock-still. I could not see his face, but I could see the flush of his neck. How could Boscawen order this? There was no reason to think William had been poisoned; Boscawen had only asked for the post-mortem to try to test Tremain in his assertions. And so Father would suffer, and Edward would, at the thought of what Father must do.

Jake got up, his face scarlet, and, before I could speak to him, followed Boscawen out. Mrs Bly had taken herself off to a corner, Mrs Mason with her. Father had gone out with the Reverend Green. Tremain was pushing through the crowd towards the front parlour when Edward, who had seemed rooted to his seat, stood up. He walked jerkily to the door, like a puppet. Agnes waited a minute, and then moved after him. Men parted around her, as though no one could have borne so much as to brush her elbow.

In my pocket, I felt the weight of the key.

I followed, pushing through the shocked and gossiping jurors to the front of the inn, where Agnes was waiting by the gig, the cold wind blowing the dark ribbon of her hat. This time one of Boscawen's men was at the reins. Edward was already walking away up the lane, staggering a little, and Tremain was watching him go. Jake was following, for that way lay his father's house, too.

At his departing back, Tremain called, 'You needn't work your notice.'

Jake did not turn, and I was glad. I could not have stood to look at him.

It was then that Boscawen came past me. He must have remained inside, settling something with Mr Mason, perhaps, but now he was here, trudging by me towards the gig. I felt the key in my pocket. I ought to tell him about it. I didn't want to believe it. But to conceal it would be wrong . . .

'Sir,' I said.

He stopped. He looked, now, tired and harried.

'What is it, Miss Cardew?' he said.

I glanced about, to make sure no one could hear. Tremain was watching us. I ought to say, now. In my pocket, I touched the key.

'You might have spared everyone the post-mortem.'

'Spared who?' Boscawen said. Then he looked up at the sky, brought his hand up to the back of his neck. 'It wasn't I who wanted your father for it.'

'You know as well as I do that the maid didn't poison William,'

I said. 'Whatever happened, it's hardly likely it was that – Tremain's feelings have run away with him. It's needless, cruel – think what Mr Edward is feeling –'

'I don't much care what Mr Edward is feeling,' Boscawen said, and then looked about us, checked his rising voice. Said, curtly, quietly, 'And the dead are dead, Miss Cardew. They can't feel.' Abruptly he turned, and made for the gig.

I didn't stop him. Someone was touching my arm; it was Father. Agnes was standing quite still, on the opposite side of the gig from the others. She watched Father take my elbow.

Boscawen helped Tremain into the gig, and then Mrs Bly, and last of all Agnes.

'Surely she can't stay there now,' Father said.

'I don't know,' I said, wearily. I thought of Boscawen saying, *she won't be harmed. Tremain knows I'm watching.* What did he think now? 'But it seems they're taking her. I'll have to go back,' I said.

Father said nothing.

After a moment, I said, 'Can you do it?'

'I spent six months attached to an asylum, when I was training,' Father said. And then, 'You didn't mention the nightshirt.'

'I didn't want to trouble you with it.' I paused. 'I can't believe it of Jake . . .'

I could feel Father's carefulness as he considered his reply. 'There is nothing to suggest that Jake set the fire . . . but Jake is a young man, Ivy,' he said. 'He is not bound to behave as a gentleman would.'

I didn't answer. I thought suddenly of the day, I was fourteen, when Mrs Humphrey must have finally had a word with Father about Jake, and Father had spoken to me. It seemed that, while children could only be divided into the good and bad, there were other ways in which men and women might be divided. Father had said I would embarrass Jake, clinging about him like that. I had never sat on Jake's garden wall to wait for him again.

'In any case,' I said. 'I wasn't asking about Agnes. I meant William. Can you do it?' I nodded towards the inn, where the body was still lying in the storeroom.

Father nodded. 'I suppose so. I did several, in my youth.'

I looked at Boscawen, conversing with the constable beside the gig. I knew what it would cost Father. 'You could refuse.'

'Mr Boscawen has asked for my help. We must trust that he knows what is necessary.' But his hand, as he laid it on my arm, was shaky, and he was frowning, as he had frowned that morning at Polneath, coming behind Agnes down the stair.

I almost asked why he had kept it back, about the paint, the fingernails. But Father had always taken seriously the particulars of his calling. Including the keeping of secrets.

The post-mortem seemed so cruel. Yet it was clear, and there was no more shirking the fact, now. The truth was cruel. William Tremain had been locked in to die. And perhaps it warranted the most intrusive and lonely of investigations, if it might be confirmed who had turned the key.

'Must you go back?' Father said then.

I looked at him. 'Mr Boscawen asked for my help.'

Father dropped his head, nodded. He was clutching his brown leather bag, the bag he carried everywhere such that I hardly saw it any more, and this made me think of his other bag – the black one. He didn't have need for it often, but I had seen it, and seen him lay the implements out one by one and name them. Bone saw, short knife. Forceps. Brain knife. Cold steel through inert, unflinching flesh.

At last, Boscawen was climbing up into the gig.

Again I touched the key in my pocket. Let him search, I thought. Then felt a stab of guilt. Wondered whether he would be angry, when he knew I had impeded him.

10.

1918

Before me on the desk are several piles of correspondence, and a plate empty of all but a small, neat pile of fish bones, fine and sharp like needles made of glass. Mrs Fossett has been making the penitential sort of food which would, most years, be unsuited to the season. It makes me think of Mrs Bly at Polneath all those years ago, that other dark Christmas, fretting about the suitability of goose, of salmon.

I am avoiding the dining room – having made the fireplace garlands, I now can't bear to look at them – and so have eaten sitting at the desk in the study, picking the bones one by one from my mouth, staring at the uppermost sheet on the pile of correspondence which concerns Richard. It is a short note, from the vicar. I always think of him as quite a child, because he succeeded Edith's father, although he is probably not much younger than myself. The note is neat, with a proper letterhead, and says that the Reverend Benson heartily approves Mr Boscawen's design for a monument to the fallen, and will be pleased to support it at the next meeting of the parish council in the new year.

Today is the 29th of December. Three more days, still, until we can turn the calendar. The 29th, and the last time I spoke a cross word to Richard was exactly a fortnight ago, and I can hardly encompass how much has happened since then.

I must offer it in pieces.

A fortnight ago. A Sunday morning. I had been out walking, and was taking off my boots when I heard Richard calling me upstairs.

He wanted to show me some sketches he had made. In the summer, I had borne patiently with this preoccupation of his, about the erection of a monument. But of course things had been different, since before Armistice Day. Since I had learned of Mrs Smith.

Now, Richard was sitting up against his pillows, in pyjamas with a stripe of an almost military green, trying to provoke in me the forbearance I had shown him before, pushing a piece of paper into my hand.

The sketch was of a sort of hexagonal spike of stone, with some ornamental business around the base. He had managed to make it surprisingly neat.

I wanted to run out of the room. I wanted to say that if you wish people to remember the dead, better to dig a deep hole in the middle of the village green, and neglect to light or fence it.

I handed back the sheet. 'I suppose it's not offensive. It will do very well for a place to weep.'

He looked affronted; did not answer instantly. He looked down at his design. 'It's not for us,' he said, in an infuriatingly wounded voice. 'It's for *them*.'

I must have made a sort of noise, a noise which sounded enough like derision, for he looked up at me, sharply.

'The dead are dead, Richard,' I said, meeting his eyes. 'They can't feel.'

After his reply on Armistice Day, I began writing and writing to Edward. Every morning, I performed a feverish search of the post. I read each of his letters at my desk, compelled, unhappy, and then put them in the fire. I could not risk leaving them lying about – I was sure that Mrs Fossett would spy around my desk now and then, glance through my waste paper. But I allowed myself to tear off and keep a strip from the top of each letter – *My dear Ivy* – and spent minutes together studying the swooping 'y', the generous 'v'.

My name, in Edward's own hand.

It brought to mind when I was young, and wrote an 'E' on a misted mirror in the bathroom at my father's house. It had come back to haunt me, the next bath time, and had me scurrying downstairs for vinegar and a cloth.

I confided everything to Edward, in our correspondence – everything, except Mrs Smith. Murray did not mention turning up an address, and I did not press him. I told myself that it did not matter, now. Hang Richard, and hang his obligations – they were nothing to me. Besides, what if Edward were to think that I had given Richard reason to stray? And so I did not mention her, nor, for that matter, my dream, nor my account of the Polneath business, which was lengthening by the day . . .

Now that I think about it, perhaps I kept back rather a lot of things.

But Edward confided in me, in his turn. He told me about his son Archie, who, he said, had been on his way to the Bar. Constance's people had helped him. He'd been studious, but neither weak nor sensitive: stolid, was what he was, Edward said. He had hated fighting, mostly for the mud and the wet. But he was not a shy boy . . . You could see the pause, where Edward had shaken his pen again. Not at all like William.

My heart broke for him, reading that. To lose wife and child within a year: not once in a lifetime, but twice.

It had been Archie's death, Edward wrote, which had led him to give up his work at the War Office. He still had friends there, but the work had all been froth. How to grow carrots in window boxes. Fiddling while Rome burned.

Besides, Constance had been ill. She had been dying rather slowly, of a tumour. That second marriage, Edward said, had not been what he had hoped. Though she had been a good enough woman; the fault was all his. A man was supposed to grow more hard-headed with age, but he thought he had been more practical, dare he say it, more mercenary, as a young man. Now that he was old, he wished he had lived more for his heart.

I still think, he wrote, *so often I think of the day I left you behind, Ivy – and, though I realize it's too late now, every day I regret the mistake.*

Nonsense, I wrote back. *I mean, mistakes can be corrected.*

*

His mentioning the War Office gave me a jolt. It was true, then: here was my opportunity, at last. Edward, who knew people, who wanted to oblige me, who stood a solid chance of finding out for certain what had happened to Tim. And I still wished to know – surely I still wished to know, even though Theo Stainforth and his insinuations seemed so long ago that I had all but convinced myself he must have been mistaken.

I told Edward about the telegram, and hinted at what Stainforth had said. *I wonder*, I wrote, *with your connections* – and left that sentence unfinished. *Richard doesn't wish to know what happened*, I told him. *But it has been weighing on my mind. I always tried to keep Tim from harm*, I wrote, *and I tried to teach him to be good, to do good, and I fear that did not fit him for what was coming. For the world. For acts which might not bear close scrutiny. I sometimes fear that I made him* – I paused, and my pen dripped – *unusual*.

Edward said that he would certainly ask around amongst his friends at the Office. Surely some brother captain or other could be turned up, who might be able to shed a little more light – but in the meantime, I really ought not to trouble myself. What was a mother for, but to keep her son from harm, teach him to be good? And as to the telegram, there were so many foul-ups with the administration of these things. There was surely some perfectly natural explanation.

For whole days together, I managed to calm myself into certainty that Tim's death had been an ordinary soldier's death. Other days, the guilt of the correspondence – the strips of paper, *My dear Ivy* . . . , lying thick as fallen leaves now in the drawer of the desk – made itself impervious even to the ready excuse of Richard's Mrs Smith, and I found myself jumpy, nervous, prone to remembering.

I had hinted that, were Edward to visit our part of the world again, I should be very pleased to renew our acquaintance – but Edward made no further mention of coming, beyond a suggestion, once, that it might be proper, perhaps, to postpone his visit until things were 'as before' – with the country, he meant. That made my heart sink, because by then I was far from certain they ever would. But I waited: as is my talent. Gently dismissed his objections, told him he would be welcome on any day, at any hour.

While I was waiting, I told him about Tim.

Tim had only come home for his first leave, I wrote: 1916, such a poor summer. I had tried to get his favourite foods all ready, but the broad beans had all blown down, and there was no cream to be got. I had not known what to expect, with his coming: his letters were determinedly cheerful. A great deal on the small ailments of his men, as though he were doing me a favour, giving me something upon which I might be able to pronounce. But the letters said nothing of his own discomfort. Nothing of death. It was all weather and inflamed louse bites and things his servant – he called him a 'batman', the military term – had said.

Then Tim came home, I wrote to Edward, and he would barely sit down to dinner, barely come indoors – had walked about, even in the rain, even at night. People in the village had seen him. He wouldn't come to church.

He stayed five days before he had to begin his journey back, and on the fifth day, I found him sitting on the bench in our garden at the back – where we had been always accustomed to have our talks. He asked after his friend, Theo Stainforth, who had married very lately during a short stretch of leave. I had gone along, Theo's mother had invited me, I wrote to Edward, and there on the bench I told Tim a little about the wedding.

Then I attempted to say what I had failed to say, before Tim had first gone to France, six months before. 'I hope you are not trying to be heroic.'

And he shot me a sort of look, and said, 'I'm doing my duty, Mother, if that's what you mean.' He sounded almost angry.

And so I only replied, 'Well, come back again. That's all.'

But he didn't answer.

After that visit, Tim had written to Richard, at last, that with the journey so far and the train timetable so reduced, he thought he ought to spend his leaves in future in London, with a friend. He knew Father would understand.

Richard left the letter lying on his desk. I confessed that to

Edward; said I hadn't intended to pry, had only gone in looking for stray teacups.

The war had begun, I wrote to Edward, by the time Tim went up to Oxford, but at that time he was only just eighteen, almost a year from being old enough to volunteer, and besides, there was all that over-by-Christmas nonsense.

It wasn't until the end of his first year – a brief visit, June, 1915 – that he had come home insistent that he was going to enlist. It wanted two months off his birthday, still, and I told him so.

'Mother,' he said, putting down his fork.

Richard said nothing.

'What I mean is, you can decide when you're old enough.'

'Everyone is going,' he said, 'everyone from Oxford –'

I put my fork down. 'If you want the truth, Tim, I wish you'd never gone there.'

'Ivy,' Richard said.

But I became quite upset then, and that brought a headache on. I took something for it, something old which Father had given me once.

I went up to bed early, and when I woke in the morning, Tim had gone.

Tim's going to Oxford had been settled upon before the war was even thought of. Early summer heat. 1914. The clock had just struck four. Tim was lying on the sofa in the little parlour, his legs over one end and his neck cramped at a terrible angle at the other. When I came in, he looked up, saw that it was me, and left his feet where they were.

'What's that?' I said.

He smiled, pulled his eyes from the page. 'Only some tosh.'

He was friendly, and I was still getting used to that, for he was not long out of one of those phases where one didn't know if one was likely to get a cheerful word from him or an irritable one. His particular friend, Theo Stainforth, had gone up to Oxford ahead of him, and he had been doleful that year.

Our maid then, Sarah, came in with the tea. Tim swung his

feet down, and Sarah moved about the table by the window, deftly laying out the things. It was rather an elaborate tea, for summertime, and I suppose she had cause to overhear when I asked him again about the exams he had lately taken. I suppose it was the third or fourth time I had asked about them, and each time I half remembered the details, but I liked to hear the names of the subjects rehearsed – mathematics, Latin, history – and was perturbed, I suppose, by how lacklustre he seemed when speaking of them, these tokens which could very soon be changed for a future.

I said, 'I suppose the Latin will be the most useful, if you decide to read the law.'

His left knee moved, and he rubbed it. 'I suppose it would.'

Richard came in. 'You could wait a year, if you're not certain,' he said. He frowned, and threw a folded newspaper down on the coffee table.

'Of course he's certain,' I said.

'Are you so very anxious to be rid of me?' Tim said, lightly.

And at that my heart gave a kick, because I knew how shapeless the days would be without the scaffold of his comings and goings. We'd never boarded him. He had kept on at the Truro Grammar School, back and forth every day on the ferry. When he first began there, he'd been so small and thin that I had insisted upon winter vests, even in full summer. Now he had finished his last exams, taking himself off in the mornings to that same ferry with rather a distracted air, thin still but rangy, stooping to negotiate the doorways upon which he could now have easily hit his head.

But he was so very on the brink of going that his holding off was the keeping of a torture in store. I had been losing him by inches, since he had moved from the tutor at the vicarage to the grammar school. Losing him first to the vicar's sons and the young tutor and their word games, their knowledge of bloody battles and the names of antique kings, and then to the great school, the crowd of unknown boys, losing him to the masters' sense of his aptitudes and to which boy could best everyone at conkers and to the kind of thing that I knew would be said whilst one was getting changed for rugby.

At Oxford he would be less cooped up, and there would not be women around. That was what concerned me, then.

'Don't be silly,' I said. All the time I was aware of Sarah, surely finished by now with the tea things, twitching the positions of plates and turning the cups about.

Tim was looking at me. His eyes had followed Sarah to the door, quite naturally, not with any discernible interest, but only as though he were watching a green boat pass by, a long way out in the estuary. Still, I was sure his eyes had not followed her so, the year before. It was as though she had gone from being invisible to visible. Simply that.

I got up to pour the tea. It was a splendid spread, Mrs Fossett had outdone herself. There were two kinds of cake. Sarah had arranged them very prettily, and the tea things, too. Two of the cups she had left with the handles pointing right, and one pointing to the left. Tim, of course, was left-handed. I took that one, before either he or Richard could see.

It was me, I told Edward. *I pushed him to go, and he went.*

II.

That morning a fortnight ago, upon which I spoke so unkindly to Richard about his memorial plan, I had been mulling over how to reply to a letter which had come from Edith. Quite a nice, inconsequential letter, simply asking how Richard was.

I had eased myself away from all correspondence but Edward's, such that even to see Edith's handwriting made me feel strange: those copperplate rows that we had worked so hard to perfect as little girls, and then to render careless and fashionable as big girls, and applied as adults in trying not to say anything to one another that would be of too much significance.

We had remained in touch, of course, across the years, Edith telling me her daughters' news, and about John's small infractions, a late dinner at the club, a harsh word to one of their servants. In return, I had always sent her the small gossip of the village. Our letters had grown infrequent – once or twice a year at most. But she had come in March, to condole, arriving in her good boots, in her cousin's car from Falmouth, smelling of London – expensive scent, and coal smoke, and the powdered milk they put in the tea on the train. She had come, and brought me solace with her company – and then she had made that face about Tim's telegram, which she was then so reluctant to explain.

Seeing her out to the car when it was time for her to go, I found myself wondering when we had last been frank with one another.

Perhaps the year we were eighteen; the year before William died, the last time Emily Tremain had given the Polneath tea. For the first time that year the invitation for the smaller tea, given on the terrace for local gentlemen and their wives, had extended beyond the Reverend Green and Mrs Green to his daughters, and beyond Father to include me. Mrs Green had pleaded a headache, and stayed at home with the younger girls – she couldn't be standing about in that heat, she said – but Edith and I went.

Edith had always known my hopeless preference for Edward Tremain, though by then she had left off pinching me when he passed us coming out of church. We had arrived a little late at Polneath – Edith having forgotten some ribbon or other – to see, beside the pond, the several small huddles of those who had arrived before us, and the tables spread out with finger sand-wiches, a fruit jelly and small cakes, everything neat as a pin. Upon the green-brown pond itself, several objects had been float-ing, white, almost like the paper boats that children might make. One of them had started to sink.

Edith and I were hovering awkwardly when Emily Tremain emerged through the French doors of the dining room and swept over to us, saying, 'Aren't they a fright? They're supposed to look Oriental.' She led us over to the nearest clutch of guests.

She was wearing a frock which even I could tell was wrong for the country. Pink, with various filmy trailing pieces.

'But I suppose one must keep an eye on current developments,' one of the men in the little group was saying.

He was a young man on some sort of survey for the railways, putting up at the King's Arms, but quite well spoken, and though that day Edith hardly knew his name, in a year or so's time she would be on his arm, dressed in white, walking out of church in her turn.

'I am certain there will always be a use for gunpowder in small-scale blasting,' he said, 'but we must surely entertain the possibil-ity that dynamite will become the preferred method for anything of a larger scale –'

'No, no, sir,' Tremain broke in. 'Fiendishly expensive. Every mine in Cornwall wants gunpowder –'

'How fortunate for you,' the young man said.

'Aye. Well, the price isn't what it ought to be,' Tremain replied.

'All will be well, though, won't it?' said Emily Tremain. 'Men will always prefer what they're used to.' She glanced nervously at Tremain. It was clear that she was hoping the young man would back down, wouldn't put him out of temper.

But Edward looked embarrassed. 'Now, my dear,' he said. 'I'm sure Mr White knows his business.'

Emily smiled, and then dipped her head. 'Of course. Forgive me. Really, you know I don't keep up with these things.' She laughed.

One or two other men had joined the group, and joined in the laughter – which was, I thought, slightly tense laughter – without having known what had passed. Emily hitched up agitatedly one of the pink, trailing pieces of her dress, and over Mr White's head made a sign to one of the maids, who produced a fly whisk from her apron pocket and moved back to guard the sandwiches. The men were all looking at the floor, and Edward rather stricken.

That was when I piped up.

'I read once,' I said, 'that for slate mining, gunpowder is preferred in any case. That what signifies in slate mining is not the strength, but the quality of the explosion.'

Mr White nodded, looked rather glad to be offered a point to concede. 'I've heard that, too,' he said.

Edward looked at me. I was wearing white, very simple, the kind of thing one wore at Whitsun.

One of the men said that he supposed that to branch out was rarely an ill-conceived plan.

And Tremain said that, in any case, they had already begun making sporting powders.

Edward turned his eyes to him, and I turned mine away to the moss and ferns of the blast wall, the many finely glazed windows of the house. At one of which, a child was standing. Little William in his nightshirt. For a moment, I was certain that I was the only person looking upward, and our eyes met. He looked doleful, sad almost. But he waved.

I waved back, and William grinned.

Everyone turned to look up at the window.

'He was rather tired –' Edward said, and broke off.

The little boy in the window seemed to stand for every hot afternoon on which I'd been instructed, as a child, to rest. The itchy discontentment of being upstairs, when everyone else was down.

'We were dipping, you see, the two of us, this afternoon,'

Edward said, gesturing to the pond. 'We caught a water boatman, and put it in a jar; but I suppose he didn't like to see it trapped –'

'And so he had a fit of temper,' Emily said, in a way which invited laughter.

Kindly, one or two in the little party laughed. Tremain laughed. I looked at Edward, looking for the strain of his laugh, the edge of distaste.

'And I did what I always do,' Emily said. 'I sent him off to get rid of it.'

I waved again, and William waved back.

Then someone appeared behind William, in the window. A maid in a dark frock, which looked hot for the day, her hair put back under the cap. The maid, who was Agnes, put a hand on William's shoulder, and he stepped back from the glass. Looking up at Agnes, Emily gave a nod, then turned to answer the young man who had asked when they planned to return to Florence. Presently, William appeared on the terrace – neatly dressed, now – and Edward suggested we might all stroll around to the stables.

As we went, William came up beside me, and I asked him his pony's name. He asked me if I had a pony, and I confessed I did not. I told him he was very lucky.

'I know,' he said, with his serious little face.

Edward found us, and gave William a wrapped napkin. Inside was a quartered apple. The pony was a chestnut, nicely kept; at William's voice, it put out its head over the half-door.

William tugged at my sleeve, and gave me a quarter of the apple. 'You must keep your hand quite flat like this,' he said, 'or Floss will bite you.'

'She won't bite, Will,' Edward said, gently.

But I extended my arm, and the pony began to reach with its lips.

'Quite flat, mind,' William said fretfully, 'or Floss will take it wrong, and choke.'

'It's alright,' I said, 'she's alright – look – there we go.'

The pony had taken the apple and turned its lovely head, chewing and watching the other guests, who all stood about with their drinks. William grasped my hand, his own sticky with apple.

'You're favoured,' Edward said to me, and smiled. 'He doesn't take to everyone.'

Edward looked at me for what manners would have said was exactly five seconds too long. Everyone else was drifting back towards the food. A cloud passed over the sun, which then emerged again, hotter than before.

On the way home, Edith chided me. Gently, the only way she ever had. 'You were making cow eyes,' she said.

'I can't help thinking well of him.'

Edith pulled a stem of grass out of the hedge. 'Yes, but Ivy,' she said. And then, 'He's married. Nothing good can come of it, so why waste –?' She broke off.

Moodily, I pulled my own stem of grass, tore at the seeds. 'One can't simply *decide* how to feel.'

'Can't one?' Edith said.

I looked at her savagely, but she was trying to make me laugh, and I did, I did laugh.

But then Edith married. And then, after the Polneath business, I did. By the time Edith visited again, I was six months wed.

She had come to stay with her cousin, who was the wife of a Falmouth seed merchant and was giving a charity tea. Edith came for me at home, in the cousin's gig. She complimented the garden; said she had always loved this house; that she was quite envious of me. Then she complained, all the way to Falmouth, about being in this part of the country again, about the state of the roads and how dreadfully she missed John. As we approached the cousin's gate, she clasped my hands.

'It's so dreadfully good to see you, Ivy. I've talked so, haven't I? Forgive me, how monstrous of me. On the way home, you must tell me how things are with you – you must tell me everything.'

There were a dozen other ladies there for the tea. They sighed over Edith's hat, the cut of her skirt, her neat London gloves, and she named the shops from which they had come. The tea was for St Margaret's – the institution for boys and girls – and once the sandwiches were demolished, the cousin announced that we were going to visit the girls' wing. They were going to sing for us.

I had never been inside St Margaret's before. It was dark and clean, the girls quiet and starched within an inch of their lives, though none of them looked hungry. They sang us 'God Save The Queen', and then we were taken to inspect the dormitories, rows of little humped brown beds. Edith and I lagged behind, with one of the mistresses. A kind-looking woman, older, though it was hard to say how old, with her hair tucked out of sight under a neatly embroidered cap. Edith had spotted a doll perched on one of the bolsters, and had gone over to inspect it.

I could not resist.

'Might I ask,' I said to the woman, 'whether you remember an Agnes Draper?'

I had thought the name would bring a guardedness, a narrowing of the eyes or a sad shake of the head, but she only said, 'Agnes Draper. Agnes . . .'

'Reddish hair,' I said. Perhaps, somehow, she had not heard about it all. Or she had, but Agnes's name had escaped her.

But now the woman nodded, though she only said, 'Agnes. I do remember. Quick at her sums. She went into service –'

Edith had wandered back to us. 'Agnes Draper?' she said, now. 'Isn't that –?'

'Never mind,' I said. I nodded after the other ladies, smiled at the mistress. 'We mustn't fall behind.'

Later, as her cousin's gig was driven carefully around the steep corners of the St Rumon's road, Edith said, 'Quick at her sums.' She was looking out at the passing trees. Then she turned to me. 'I wonder she said nothing of her character.'

'Miss Draper's?'

Edith gave a nod. 'She must have shown some fault, mustn't she . . . ?' She paused. 'Something that showed how she would turn out. I thought that was why you were asking.'

Now it was my turn to look away into the trees. 'Perhaps she thought that to speak of it would reflect badly on the place.'

'Perhaps.' I felt Edith watching the side of my face. 'You had to nurse her, didn't you? After William died? Papa mentioned it . . .' She paused. 'What was she like?'

I turned back to her, gave a vague smile. 'Hard to say. She didn't talk much –' I stopped. 'I only . . . I only asked before, because I was wondering where she was sent. Afterwards.'

Edith shook out her skirt, and smoothed it. The fabric really was lovely.

'Goodness,' she said, lightly. 'To think how jealous I'd have been, once, knowing you'd had the chance to stay at Polneath.'

12.

I suppose, when I spoke unkindly to Richard about his memorial plan, that ordinary, inconsequential letter from Edith had put me out of sorts: thrown into sharp relief, for a moment, what I was doing. For I had also heard again from Edward. On Monday, he said, he would be in Falmouth.

At last, he was coming.

He had turned up some information. About Tim. That is, he had turned up a person, who had a little information – a man who had served with him. He could bring him up to see me. He suggested the Grand Hotel, at three. I would have preferred the morning: eleven o'clock, tea, a cool white light, a low hum of chatter, a certain decorousness. But at least the hotel was the right sort, and not heavily frequented by Richard's friends. In any case, there wasn't time to reply. But how to wait out the agony of the intervening day?

Early on the Sunday morning, I had suddenly remembered what Edward had said, about wishing to have another look at Polneath. I ought to go, I thought, and check it is not in too dreadful a state. In case.

I had not been down into the old mill woods in many years, for all that it is Richard's land, now; our land, I suppose. While the first fire damaged only the north wing, the second devastated the whole house, and parts of the structure are not wholly safe. The Polneath woods, what is more, have always been damp woods, deep woods. But I made myself go. The drive from the top road down to the house is quite overgrown, now, so I went by the village, passing my father's old house and the quay and along the lane.

The sign beside the rusting gate proclaims 'REMAIN OWDER WORKS'. The gates are still kept padlocked. Rather than ask Richard or Murray about the key, it seemed easier to cut along the outside of the wall, to one of the places where a falling tree has tumbled the stones, and then pick my way back to the track.

The lower drive is all weeds. Perfectly passable, but no longer carriage-wide. Young trees have been opportunists, and crowded into the gaps. The first impression, that morning a fortnight ago, was so much of a profusion of spindly branches that when I caught a glimpse of the roofless, ruined mills, they were startling, like bad teeth in an otherwise empty mouth. The sound of running water came from all sides: the sound I remembered, the fretwork of troughs and runnels still working redundantly to soften the air. Though some of them had burst, so that in places water seeped away into the ground. I wished I was wearing better shoes as I picked my way through the mud towards the house, and the rhododendrons closed in about me.

In amongst the bushes, here and there, I spotted snares – one or two rusted, one or two freshly laid. Poachers, getting in where the wall was damaged. I wondered whether Richard knew, whether he had turned a blind eye. He had never done anything with the woods since buying them, never done anything with the remains of the mills or the house, had let them crumble almost stubbornly into disrepair.

I went on, almost went over on my ankle once, and that calmed me. But as I came through the blast wall and within sight of the pond, my heart beat faster again. Underfoot were damp cigarette ends, old ones. I wondered whether they belonged to Tim, for Tim had been in here, I suspected, when he'd come home on leave. He knew I'd never liked him smoking.

The main house has more broken panes than those still intact, and birds have found a way to nest on some of the windowsills, streaks of white giving them away, some faint, some clear below the nests from this past spring. Above each window is an upward breath of black, from the second fire, and the roof is almost gone: only a handful of dark silhouetted ribs, open to the sky. I watched a pigeon burst upward from one of the rafters, and paused for breath beside the thick green pond, on what used to be the terrace. Amongst the gravel was a quantity of broken glass.

I tried to tell myself that I simply felt sad, standing there on the old terrace, ruined and disrupted now by weeds, the pond filmy with scum, the black scraps of birds lifting amongst the trees. But my heart was beating hard. I fairly ran back through the woods, removing a neat segment of skin from my leg as I got over the broken wall, and I was in quite a state of disarray by the time I gained the St Rumon's lane again.

I was still smoothing myself down when Mr Murray appeared, with one of his dogs.

'Murray,' I said, catching my breath. 'Murray, you startled me.'

'Forgive me, madam,' he said. 'Are you quite well? Were you . . . ?' He looked at the rusted Polneath gates and my dishevelment.

'I thought I ought to look at the old place,' I said. I regained my breath, and swallowed. 'You know, as we were discussing. I thought I ought to be taking an interest.'

'I could have opened up for you, madam,' Murray said. He was patting his dog, who wanted to be off. 'I think you've torn your skirt, there –'

'I'm quite alright,' I said. 'It's nothing. I'd better . . .'

'Of course,' Murray said, and moved his hand to raise his hat to me, but paused. 'Although – while I have you, I ought to – I got across to Falmouth at last,' he said. He ducked to pat the dog again. 'Yesterday. I went to the bank. But I'm afraid they declined to give me Mrs Smith's address.'

'Never mind,' I said.

'And how is –?' Murray asked, after an awkward pause.

'Oh. He's the same,' I said.

Murray looked down. 'Well. I suppose it was sense. His resigning as coroner. Although it must have been a hard blow for him.'

I nodded.

Murray looked at me. 'I'm terribly sorry, madam,' he said. 'About the address.'

'Not to worry. I suppose it can't be helped. I suppose there is nothing to be done, now. Really, Murray, I ought to –'

'Of course,' Murray said, raising his hat now. 'Dreadfully sorry to have kept you. Mind how you go, Mrs Boscawen.'

And I walked home, my leg bleeding very slightly, arriving to hear Richard's shout floating down the stairs. He had a plan for a memorial which he wished me to see.

After I had been beastly to Richard, I went down to the study, to fume, and justify my actions. I looked about me, at the inquest files which Richard had kept so close at hand, arrayed above the books in the study, all the many years of his long career. I had always suspected that he was comforted by the bulky mass of them – evidence of competence, the capacity to tidy all those different deaths into buff, quarter-inch sameness.

Taking the Tremain files down from the shelf, however, I could feel with finger and thumb that these were different from the rest. The first was thicker than most – the other, second file, rather thin. William's file I had opened many times since the Armistice, wishing to refresh my memory of the Polneath business, to help my account. Everywhere I had found Richard's notes: underlinings, question marks.

He had only ever wanted those elements of the truth which made sense, I thought. Which could be proved, which were safe to write down.

Theo Stainforth's visit, by now, was a dim memory. But the dream, of Polneath, that waking sense of Tim under the bed each morning, had grown clearer, more insistent than ever.

I was stronger than Richard, I thought. It was up to me, to conduct Tim's inquest.

Me.

And Edward, who would be here tomorrow, who might even now be packing his bags.

13.

The dream was almost unbearable, that morning of Edward's visit. I woke with the sense of Tim stronger than ever. When Mrs Fossett came up to draw me a bath, she said that she thought she could get hold of some currants from her sister-in-law, in Truro.

'I beg your pardon, Mrs Fossett?' I said.

'Currants, madam. You wanted to know about Christmas fruit.'

'Oh, I did, didn't I?' I said. 'Mrs Fossett, I'll be going into Falmouth this afternoon.'

'Very well, madam.' She looked at me. 'Mr Boscawen was asking for you,' she remarked.

After the bath, I got out one of my older girdles. I managed it alright, and then slipped one of the petticoats over the top – the rather nice grey one I got when I was first married. It's silk, and has that rustle, that thin strength. It was the old length, but there was nothing to be done about that.

I was embarrassed, as I fingered the lace in the mirror, trying to tell whether it had yellowed as I smoothed it down, my hands slipping. For a moment, I felt linen against my cheek, remembered the way Richard would reach to put out the light. I tried three different things with my hair, which I told myself were simply a change but really were methods of twisting it to hide the worst grey at the temples. I was more careful than usual about my cold cream. My face was not the face that had looked back at me from the mantel glass in Father's kitchen. Thirty years have made my ordinary blue eyes larger, my chin firmer. They have stolen my ability to meet my own gaze.

My stockings kept catching, where I had grazed my leg, the day before, at Polneath.

I waited so long for Tim. Six years of that cheek to linen business, before he finally came along. So I was reluctant, at first, for him to be sent to school. When he was seven, however, Richard had insisted that he ought to have some education: but we would not have to send him away, for he had arranged with the vicar that Tim could share his boys' tutor. He could simply walk to the vicarage every morning, and back every afternoon.

Readily I agreed, but soon Tim began to find diversions, amusing reasons not to come straight home. He began to stay out, playing with the vicars' sons, until at last I had to go and retrieve him. One day, I could not find them, and went right down to the vicarage to enquire. Summer, one of those light evenings. Their eldest girl admitted that the boys had taken to playing in the old mill woods. Telling myself that I was only cross that Tim's tea was wasting, I went after him.

The house had never been made safe, after the second fire, and I had complained to Richard before that, with the state of the wall now, children might go playing there, but Richard had always brushed me away. 'They must have some latitude,' he said. 'Some freedom, or they never learn.'

It was not the thought of a falling beam, however, which caused me to go looking for Tim, as the sun dipped just below the line of the trees, nor his wasting tea. I thrashed my way up the track, made my way around the pond, heard the strangled sound of my own calling as damselflies skipped over the surface. It was a sense that made me go; the sense that there might be something waiting there, at Polneath, even now.

Listening.

I knew the boys were there, crouched amongst the ruins, their backs to the trunks of trees. But they would not come out, and I had half destroyed my shoes. So after a few minutes of calling, I gave up and went away. When Tim came back that evening, shamefaced but happy, his clothes full of grass seed, I forbade him his supper. And that was that.

Or, not quite.

Because a few days later, I noticed Tim out in the garden, engaged in some game. He was talking to the bench, to somebody upon the empty bench, waving his arms as though there were somebody there. I went out, and, smiling encouragingly, asked him what he was doing. He said he was talking to his friend.

'What friend is that?' I said.

'He's my friend,' Tim said. 'Not yours. It's a secret.'

'Is he a little boy, your friend?' I said. 'Is he a little boy, like you?'

'He's got white hair,' Tim said. 'He's gone now. You made him go.'

I felt cold. Cold, all over. And that had at last decided me.

'Tim?' I said. 'Tim – you shan't be going to the vicarage any more. You shall be going to the big school, the grammar school, in Truro. Won't that be nice?'

It would give him a longer day. Mrs Fossett would put him on the ferry early each morning, and retrieve him each afternoon; there would be no more playing at Polneath.

Tim wouldn't answer.

And a few days after *that*, I found him hiding under his bed.

He had always enjoyed small spaces: tucking himself on to a window ledge, or beneath the kitchen table to read his little books and suck the barley sugars which I discouraged but Mrs Fossett slipped to him frequently. But that day – was it a Sunday morning? It might have been. I needed Tim for something, we had to go out and he needed to wash his hands and face – he was not to be found. I called and shouted all over the house. Perhaps it wasn't church, wasn't Sunday, for I remember Richard calling exasperatedly to leave him, that he would come out if I would only stop fussing.

I looked in the garden, but the old gardener had been out there since seven, and hadn't seen him. I returned to the house, and – I'm not sure why – stopped calling. Instead, I crept from room to room, checking behind sofas, inside wardrobes. At last, and my heart was beating rather hard, I went into his bedroom, almost hitting my head on a dangling model owl. I took a deep breath, and sank to my knees, my palms on the rough carpet, and I peered under the bed.

There were Tim's two eyes, quite open, looking at me. I suppose I made a sound, and his eyes widened and he blinked.

'Get out from there,' I said, and I'm afraid I gripped his arm rather hard.

I yanked him out, and he began to cry. I discovered later that during this operation he had swallowed his barley sugar.

'You mustn't hide from me,' I remember shouting. 'You mustn't hide.' My heart was hammering in my chest.

Richard came up to see what the matter was, and I was weeping, uncontrollably, and that stilled Tim's tears and he crept close.

'Don't crowd her,' Richard said. He looked rather alarmed.

'You mustn't frighten me,' I said to Tim, hardly able to get out the words between the sobs.

Tim's wrist swelled, and we did not go out that day. I made a frightful guilty fuss of him. He had enough barley sugars that week to empty his head of teeth. A few days after that, I enrolled Tim at the grammar in Truro.

Richard couldn't object. After all, it was he who had insisted that Tim ought to have some education.

I covered the grey slip with a dress, black of course and as nice as I could reasonably choose for daytime.

There was still a whole morning to pass before the ferry. Leaving my appearance, I went to see what Richard wanted. As I went in, he ever so slightly lifted his eyebrows.

'Have you done something to your hair?'

I touched it. 'I haven't decided whether I like it, yet.'

'It's very nice,' he said. And then, 'Are you alright?'

I'd taken hold of the smooth rounded end of the bedstead, feeling hot suddenly and faint. The old girdle was tight. He was being gentle, and after I had been so horrid yesterday.

'I've not been sleeping terribly well,' I said.

Richard was looking at me, looking at my face. 'Well, I'm glad you're going out,' he said. 'Fresh air, you know.'

Now he looked away, out of the window, and I said, 'Did you want me for something?'

He looked back at me. 'I've been thinking about Tim.'

I felt a sort of jolt, as though he had somehow found out my purpose in going to Falmouth.

But then he said, 'In April, you know, after his friend came – and

I was thinking about his volunteering, you said I didn't stop him. And you're right. I didn't.'

I moved my hand from the bedstead. 'I'm not sure there's much –'

But Richard raised his hand. 'No, no. You were right. I didn't stop him. I wanted to . . . I hoped, you know, I suppose I hoped there might be some advantage to be had, from volunteering. I suppose I thought, if he only plays by the rules, if only he sticks to that, then –' He broke off.

A tear was finding its way down his cheek. It fell, and spotted the counterpane, and I turned aside to let him collect himself. This was not how Richard was.

In that girdle, with my hair done up like that, I was too hot. I wanted to sit down. But instead I found myself saying, 'Every morning, when I wake up, you know, I think he's there. Under the bed. I can almost hear him.'

Richard shuffled against his pillows, putting his handkerchief away. 'You mean you dream of him?'

I shook my head. I didn't say, about the fire dream, but replied, 'By the time I . . . I'm quite awake. Sometimes it's as though he's hiding. Sometimes as though he's waiting to tell me something.'

Richard looked at me, slightly troubled. Kind. Gently, he said, 'You mustn't suppose it means anything.'

'No.' I sniffed, and gave a brisk smile.

This was the Richard I knew. When we'd first married, I remembered, he'd mentioned once that he never had dreams – nor nightmares, either.

'I'm terribly glad you're going out,' he said, again.

Just after one, I put on my good coat.

Jake was limbing one of the old apple trees, and asked whether I was off to town. I lied smoothly about going to meet a lady of my acquaintance, whose name I knew Jake would recognize; I even named the Grand, in case I was seen. My only pang of conscience came as he asked whether I was sure I would not prefer him to bring round the car, and I insisted that I wanted the fresh air.

Waiting at the ferry, I watched the ducks in the estuary,

frightened by the approaching boat. They lifted, moved all in unison, and settled further away. There was a cutting wind. I wasn't warm enough in the silk. The boat docked, and one or two boys began to help with the goods off.

The hand helped me up, and said he hadn't seen me in some time, and he hoped I was keeping well, and Mr Boscawen, too.

Falmouth felt strange, after so many months. There were too many sounds as I walked up from the docks to the Grand. I walked, conscious that Edward's eyes might be on me, for of course he would be here already, might be anywhere. I wondered whether he would be recognized now in Falmouth. I had not considered that. Although, he would look different than he had as a young man. I had not considered that, either.

Of course, I should not agree to go upstairs. We would have a glass of something, and that would be all. Besides, he was bringing this other man, who had known Tim. That was why he had come.

It had crossed my mind, of course it had crossed my mind. Sometimes, I had watched Jake in the garden – not digging, no such brute effort, but doing something complicated with his hands, mending something – and I had felt: something. I had felt something. But that is a very different matter from the immediate prospect of a hotel room on a rainy afternoon.

Perhaps the war had changed things, for young people. But we were not young people. I looked different now.

And it had been so very dark, that other time, all those years ago.

Edward arrived at half past three, alone. I had let a cup of tea sit until it was cold, because I didn't wish to be in the powder room and miss his coming. He was framed for a moment by the revolving door, which seemed to bring in a little wind with him, and he rearranged his scarf as he looked about for me. His face was just as I remembered it. Well, the folds were more strongly marked, and there was a more pronounced softness about the mouth. But his eyes were the same, different than the eyes of most men. They observed you, gently but attentively; they waited, looking to take their cue from you.

I stood up and put out my hand. He took it and kept it for a moment. His hands were cold, but his nails were exquisite, almost like a woman's: city nails for certain. He stepped back, and began to unbutton his mourning coat, which was good but small, worn at the elbows. I smiled. He'd never known how to dress himself. In my best fur, I felt how we were equals, now, at least. I was no longer the nineteen-year-old with the three decent frocks. Now, for the first time, we might meet on even terms.

'I'm late,' he said. He was rubbing his hands together, chafing them.

'No, no.'

A waiter was coming.

'What would you like? They've decent coffee again . . .'

The waiter had made two or three pleasantries since I had arrived, perhaps thinking that whoever I was meeting would not come. Now he ignored me, and looked at Edward questioningly.

'Sherry, I think,' Edward said. He looked at me. 'Sherry?'

I glanced, nervously, at the waiter. 'Why not?'

Edward asked what they had, and the waiter explained. Edward replied with something about Cadiz, and something about Oloroso. In the end, they settled upon a bottle. 'Open it for us,' Edward said. 'And we'll come back another day, and finish it.'

I blushed at that, and wished he wouldn't, and felt, at the same time, thrilled. My hand still felt different where he had touched it.

We sat down.

The man had not come, then, after all, who'd known Tim. It was such a long way. Perhaps Edward would suggest I go up to London to meet him, instead – but he himself had kept our appointment, anyway. Had wanted to keep it.

'It's wonderful to see you,' he said. 'I'm sorry I put off coming. I didn't *want* to put it off, you know, even for a week.'

'Not at all,' I said.

And he smiled, as though he were grateful for my forbearance, but knew well that I had been waiting. 'The truth is, I had a particular reason for not coming at once.' Edward crossed his legs, carefully. 'It's rather old-fashioned. But I wanted it to be a year, since Constance . . .'

I felt myself flush. 'I quite understand,' I said. 'And it's wonderful to see *you*.' I looked at him. 'The man you mentioned –'

He pressed my arm. 'Yes,' he said, 'but first you must tell me how you are. For letters really aren't any use, are they?'

'Oh, I hardly know,' I said. And then, 'Well. I'm well –' I stopped. 'The truth is, I'm not sleeping as much as I ought to be.' I swallowed. 'You see, I keep thinking Tim is in the room.'

Edward sat back in his chair. 'Of course you do,' he said.

I felt absolutely washed with relief. 'Do you get it, too?'

He nodded. 'Occasionally. To tell you the truth, I've felt a great deal less troubled about Archie since the memorial service.'

'Of course.' I looked down at my cold teacup. 'I was dreadfully sorry not to come. I saw the notice, of course, but – but by the time I was able to write to you, the date had gone.'

He smiled. 'I was wondering about that.'

I looked down. 'One asks oneself, I suppose, what one might have done differently.'

When I looked up, Edward was studying my face very closely.

'One can think of plenty of things,' he murmured, 'that one ought to have done differently.'

And just like that, as easily as that, we sat, smiling like lunatics.

The waiter came, with the sherry. He appeared to have misunderstood, and had brought us the bottle, there and then. Edward poured me a measure, and it was too generous, but I didn't care. I felt the happiest I had in years, perhaps the happiest I had ever felt. Edward toasted the future, and that seemed right, and I drank.

'Wonderful stuff,' he said. 'I'll be passing through Jerez, in fact. I'm planning a tour of Andalusia, in the spring.'

I nodded, and smiled. It was impossible to say whether he was mentioning it because he hoped I'd come, or to warn me that I had got matters tangled, or whether he was simply mentioning it.

He smiled at me, met my eyes, and then looked into his glass. 'Constance didn't care to travel, so.'

'Nor Richard,' I said.

'Though we met in Ravenna, you know. She was there with her aunt. It turned out she was simply trying to keep the old lady happy . . .' He paused. 'I suppose you knew that Boscawen would prefer his home comforts.'

I looked down, embarrassed. He was behaving as though I had chosen Richard; could laugh about having done so.

The waiter came back, to ask us whether everything was to our liking. Edward seemed to feel that he had said something wrong, because he told the waiter that everything was very much to his liking, and met my eyes as he did so. He turned the subject, then, away from Richard. He told me more about his work at the War Office, and how pointless it had often been, and occasionally how crucial, but that he had been glad enough to stop in any case, after Archie's death. He asked me about Father, and said kind things about him, and that he was sorry things had gone hard with him at the end. He made me describe Mr and Mrs Fossett in detail, and then at last we got on to the fates of various people he had known in St Rumon's.

'And I suppose Polneath is quite a ruin,' Edward said, carefully not looking at me.

'Yes,' I said. I was somewhat drunk, and knew very well that I was, and was quite on the brink of asking him why he had left me that last day, after all the horror. Why he'd never come back for me –

When he looked over my shoulder, at the entrance to the dining room.

There was a man, framed as Edward had been in the doorway. He had a shabby look, and already a waiter was moving discreetly towards him to shepherd him out.

'Here he is,' Edward said – and then, seeing my surprise, 'I wanted to have you to myself for a little, first. I hope it wasn't too dreadful of me.' He glanced distractedly again at the scene by the door. 'I'd better go and – why don't you powder your nose?'

When I came back, the man at the door was sitting with Edward at our table. He was out of uniform, but you could see where his uniform had sat, the white places on his neck and wrists where his civilian shirt sagged to show where France had stripped the flesh from him. He looked uncomfortable in his ordinary clothes, as though he had only very lately taken them up again. He was smoking nervously, as Edward spoke to him, leaning gently forward and looking about him, as though he did not often find himself in places with so much white linen and polished wood. As I approached the table he nodded, spotted me, stubbed out his cigarette, and stood up.

Edward stood up, too. 'Mrs Boscawen,' he said. 'This is Sergeant Fred Campbell.'

'Freddie,' the man said, and offered his hand. 'I'm not a sergeant now. I'm not an anything. I served with your son, Mrs Boscawen,' he said, and glanced at Edward.

We all sat down. He had the accent one rather expected a sergeant to have: East End, of some sort. It was hard to believe that I was sitting so near to someone who had known Tim, who had lived with him, eaten with him, fought with him. He looked around too much: at the table, at me, at my handbag where it sat beside the sherry bottle, at the waiter as he came to see what he wanted, and then at Edward.

I tried to think more kindly of him. A glass of cider was settled upon, and I asked whether he were hungry. He said he was not, but that it was very decent of me, very decent indeed.

I wondered where he had been waiting the hour or more Edward and I had been together. Somehow, it troubled me, the thought of him loitering outside on a bench somewhere, or in one of those pubs nearer the docks.

He picked up his glass, a crystal one, rather gingerly. Sipped the cider, seemed to be reassured to find it, in fact, cider, and then put it down. 'I suppose you want to hear how he died, madam.'

I tried to smile. 'Of course,' I said, 'anything you can tell me.'

Edward put his hand on my arm, but, when I didn't look at him, moved it away again.

'It was evening,' the man said. 'I don't know, half an hour off sunset. The mess had gone round, and I was having a smoke, with Jack Ingram, he's dead now. Captain Boscawen must have been round the corner. You know the line dog-legs –' He looked at me, and drew it with his finger on the tablecloth, and I nodded. He glanced at Edward, and went on. 'Well, it was flattish there, so we were sat against the back wall of the trench and on a

135

sudden we just saw this head pop up. Head and shoulders. And then – well. Say what you like about the Germans, but they don't kip on the job.'

Edward was looking at me. He made a sympathetic sound, but I shook my head. A feeling of cold confirmation was spreading from my stomach, out into my limbs. I felt light, nerveless.

To the sergeant, I said, 'Was anyone with him, at the time?'

The man shook his head. 'Me and Jack, we were round the corner sharpish. Then some of the other lads came.' He glanced from me to Edward. 'After a bit, another officer turned up, from the next unit over. I reckon it was him that dealt with the stretcher bearers, and all that.'

'I see,' I said. 'And – what had it been like, in the line just there? Had anything of note happened that day?' I swallowed. 'Was anything of note due to happen the next day?'

The man took a swallow of his cider, and slowly shook his head. 'You mean, was there anything hot coming? Not that I knew. Things got bad once we were moved, but there – it was just, average, you know. But some boys, they just can't stand it.' He glanced from Edward to me. 'I mean, it isn't a pretty business.' He glanced at Edward again. 'We'd got two of theirs that morning, but that was all.'

I nodded, and took a sip of my sherry. What was that, my third? But I seemed to have found a clarity, a chill or hardness, or a gap of some sort between my brain, my lips, which were asking the questions, and my heart.

'Could he not,' I said, 'could he not have been . . . you know how men would sometimes wave.' I did it, waved slightly, trying to demonstrate how a man might do what Theo Stainforth had perhaps done: seek to have his hand shot off, in order to come home.

But it must have caught the waiter's attention, because Edward shifted slightly in his seat and shook his head.

Fred Campbell looked back at me. 'I don't believe so, madam.' He moved his hand. 'It weren't his hand, see. It were his head.'

Edward touched my arm. Gently, he said, 'There are particular –'

The sergeant took him up. 'And there were ways and means, with that – sorry, sir – you see. You'd do it during an action, or just before maybe, when they hadn't time to martial you.'

I had withdrawn my hands into my lap, and I think I was biting my lip. That was when I felt Edward take my hand, properly, under the table.

'Jack did say,' the sergeant said, then, tentatively, and I looked up. 'Jack Ingram, the corporal, he did say,' he moved in his chair, and dropped his gaze, 'as how he thought Captain Boscawen was troubled.'

'Troubled?' I said.

Sergeant Campbell looked embarrassed. 'The trenches aren't for everyone, madam. They're a deal to stand, for a delicate man.' But Edward must have shot him a warning look at that, and he left off.

I had to get my handkerchief out. Around me the hotel dining room was wobbling. There was too much glass, too much whiteness, too much light.

Edward was thanking the man, and telling him that he had arranged his train ticket home, as he'd promised. He was telling him how very much I appreciated him coming. I lifted my head up, and agreed. After a moment, Edward went to see about the bill, and our coats. Fred Campbell and I stood about, awkward. He had taken out another cigarette. They were rather nice ones, better than the quality of his clothes. He was stroking the cigarette, as though he were anticipating smoking it in solitude.

'How close were the Germans?' I said. I was holding my handkerchief, clenched in my pocket. 'How close were they, in that part of the line?'

He met my eyes for a moment. Then he said, quietly, 'Close enough, madam. I never put my head up, myself, to see.'

At that, I felt embarrassed, and I don't believe I met the man's eyes again as Edward thanked him once more, took our leave of him, and helped me into my coat. We watched him walk away down the steps, and into the Falmouth night. The clock on the reception desk read half past five.

'My hotel is only just up there,' Edward said, nodding in the direction.

'Oh, that one,' I said. 'How is it?'

He laughed. 'Oh! The press is a dreadful old thing. I fairly trapped a shirt in it. That's why I was so late. I forgot how things are, in the country.'

I smiled. 'Falmouth is hardly the country.'

He looked at me. He must have seen how the sergeant had unsettled me, how raw I felt.

There was an awful quiet.

'Well, the ferry won't wait,' I said.

But Edward dropped his voice. 'Ivy, I'm terribly sorry,' he said.

'No, I –'

'I feel dreadful. I thought – I thought you wanted to be certain. I didn't know he would be so . . .'

I put my hand on his arm. 'I did want to be certain. I did.'

And now I was. Tim had gone to the war, and it had broken him.

I had mothered him, given him fine and exacting principles, kept him with me always, made him a sensitive boy, a strange boy, ill fitted for the rigours of war. I had made him – and then he had been sent to the trenches, and got himself out of them, in the only way open to him.

'It's only,' I said to Edward, 'it's only that it's difficult.'

'Of course it is.' Edward nodded. 'Listen, I – I must see Campbell off tomorrow morning. But my train isn't until four. Are you terribly busy?'

I glanced at the man behind the reception desk, who had his head bowed over a ledger. 'I'm not sure.'

Edward looked at me for a long moment. 'Not to worry,' he said. He took my hand again.

But I removed it, with another look at the man at the desk.

'Forgive me,' Edward said. 'It's only that it's wonderful to see you –' He stopped. 'Forgive me.' He searched my eyes once more, and then nodded, and was away down the steps and up the street, in the same direction the sergeant had gone, back towards the lights of the town.

Rain had begun to fall, lighter than light. You could not see it, but you could feel it on your extended hand. It would soon make my fur useless.

I would be rather early for the ferry. But the man at the desk looked up from his ledger again, and so I stepped out. I walked slowly down to the docks, towards the rough shouts of men, and night on the water.

14.

I had to pretend to Jake, when I got home and he was still burning branches in the dark at the side of the house, that I had passed a merry and inconsequential afternoon. I could barely keep my smile for long enough to escape him, and indoors I had to deal with Mrs Fossett.

The doctor had been, because she hadn't liked the sound of Richard's chest. I didn't think much about it: she had found a reason to send for the doctor fortnightly since the haemorrhage. This time there was some syrup, to help with congestion. But all I wanted was some solitude. I told her she and Fossett might take tomorrow mostly for themselves, and mentioned an errand at the Truro haberdashers, hoping to get them out of the house. Mrs Fossett looked rather doubtful, but agreed, said they might go and hear the carols at the cathedral.

The dream came that night, and the sense of Tim the next morning, just the same.

Poaching some eggs in the kitchen, with the Fossetts out of the way, I at last felt foolish. How could I have been so ungrateful towards Edward? At the Grand I had felt almost angry with him. Of course it had been difficult to hear what the sergeant had had to say, and of course he had been a rough fellow, but what did I expect? Did I think someone promoted from the ranks – promoted for his merit, no doubt – would have delicate manners, make little jokes about Shakespeare? The fellow had come all that way, and Edward had gone to the trouble of finding him, to give me some certainty. It was not the sergeant's fault, nor Edward's, that I was complicit in Tim's sad end. I ought to have been grateful, to have the truth at last.

When Theo Stainforth had first said about Tim's standing up, I had been possessed of an instinct, almost a superstitious one – that I had done a very particular wrong, long ago at Polneath, and therefore my son had killed himself. But I saw now that, though Polneath was at the heart of it, it was not by some supernatural mechanism, but simple cause and consequence.

Tim was the way he was, and I had made him that way.

I was the way I was, and what had made me that way was Polneath.

I had eaten my eggs, and was rinsing the plate of yolk, when there came the sound of a car in the lane, slowing, stopping, and then a tap at the front door. I went to answer it, wiping my hands.

It was Edward.

I felt twelve things at once. I stepped out, half closing the door behind me, though it wasn't Jake's day.

'Edward,' I said, whispered. 'What are you –?'

'Oh, forgive me,' he said. 'I didn't think you'd . . . that is, I simply intended to leave a note. I supposed that Mr Boscawen would be upstairs, and . . . and your servants don't know me, so. I wasn't going to leave my name.'

'A note?'

Edward had stepped back rather. He was pushing a folded scrap of paper into his pocket. 'To apologize. About yesterday. I oughtn't to have brought him.'

I glanced about again, I couldn't help it. 'No. Edward, listen to me, I – it was hard, of course it was, to hear it spoken of. But I'm terribly grateful to you for bringing him, and it was generous of Mr Campbell to come . . .' I paused. 'I imagine you laid out something in expenses. Might I . . . ?'

'Certainly not,' Edward said. 'Certainly not. I'm –' He smiled, pushing his hand back over his hair, for he had taken his hat off. 'I'm relieved.'

We looked at one another.

'Would you care for a stroll?' Edward said, helplessly.

'Yes,' I said. 'Yes. That would be better. Give me a moment.'

I left the door slightly ajar, ran upstairs. Richard was asleep. He looked rather flushed. I settled his pillow a little. He wouldn't need his next dose for another two hours.

In my own room, I looked out some shoes, and glanced in the mirror. Patted my hair.

'I thought we might just walk down and see William's grave,' Edward said, downstairs.

'Of course we might.'

I waited for him to get back into the motor, for his stick. I felt relieved that he had not, after all, asked to go and see Polneath; and tender-hearted, suddenly, at how gingerly he bent to search for the stick. There was nothing to fear. We were both older now. And, though our correspondence had felt long, it had not been – hardly more than a month, we had been writing letters. We didn't really know one another; there was all that ahead of us, perhaps.

A chilly little wind swirled about the car, and picked up the leaves and flung them down again.

We set off. Edward prodded into a pile of leaves with his stick. 'I told him to be delicate. I would never . . . if I'd known he would be so coarse, I'd have spared you . . . but I thought you would want to see him for yourself.'

I put my hand on his arm. 'You were right. And I wouldn't have wished to be spared.'

He looked at me.

'Truly,' I said.

We were passing Jake's house, though there was no sign of him. 'It's dreadful, of course it's dreadful, that Tim . . .' I said.

Edward nodded. 'Dreadful.'

'And I suppose one worries that – as a mother, I worry that . . .' He stopped. 'Ivy.'

I half turned away, but he took my shoulder.

'You must make a life now,' he said. 'You must make a new life, in spite of it.'

We had reached the churchyard. It looked just the same as it had the day William was buried, or the day I emerged from the little carved stone porch as a newly minted bride.

We paused at the gate. The river was hidden, but one could see the winter dun of the reed bed, and the green of the hill beyond, the blue of the sky, a flight of ducks going over. Nearer at hand, there were the older hummocked graves, and the grassy mound of the churchyard wall.

Edward led the way, through the older graves to where a willow leaned into the wall, as though it were resting its elbows. Some of the graves further back from the path were, under closer inspection, in rather a sorry state. Jake had not been keeping up with things. I felt a flush of guilt. He could not bend as he used to, and he had been doing a great deal for Richard and for me.

Edward stopped at William's place. A short grave, and a modest little headstone, considering that the Tremains had always had a crypt inside the church. But Edward, I remembered, had not wanted him to be inside. The usual wording: *beloved child of*, and his brief dates.

I put my hand on Edward's arm. To think he had twice lost his only son, and there I was, talking about my own pain.

'Do they ever leave you?' I said.

Edward looked at me. 'No.'

We stood looking at the grave for another minute, and I stooped for a couple of dandelions, growing flat to the turf. No point in those taking hold. I crouched, dug my fingers in to get the whole white root.

'There's no need,' Edward said, gently. 'It doesn't matter, you know.'

I turned, and looked up at him. 'I don't mind,' I returned. 'It's good for me.' I pulled four or five dandelions, making a little pile by the grave end, and then stood up, dusting my hands. 'Richard is consumed with the idea of a memorial for them,' I said. 'You know, all the fallen. But the designs, they're –' I looked at my hands. 'They're so *clean*.'

Edward took one of my grubby hands, gently, in his. He licked his thumb, and rubbed at a bit of dirt, but it had got into the whorls of my fingerprints, got into the cracks where my skin was not what it had been.

I looked up at him, into his eyes. 'He was paying a woman,' I said. 'Richard.' I broke away, looked off towards the river, and gave a mirthless laugh. 'What am I saying? He *is* paying a woman. Some Mrs Smith, a small living, since we were married.'

Edward caught my hand again. I imagine I wanted him to say that Richard was a fool.

'Murray was trying to find out her address. But what would I do with her address?' I wiped my eyes. 'The whole thing is ridiculous.'

Edward looked serious. 'Has he traced her?'

'Not yet. The bank wouldn't – I've told him not to bother with it.'

'I'm sorry.'

'I don't care.'

Edward clutched my fingers, rather firmly. 'No,' he said. 'No.'

We were standing extremely close together. Even as I could feel his warm sweet breath, his tobacco and outdoor smell, I was thinking about how Mrs Fossett would not have approved of my leaving Richard alone for so long. Thinking about how exposed the churchyard was. The ferry was in, and I could hear men calling to one another as they dispersed. I was thinking about how old we were now, and what it would be, at almost fifty, to be discovered behaving improperly in a graveyard . . .

But the kiss was just, just as I remembered. For a moment, I felt nothing else. The warmth of him, the momentary shelter. I could taste mint, warm mint. He had been chewing something, he had been *planning* to kiss me –

Then Edward broke off, and pulled back, with a little intake of breath. His eyes were bright.

'I shouldn't have left you,' he said.

My heart was thudding in my ears.

'But you must understand that, afterwards – I had nothing.'

'That wouldn't have mattered.'

'And then, when I heard that you'd married –'

'What else could I have done?' I said.

'I know.'

'You married, too.'

'I know. I know,' he said. 'Though I was alone for three years, before I met Constance.' He looked at me for a moment, and then stooped for the weeds, gathered them easily in one hand. 'Come on.'

We skirted the church, entering the cold shadow on its north side, I at Edward's shoulder, my hand in his, though I couldn't fit on the path beside him. I knew where he was heading. I had never once, in all those years, been to look at his father's grave. Moss had crept over his stone, enough to obscure his dates, but not the name.

Strange to say, but I thought Edward was going to ask forgiveness: out loud, perhaps, offer some kind of ritual. Then, without looking about him, Edward threw the weeds down on Tremain's grave. They sat there, their roots tooth-white and dirty.

I touched his shoulder, and made him turn to me. His face was alight with something like rage.

'Shall we go?' I said.

Edward walked ahead as we thrashed back through the overgrown portion of the churchyard. Watching him stride towards the gate, I thought, with a sick sort of feeling, he is still angry with him. Even now. Even after what we did.

He waited for me outside the lychgate, and I couldn't help it.

I said, 'I've been thinking about that day. About the second fire.'

He stopped, and turned to face me.

I nodded back towards the graveyard, Tremain's neglected stone. 'When you quarrelled with him. You never said what it was about.'

'What do you suppose it was about?' Edward said, and started on, but then stopped in the lane, and wheeled about. 'We exposed him. We both did, we showed them all what he was, and he –' But now he stopped.

I could feel his breath on my face.

'Ivy,' he said, and his expression smoothed, as his gaze moved over my shoulder.

Coming towards us, up the lane, were Murray and Jake.

'Good morning, Murray,' I called out.

'Good morning, Mrs Boscawen,' Murray replied, looking curiously at Edward.

His dogs were with them, and got rather excited, and of course then I had to introduce them and tolerate their small talk while we lingered in the road. I avoided Jake's eyes.

I supposed Edward had not recognized him. 'And this is Mr Feltham, of course. Who –'

'Of course.' Edward put out his hand. 'Good to see you, Feltham. I hope you're keeping well.'

Jake shook, and said he was, thank you. But he was swift to take his hand away, and there was a chill in his tone which was more than awkwardness.

A silence was left, which was just becoming embarrassing, when Murray said, 'Mrs Boscawen. Might I look in tomorrow? There are one or two matters . . .'

'Of course,' I said. 'I'll come up to you.'

'Are the Fossetts back?' Jake said, suddenly. 'I saw them, waiting for the ferry.'

'Not yet,' I said. 'And, as it happens, we ought to be going.'

Murray raised his hat; a beat later, Jake touched his.

I hurried Edward away, back up the lane towards home. Murray had been too polite to ask what he was doing there. But Jake, I suspected, had guessed.

When we were up the hill and out of sight, Edward said, 'He offered to marry her, didn't he? Feltham. Marry Miss Draper, afterwards . . .'

'I believe so,' I said. 'But she declined.'

'Did you ever hear what became of her?'

'No.'

I stopped, and the strength seemed to go out of him. Our faces were very close together again. Under the moving boughs of the oaks, he leaned against me. The wind blew about us.

'Whatever are we going to do?' I said.

'What do you mean?' He held me away from him, by the shoulders, to look at me. 'We'll go away. Not yet, but . . .' He paused. He meant, when Richard was finally dead.

I took a half-step back, the better to look at him.

'Tim wouldn't wish you to be miserable,' he said.

'Sometimes,' I said. 'Sometimes I wish I had never found that key.'

Edward pulled me to him again. 'You were meant to find it. Will meant you to find it. I do believe that. My father was a monster, Ivy.'

I wanted to say, *but he wasn't, was he? He was a man.*

As it was, I didn't answer, only pressed my face into his shoulder. The wind moved in the branches above us.

'You do forgive me, Ivy, don't you?' he said, into my hair. 'For –' He nodded back towards the graveyard. 'Because honestly, all I have clung to, all these years, is that you would forgive me.'

I let him lean on me.

'Of course I forgive you,' I said.

Edward said he'd come again after Christmas. He stood, his palm against the door of the motor, and looked up at the windows of the house. Then he began to ask about rather practical matters, such as whether the Fossetts usually took any of their days at Christmastime.

I said I could not say, I did not know. I said I would wire.

He kissed me then, again, rather roughly. I felt his whiskers this time. I had to remind myself that there was no one to see us. The Fossetts had not come off the ferry; it had been eight months since Richard had left his bed.

It came over me that this might be what it would be like, to be kissed by my husband. Would Edward really be my husband? It was all very well, to marry a stranger when one was practically a child, but –

Yet I knew that it was no use doubting. Edward was right: I had been meant, *we* had been meant for one another.

And there would not be so very long now to wait.

Upstairs, Richard was still flushed, still asleep, just as I had left him. He did not seem any worse, though he had declined in the last month. I seemed to see him suddenly afresh. His face was reduced, and that made me feel guilty again.

I went slowly back down the stairs, and stood uncertainly in the hall. I needed occupation. A week and a day until Christmas, and I had done nothing, nothing whatsoever about it. So I made pastry for the small quantity of mincemeat I had bottled in the autumn. I decorated the pies with ivy leaves, cut out of pastry. Tim had liked helping with that bit.

While the mince pies baked, it grew dark outside. I stopped

wondering where the Fossetts were. Richard was still sleeping, but there was a sort of catch to his breathing which had not been there a week ago. Perhaps Mrs Fossett was right.

When the pies were ready, I put most on a rack to cool, and three on the little chipped plate on the sideboard where Mrs Fossett would always leave Jake his sandwich at lunchtime.

As I set them down, Jake came into the kitchen.

'The ferry's snarled up. Another boat ran into it, at the docks. It'll be two hours for them by road, on a night like this.'

I turned to the range. 'We'll have soup,' I said, exhaustedly, peering under the lid of a pan. And then, 'It's good of you to come.'

Jake opened his mouth, and shut it again. 'How would it be,' he said, at last, 'if Mr Boscawen were to find out?'

I turned away, in frustration.

'If it got to be *known*, Ivy.'

Jake had guessed, then. He had guessed that Edward had come back for me. And that meant he had guessed more, long ago, as I had always suspected. He knew.

I rested my hands on the table. I thought about lying to him, but I was too tired. 'Do you not wish,' I said, 'do you not wish, after everything, Jake, for me to have a little scrap of happiness?'

Jake looked away. 'He's not a good man.'

I made a sort of wild gesture upwards. 'Oh! And is *he* a good man?' I paused, looking at him. 'Are you?'

'A better one than Edward Tremain,' Jake said. He'd turned red.

'Well, I don't recall asking for your opinion,' I said. 'Nor does it seem to me that you are in the position to offer one.' I didn't mean to remind him that he was a servant. That was not what I meant. But it was how it came out.

In reply, Jake only offered me one hurt look, and then went, slamming the door behind him.

The Fossetts were back late, and apologetic. I told Mrs Fossett that Richard seemed – I groped for the word – *different*.

She nodded. 'That was what I thought, madam. I'll sit up with him, I think.'

'Would you?' I said. I felt a wave of gratitude. For I was suddenly quite exhausted.

I slept deeply, and dreamed, as usual, of fire – the shattering of glass in the heat, and perhaps a distant shouting – and woke, as ever, sensing Tim beneath the bed, solid, alert. I crawled out from under the blankets, bone weary, fastened my dressing gown; knelt, as ever, to look into the empty gap. There was such a sense of him, almost annoyed, just the kind of irritated silence as when he was deep in a book and I would ask him some question simply to draw him out of it and make him talk to me.

But this time I did not get to my feet, upon beholding the empty space. This time, I lowered my cheek to the floor, felt the harsh texture of the floorboard. I rolled and shuffled myself under the bed, and looked out from there. A sidewards world of wood grain and tiny dropped hairs, the grey morning light on the boards. I was a child again.

Time passed. Feet came into the room, and I said nothing. They went away.

At length I heard calling – 'Mrs Boscawen?' – and scrambled out, grazing myself.

Mrs Fossett hesitated as I came out on to the landing, staring at my dark brocade dressing gown which was white all over with dust.

'Madam? I think the doctor ought to be fetched again.'

Richard's breathing was shallow, and his chest was flushed. Half asleep, he began to cough, and it didn't stop this time, heaving and hacking as though it would never end.

I went back to the door. 'Doctor,' I said to Mrs Fossett.

I waited with Richard, holding him through the fits. I wanted to tell him about the sergeant. But he was hardly awake. I think he thought I was Mrs Fossett.

When the doctor arrived, he shrugged immediately out of his coat and handed it to me, and went away up the stairs, carrying a brown bag that might have been my father's.

A while later, he came down with a grim face, and told me what he needed to tell me. Richard would need someone with him every minute.

Mrs Fossett was saying that if a kitchen girl could be obtained, she would do it herself.

I went into the study, sat down rather suddenly. I hardly heard her seeing the doctor out.

Both the inquest files are still here on the desk. I can touch the slimmer of the two: Old Tremain. I know the contents off by heart, now. The inquest convened on the 30th of December 1888, following the events of the 27th. I can touch my husband's signature at the bottom, while upstairs, his breathing labours to its end.

The verdict, suicide.

15.

1888

I walked alone back to Polneath, after William Tremain's inquest was adjourned. Dimly, I saw ahead of me my breath's regular cloud. Christmas Eve.

I carried a bag containing the two spare changes of linen for which I had scrabbled about at home, and Edith's latest letter, which I had been saving as a present to myself. In my pocket was the key I had found in William's school blazer. I grasped it, the brass warming in my hand. I perceived nothing of my surroundings, not the trees nor the sky. I was dazed.

William had been locked in. His death had been no accident.

Every time I thought of Jake, of Agnes and Jake, my mind flinched away. I could countenance that they might have been sweethearts. I did not wish to countenance it, but I could do it. The idea that they had been together that night – in the gardens perhaps – and that William had come down, and, finding Agnes gone, had simply waited rather than make the dark walk back upstairs alone. Very well, then. And could Agnes have set the fire? Angry, at having her notice given? Possibly, just possibly.

But could she have locked William in – opened the door again, once he was dead, to conceal her crime – and hidden the key later, amongst his school things, to be shut away and forgotten? Could she have killed the little boy, simply to spite her master? I could not believe it. But I must believe it.

I was certain that the key in my pocket, the key I had found, belonged to the door of Agnes's burned-out bedroom. That Boscawen, who would even now be completing his search, would find nothing.

Yet when I saw his gig, coming down the track, I sank back

amongst the rhododendrons. There was too much confusion, everything seemed suddenly to be moving too fast. I needed to be certain of Agnes's guilt, before I handed her to Boscawen.

Jake, I must simply not think of. Whether he had known. Nor must I think of Father, reaching his black bag down from the high shelf, flexing his trembling hands. In the morning he was supposed to be coming to speak to Agnes, in order to report to the inquest on her state of mind, but the hours until he came might as well be years: I would need to act sooner, and first I must prove for myself where the key belonged.

I hurried around the pond, glancing up, to be sure that no face regarded me from the windows of the house. I went in at the north wing door. The thumping of a copper sounded from the laundry – Mrs Bly must be in there – but nobody came out into the passage as I slipped up the end stairs. The upper passage was as blackened and desolate as it had been the day before.

I took the key from my pocket, and fitted it into the door.

But it wouldn't go: only hung limply from the keyhole.

I tried again, crouching, but it wasn't right. The key simply hung there.

It did not fit.

I stood quite still for a moment, before I withdrew the key, and pocketed it.

If it did not unlock Agnes's old room, to what door did it belong? Slowly I climbed the north stair, to the upper floor. Agnes's door was standing open, the key in the outside as I had left it that morning. Where was she?

In my room – William's room, rather – I put down my bag, and hung up my coat. The key I moved to the pocket of my frock. I smoothed my hair, and went down to see Edward.

When I tapped at the door of his study, there was a weak but definite 'come', and I opened it.

Edward was laid out on the sofa. He had grasped the tartan blanket up to his chin, but seeing me, he cast off the blanket, and lowered his feet to the floor.

'Miss Cardew,' he said.

'Forgive me –'

'No, no,' he said, and shakily indicated the chair by the desk.

I sat, and watched him look at his hands, and then glance at me. His eyes looked sore.

'I'm so terribly sorry,' I said.

He bit his lips. 'I can't – I simply can't believe . . .'

'No.'

He looked at me. 'Has Boscawen gone?'

I nodded. 'I saw him departing.'

'He was talking to Father . . . He found the key, you know. In her room. Miss Draper's room. Under her bolster. Father and I went up with him. He put back the bolster, and – staring us in the face.'

I sat back in my chair, and we looked at one another.

So she *was* guilty.

'I didn't know,' I said then. 'About the paint, under his fingernails.'

Edward closed his eyes. 'Perhaps she is. Perhaps she is mad.' He opened them. 'You did know, though, about this business with the nightshirt.'

I looked down. 'I thought it was Mrs –' I stopped, met his eyes. 'I didn't wish to upset you.'

Edward watched me steadily, his face bleak. 'You're a good girl, Ivy,' he said. 'Too good to be caught up in all this.'

I felt myself turn red. 'I only wish to help, sir,' I said, and saw him flinch.

'Edward.'

I studied my hands. 'Anything I can do, I will do.' I moved in my chair. 'I thought to stay at least until the morning. Father will come then, to speak to Miss Draper.'

Edward bunched his handkerchief. 'And then go home again, to his other task.'

He looked up at me, and I nodded. He brought his hands up to his face, and sniffed, and seemed to gather himself.

'I should be very grateful, then, if you would stay, Miss Cardew,' he said.

'Ivy,' I said, softly.

He looked at me. 'Ivy.' He bowed his head. 'Miss Draper must be treated humanely. I still can't believe –' He broke off.

'No,' I said. 'And Jake Feltham. I've known Jake all my life.'

Edward seemed to recollect himself. 'Of course. No, I think – I am firmly of the belief that Feltham is clear of this. There is nothing to suggest that he – even if they – though, of course, it is better that he should go. But something must be done for him. I will do something for him, you may be assured of it.'

I shifted in my chair. I felt a flush of relief. Father had said the same; perhaps Jake had been with Agnes, but had taken no part in her crime. 'It is kind of you even to think of it.'

He lifted his head. 'If he matters to you, Ivy, he matters to me.'

I could feel myself blushing again, and looked away.

'Only, don't keep anything more from me, if you can bear not to,' he said. 'Not even to spare my feelings. I had rather face it all. I had rather know.'

I looked at him. 'Of course.'

A silence elapsed between us, in which he began to fidget with the blanket. I wanted to tell him about the key in my pocket, the one I had found in William's blazer, but he looked so tired. I rather thought he was waiting for me to go. And in any case, it appeared that the mystery was solved, now.

'Forgive me,' I said, 'but where is Miss Draper?'

'Down with Mrs Bly, I should think,' Edward said. 'Boscawen asked her to keep her away, while we were searching.'

I stood, and he looked up at me.

'If you see Mrs Bly, could you tell her that we shall dine downstairs after all? I told her Father and I would take separate trays in our rooms, but –' he looked wearier than ever – 'I must make certain that Father eats, as well as drinks.'

I let myself out of the French doors, wanting the air on my face for a moment. Going in again at the north wing, I heard sounds still coming from the laundry, and I went in, ready to give Mrs Bly Edward's message.

But it was not Mrs Bly. It was Agnes. She had her back to me, working in the steam. She was washing curtains; I had heard Mrs Bly bemoaning the previous day the way they all stank of smoke. When I made a sound, Agnes wheeled about, wiping the back of her wrist across her face. Seeing who it was, she set down the wooden dolly-pin with a thunk, letting it lean against the steaming copper.

I had not known how it would feel to see her – a murderess, I reminded myself, a woman who could lock a child who trusted her away to burn – but somehow it felt no different.

She was studying me: coldly, angrily.

'Where is Mrs Bly?' I asked.

'Kitchen . . .' She paused. 'She'd rather not look at the chicken she's thrown to the dogs.'

I did not answer that.

Agnes lifted her chin. 'When's your father coming back?'

'In the morning.'

She touched the dolly-pin. 'I suppose you heard your sweetheart found the key.'

I swallowed. 'You did not help yourself,' I said, 'not telling them where you were.'

At that, she looked at me. 'I was not with Jake Feltham,' she said, fiercely, and then shook her head. 'You'll believe what you want, I suppose.' She turned back to the heavy, soaked cloth.

'You ought to be upstairs,' I said.

That made her turn back to me, and her face was fearful now. 'Don't shut me away,' she said. 'Please, not yet. I really shall go mad, if I stay up there with nothing to turn myself to.'

After a moment, I gave the smallest nod. She began to work the copper again, and I backed into the passage. Perhaps there was no harm in letting her keep downstairs for as long as I was down here. Perhaps I was frightened, now that the charge might be murder, that if I locked her up she might do away with herself.

I expected to find Mrs Bly triumphant after her denunciation of Agnes and Jake at the inquest, but she was subdued, and did not meet my eye when I stood at the kitchen door to tell her that I had given Agnes permission to continue with the wash, and that the gentlemen would dine downstairs, after all. She only looked up at me when I asked what was to be done for dinner, and then looked at the floor again as she pointed me towards a heap of potatoes and a paring knife.

I couldn't help but grow calmer, as I worked on the potatoes. They must have just come from the cellar, for soon they numbed my hands with cold. Against my leg, through my petticoats, I could feel the mysterious key. On the other side of the kitchen, Mrs Bly was kneading dough.

The house felt different, without Jake. As if a layer of safety had been removed.

As my hands lost their feeling, I thought of William. Waking, in that little room at the top of the north stair, perhaps from one of those bad vivid dreams which can trouble the early part of the night. Padding down – his feet bare, the cruelty of the cold stone – and the lights of the house almost all out. Looking for Agnes.

I peeled, and thought about Agnes.

It's my fault.

I knew what Mrs Mason would say about her reserve, through the inquest. Guilt, she would say. Lack of proper feeling. But it had seemed simply like her usual reserve, her reticence. I had thought about the nightgown. Her fear, which had *seemed* real. Her professed affection for William.

The key to that room, found so easily under her bolster. Tremain had said it would be there: there it had been. That was when the ghost of an idea began to form.

How vehement Tremain had been, wielding that bunch of keys. How certain.

What if Tremain had planted the key, to divert suspicion from himself? But then, why would he have wished to kill William? Nobody had wished to hurt William. And as I peeled, it came to me.

Nobody had wished to hurt William.

I put down my knife.

What if William had come down, looking for Agnes, and found only an empty room? Had decided to wait? What if Tremain had been in his office? Heard steps in the room above, set the fire amongst his papers, then crept upstairs, and locked the door.

Then William, recognizing the heavy boots of his grandfather – knowing that Tremain disliked Agnes doting upon him – would have panicked, hidden, kept silent. Heard the evil click of the key in the lock, and only afterwards smelled the smoke. Understood.

I felt a horrible sort of triumph in deducing it. But there was also relief. Tremain, about whom I had always had a bad feeling. And Jake was clear, guilty at most of a love affair . . .

Across the kitchen, Mrs Bly had embarked upon some sort of ridiculous fancy pudding – a blancmange, perhaps – with preserved peaches sliced artfully around the edge. Some of my potatoes were starting to turn brown, in the warm air of the kitchen, and my hands as they thawed were painful.

And perhaps Jake was wholly innocent, after all. For there was one easy reason why Tremain might have wished to harm Agnes. Why a master might wish to get rid of a maid.

I must talk to her. When we retired for the night, I would do it then.

And Edward, I thought, as I asked Mrs Bly what to do with the potatoes. If I was right, I would have to tell Edward. And that turned me cold again. He would be beside himself. What if he hurt his father – killed him, even? Away from the house, I must do it away from the house . . .

And that was how I went on, until the dinner hour.

I could hardly stand the thought of seeing Tremain. I felt sure that my knowledge would show on my face. That Edward would guess.

Mrs Bly served up lamb chops and mashed potatoes, and a dark, shining sauce.

I carried the heavy tray up the three steps, and opened the door to the dining room with my hip. Edward was at the near end of the table, Tremain at the further end. He was slumped in his chair, a mostly empty wine glass at his elbow, his coun-tenance turned even redder by the flickering of the fireplace behind him. His white hair, standing up in tufts, made him seem harmless.

I moved to Edward, and he glanced at me, met my eyes. 'Thank you,' he said, as I moved his plate from tray to mat.

That seemed to rouse Tremain.

'Still here, Miss Cardew?' he said. His voice was thick with drink.

'Father,' Edward said, with a tone not of appeasement but of warning.

I was grateful, and surprised when Tremain only grunted and turned his attention back to his wine glass.

'Leave the tray,' Edward said.

And I went.

'She shouldn't still be downstairs,' Mrs Bly said, as I came back in.

But I didn't answer, only took up my knife again. She wanted the apples cut into very thin slices, and I preferred to keep Agnes within earshot. That way, she would be safe.

After a quarter of an hour, Mrs Bly said, 'Pudding,' and disappeared.

A few moments later, there came a shriek.

I was on my feet and out into the passage. 'What? What is it?'

Mrs Bly was backing out of the gun room. 'I only put it in there to chill,' she was saying.

Agnes was inside, her hands still wet from the wash.

'What's the matter?' I asked.

'She's done a mischief,' Mrs Bly said.

Agnes was standing beside the large wooden table that filled most of the room, quite still, almost in the dark. She was staring at the pudding, which was smashed, spattered across the floor.

Mrs Bly had come to me, where I stood in the doorway, catching at me with her hands, imploring. 'I just put it in here to catch a bit of chill –'

'What's this?' Edward said.

The commotion must have carried, along the echoing passage to the dining room.

'Look, sir,' Mrs Bly said. 'I dropped it when I . . . look what she's done.'

'I didn't,' Agnes said. She wouldn't look at Mrs Bly, but she turned to me. 'You know I didn't,' she said. Her face was open with fear.

I looked back at the table. In the low light of the gun room, after the bright lamps of the kitchen, it was hard at first to deduce.

But now, as my eyes grew accustomed, I saw. There was a black . . . shape, on the table. Like a shadow without a person.

Mrs Bly said, 'William. It's William.'

I felt myself turn cold. Made myself move to the table, and touch a finger to the shape. The finger came away black, as though the shape had been burned into the table. William, where he had been laid out. But the table had been quite dry and clean, only yesterday.

Mrs Bly was looking at Agnes.

'Mrs Bly,' Edward said, firmly, 'you might take some brandy up to Father.'

She looked at the table. 'Shall I not –'

'Leave it,' I said to her. 'Mr Boscawen may wish to examine it.'

'Brandy, Mrs Bly,' Edward said, gently. 'A small one.'

Edward and I looked at one another.

He looked rattled, but not so much as Agnes, who was the only person who had not stood back from the table, and that was because she had a tight grip on the edge of it. She looked as though, if she did not sit down, she would fall down.

When I took her arm, it was cold. 'Come on now,' I said.

Agnes did not resist. She seemed exhausted, suddenly. Utterly drained.

I led her away, leaving Edward in the passage, gazing at the gun room table with its dark stain.

Upstairs, Agnes, all the fight of earlier gone out of her, submitted to help with her buttons, and climbed into bed.

'Can I –?' I said, and nodded at Agnes's wrist.

'If you want.'

I took her wrist, which was cold, and felt for a pulse.

Agnes watched as I counted, her face wary, thinking perhaps of the chill of our exchange in the laundry.

When I was satisfied, I lowered the arm to the counterpane. 'You've overexerted yourself,' I said, gently.

'I wasn't seeing things,' she said.

'No.' I put down her hand.

Agnes's eyes wandered away. 'Your father was kind, this morning. And the other night, he was kind then, too.'

'He is.'

'Will he be kind tomorrow, do you think?' Agnes began to pick at the blanket. 'You're all kind, till it costs you something.'

I leaned forward. 'Agnes –'

But she turned away. 'I keep thinking I've heard him. Will.'

'That's very common,' I said, in a soothing voice.

'His hoop, up and down.' Agnes nodded at the door.

'Very common,' I said.

She looked at me. 'What if the thing on the table –' She stopped. 'What if it *was* William?'

'Agnes.' I put my hand on her arm. 'We must keep our heads. We must hold on to what we *do* know.' I sat back. 'And I know who put that key under your bolster.'

Agnes looked at me, for a long moment, eyes filling. 'Thank God,' she said, and burst into tears.

I made sounds, and brought out my handkerchief. I watched her weep, feeling horribly guilty. To think that I had grown to suspect her – when, not only was she innocent of William's death, but she had been suffering alone herself.

When she was sniffing and breathing again, she said, 'I thought the fire was an accident, see. Or if he meant it, then he meant it to frighten me, not to . . . but he *locked the door* –'

'I know,' I said, gently. 'How long had it been going on? How long were Tremain and yourself –' I stopped. 'I shall not call it lovers.' I could feel myself turning red.

Agnes had grown still. 'About a year.'

I leaned forward, made Agnes look at me. 'And where were you? When the fire started?'

Her eyes had filled again. 'I was in his bedroom,' she said, thickly. 'We'd quarrelled.'

I worked to smother my shock, my disapproval. 'You were waiting to make it up.'

Mrs Bly had lied, then, at the inquest. Tremain had not been in his bedroom, and therefore she could not have rescued him from it. Tremain must have lurked somewhere, outside perhaps, out of earshot of William's shouts; then come up for Mrs Bly, after the blaze had taken hold.

She had not rescued him: he had rescued her. Mrs Bly had lied, and so she must know something. Perhaps she had heard Tremain, coming to Agnes at night.

'That was why you were moved downstairs,' I said, now. 'Away from William's room. So that he would not hear anything.'

As I turned red again, Agnes nodded. I forced myself back to the problem. For it comforted me to turn my mind from that shape on the gun room table, that shape meant to frighten, to clearing·Agnes when the inquest reconvened.

'How did you know?' Agnes said. 'How did you know I didn't do it?'

'When the key didn't fit,' I said, distantly. And then I explained about the key I had found in William's blazer.

'A key?' Agnes sniffed again, and unfolded my handkerchief, made a face at the mess she had made of it, then looked at me in apology.

I produced the key from my pocket, and her face changed in understanding.

'I should think it's to *his* room,' she said. 'Tremain's. Will stole that key.'

Tremain and Mr Edward had quarrelled often, she said. One night, Tremain had been raging, destroying his room, and found himself locked in. Mr Edward swore he hadn't done it. William wasn't to be found. Tremain had shouted and cursed, but Mr Edward had given Jake permission not to pick the lock that night, but to do it in the morning when his father had worn himself out. In the morning, though, the door had been standing open – but the key had not reappeared. Tremain had ransacked Agnes's room and Mrs Bly's, Mr Edward's room and finally the boy's, and still not found it.

'Will thought he could lock him in,' I said. 'If he became enraged again –'

Agnes sniffed, and nodded. 'He was always uneasy about leaving the master alone with Mr Edward,' she said. She looked at me. 'And about me. That's why he worried so, about being sent away to school. He wasn't scared to go. He didn't want to leave.'

I nodded. 'And what about Mr Edward?' I said. 'Did he know about Tremain's behaviour towards you?'

She looked down. 'I don't know.'

'We must tell him.'

She shifted, clutched the counterpane. 'No. No, you mustn't tell anyone. They'll not believe it.'

'But –'

'Please, Miss Cardew.' She was becoming agitated.

I made a soothing sound, and we lapsed into quiet. We sat, listening to the wind amongst the chimneys, and thinking our separate thoughts. When I glanced at Agnes, she was watching me.

'And what about after all this?' I said. 'Have you any family?'

Agnes looked down. 'I've an aunt. She had eight of her own, when I was little, so she couldn't . . . All grown up now, of course. But she won't want to know, not while there's a question of the law.'

I pressed her hand, and she looked at it.

'They don't use the short drop, for women, any more,' she said. 'Do they?'

I told her to hush. I told her that could never happen, that I would not let it happen.

But she became more and more distressed, pulling up the blanket about her chin, the rope of her plait flung out across the bolster. 'You'll take my key when you turn it?'

I promised, if she would take some of what Father had left, and she agreed to that. Her eyelids were dropping, in any case. Whether it was the morning's inquest, or her exertions at the wash, or the fright she had had, or whether it was some delayed influence of the fire and water which had marked her recent days – whatever it was, she was evidently exhausted, and after the first unsettled flickering of eyelashes, went directly to sleep.

I paused in the passage, wishing to go to Edward, for surely he had known, surely suspected something. And yet, perhaps not – for if he had known, then he must have guessed, too, at what his father had done. And how could he sit at table with him, if that were true? Perhaps, then, he did not know. But I could not tell him while his father was nearby.

I went into William's room, and took out the key I had found, the key to Tremain's room. I could not try it now, of course. But poor William. Trying to keep his father safe, to keep Agnes safe.

I could tell Father, when he arrived in the morning. I held the key in my fist. The room was cold. I lay down in my clothes, thinking of Mrs Mason at the King's Arms, once demonstrating covertly how a key held in the right way might serve a woman for a weapon, when she had none other to hand.

I was late to sleep that night. I heard Agnes get up more than once for the chamber pot, as I lay awake.

William had not been afraid to go to school, but afraid to leave.

Tremain was one matter, I kept thinking of that black shape on the gun room table – so perfect, so silently done. Could Tremain have made it?

William had been afraid to leave, I thought.

Perhaps he never had.

16.

I was woken next morning, Christmas morning, by a knocking at my door, and Father's voice outside.

'Ivy? Ivy, my dear?'

I found myself dressed, outside the bedclothes. I had slept long past my usual hour.

'Father,' I said, slipping on my shoes. 'Just a moment.'

He was standing in the passage, holding a tray with a dish of bread and dripping, and a cup of tea. He looked pale, and the tea was slopping as the tray shook.

'It's for Miss Draper,' he said. 'How is she?'

'Agitated,' I said. 'Up and down to the chamber pot, though her chest seems better.' I dropped my voice. 'But I wanted to speak to you, Father –'

'About Miss Draper?'

'No. Yes. About William's death –'

But now I heard feet on the south stairs, and Edward appeared at the end of the passage.

'Dr Cardew,' he said. 'Thank you for coming. You're here to speak to Miss Draper?'

I took the tray from Father, and he shook Edward's hand. I wondered whether Father's would be cold, sweaty, as it often was when his shakes were bad. But Edward grasped Father's hand warmly.

'Let me wake her,' I said.

I tapped at Agnes's door, and unlocked it at her answer. She was up and dressed. She sat, and I handed her the tray. Father came in, and I made to shut the door.

But then he said, 'You might leave us, my dear.'

'Oh?' I said.

I looked at Agnes, and she nodded, glancing at Father.

I handed Father the key, and closed the door behind me. Perhaps Agnes would tell him about Tremain.

Edward was standing at the end of the passage.

'Let us wait downstairs,' he said.

I nodded, and followed him down the south stairs. I could not speak to him now, not with Tremain in the house, not with Father here. I knew I must wait.

We emerged into the hall and Edward led me through to the dining room, out of the French doors and on to the terrace, as I tried to answer calmly his polite enquiries as to how I had slept.

Outside, it was chilly but bright, the thinnest skim of ice on the pond. In the village, children would be waking up to their oranges and toys, would be being laced into their best things, ready for church.

'I hope you slept well,' Edward said again.

I tried to smile, resisted touching his arm. 'I did.'

'And that you were not unduly alarmed by that business last night, in the gun room.'

I met his eyes, but he looked only worried.

'You mustn't worry about me,' I said. 'I hope *you* were not alarmed.'

He frowned. 'No. No.' And then, 'I am quite certain that there must be a sensible explanation.'

He looked at me, rather desperately, as though I might offer it then and there, but I only bit my lip, and looked away across the ice. We sat quietly like that, until I heard the French doors behind us open.

I turned, and stood up.

'Father. How did you get on?'

'Well,' he said, 'well enough –' But he was white in the face, and, somehow, as he said it he missed his step, and pitched forwards into the gravel.

By the time we had got him up and into the kitchen, into a chair by the stove, the shaking had abated somewhat, but he still looked dreadfully white. Edward got it out of him that he had come on foot – 'I didn't feel up to tacking the horse, my dear,' Father said, clutching my hand – and so Edward would accept nothing but that he would run down himself to the King's Arms, to send for their carriage. He had mumbled something, too, about whether a doctor ought to be fetched: but Father pointed out that there was no one *to* fetch, and that in any case Dr Graves was coming that afternoon, to –

And there he broke off, and Edward paled, himself. Coming to give his second opinion, Father meant. Of the post-mortem.

After Edward had gone, Mrs Bly flapped around Father, while he avoided my eyes.

She was presenting him with his third cup of tea when she said, 'And so, Doctor, what do you think? Is she mad?'

She asked it not avidly, but fretfully, and a strange look came over her when Father said, 'Not mad, Mrs Bly. Fragile. But not mad.'

Mrs Bly turned away. I thought then that she would speak to Father about the gun room table, but she did not.

With Father waiting quietly, I could not resist slipping along the passage, to look again in the bright morning light. The gun room door was open, and the table was clean. Quite clean, as though no stain had ever marked it.

I felt the hairs rise on my arms.

Back in the kitchen, Mrs Bly stayed bent over the sink, as I waited with Father, who seemed to have fallen almost into a doze. Mrs Bly must have cleaned the table. But if she thought Agnes mad, why would she have removed the evidence of it? I watched her movements at the sink, quick and nervy, as Father breathed quietly beside me.

After an hour, perhaps, Edward reappeared. 'Now then, Dr Cardew,' he said, kindly. 'I'm sure you won't object to taking my arm . . .'

He helped Father up. Already his legs were steadier. When they had gone from the kitchen, I spoke to Mrs Bly.

'I told you to leave the gun room table,' I said. 'For Mr Boscawen.' Her turned back was frightening me, so I said, 'Mrs Bly? Look at me.'

At that she swung around. Quite calm, she said, 'Miss Cardew, I haven't touched the gun room table.'

I stepped back and back again, up the steps and through the swing door to the hall, where Father and Edward were just reaching the front door. Father climbed easily enough into the carriage, and remembered to press the key for Agnes's door into my hand. He assured me three times that he would rest when he got home, and then the carriage was going. As it moved across the gravel, Edward touched my arm.

'Are you well?' he said.

'I am.' I looked at him. 'I am. But I need to speak to you.'

Tremain was somewhere in the house, but he suspected nothing, and there was a locked door between him and Agnes.

Edward was nodding. 'I have to make an inventory of the works,' he said. 'If you'd be kind enough to assist me.'

'Of course,' I said.

We would be alone, and away from the house. Now I would find out whether he knew what his father had been doing. If he lied, I would know it, by his face or his voice. Either Edward must discover a terrible truth about his father, or I must discover one about Edward. It was horrendous, waiting for him to gather his papers, not to know which it would be.

When he was ready, Edward joined me on the terrace, and handed me fresh paper, a clip and a board to rest on, a stub of pencil. I followed him around the pond and through the blast wall, not knowing how to begin.

Edward nodded at my shoes, as we walked down the track. 'No nails?'

I shook my head. The regulations in the mills were stringent, and deservedly so: almost anything could make a spark.

I said, 'You didn't . . . you didn't clean the gun room table, did you?'

Edward looked at me. 'Did I . . . ? No.'

'No,' I murmured. I looked at him. 'Is it for the insurance? This inventory?'

Edward glanced at me, shook his head. 'Father says they may not pay out. We will need a bank loan. He has been wiring to the bank in Falmouth, but they want to see an inventory of the security.' The broad daylight showed up the flinching sleeplessness of his eyes.

'Edward,' I said, at last.

He stopped. But it was as though he hadn't heard me. He said, 'Dr Cardew – your father – that is, I'll be able to see him, won't I? Afterwards?'

He meant William.

'Father will be as careful as he can. But there will be some damage.'

Edward pushed a hand across his face, and walked on. 'Reverend Green asked me to look in, about the burial,' he said.

'Edward.' He stopped again. We were beside the storage houses for the powder's separate ingredients: the sulphur, the saltpetre, the charcoal in its pressed barrels.

I swallowed. 'This might be a shock,' I said.

He looked at me.

In a rush I said, 'It was your father, Edward, who set the fire. Who locked the door on William.'

Edward stood quite still for a moment, and then reached out for the door of the charcoal store, sat down rather suddenly on the step. For a moment I felt elation, relief – he had not known. But then I saw his face, in which there was not only shock, but bitter confirmation.

'You knew?' I said. 'You knew, about him and Agnes.'

Edward's eyes, which had been roaming the floor, met mine, and he gave a quick nod. I could feel myself turning red.

'And you knew what your father –'

But now Edward shook his head. 'I hoped it was her,' Edward said. 'The fire – after some quarrel perhaps. Before we knew about the locked door, I hoped it was her, and that Will being down was only a horrible chance. But then, after yesterday, I didn't know what to . . .' And at that, his face crumpled, and he reached for me.

I held him as the sobs racked him, there on the step of the charcoal store, until the fit had passed.

His face wet with tears, he said, 'How did you fathom it?'

I felt in my pocket for Tremain's door key. 'In part, because of this. The key to your father's room.'

Edward took the key, and looked at it.

'William had hidden it, amongst his things . . .' I paused. 'I suspect William knew. About his grandfather and Agnes.'

Edward's eyes were filling again, and I put my hand on his arm.

'He was softer with Will than with me,' he said. 'But Will was still frightened of him.' He looked at me. 'I never fought back as a child, you know. Father beat me for having mud on my boots, for forgetting to trim a lamp, for leaving the gristle from my meat, and I never struck him back.'

I did not know how to answer him. I wanted to bring up Agnes, but for a moment there was only sadness: his childhood wasted, William's snuffed out. It was cold on the step. Edward's hands were cold. He needed time to recover.

I gestured to the blank paper I carried. 'Shall we do this?' I said, gently. We would need to decide, precisely what he must say when the inquest reconvened.

We moved through the mills, Edward counting and I noting, and now and then he would stop, and out would pour more. How Tremain had made him recite Shakespeare, and if he fluffed a line, twisted his ears until they bled. How once a puppy had followed him home, and Tremain had drowned it. How he had gone away to school at last, and only known how poor his learning had been when the other boys had laughed at him, for thinking that King Lear was real.

In the carpenter's shop, *a bench, a level, a lathe*, I wrote. *Lightly used*.

Edward was counting some boxes of brass nails. 'Mrs Bly has always been his creature,' he said. 'Do you know she came from the same place as Agnes? St Margaret's. Before I was born. She's been at Polneath for thirty-five years.' He looked at me. 'Twenty boxes,' he said, and I wrote it down, and we stepped back into the open air.

'Do you suppose it was she who made the shape on the gun room table?' I said. 'Or your father?'

Edward spread his hands. 'She does whatever he asks. And if they wanted Agnes to seem mad . . .'

We were beside the incorporating mills. Outside each mill was a small dry space, pocked with discarded wads of chewing tobacco, where the men could squat and listen to the charge grinding away inside. Edward stood still for a moment, looking away into the grouped buildings amongst the stark, graceful branches of the winter trees. The soft sound of the damping channels, falling as a gentle trickle further along the path.

I glanced at the inventory, almost complete. There was something troubling me about it, but I could not tell what. I tucked it under my arm.

'I suppose I hoped it was Agnes,' he said again. 'I suppose I hoped it was her, but I knew it was not.'

'From the first, you wished her treated decently.'

He looked at me. 'So how *did* you fathom it? Did she confess it to you? About the affair?'

I assumed his mind had turned to the inquest, to how we would prove her innocence.

'She has told me a little, but even before that . . . either Agnes set a fire for which she knew she'd be caught, and set out to kill William, whom she loved . . . or, it was your father who set the fire. And it was not William he intended to kill at all.'

Edward was looking into the trees again. 'Will was too frightened,' he said, bleakly. 'He knew who it was in the passage, who turned the key, and he was too frightened to call out.'

I nodded, though Edward was looking away. As he brought his hand up to his face, I did not speak. But then I asked, I made myself ask, 'What will you say? At the inquest?'

He turned away, into the expense magazine, and I followed.

'What do you mean?' he said, carefully.

'At the inquest. You'll need to speak out against him.'

He bit his lip. 'The scandal alone would ruin the business,' he said. He was counting the barrels of finished powder.

'But after what he has done.'

'There's not enough proof.' Edward looked at me. 'Not against him, nor against Agnes.'

'What do you mean?' I said.

I had followed him into the pressing house; he was running a hand over the blocks of lignum vitae, heavy enough to crush a thumb blunt. I thought of Agnes, up at the house, alone.

'You can't mean it.'

He wouldn't look at me. 'She won't be convicted.'

'But what of her reputation?' I stopped. 'Jake Feltham's reputation?'

He shook his head. 'Her reputation will be whatever I say it is, Ivy . . .' He paused, breathing hard. 'Miss Draper shall have her character, and that will be the end of it.' He turned to me. 'You don't know the world as I do. No one will have heard of any of this, certainly not beyond Cornwall. She can go somewhere else. Begin again. And so can I.'

I turned away, angry.

'What would you have?' he said. 'The whole village out of work, so that a villain can be called a villain?' Then, more gently, 'Is it even what Miss Draper wants, to have it exposed? Would that help her reputation?'

Suddenly I doubted. Whether it *was* enough, by itself: the paint, William's little bruised hands, Agnes's testimony.

Edward was looking up into the canopy, the lattice of branches and sky, as though we were talking about the weather. 'I'm sorry about Jake, of course,' he said. 'So long as the loan is approved, I would like to compensate him.'

I turned away, and though blinded by tears, I saw we were watched from the mill gates. Two of the men who worked mixing up the green charges were standing out in the lane, hands in pockets. Come to look, come to gawp, even when there was nothing to see: it is how people are, after a disaster. One could sense them, half wondering whether to shout 'Merry Christmas' or not.

Edward lifted a hand, uncertain.

One took off his hat.

I turned away, back towards the house, and began to walk fast so that he wouldn't see my face, but it was then that it came to me. The inventory had been perturbing me, all the time we had been talking.

Unwillingly, I stopped. Edward caught up.

'There's too much.' I handed him the paper. 'There's too much powder in the separating house,' I said. There were strict regulations, for how much might be in each of the buildings of the mills.

Edward looked at the list. 'Eighty pounds,' he said.

'A barrel.'

Edward looked through the trees. 'We could change it on the list,' he said, studying the inventory. 'Add it to the tally for the pressing house.'

I looked at him. 'It's not safe,' I said. I turned back, and marched ahead, down to the separating house, too quickly, almost falling as I went.

Edward arrived as I was trying, like a fool, to lift a barrel by myself, my face to the wood.

'Ivy,' he said. He touched my back. 'Ivy, stop. Let me.'

I looked at him, and stepped away, but I couldn't refrain from helping as he lifted it, holding his breath, at the limit of his strength. I steadied him as he carried it the fifteen yards to the pressing house, and I hardly let my own breath out until he had set it safe on the floor.

He looked at me. 'Forgive me,' he said.

I bit my lip. 'Miss Draper has been alone too long. I must get back up to the house.'

We walked back together in silence, Edward a pace behind me.

When we reached the blast wall, he paused, and I thought he was about to speak, when, at the same moment, we looked across the pond to the house. The day was a dark one, and there were lights burning in the drawing room.

Clearly I could see Tremain, talking to a lady, fine-looking, older, in a wide skirt. And nearer, looking out of the window, a younger lady. Looking out at me, across the pond, where Edward and I stood side by side.

17.

We stood like a pair of gateposts, Edward and I, staring for one long moment at the young lady in the window. Then I turned, to see him lifting his hand.

He looked at me. A guilty look.

'Forgive me,' he said. 'Forgive me. I must –'

And he was gone, around the edge of the pond, and in at the French doors. I made for the north wing door.

In the kitchen, Mrs Bly was moving things about, looking shocked and hot. 'Where were you?' she said, forgetting herself. She took in my rolled sleeves, grubby hands, the mess of my hair.

Before I could ask what was happening, Mrs Bly was telling me.

'That is Mrs Albertina Myers. The other lady is her daughter, Flora,' Mrs Bly said. 'And now they want tea, and as far as I know they're staying for dinner, though what I'll give them – and now I can't for the life of me remember where I put the best tea service away.'

She was so agitated that I found myself offering to help her. After I had washed my hands, I helped her search three cupboards, while on the stove the water boiled and boiled.

'He said he'd telegraphed. With warning, I could have – no, not that one.'

When it was found, I ran up to Agnes with a plate of sandwiches, which I had clumsily made myself while Mrs Bly was arranging the trays.

Agnes was sitting on the edge of the bed.

'There's visitors,' I said.

'I know,' Agnes replied. She had picked up a sandwich, and was examining it. And then, 'Tremain took them out by the pond, as far as the blast wall.' She was chewing, swallowing, her eyes on her plate. 'The young lady is Mr Edward's fiancée.' Then she flicked her eyes up at me. 'Is something the matter, Miss Cardew?' she asked. And then, 'Where have you been?'

'With Mr Edward,' I said. But at her look, I added, 'Later. You ought to eat. I'm needed downstairs.'

Back downstairs, I went ahead with the pot, cups and saucers on one tray, Mrs Bly following with the milk jug, sugar tongs, a plate of small biscuits, arranged in overlap.

I was telling myself that I did not care, did not care that there was a fiancée. That Edward all too evidently lacked strength, lacked a certain resolution – that should be all too clear from his refusal to speak up against his father, to speak up for what was right. In my distraction, I had agreed to put on a maid's cap which Mrs Bly had found somewhere.

'There she is,' Tremain said, as we came in. 'We thought you'd fallen down the well.'

'Nonsense,' the mother said. 'Mrs –?'

'Bly,' Edward supplied.

'We'd never have imposed, Mrs Bly,' the older lady said.

I moved to help take the things from the tray, and there was genuine kindness in how she arranged what I set down. I didn't dare look at the younger lady, but from the corner of my eye I saw her shoot her mother a look as Edward said, 'I'm terribly sorry, I did wire –' He was rumpled. A dead piece of bracken was stuck to one of his sleeves.

'To the London house?' Mrs Myers straightened. 'Oh, my dear. But we were in Devon, you see. With the Killingtons.'

The tray unloaded, I stood back. Somehow, in all I had done at Polneath, I had not felt like a servant. But suddenly now, present but disregarded, I felt like one – except for the way in which Edward would look anywhere except for the corner in which I was standing.

Mrs Myers was perhaps fifty. She had bright blue eyes, considering eyes. She was small and slight, but her husband, I thought, must have been a larger, taller, creamier person, for everything about Miss Myers was softer and fairer. Her hair was more simply done, but she had a little white fur at her throat, which she kept touching, as though to check it were still there. On her face was a small, worried frown. On her left hand she wore the nicest diamond ring I had ever seen.

'We're a bit piecemeal today, I'm afraid, madam,' Mrs Bly said, in a strained voice. 'Some of the girls have their half day –'

The scale of the lie made me glance at Mrs Bly.

'Not at all,' Mrs Myers replied.

Both the women, despite being in their travelling things, still looked extremely fine. The stainless dove grey of their skirts, their beautiful gloves and neat boots looked peculiar against the backdrop of the faded drawing room, and made me notice afresh its shortcomings. Scuffed woodwork, dull brasses, dead leaves in corners where they had been sent by the perpetual draught.

Tremain looked on edge; he was watching Mrs Myers as she subtly appraised the beautiful teacups, the rather coarse sugar. Even with Edward there, glancing stricken at Miss Myers in her wonderful clothes, I felt a flush of hate towards Tremain. His large, watery eyes. His fleshy hands.

'You're cold, Miss Myers,' Edward said, and moved to the hearth.

But loudly she said, 'No. It's only – that is –' She glanced at her mother. 'Edward, it's such a dreadful thing. I'm so terribly sorry.'

They had not known, then, about William. I remembered, now, Edward telling Mrs Bly, the day I had come to Polneath – could it be only two days ago? – that he had wired to put the Myerses off. They had been coming for Christmas, then. Edward's future mother-in-law. Edward's fiancée.

'It's lovely of you to give us tea,' the mother was saying. 'But of course, we won't impose –'

'But surely you'll stay for dinner,' Edward replied, desperately.

'If you'd like us to,' the young woman said, glancing at her mother.

The mother only smiled. 'We ought to leave you in peace.'

Tremain was glancing anxiously from Edward to the ladies. They must not know, I realized, what had passed at the King's Arms yesterday. They must know only that there had been a fire; that William was dead.

'Edward is right,' Tremain said. 'And in any case – Christmas Day – there's no good hotel nearer than Falmouth –'.

'I'll pour,' Mrs Myers said to Mrs Bly, who was just fussing with the plate of biscuits. 'But, if Flora might –' She glanced at Edward.

'Miss Myers would like to tidy herself,' Tremain said. 'Perhaps Mrs Bly might show her up to Mrs Tremain's room.'

The pink room, he meant; somehow, from the way he said it – 'Mrs Tremain's room' – I felt sure that it had been Edward's mother's room, too, long ago.

'Allow me,' I said.

Miss Myers smiled a slightly tense smile, and came towards me. Carefully, I avoided Edward's eyes.

I led the fiancée upward through the house. Something in her seemed to drop as soon as she was out of sight of her mother. I had to wait for her at the top of the stairs. Her dress must have been a tight one, and I slackened my pace as I led the way up the passage, letting her breathe. It wasn't her fault, I reminded myself, as I held the door into Mrs Tremain's room. Miss Myers had probably never even been alone with Edward before – probably only traded nothings in a London crowd. Dropped her handkerchief and allowed him to pick it up again, or some nonsense of that sort.

I opened the door, allowing her past me, and then moved across the room to open the shutters. There were the small soft slippers beside the bed; the great wardrobes, with their hat boxes; the dressing table crowded with scent bottles.

Miss Myers took a seat there, looked at the silver jewellery box, the old church flower rota, the dust. 'What a queer house this is,' she murmured, and then, 'Forgive me. No doubt any house would feel queer, after such a terrible blow.' The recovery was an elegant one, and sprang from kindness.

'This is your first visit to Polneath?'

'It is. Poor Edward. What a dreadful thing.' With shaky fingers, she began to unpin her hat, laying the pins in her lap to avoid the dust. She met my eyes in the mirror. 'This one hurts my head. I can't get it to sit straight.'

It was another piece of elegance, an excuse for her flushed face and the wobble and catch in her voice. Perhaps it was William's death, but I suspected then that it was more the suddenness of the reversal, of coming here and hearing of the death; of coming here and seeing, unadorned, the Tremains' financial position. She was beginning to suspect, I thought, that she ought not to marry Edward, and now she was crying. As when a child falls, they cry, even when there is no damage: that is what I told myself.

I knew that I might say something to soothe her now, to change her mind, to convince her that matters at Polneath were not so bad as she thought. But if a blow must fall, better that it should fall quickly.

'Allow me,' I murmured, as the hat came free, and took it from her.

It was the velvet which made it heavy.

Flora Myers pushed her fingers into her hair, easing her scalp, and I noticed again the diamond. It looked an old one. I wondered if it had been his mother's. If it had, after that, been Emily Tremain's.

'It is a sad business,' I repeated. 'And it seems doubly cruel, after losing his wife at such a young age.'

Flora raised her eyes. 'Did you serve her?'

'I met her. She's not been gone a year. Those are her slippers, just there. My father treated her, once or twice.'

Flora had begun repinning the hat, but now she stopped, looking at me.

'Father's the doctor. I help him sometimes. I only came to sit with one of the maids. Smoke inhalation, and a chill. The night William died . . .' I paused. I saw that she was looking at my white servant's cap. Slowly, I took it off, held it. It was a dreadful stiff thing. 'The little boy was locked into her room, it seems.'

Flora must have missed with a pin, for she winced. 'I'm sure the family are grateful – it's very kind of you to help, Miss –?'

'Cardew. I'm glad to do it. We're all very fond of Mr Edward, in the village.'

'I'm sure,' Flora said.

'It's terribly difficult for him, with the works struggling, too. And now the inquest.'

'Yes,' Flora said.

She had left off the pinning – was simply looking at me, in the mirror. I told myself that I was doing her a kindness. I would not have admitted, in that moment, to the slightest shred of an intention of my own towards Edward. He would not speak up against his father, had said not a word about Miss Myers. I had hoped he would be bold as well as gentle, but my hopes were disappointed, and now I was merely shielding Miss Myers from the same disappointment.

She dropped her eyes. 'Forgive me,' she said. 'I mustn't keep you. I can find my own way back to the drawing room.'

I nodded. 'When you come down the stairs, turn right down the hall for the convenience,' I said.

She nodded gratefully, and I left her.

In the kitchen, a pair of ducks lay unplucked on the table, sprawled out with dull eyes and bright feathers. On another board lay a mound of carrots, and Mrs Bly was wresting the lid from a large preserving jar. Perhaps it contained plums, but in the low light of the kitchen, it looked redly medical. Suddenly, she gave up on the jar. She was moving from side to side, as she did when her foot was bothering her.

'I shouldn't think they'll stay for dinner,' I said.

'I ought to be ready,' Mrs Bly replied. But then she stopped. 'Jake Feltham shot these,' she said, touching one of the birds. 'Handsome, aren't they?'

I nodded. Their heads were chestnut, their feathers glossy and detailed and beautiful. Mrs Bly seemed uneasy. I thought of how she had lied for Tremain at the inquest. Betrayed Jake. She must feel guilty. Perhaps I might force her to let something slip. Enough to clear Agnes.

'Well, *they* know they're very fine,' I said, tilting my head at the ceiling, to indicate the Myerses.

Mrs Bly frowned. 'As bad as the mistress. Mr Edward's wife, God rest her. They come here and expect it to be like Mayfair. And that only gets his back up.'

She meant Tremain. I thought of what Edward had said. That she had always been his creature.

'You were a great help with my father this morning,' I said.

She looked down. 'Dr Cardew has always taken trouble with me.'

I lowered my voice. 'Mrs Bly,' I said. 'If you did not clean the table in the gun room, then who did clean it?'

She had her back to the door. Suddenly, over her shoulder, Tremain appeared. She saw my face, and turned.

Coldly, he looked at us both. 'Didn't you hear the bell?' he said. 'They're going. They want coats.'

'Coming, sir,' Mrs Bly said, wiping her hands on her apron. She followed him out.

I stood in the kitchen for a minute, catching my breath. Then, silently, I ran upstairs, to watch how Miss Myers would say good-bye to Edward, and how he would say goodbye to her.

In Mrs Tremain's bedroom, the pale daylight illuminated the draped bed, the screen, but something caught my eye on the dressing table. A point of light. I went closer. It was the ring. I picked it up. The larger diamond was surrounded by other, smaller diamonds. I did not know the words for such things. Edith knew all that, about brilliant cut and cushion cut. I could never remember the difference, but that did not prevent me from, for a moment, coveting the ring. It glittered in the low light. I took it to the window, to see it better, and slipped it, without thinking, on to my finger. The band was tighter than I expected. I held it up, went nearer the glass.

Below, Mrs Myers and then Miss Myers issued forth on to the gravel. Fur and velvet blobs. If anyone came, I would say I had come up to tidy after Miss Myers.

Edward and Tremain stood on the gravel, the wind moving their hair. Then Tremain bowed, and stepped back. Either from cold or delicacy, Mrs Myers allowed the coachman to hand her up quickly, leaving Flora alone with Edward. I squinted to see his expression as he spoke to her, she with her hands tucked away into her muffler. He looked earnest, certainly, but I could deduce no particular pain or affection. Then Mrs Bly ran out with his hat and coat, and he took them, and got up beside the coachman, and the coach moved off.

I was stunned. Why would he be going with them, if the engagement was broken off? Perhaps she had not told him. But to leave me alone here – and surely he need not see them all the way to Falmouth –

There was a noise in the passage outside. Tremain, I saw, was gone from the gravel sweep. Quickly, I turned. The door swung open, and I barely had time to push my arms behind my back.

It was him.

'I was just seeing,' I said, 'whether everything was alright with the room.'

Tremain advanced towards me; outside, the coach was disappearing through the top gate.

'What did you say to her?' Tremain said. His voice was soft, almost reasonable. He was halfway across the carpet, and had allowed the door to gently close behind him.

My heart was beating hard. 'To Miss Myers? Nothing.'

He stopped.

I wanted to bring my hands in front of me, but then he would see the ring. I was considering and measuring the distance around him to the door, measuring his stupid watchfulness, like that of a bull from across a field. I might be quicker. He was certainly stronger.

He was studying me minutely. 'You must be fond of Agnes, Miss Cardew, to have stopped with us so long.' He leaned nearer.

'She needs nursing –'

'Now, Miss Cardew, no untruths. But perhaps it's not her you stay for, eh?' He was close, now, very close.

I found that I could not have moved, not a step, could only stare at the pale grey-pink of the old carpet and feel my hands sweating into one another, aware of the bulk of the ring. The stone was sharp, but not sharp enough to make a difference. If I had to defend myself.

I could smell his breath.

'Mrs Bly is very busy, Miss Cardew,' he said. 'She's a good servant – very loyal. And very busy . . .' He paused. 'I won't have her upset.'

I nodded, very slightly, hardly daring to move my head in case it caused our cheeks to touch. He smelled of sleep and old liquor. He moved behind me, now, to the window, to look out. I wanted to dart for the door, but my feet were still stuck to the carpet.

'Boscawen can ordain as he likes out there, but that stops at my gates,' he said, very softly. 'I know what you're trying to do. Miss Draper will hang, for what she's done. And you're a fool if you think either the village or my son will risk their futures to stop it.'

I nodded, for what felt like the fiftieth time; and then he strode past me, and out into the passage, and I heard him go away down the stairs.

I breathed. I brought my hands in front, and twisted and pulled. At last the ring came free. I went to the door, and listened.

Silence.

I put the ring into my pocket. The diamond had warmed against me.

Somehow, I got myself to William's room, and sat there on the floor, my back against the door, in the half-dark.

Agnes must have heard me, for she asked me if I was well, twice, through the wall.

I did not answer.

When my breathing slowed, I crept around, putting my things into my bag. Not knowing what to do with the ring, I hid it in the pocket of my coat. But I knew I could not go. I could not leave Agnes. I sat on the bed. Slowly, I calmed. I could not pretend, any longer, that my feelings for Edward had disappeared. The brush with Tremain had given me a horrible reminder of his tyranny, and it occurred to me, now, for the first time, that perhaps Edward was scared.

But whatever he was, and whatever the state of his promises to Miss Myers might be, I knew I must put my feelings for him aside. Agnes must be cleared, and Tremain brought down, and there was only me to do it. I must have sat thinking for some time, for when a tap came at my door, it was Mrs Bly with a dinner tray.

'This is hers,' she said. 'Are you coming down for yours? Mr Edward's back. I fear he's had his hopes dashed. He took his tray straight up to his room. But then a telegram's come, and the master's in a fearful mood, says he must go to Falmouth in the morning, and I don't know now whether to trouble Mr Edward with it . . .'

She stopped, looked at me. I suppose I looked pale.

'I'm sorry, Mrs Bly. I'm not hungry,' I said. I took the tray. 'I'll take this in.'

When she had gone, I unlocked Agnes's door. I waited for her to sit up, then put down the tray in her lap, and lifted the cover. Duck, in a sauce. Some silly, fancy turned carrots. Agnes picked a carrot and put it in her mouth before reaching for her fork. I put the dish cover aside on the chest of drawers, but when I turned back Agnes was quite still, not chewing. Then she spat out what was in her mouth, on to the plate.

'What?' I said.

Agnes looked up, pulling the back of her hand across her mouth. She looked almost triumphant. 'It's been mucked about with.' She spat again, and at last swallowed.

I took the tray from her, and as soon as I did, she drew up her knees and held them. I put the tray on the chest of drawers, and sniffed the plate myself. Put a finger to the surface, licked it.

Bitter.

I spat in turn, into the plate. It was saltpetre, like they put in the powder. Not a poison; they put it in sailors' food, sometimes. To kill lust.

Not a poisoning. A warning.

I met Agnes's eyes, and tried to ignore the chill that was going through me. There was no ghost at Polneath: or, if there was, it had not tampered with a piece of duck and some carrots. Whatever I might once have thought about the nightshirt or the gun room, this could not have been Agnes, and I thought of Mrs Bly's frank chatter, when she'd brought up the tray. I did not believe this was her, either.

This was Tremain.

I drew the stool closer, and sat down. 'I told Mr Edward,' I said. 'About you and Tremain.'

Agnes looked at me. She swallowed. 'Did he believe it?'

'Yes,' I said. 'I know you didn't want anyone told. But believe me, Mr Edward holds little love for his father. I thought he would help us –' I stopped. 'But he was reluctant to speak against him.' I looked into my lap. 'He says he must think of the mills. He believes that there is not enough evidence, that there will be an open verdict, that there is no risk to you.' I put a hand on Agnes, on her leg, over the blanket. 'You could speak out, anyway.'

We both sat still a moment.

'Nobody would take my word, over Tremain's,' she said. 'And with Boscawen finding the key –' She was silent for a moment.

I gripped her leg more fiercely. 'There will be some other proof,' I said. 'There must be. I'm going to help you . . .' I paused. 'Can you think of nothing, nothing else we might use?'

She didn't answer.

We sat like that, for some time.

I asked her if she'd have me go down and find her something else to eat, but she told me she wasn't hungry. After a while, I locked her safely in, and went back to William's room.

The wind was getting up, loud in the chimneys. Edward was back. But I must not think of him, I must not expect his help. I had one day, and then the inquest. One day to save Agnes. In the morning, I would go to Father at last. I would tell him all of it, and he would know what to do.

It was cold in William's room. To comfort myself, I took out my letter from Edith, and opened it. My Christmas present.

My dear Ivy,

You will forgive, first of all, how late this is. You do forgive me, don't you, sweetheart? For I know we said I would not write during the honeymoon, but I have been back a month now, as you very well know, and so all I can do is throw up my hands and confess myself guilty, for I have no good excuse but lack of time . . .

She implored me to visit in the spring. The spring; as if that existed, would roll around again, as it had in other years.

*What is more, when you come, I can give you your presents. I got you
a little glass horse in Venice and I have brought you a piece of the
Colosseum. John said I oughtn't, but really it is a very small one.
Truly, Ivy, Italy is everything we used to speak of. The food is marvel-
lous, and it costs almost nothing. I am quite sunburned.*

I folded the letter. I felt further away from Edith than London,
than Venice. Further away than the moon.

I thought of Boscawen. Edith had had two sisters to leave
behind her at the rectory, and her mother alive, her father still
working. She had been free to marry away.

I undressed, and climbed into William's little bed. With the
moan of the wind, I almost thought I heard the sound of a hoop,
up and down, up and down in the passage outside. And that was
when I realized it: the yellow nightshirt, the black shape on the
gun room table, the strange taste in Agnes's dinner.

Yellow sulphur. Black charcoal. Saltpetre. Gunpowder's three
components.

What had seemed like hauntings were nothing of the kind.
William was gone. But his grandfather still thought he could
silence Agnes by putting a bitter taste in her mouth.

At last I slept, and dreamed that years had passed, and I had forgotten to let Agnes out. I dreamed of Agnes, her hair flecked with
white. Like an illustration I'd seen in a book once, with cobwebs
woven over her brimstone-yellow mouth and eyes.

18.

I waited, in the morning, until I had seen Tremain leaving on foot for the Falmouth ferry. After another half an hour, I took Agnes's uneaten dinner out in her chamber pot. Finding the kitchen empty, I took bread and cheese to last Agnes the day, trying to smile in reassurance as I handed it over. Then I locked her door, and crept down the north stair. I set out for home the front way, so that Edward might not see me from his study window.

As I walked, I felt shaky, hollowed out. Father would know what to do. I didn't wish to burden him, tax his strength, but now I had no choice. I put my hands in my pockets, to warm them, and there was the ring: I must find a time, I thought, today while Tremain was out of the house, to drop it somewhere, in the pink bedroom.

Home looked odd, as I approached it. Even two days had made it different. Smaller, and its shortcomings more visible. The bleary panes of the little window high up at the turn of the stair, and the moss on the front path. The boot brush at the front door, worn and splayed past usefulness. Father could just be seen in his bedroom window, wiping his face with a towel.

The window of the consulting room was open, admitting the freezing December air. Father fairly lived in his consulting room, usually; he had an easy chair, where he read the *Lancet* in the eleven o'clock sun, and ate humbugs slowly from a brown paper bag, and if the heat was particularly insistent and no patient had called, slept. But now I realized what the open window meant. I was drawn helplessly towards it. Through the gap I caught the sharp scent of rubbing alcohol, and was reminded for a moment of Tremain.

There were tools laid out, in a metal tray – messy – and I looked away from them. Nearer there was the white hummock of William, covered in a sheet, mercifully clean. I could only see below his knees, his pale shins smudged with ash, his feet flopping outward, relaxed.

The thought of ghosts seemed foolish now. Here he was, real enough.

When I went in at the front door, Mrs Humphrey bustled out instantly and held my shoulders, asked whether they had been feeding me, exclaimed over the state of my hands and waved me into the parlour where there was a good fire. She appeared again, a minute or two later, with a large tray of tea, and currant buns. She put down the tray, and then twitched it so that it was squarer to the table. Mrs Humphrey never scowled when she was angry, only when she was nervous.

Looking at the buns, I realized how hungry I was.

'How is he?'

'He's washing. I made him stop for a bit,' Mrs Humphrey said.

'He had a turn yesterday morning. When he came to Polneath.'

She nodded. 'He couldn't keep it to himself – I saw Mr Edward running to the King's Arms, and then when he came back in their gig . . .' She paused. 'I made him rest till lunch, but then he had that to do.' She nodded in the direction of the consulting room. 'That Graves was here last evening. For his second opinion.' She frowned. 'I didn't take to him.'

'Didn't you?' I said, and smiled.

And Mrs Humphrey tutted, but smiled too, and told me to make sure Father had a bit of something, and bustled out.

For a minute I watched the tea steaming, the fire crackling. Garlands of holly and ivy were ranged about the fireplace. I myself had put them there, only days ago. On the mantelpiece was the little silhouette of my mother. Father said that someone had cut it once at a small house party, and they had blunted the tip of her nose – but it did have the look of her. We had no other portrait, but that one had always felt strangely apt, the little trimmed black shape, perhaps especially at that time of year. The dark blank of it, when every chair was a chair she was not sitting in.

Then Father came in, shaking his hands. It was impossible to tell whether they were wet, or troubling him.

'My dear –' He came forward to kiss me.

His touch was cold. I held his hands to warm and steady them.

'Edith's Rose came looking for you – she has postponed her party.'

'How are you, Father?' I held his hands for a moment.

He smiled at me, in a vague fashion. 'I'm very well, my dear. Don't fuss.'

I made a dissatisfied face. We sat, and I poured out the tea.

'I did the examining yesterday. A sad task on Christmas Day, but I thought best not to leave it any longer.' He gestured towards the consulting room. 'This is the repair.'

'Yes,' I said, adding milk.

When I was a child, the forbidden books had not been novels but the anatomy texts on my father's high shelf, with their detailed diagrams. I thought of William, in there now, the front of his body parted like curtains. Passing Father his cup, I tried not to examine the beds of his nails.

Somebody laughed, going by in the lane outside. Boxing Day visiting.

'Did you find anything?' I asked.

He shook his head. 'All healthy,' he said, sadly. He took a sip of his tea, his eyes gripping the cup until it was back in the saucer. He looked up. 'His wisdom teeth would have given him trouble.' Father gazed into his tea, as though he had forgotten I was there, or was thinking of something quite different.

'Do you not want to know,' I said, 'how things are at Polneath?'

Father looked up, then stood. 'Can I not first give you your Christmas present?'

I put down my cup. 'My Christmas present?'

He sent me upstairs to fetch his, and I allowed myself a moment, in my bedroom, to breathe.

Back downstairs, I handed Father his little parcel, and he unwrapped it. Handkerchiefs, as usual. He liked new ones. The ivy motif looked childish now. He thanked me and kissed me, and handed me a little parcel in return.

I opened it and something dropped into my palm, heavy and

satisfying. It was a hair ornament, in the Chinese style, a pink butterfly. 'Thank you, Papa,' I said, and got up to kiss him.

'That's not half of it,' he said, but then he held up a finger, because there was a tap at the front door. Whether with the cold or the gravity of the week's events, he refrained from putting his head out of the window to see who it was, but went out into the hall.

I looked at the ornament. Edith had had one just like it, a year or so before, and I'd had a kind of mania to own one, too. It seemed a foolish thing, now. I wondered whether Edith had worn hers, since she had been married.

In the hall, someone asked Father a question, and now he was answering. Someone from the village, with those long vowels Edith and I had worked so hard to avoid.

He came back in. I raised my eyebrows, and he said, 'They'll keep.'

Swiftly, I poured us out a little more tea. It was rather dark. 'Father –'

'Now,' Father said, 'the other half.'

I tried to look expectant, and he looked almost grave; nervous, as though he didn't know how to say the treat. For a moment, I thought of Italy, or Paris at least. Could it be?

He rubbed his hands together. 'Well. I have put, a certain amount, against an account at a dressmaker in Falmouth. And another certain amount at the milliner's.'

'Father,' I lowered my teacup, smiled as best I could, shaking my head.

'It's high time you had nicer things.'

I rose, kissed him. 'Thank you.'

I never asked for anything new, even though I had heard Mrs Humphrey complaining to Mrs Mason that you could see six inches of ankle in half my dresses, even though everything had been turned and mended twice. But it would be a relief, to have a dress I could hold my head up in.

'And as regards linen and so on,' Father said, 'I thought, Edith could advise you?'

And now I saw the reason for his nerves, and saw what was

meant. Nicer things did not mean a new walking dress, or a summer hat less childish and faded. Nicer things meant caps, such as those matrons wear, and bedjackets and pillowcases to be marked with new initials. Nicer things meant my marriage, to Richard Boscawen.

I put my cup down. Suddenly my stomach hurt. 'Oh, I should think so,' I replied, broadly, and tried not to hear the false note that had come into my voice. 'But Father, I must talk to you. I have discovered who lit the fire at Polneath. It is – delicate.'

Father was watching me.

'It was not Miss Draper. It was Mr Tremain. They were . . .'

Father closed his eyes. 'It's not Jake's.' He reached for my arm. 'Thank God –'

I stopped still. 'What's not Jake's?'

He met my eyes, and I swallowed, studied the tea table.

Agnes was with child.

I thought of her visits to the chamber pot, her inconstant appetite. How, the day before, Father had asked to see her alone.

'I wish I'd known sooner,' I said, unable to keep the reproach from my voice.

'I only confirmed it yesterday morning,' Father said. 'I suspected, when I came to check her over before the inquest. But now I am certain.'

'It wasn't an accident,' I said. 'Tremain set the fire. He wanted to be rid of her. Now we know why.'

Father looked down. 'It's early, still. Perhaps three or four months.' He looked rather embarrassed. 'I'm sorry you should have to begin to discover that such things go on.'

'Father, that's not – I mean, I'm shocked, of course.'

'Of course.'

'Mr Edward knows,' I said quickly. 'Not about the child, but about the – connection. But he doesn't believe there is enough evidence. He thinks Agnes will be able to walk free, despite the key Tremain hid in her bed. He thinks the evidence insufficient to convict either her or Tremain, and that if Tremain's reputation is tarnished then the mills will go, too . . .'

Father was frowning as I fell silent. 'Perhaps he's right.'

'But she's with child.'

'He'll say that it's Jake's.' Father spread his hands, helplessly.

'So you mean to do nothing.'

'My dear,' he said. 'You cannot right every wrong.' He swallowed.

I looked at him, perched nervously on the edge of his chair, his trembling hands holding on to one another.

'And what about Jake?' I could have sworn he was about to say what Edward had said. *I'm sorry about Jake*.

But Father only said, 'I should be grateful if you would give him my apologies, my dear. I saw him, yesterday – he passed in the lane, just as Dr Graves had taken his leave, and – I'm afraid I spoke rather severely to him. Said he ought to marry her.'

I looked at him. 'Of course.'

'My dear –' he said.

But I got up and went out, closing the door behind me.

In the hall, however, I was caught by Mrs Humphrey, who hauled me into the kitchen, wanted to tell me things and point at things. The washing, dusting, polishing, everything was behind. I felt a rush of fierce fondness as I listened, as Mrs Humphrey moved a pan of potatoes expertly from the heat. As she drained the potatoes, her face reddened. I had a sudden sense of how she and Father would exist together, after I had gone. Breakfast, dinner. Her grumbling over the state of his sleeves. I could hear Father in the parlour, the rattle of him clearing the tea things on to the tray.

'If you ask me, it's a crying shame,' Mrs Humphrey was saying. 'But I told your father not to go to that inquest – I said, it'll be full of gossips and meddlers – and now look.' There was a brief cloud of steam as she returned the potatoes to the pan. 'He's tiring himself out.' Mrs Humphrey turned.

With my cuff, I wiped the window. 'Why is the pudding bowl out in the yard?'

Mrs Humphrey snapped the dishcloth once and folded it. Then she moved behind me and squeezed my shoulders, as she did very occasionally. 'I'm going to scald it out there,' she said. 'It's been used.'

'Oh,' I said. The large white bowl sat innocently waiting.

Just then, Father appeared in the kitchen doorway, holding the laden tray.

Swiftly, Mrs Humphrey moved to take it from him.

'My dear,' he said to me, with a glance at Mrs Humphrey, 'ought you to go back?'

'I have to,' I replied, rather coldly.

By the sink, Mrs Humphrey raised her eyebrows. 'He's right, miss. You're running yourself ragged.'

Father said, 'My dear . . . do you suppose you are quite safe?'

That made Mrs Humphrey look at him, but I was buttoning my coat, and, before either of them could stop me, moving for the door.

'I must go,' I said. 'I must go and see Jake.'

Instead of knocking, I went through the little side gate at Jake's father's house, and around the back. A man was bending to throw a tangle of branches on to a small bonfire, and for a moment I took it for Mr Feltham, until the figure straightened, and I saw it was Jake himself. He saw me and began to wipe his hands on the thighs of his breeches. Smoke was coming up from the damp branches. Tremain's gun dog was nosing amongst the piled leaves waiting to be burned.

Jake turned as I approached. 'I sent him home, but he came back again.'

'I won't tell anyone,' I said.

He must have seen me glance at the windows of the cottage, for he said, 'Father's out.'

I looked at him. He pulled his arm across his forehead. He was warm.

The garden looked denuded of all of its winter weeds.

'He's along digging,' Jake said, and nodded towards the churchyard.

'Oh,' I said. William Tremain's grave.

'Are you alright?'

'I know it wasn't true,' I said, 'about you and Agnes Draper.'

Jake looked at the fire. 'I'd have owned to it, wouldn't I? I'm as good as she is, there'd be no impediment.'

'Why didn't you say it was Tremain?' I said. 'Did you know?'

He stooped for another branch to burn – gently batted at the dog, who thought it was a game. He was frowning. 'I wasn't certain,' he said.

'Half the village will think –'

'They can think what they like.'

'Mr Edward won't speak out, nor Father. They think that we need more evidence. I'm going to see Boscawen, now.'

'He spoke to me again yesterday. Came here. He was asking me about the fire, when we were trying to put it out, exactly how it went. I don't know if it was any use.'

I paused. 'Mr Edward said he wished to compensate you.'

Jake frowned. 'I don't need his charity. Besides, I'd be surprised if he has much left to compensate *with*, when all's said and done.'

We watched the blaze.

'Is there nothing? Nothing you can think of that points to Tremain's guilt . . . ?' I paused. 'She's with child, you know. Father says. They might not kill her, but . . .'

Jake glanced at me, and then frowned at the fire for a long time, and was quite absent when the dog came back and put her nose into his hand. But I was long used to his pauses, and I waited it out.

At last, he said, 'They had words. Agnes and Tremain. Earlier on, the night William died. I didn't mention it to Boscawen. I wasn't sure . . .'

'What do you mean?' I said. 'What words?'

Tremain had been out on the terrace, Jake told me, with his last cigar. Jake had been waiting up in his own room for Tremain to go in, so he could go and put out the lamp on the terrace. But after a few minutes, he'd heard muffled voices, and when he looked out, Agnes was there, speaking low and urgently to Tremain, and he replying irritably. He could have told Agnes, from the abrupt way Tremain kept flicking his cigar, that this was not the night to bend his ear, about William or anything else. He couldn't hear, himself, what it was about, but Mrs Bly had been clearing in the dining room behind them, near the glass, and she had taken long enough to load her tray.

When Agnes had finally gone away indoors, he'd felt relieved, because surely soon now Tremain would put out his cigar and turn in, too. When Jake looked out a few minutes later, though, Tremain had lit a second cigar, and when he looked out after an hour he had lit a third. Jake had lain down on his bed, and closed his eyes, just for a moment.

'I woke, must have been an hour later,' he said. 'To Mrs Bly's shrieking.'

The half-damp leaves burned with a red smoulder. Jake shook himself, as though the smell had made him shudder.

'This might help,' I said.

Jake looked at me. 'Won't Tremain just say I'm trying to turn suspicion off myself? Mrs Bly won't speak against him.'

I put my hands in my pockets to warm them. Felt the ring. 'Boscawen will make her,' I said. And then, 'I wish Tremain might be exposed, without harming the mills.'

'The mills'll be gone soon, either way,' Jake said. 'My father's going to retire at the church. He thinks they'll take me, in his stead.'

'Mr Edward thinks he could save things.'

Jake looked at me queerly. 'Mr Edward will be gone too, Ivy,' he said.

Rarely since we were children had he called me Ivy.

He looked serious. 'You need to get yourself clear of this.'

I looked away. 'Someone must look out for Agnes.'

'Agnes can fend for herself,' Jake said. 'She has till now.'

We watched the dog follow a blackbird down the garden, and then I touched his hand, just once, and left him there.

Agnes must have realized her condition, and told Tremain. And later, he had kindled the blaze, and turned the key. He must have been astounded to see Agnes, her skirt on fire after her attempt to rescue William. Perhaps he had thought she'd broken down the door somehow. He must have been bewildered when he'd slipped up to look at the door as he and Jake had fought the fire, and found it intact, still locked. Dumbfounded, when he'd unlocked it and discovered what seemed to be an empty room.

When William had failed to appear, however, then he must have known what he had done.

As I passed home, I felt a sort of pang, but there was no use in going to Father with this. He could not help me. I realized that I had been keeping things from him all my life, and it was so easy, like breathing, that I had not even known I was doing it, until now.

At the crossroads, I turned up the steep lane to the large white house on the top road.

I was shown into Boscawen's study by his housekeeper, a sour-faced young woman. As Boscawen stood to greet me, I was impressed by the gold-tooled books ranged about the walls of the room, the ranks of buff card files.

'I need to talk to you,' I said, 'about Agnes Draper.'

Boscawen gestured to a chair.

I sat, and looked at him. 'Father told you she's with child.'

Boscawen folded his arms. 'I am aware.'

I looked down. 'Well, it is not Jake Feltham's.' The urgency was so great, now, that it did not even occur to me to be embarrassed.

'I did not suppose it was.'

I looked up again. I'd always thought that Boscawen didn't like Jake. He had been close by, once, when Jake had slipped, and called me Ivy.

'It is Tremain's,' I said. 'She and he were –' I stopped.

Boscawen nodded, thoughtfully. He was nudging something to and fro across his blotter, and I saw that it was a key, a Polneath key. The one he had found under Agnes's bolster. The one which had locked William in to die.

'And she was unwilling?' Boscawen said. He dropped his eyes. 'Girls of her station, you know, do sometimes make . . . arrangements.'

'You have seen Tremain,' I said. 'You've met him. I don't suppose it was willing.' Boscawen looked away, and I swallowed. 'I believe that Tremain set the fire to be rid of Agnes. That she'd told him about the child.'

Boscawen nodded. 'Though it answered, too, his other problem. The shareholders in the works had asked for an audit in January. The records necessary for that were amongst what was destroyed in his office.' Boscawen thought for a moment. 'How do you know that she had told him about the child?'

'They'd quarrelled, that evening. Jake Feltham saw them. He thinks Mrs Bly would have heard them – but she's cowed by Tremain. She might not own to it.'

Boscawen frowned. 'Feltham did not mention this.'

I cleared my throat. 'He is not a meddling sort of person. That is, he tends not to say more than he is asked.'

Slowly, Boscawen nodded. 'So we will need Mrs Bly to testify that she saw the quarrel. Ideally, that she heard it.'

'Yes. And she's lied to you once.'

Boscawen looked up.

'She said she rescued Tremain from his bedroom,' I pointed out. 'At the inquest. But it must have been the other way around.'

Boscawen sat back in his chair. 'Does he know you've got wind of him? Tremain?'

I thought for a moment that Boscawen would do as Father had, and try to prevent me from going back to Polneath. But he only looked at me frankly, waiting for my answer.

'I don't know,' I said. 'But he's trying to frighten Agnes.' I told him about the outline on the gun room table, the saltpetre-laced dinner. 'It's gone rather beyond the yellow nightshirt.'

'Beyond the what?'

'Beyond the nightshirt. You remember.'

'Ah yes.' Boscawen nodded, and thought for a minute. 'We must leave Miss Draper where she is, for tonight,' he said. 'It will only alert him, to move her now.'

'But she must be helped. There's the key, isn't there? And she cannot go straight to another position –' I stopped. 'I would be grateful if you were to take a special interest in helping her.'

Boscawen looked at his feet. 'There's no need to be grateful,' he said.

'Then you think it can be managed?'

'I believe it can,' he said. 'What does Mr Edward know of this?'

'He knew what his father was doing. But he didn't think there would be enough evidence to convict Tremain, or Agnes, for William's death, so . . .' I broke off. 'He doesn't yet know about the child.'

Boscawen nodded again. Then he looked at me. 'Miss Cardew, do you remember what everyone was wearing? When we arrived at Polneath – you and I and your father, that night? Mr Edward, Mrs Bly, Miss Draper – Tremain himself?'

'Of course,' I said, and told him.

He nodded, and made a note. Then he stood up. 'Miss Cardew,' he said. 'I have been most particularly impressed by your courage, by your –' He stopped.

'Father thinks me foolhardy,' I said. 'He wants to keep me at home.'

Boscawen looked at me. 'Don't worry,' he said. 'I'll speak to him. And, Miss Cardew – I wondered if I might have reason to hope, after this . . .' But now he stopped entirely.

I glanced at the door. I thought it would do no harm, to allow Boscawen to hope. I could always kill that hope, later. It all felt so distant, in any case: going home to my old bedroom, taking the ferry to Falmouth to spend my Christmas present. Something so ordinary, so frivolous as a wedding. Besides, I needed him, to save Agnes.

I looked at Boscawen, as the housekeeper stirred in the hall. 'You might have reason,' I said.

Boscawen looked at me; nodded once, and moved towards the study door. 'Tell Mrs Bly I was asking after her,' he said.

As the housekeeper showed me out, I had to lift my hand to the Reverend Green, who was walking with two of the younger children further down the lane. But even as he raised his hand to me and called a greeting, I did not think about how it looked, my emerging from Boscawen's house.

My having visited him alone.

19.

Coming from Boscawen's, I arrived at the front door of Polneath. With the shutters closed, the house looked as though it was in a sleep. I climbed the three short steps under the portico, and quietly let myself in. A breeze moved some dead leaves across the tiles, and the door as I closed it gave a clang into the dim quiet. I reminded myself that Tremain had gone to Falmouth.

I had climbed half the first flight of stairs when Edward said my name from the hall below.

His face looked pale, and his eyes dark against the black of his mourning coat.

'Will you walk in the garden with me?' he said.

He looked eager, tremulous, as though he thought I would refuse.

I was still rattled, from Boscawen, from his *reason to hope*. But I felt a rush of excitement, at seeing Edward, and a rush of pity, too. Viewed in a certain light, he was as much a victim of Tremain as Mrs Bly, as Agnes. After a childhood like his, how could he not be afraid of his father?

'Of course I will,' I said. I turned back down the stairs, buttoning my coat again.

He led me through the dining room to the French doors.

'Your father isn't back?' I asked, my voice low.

He shook his head.

We went through the blast wall, and walked side by side towards the walled garden.

'The loan was declined,' Edward said. 'They wired, apparently, yesterday. So now Father has gone to the bank manager's *house*.'

'On Boxing Day?'

'I know.'

We had reached the door of the walled garden. He paused, and we looked at one another. He frowned.

'I've been thinking. About what you were saying, yesterday. And you're right. I know you're right. I will speak against him.'

'Edward,' I said. 'I'm so glad.'

He held open the door for me. 'I'm sorry I left so abruptly, yesterday.'

I remembered watching the carriage pull away, and the abandoned ring in my pocket. 'Not at all. I didn't –'

'I went to talk to the Reverend Green. He says the funeral ought to be able to be tomorrow, after the inquest. He says I ought to choose some flowers.' He looked at me. 'I hoped you might help me.'

I felt a wave of relief. He had gone to the vicar. 'Yes.'

We had emerged amongst the fruit trees trained beautifully against the walls, like silhouettes of themselves, each with its own little zinc label with the variety written on in Jake's very particular hand, and other hands, too, of other gardeners who had gone before.

Edward had seen the right of it. But under my relief was the burden of what I must say next. For I could not leave him, now, to be blindsided tomorrow by news of Agnes's child. Not after everything he had suffered.

I cleared my throat, thinking of how tender he had been to his wife when she'd been carrying William. He might even wish to help Agnes, when he was over the shock of it.

'Miss Cardew,' he said. 'I want you to know that Miss Myers and I –'

I held up my hand. 'Please,' I said. 'I must – first I must – that is, it ought to go rather more smoothly than we feared, tomorrow. There is new evidence.'

Edward stopped, looked at me. 'What evidence?'

'Agnes . . . she's with child.'

'She's –' He blinked. 'And he –' He turned away.

All I could see was his back, hunched with emotion, and the splayed, still fruit trees, and the hummocks of earth. Portions of the garden were dug over, and others waiting under tarpaulin. Only here and there were hints of what it could be in summer, in the form of the glossy dark mulberry bush, and the stalks of last year's artichokes, dried out and leaning at crazy angles.

'Will is dead,' he said, muffled. He turned, and his eyes were wild, amazed. 'And she –'

'I know,' I said. 'I know it must be a shock.'

He spent a few moments with his face turned away. When he had recovered himself, he nodded at the glasshouse, in the opposite corner, along the sunniest wall.

As we moved towards it, he said, 'Are you certain?'

'Father confirmed it.' I looked at him. 'And Jake Feltham says that he saw them arguing. Before he went to bed. The night William died.' We had stopped at the door of the glasshouse; Edward was fumbling with the catch. 'Boscawen will find her a place, for her and the child, elsewhere –'

'Of course.' He touched my arm. 'Thank you for telling me.'

There was a rush of hot, damp air, and I stepped in before him. Jake had shown me the glasshouse once, when he first came to work at Polneath, and it had not changed. There was a lime tree, and one that produced small, hard grapefruits. At the tall portion, in the middle, various shrubs climbed the wall or stood in pots. At the far end, there were four white, wrought-iron chairs, and a table to match. And there were white camellias, everywhere, flowering splendidly, one or two blooms tipped over into brownness.

'I'm sorry I didn't mention Miss Myers,' he said, abruptly. 'Really, you must believe me, she was my father's plan. Never mine.'

I turned, as he closed the door behind us. 'No, it's – that is, I didn't expect –'

'You have a perfect right to be angry,' he said.

'I'm not angry.' I looked away from his eyes, at the floor, and, remembering, felt in my pocket. 'Though I ought to –' I opened my hand, and tipped the ring across into his palm. 'I found this, when I went in to tidy. She left it behind.'

Edward was looking at the ring. He tilted his hand, and let it roll a little to and fro, and then closed his fist around it. He looked at me. 'It's a relief,' he said, quietly. He walked towards the camellias. 'It was the same with Emily,' he said. He stopped, and touched one of the flowers. 'We were young. She was your age. I was only a year older –' He stopped. 'I didn't know how to refuse. And this time, well. When he began to speak of Flora, I wanted to keep the peace, for William's sake, and I had no other lady in view . . .'

I couldn't stand still, moved away into the glasshouse. The camellias filled the space, crowding out all else. 'It doesn't seem as though there is a choice to be made,' I said, gesturing at them.

'They're beautiful,' he replied, in a thick voice.

I felt my face growing warm. I touched one of the blooms, like a small lace rosette, and gently took a petal between finger and thumb. It was so warm, it might have been summer, one of those brief days which give hope of an easier way to live.

Edward turned away, and looked out into the garden. 'I don't know what I'd have done, these last days, without you.'

I joined him. 'I've only done what anyone would.'

'That's not true.' He tilted his face to the weak sun, let out a breath. 'It could be Italy.'

I smiled. 'I was just thinking something similar.'

He looked at me. 'I'd like nothing better than to take you.'

I looked down. 'I thought Father was offering to, this morning,' I said, half laughing. 'But he was offering to buy my wedding clothes.' I folded my hands. 'He wants me to accept Boscawen.'

'You've had an offer?'

'Not quite, but –'

'You mustn't make my mistake,' Edward said. Then he took my hand. 'You should think of your own happiness.'

My mouth was dry. We looked at each other for a long, long minute. Then, all suddenly, he crushed me to his chest. 'We could go away from here. Right away,' he said, into my hair.

I felt the words as a buzz through his flesh, and the feel of his shirt against my ear, and his chilled arms beneath the fabric.

He drew back, to look at me.

And then came the kiss.

My first jolt was that someone might be watching. But with Tremain in Falmouth, Jake gone, who would care? Besides, the glasshouse flowers concealed us, the garden concealed us. His mouth was warm, and his whiskers rough – and my face, tilted upwards, felt just as I had once hoped it would. It was just as I thought it would be, less like something new than something I was remembering inexpertly how to do.

When we parted, he said, 'Forgive me.'

I smiled, too broadly, and said, 'Whatever for?'

He smiled back.

We walked back from the glasshouse, hand in hand, saying nothing. My hand felt as though it might meld entirely with his own, and I kept glancing at the side of his face, wondering what he would say next. Half my mind was already plagued with questions. Where would we go? What about Father? But I hushed it with the other half. I had Edward, at last, and he had me – here was my hand in his.

He kept hold of it, even through the gap in the blast wall. Beside the pond, he stopped, and felt in his pocket for the ring. For half a moment, I thought he was going to give it back to me.

'I fear this has only brought its wearers discontent,' he said. 'Father would want to pawn it, but I think –' And he threw it into the middle of the pond. 'You shall have another one,' he said. 'A better one.'

I looked at him, smiling. 'I had better go and look in on Agnes.'

He nodded. 'Will you tell Mrs Bly,' he said, 'that we'll be dining together?'

That reassured me. And then, warmly, with a shake in his voice, he wished me a good afternoon.

I stood by the pond, in the freezing sunlight, half stunned. I could not believe it. But I must believe it. I felt a rush – of fear, of happiness – but there was still Agnes.

Before securing my own happy ending, I must secure hers.

When I went into the kitchen, there was a black stuff dress laid out on the table, with a length of black ribbon and a work basket.

Mrs Bly turned as I came in. 'One of the old maids left this. The moth hasn't got to it. It'll be short in the sleeve, but –'

The style was old-fashioned, but the cloth was good. I could make a sort of cuff, from the ribbon. It would make Agnes look less abject, but still deservingly threadbare. Still grateful.

'Is the master back?' I said.

'Not yet.' Mrs Bly had turned back to what she was doing. 'This salmon. There's another for Friday. You'd get more meat on a minnow . . .' She paused. 'I was thinking, she ought to have a bath.'

'I'll see to it,' I said. 'Before I dine with Mr Edward.'

Mrs Bly paused minutely, and then resumed her filleting. I didn't move.

'I suppose you had care of Mr Edward, Mrs Bly? When he was little?'

She nodded. 'I had the raising of him. Until he was sent to school. I cut his baby curls myself. Still got one, somewhere –' She stopped. 'The master didn't – well. You know what men are like. But he was a sweet child, Master Edward, when he was little.'

'And you would want him to be happy?' I said. 'Now?'

She turned and looked at me, but did not answer.

I let quiet fall a moment. 'You'll be taken care of, Mrs Bly. After this. Whatever happens.'

'What do you mean?' she said. She put her knife down.

I stepped closer. 'I know you did not leave Agnes to burn,' I said. I dropped my voice. 'I know you did not rescue Tremain.'

Again, she did not answer.

I touched the scarred surface of the kitchen table. 'Mr Boscawen was asking after your health,' I said, in quite a bright, quite an ordinary voice.

Mrs Bly's eyes met mine, for one moment, then another, and then they slid away.

Agnes closed her eyes in relief at the prospect of a bath. I pulled a bathtub up the stairs, and then climbed back and forth with jugs of hot water. On my way down with an empty jug, Edward emerged from the dark of the stairwell.

'Give this to her, will you?' he said. He held out a folded paper. 'My dear?'

When I came up with the last jug and the soap, Agnes was holding her hands in the warm water.

'Forgive me,' Agnes said.

'No, no. While it's hot . . .' I paused. 'Would you like help with your hair?'

Agnes hesitated.

Now, I could guess why. I pulled the stool a little distance away, and sat. 'I know about the child.'

Agnes looked at me.

'Father told me, and Mr Boscawen,' I said, then paused. 'I told Mr Edward.'

Agnes was quite still for a moment. Then she turned away, and began to unbutton herself. 'What did he say?'

'He was appalled, of course,' I said. 'At what his father has done, I mean. He says he'll speak out against him.'

Her body was a shock. How white it was, away from her reddened hands and face. I had seen women in their shifts before, of course, but never all at once like this. Her breasts were different than my own. I tried, without being caught, to assess whether she were showing yet, but it was hard to tell.

She climbed into the bath, and poured over the first pitcher of water. 'Will he truly? He said that?'

'He did. And Boscawen thinks we will win through. He says there is enough evidence, after all.' I passed her the soap. 'He was asking – to be certain – with you and Tremain – whether you were unwilling.'

Agnes passed the soap back, and looked at me, rather more coldly now. 'It wouldn't have counted a straw with him,' she said, 'whether I was willing or not.'

I looked down. 'Well. I told him you would have hardly chosen Tremain. Left to your own devices.'

'No,' she said. And then, 'You've got to survive, haven't you? That's all.'

I nodded, uncertainly.

When I'd finished helping her wash her hair, I said, 'Mr Edward gave me this, to give to you.'

I held out the corner of the bath sheet for her to dry her hands, and produced the paper from my pocket. She unfolded it, and read it quickly. She swallowed, and passed it to me.

To whom it may concern

I can attest that Agnes Draper has during her time in my employ
displayed the utmost diligence as housemaid here. She has shown
herself to be thoroughly trustworthy and I unreservedly recommend –

I left off reading, and looked at her.

'I am grateful to you, Miss Cardew,' she said.

I moved my hand. 'You needn't be,' I said.

Agnes stood up, water crashing and dripping from her, and stood still while I held out a sheet. Carefully, she climbed out of the tub. Her feet made two spreading wet prints on the mat.

'Mrs Bly has found you a dress. I'll alter it for you, and bring it in the morning,' I said. 'Everything will be fine.'

I found Edward in the drawing room, where there was a good fire. I had brought in Agnes's dress with me, and Mrs Bly's work basket. He stood up, when he saw me at the door, and only resumed his seat when I had taken the other chair by the fire.

I worked steadily away on the dress, breaking off only to carry salmon and potatoes up and down the stairs. It was different, without Tremain in the house. There would be no more hauntings.

Edward and I ate by pulling up the little drawing room table, as though we were at an inn, and afterwards I remained on the sofa beside Edward, he reading some days-old newspaper.

It would have felt like a foretaste of a quiet married evening, had Edward not kept jumping at every sound, and had I not been so nervous about the inquest. An inquest, I had heard Boscawen say once, was always also a trial. The coroner might want facts, but the people wanted blame. We had to make sure it was not Agnes on trial, but Tremain.

'He ought to be back by now,' Edward said, more than once.

At last, I paused my needle. 'You'll have to be ordinary with him,' I said. 'Or he'll suspect.'

'I know.' Edward looked pensive.

I said, 'He threatened me, you know. Yesterday. When you were at the Reverend Green's.'

Edward looked up. 'If he laid a hand on you –'

'He didn't,' I said. 'And besides. He's got his reckoning coming now.' I looked down at the cuff I had done, and bit off some thread with my teeth. 'Will there be anything left,' I asked, 'when the debts are paid?'

'I don't know,' Edward replied. He got up to mend the fire.

My heart twisted for him. Everything was ending. He had grown up here, knew every fire iron, the knack of every rickety door. Very likely the house would be sold, separated from the mills, perhaps, which might be acquired by one or other of the powder firms nearby. However painful his childhood had been, Polneath and the mills were what he had known, and should have been his, to set back on the proper course again. And I hardly dared think about what the loss of the mills would mean for the village.

Edward subsided again, into his chair.

It got dark. I finished with the dress, and went upstairs to hang it. Agnes was asleep. It was getting late.

When I came back in, Edward threw his newspaper aside. 'He'll be drinking in Falmouth.' He put his head in his hands.

I sat beside him. 'Where shall we go?' I said. 'Afterwards?'

Edward sighed. 'I hardly know. London, perhaps? The Continent again.' He frowned. 'Money will be difficult.'

'Edith says in Italy the food is free. They *give* it out.'

Despite himself, he smiled. He looked at me, then reached for my hand, and drew it towards himself. Kneaded the knuckles and fingers, as though seeing what they were made of.

I felt myself grow warm.

'I won't be able to bring much,' I said.

'It doesn't matter.'

'When should we go?'

'Soon. Tomorrow.'

'We can't go tomorrow.' I squeezed his hand. 'After the inquest, there will be William . . .'

He hung his head. 'Of course. The day after, then.'

'In the morning?'

He nodded.

'I'll come here. First light.'

He kept kneading my hand, and the kneading had taken on a different quality.

'But Edward, I was thinking.'

'What?'

'Father. I can't leave him. For a while, perhaps, but not forever.'

Edward stopped kneading. 'Then can't he come? You could convince him – the climate, for his joints and so forth.'

We were both smiling, now. But then came the unmistakable creak of the front door.

Together we stood, and I followed him out into the hall. There was Tremain, slumped on the tiles. His boots were a feast of mud.

'Where has he walked from?' I said. I shut the gaping door.

Edward poked his father with his foot, and I felt for a flash that that was callous. But I smothered the feeling. Tremain had waived his expectations of nice treatment. I watched his eyes rolling in his head.

'Bastard,' Tremain said, to the air.

All at once, with a sudden, practised force, Edward raised Tremain from the floor. They started to make their lurching way up the stairs, and I followed, hovering, fearful that one of them would fall backwards. Tremain was slurring and shouting about the bank manager. Perhaps Mrs Bly had gone to bed. At any rate, she did not appear.

We came to Tremain's room. Mrs Bly had left a lamp burning, and a window open, as Tremain liked. It was very cold. Rather than take him to the bed, Edward got free of him, suddenly, as soon as they were inside the door. Tremain wobbled, but stayed upright. Then he caught sight of me, and reached to touch my hair, to grab me by the hair. Edward moved quickly, and pushed him back.

Tremain sniffed in my direction, and closed his eyes, a dreadful smile on his face. 'This one smells good,' he said. 'She's no oil painting, but she smells good.'

'Get to bed,' Edward said. He moved me gently out of the room, by the arm, shut the door behind us.

'Edward,' Tremain shouted from inside the room. There was a thud on the inside of the door. 'Edward –'

Another thud. The door shook in its frame. Edward took hold of the door handle, and held it, struggling. Calmly, from his pocket, he produced the key. The one William had hidden away, that I had given him, down amongst the mills. He locked Tremain's door, from the outside, leaving the key in place.

'Go to bed!' Edward shouted, again, and after that there was no more thudding.

Edward looked at me, met my eyes for a long time. Something seemed to shift, decisively, between us.

'Before you turn in,' he said, 'would you help me look over my mourning? I should like not to look so much of a scarecrow as last time, tomorrow.'

'Of course,' I said. I knew precisely what he was asking.

I was terrified: but this was how it went, was it not? We were to be married, after all. I followed him along the corridor, and then he turned, nodded at me, held the door open to his bedroom. I stepped in. The room was chilly, the bed perfectly made.

'Just in here,' Edward said, and crossed to another door, where there was a room with a press, a chest of drawers, a wash stand, a copper bath. He began to hunt in the press, while I stood watching.

'They're both bad, I'm afraid.' He brought out two suits, both black, and laid them over a chair.

I stooped to flip back one of the coats to show the lining, dark silk. A good suit, once; now it was an old one. Quite grey around the shoulders. The other was better.

I took it, my heart going too quickly, and held it out to him. 'Try this one on a moment?'

He slipped out of the one he was wearing. Through his shirt, I thought I could see the slope of his back, the suggestion of apricot skin. I thought of touching him, with the flat of one palm, how warm he would be. He put the better coat on, and turned back, spread his arms to show himself. There was a sharp smell, of mothballs, things that have been shut away.

I nodded. 'That one,' I said.

I was standing very close, close enough to tip my head back to look up at him. I felt as though we were together in a box within a box within a box, buried very deep in the earth perhaps. When he turned me to reach the small button at the nape of my neck, it felt ordinary, as though now *I* were going to try something on, and he give his opinion. But he did not unfasten the button straight away; rather he held it, between finger and thumb, and steered me, very deliberately, back into the room with the bed. Then he unfastened it. He knew what buttons would be where, and was deft with them, and gentle; he had been married, of course. Occasionally there came a disconcerting thud, from Tremain's room along the passage, and once the crash of broken glass.

It was cold in the room, but I was not cold. I felt I would melt, and hoped that I would smell right. Tremain's words sprang to my head. The complicated rows of scent bottles on Emily's old dressing table.

I did not care that there would be pain.

Edward moved on top of me, and I thought that he would be rough, as puppies can be when they fight together, but I was not expecting that sharp prising, through which my limbs were liquid, like being drunk. Edward looked drunk, too, in the half dark, his face flushed red and intent as he held my arms, and I was frightened he would crush me, and I wanted him to crush me.

Then I wanted to go back to before, with the buttons.

He stopped, and his face on mine as we rested was wonderful. We lay together like that, and after a while, I realized he was asleep. I wondered whether there would be a child. If there was, it would be as well that we were not planning to wait for a summer wedding.

I knew it would not do to be found there, when Mrs Bly got up to light the fires. That I needed sleep, to weather the inquest. And so I extricated myself – clumsily, hoping Edward would wake. But he slept on. I crept down the landing, past Tremain's room, silent now.

Back upstairs, I washed in the water Mrs Bly had left for the morning. In the candlelight, it was too dark to say whether the water had turned red. I lay awake, and thought about our wedding, and then our life together, the real business of which would take place in darkness, between days drenched in a relentless golden light.

20.

1919

Old Tremain's inquest file, with its verdict of suicide, contains a slim quantity of small facts. About the likely dryness of the roof timbers at Polneath, about the risk of staying to fight a fire so large, with deposits of gunpowder close at hand. It contains testimony from the manager of the Falmouth bank, who describes the oaths Tremain swore at him when he was declined a large loan, the day before his death.

It contains testimony from Mrs Bly, that she had left Tremain's service that very day, the day his grandson's inquest was concluded; that Mrs Mason of the King's Arms could vouch she had been in her room at the inn at the time of the blaze. It contains testimony from Edward Tremain, the son of the deceased, who attests that his father had damaged his health with drink, had been prone to impetuous rages.

Not many years before Tremain's death, a verdict of suicide would have meant the seizure of the assets of the deceased. The law had changed, by then, not that there would have been much, in any case, left to seize. Before, it was accounted a crime against the Crown: a murder case is argued that way, even now. A life is not robbed from the one who lives it, but from England, or else from God, which view has taken longer to shift, in places like St Rumon's, than the law has. Tremain was buried in daylight, but on the wrong side of the church.

Edward was not present; by then, he had already gone.

I have thought a great deal, these last months, about the suicide verdict on Tremain. The only unsound verdict Richard ever gave, and he did it to save me.

*

I saw Mrs Bly, once, in Falmouth, not long after Richard and I were first married. I was visiting my dressmaker, and as I stepped out of the shop I noticed a woman, slightly hunched, carrying a full basket, and realized it was her. I had heard she had found a position in the house of a naval officer.

I followed her, up the high street. It was a filthy day, with a thin, cold rain from the sea. I followed her for a full minute before I called out.

'Mrs Bly!'

She stopped, turned. We were under the awning of a curio shop.

'It's you,' she said.

I made some awkward enquiry, about how she was settling in, but she dismissed it.

'How can I help you, Mrs Boscawen? I need to be getting on.' She hefted the basket, nodding at my left hand, in which I held my umbrella. 'My congratulations, by the way.'

I looked at her, the rain collecting on the brim of her hat and gradually wetting her shoulders.

'I suppose you're glad,' I said. 'To be free of Tremain.'

She looked away. 'Of course I'm glad.'

'I'm grateful,' I went on, 'that you were brave enough to tell the truth, at the inquest.'

She hefted the basket again. 'The first I knew of that fire was the master – was Tremain seizing my arm, which woke me, and then he saw me out. And that was all I had to do with it.'

I looked at her. 'So it *was* all him? The nightshirt, the gun room table? The spoiled dinner?'

She did not answer at first, and I stepped closer.

'You needn't fear him *now*, Mrs Bly. It's past. He's dead.'

But she stepped backwards, out of the shelter. 'I heard your husband bought the place,' she said.

'He did.'

'Then I'll say this,' she said, 'and only this. If it's past, as you say, then you tell him to tear it down.'

And abruptly she turned, and walked away, and I watched her, dwindling, from under the dripping awning.

★

Mrs Bly; I would like to be able to speak to her again, now, just as I would dearly love to speak to Father. But I would like to speak to him while he was still sharp: or, if softening, then only at the edges. Before his last decline. Before that day – years after my conversation with Mrs Bly – probably, in fact, about the time I had found Tim hiding under the bed.

I had walked down the hill to Father's house; I had taken to going, most days, so as to give Mrs Humphrey some respite in the afternoons. And I was telling Father about Tim, what trouble we were having with him. At first Father seemed to be following, but then he seemed to grow fascinated by the pattern on the bedspread.

'Who did?' he said, frowning.

My heart paused. 'Tim, Father.'

He lifted his head, and asked, as though it were a perfectly reasonable question, 'Who's Tim?'

I took his hand, so soft now. 'Your grandson,' I said. 'My son.'

Father lifted his eyebrows. 'Don't be silly, my dear. How can you have a son, when you're not married yet?'

That stunned me, and I did not answer, only squeezed his fingers a little; said, 'Oh, Papa.'

But he was fidgeting, as though he had something else to say, something serious, and then he took my hand in both of his.

'My dear,' he said. 'My dear, I've been thinking. I know – I had a hunch, you see, and then Mrs Humphrey mentioned something about it – that you have a . . . an inclination for Edward Tremain.'

'Father,' I said.

But he held up his finger. 'My dear, you mustn't take Boscawen if you don't want him,' he said. 'You musn't take him only on my account.'

His face was so open, so urgent; his grip so very weak.

When I began, in November, my account of what happened at Polneath, I believe I wished to justify it. What I did. What Edward and I did together.

Then, when I picked up my pen again, in those days between Christmas and the New Year, when I began to write about

Richard and Tim and this past dreadful year, it was out of a wish to correct the record. To explain.

Now, as I make a third attempt at the truth, it is from an altered and altering world. Men are streaming home. The ghosts are coming back, and I have not finished.

I take up my pen again, now, for Tim in his unknown foreign corner, and for William Tremain, holding his breath beneath the bed. I take it up for Mrs Smith, and for a Mrs Sewell of Mayfair . . .

But most of all, I take it up for myself, for I wish to understand, at least, where I went wrong. My soul has grown dark to itself, like an old stove, too smoked to see the light inside. And I am resolved, now, if I can, to open the door.

As coroner, Richard did not only deal in deaths. His other duty was that occasional relic, the administration of treasure trove. Many times over the years, he was called out to settle the question of whether a wreck was above or below the tideline. But there was only one occasion I recall upon which someone turned up with real treasure, disinterred from the earth.

A winter's afternoon, and the ploughman from the top farm came in, right into the drawing room, with Mrs Fossett chewing her cheeks at the state of his boots, and deposited on to the cloth amongst the tea things a handful of bright gold coins.

He said he had checked the hole carefully; this was all. Two dozen, achingly shiny. Richard could talk to Mr Pickering about them, the ploughman said. He wanted no part of it.

Richard asked him whether he was sure, then thanked him for his honesty.

The man went, and Tim sprang up to poke through the coins, exclaiming.

Richard said how peculiar, and something about superstition, smiling over it, and waiting for my agreeing smile, which I gave. But secretly I well understood the ploughman.

It is a relief to hand over the past to someone else.

And there is only a little more of it to come. For which I suppose I should be thankful, as everything that is done in the house, now, I do myself. A few days ago, the Fossetts took their leave, with my good wishes. Mrs Fossett, with whom for so many years I was locked in a trivial, exhausting war, clasped my hand with full eyes before she went. Her kitchen and linen cupboard are my domain now, and when Jake is not about, I impinge upon his work, too, lugging baskets of logs about in the cautiously lengthening afternoons.

I will keep to the kitchen, where it's warmest. Look out of the window, and write the last of it down.

21.

Once the doctor had gone, the day after Edward had surprised me like that at home, I found I could hear Richard's breathing all through the house, quite distinctly, even when I was shut away in the study.

The stertorous intake. The pause. The letting go, like peas shaken in a tin to entertain a child.

I couldn't settle to anything. My lips felt raw where Edward had kissed them in the graveyard and then again by the front gate.

I went upstairs, but Mrs Fossett was sitting with Richard, still perhaps castigating herself for having gone out to enjoy the carols, for having trusted the Truro ferry. She offered a tense smile as I came in. Jake mustn't have told her yet, that he had seen me the day before. Who he had seen me with.

'I thought I might go out for an hour,' I said to Mrs Fossett, in a low voice. 'Mr Murray asked me yesterday to look in . . .'

She had already turned back to Richard. 'Do, madam. You can see for yourself there's no change. Get some air.'

Outside, the morning was damp, not too cold. At Mr Murray's, one of his daughters had hung up mistletoe in a bit of red ribbon above the front door. It was early still, but his motor was there at the side of the house, and I knew Murray liked to be up and about.

The maid looked rather surprised to see me, but she asked me to step in, and Murray put his head out of his study.

'Mrs Boscawen,' he said. He took my elbow, and steered me in, and asked the maid for another cup for coffee.

It was a pleasant room. I had not been in it since Father had died, when Old Murray had still been Richard's agent, and had handled everything when we wished to let Mrs Humphrey stay on at the house, to see out her own last years. The room was just the same, now that the son occupied it, except for a fleet of toy boats sailing across the rug.

'Forgive the mess,' he said.

I shook my head. 'Not at all.'

The maid came back with the cup, and Murray nodded to her, and began to pour my coffee himself.

'How is Mr Boscawen?'

'Rather worse, I'm afraid.'

'I suspected so. I'm sorry for it. I'm glad you've come here; I didn't want to present myself at your house uninvited. Two of the children have had colds –'

'No, no, of course.'

I was certain that he was going to ask me about Edward, yesterday's visit. I hardly knew whether to be coldly or hotly affronted, or whether to do as I wished, and confess my guilt, my uncertainty.

But then Murray handed me my coffee. He waited until I had taken a sip and put down the cup, before he said, 'Forgive me, Mrs Boscawen, but . . . have you ever seen your husband's will?'

I thought I saw, then, the reason for his delicacy, and I said, 'I haven't. Of course, with Tim, there's an amendment to be thought of, I imagine.'

'Not as such. It turns out that Tim's death is provided for. It was my father who drafted the will. The latest version is dated when Tim was seven, when a bequest was added for Truro Grammar, to pay for a scholarship. No, it's . . .' He had pulled a sheet towards him, and his eyes moved over it. Then he looked up at me. 'Don't be alarmed, madam. It's not – that is, you are amply taken care of. There's a small amount to the Fossetts, something for Feltham, but . . .' He looked at his coffee cup. 'I wouldn't have dug it out, but that I know the doctor has been back and forth of late.'

'I'm not alarmed,' I said, bluntly. 'He was here again this morning. He says it won't be long, now.'

Murray seemed agitated. He had got up, to see to the fire, and now he turned, and used a lower voice. 'I enquired with the bank, madam. As I told you. About . . . about Mrs Smith. They wouldn't give me an address.'

'I know.' I set down my coffee again. 'I didn't expect they would,' I said, calmly, but I did not feel calm. For suddenly I suspected the reason for Murray's agitation.

Murray pushed the sheet towards me, and pointed. 'But look,' he said.

I looked.

The whole of the Polneath woods, either the deeds themselves or the value thereof, to James Smith, of 12, Rope Walk, Plymouth.

There was silence, while I took it in.

Smith.

Then Murray said, 'I haven't been. It was only yesterday that I . . . but I thought –' Then, 'Of course, he too may be deceased.'

'Indeed,' I said.

Distantly there echoed through the house a voice – 'Darling?' – and Murray asked me to excuse him. I remained in his study a few minutes, alone with the cheerful crackle of the fire, staring at the fleet of small boats bravely sailing the hearth rug.

At length, Murray reappeared, and delicately enquired whether I intended to ask Mr Boscawen about it. When I said I wasn't sure, he began to talk too fast, tripping over his words, saying how if I wished him to he could simply deal with it himself, how I never need hear about it again, or else – he swallowed – we could leave it for the time being, but discuss it again another day.

Another day, when Richard was dead, I knew he meant.

Half distracted, on the brink of tears, I made myself look at him. 'Forgive me, Murray,' I said. 'Yes, I think another day . . .'

Then he asked if he mightn't drive me home. It's a short lane from Murray's, but steep. I agreed, but once we were in the motor I suddenly asked if he could run me into Truro, instead.

He looked taken aback, but he said of course, that it was quite alright, that Alice wouldn't mind so long as he was back for luncheon, that in any case he had a pair of rubber boots to pick up that ought by now to have been repaired. It would be sensible to fetch them before Christmas. He drove, and subsided into silence, his fingers nervously tapping on the wheel.

I let him set me down by the cathedral, and from there I walked up to the station, and got on the ten o'clock up train.

Perhaps I had vaguely thought I would telephone from the station – to Mrs Fossett that I was going, to Edward that I was coming – but somehow I did not. Soon I was ensconced in my seat, looking out on the sea. All that unyielding blue.

That it should be in his will like that – all open, black and white, for me to find – as though it ought to trouble me no more than a Truro Grammar scholarship. The thought of Richard gaining a son, now, this year of Tim's death. Or not even gaining one, but simply having had one stashed away all the time, like a spare handkerchief.

All I wanted was to see Edward; he would hardly have set his own suitcase down, but that did not matter. I would tell him that of course we might be together. I was a fool to have hesitated. I saw that now.

The train, I knew, would stop at Plymouth, and every station until then was a torment. As they counted themselves away, I thought about how I could get off, could go to Rope Walk, and find this boy, find his mother. What if I went there, and the boy was alive, and he insisted that, as Richard's only son, the Polneath woods were not half what he was owed? What if I went there, and the boy was dead, and the woman wished to commiserate with me over our lost children? I kept imagining her hair, her eyes. She could not be young, if Richard had been paying her since the year we had married. She might be very nearly my own age, or older, even. Perhaps she would seem quite an old woman, and I would have to feel sorry for her . . .

But I did not alight at Plymouth.

As the train pulled on towards London, I was calmer. I would go to Edward. He would be surprised, but he would get over his surprise. Perhaps I would tell him what had precipitated my journey; perhaps I would not. Perhaps I would stay a few days. I could buy some new things. When a woman is my age, people hardly care.

Even remembering that I had been writing to Edward at his club, that I did not know his home address, did not dismay me.

Perhaps he would even be there, at his club, picking up his post after his few days away.

At Paddington, I put my coat over my arm and walked out into the open air. Outside the station it took me a moment to remember right from left. But I had soon engaged a cab, and given the address on the Strand.

The doorman's face moved somewhat when he saw me – I hadn't come up in town clothes, of course, and was wearing a thick winter tweed. Only two days earlier, I had still been in black, for Tim. It was seeing Edward which had made me put it aside; but now, I realized, I looked ridiculously countrified.

The doorman frowned, when I asked for Edward. 'We've not seen Mr Tremain in a week or two, madam.'

I asked if I might have his home address.

The doorman gave me a measuring look, and seemed to decide I did not look criminal. He turned to a ledger, opened the page for T, wrote something down, and held it out. 'Tell Mr Tremain he's welcome to come in, at any time, and settle his account,' the doorman said.

I did not know the address myself, and perhaps I was downhearted when my second cab stopped in one of those squares not quite in Bloomsbury, that are too small, and rather dark in aspect. Where sounds, as a consequence, echo rather desolately from the walls. I paid the cabman to wait, in case I had the address wrong.

Edward's door had a knocker but no bell. I knocked, waited, and then knocked again. I could feel the cabman regarding me from his post.

A woman opened, and looked me over. Her sleeves were rolled up, and her apron grey with muck. I asked whether this was Mr Tremain's residence. When she said it was, I waved the cabman off. But he was out, she said. I was lucky it was her day.

'Out,' I said. I must have looked rather hopeless.

'Yes, madam.' And then, rather pityingly, 'Have you a card, Mrs –?'

'Boscawen,' I said. 'I'm afraid not. But if I might leave a note . . . ?'

I could feel how deep a red I had turned. I couldn't even ask Edward to ring me up somewhere, for I didn't know where that would be.

The woman went away. The hall was dreadfully shabby, a taupe sort of paper, peeling with damp near the skirting board. The woman came back with a pencil and an old envelope.

'I think he was taking tea with a Mrs Flora Sewell. Mayfair, you know.'

I took that in. 'Do you know, I'm not sure I need to leave a message. I was simply passing, and I –' I screwed up the envelope in my hand, held the pencil out to her.

'As you like.' She half stepped out, looking me over, the thick country cloth of my skirt. She paused. 'Mrs Sewell is a widow. Lost her chap last year, about this time. I believe Mr Tremain knew her, when he was a young man.'

'Yes,' I said. 'Yes, I rather think I met her, too. Only once.'

The woman nodded. And then, 'Are you sure you won't leave a message?'

'Not to worry,' I said, already several feet away.

I walked, after that, for a long time. It began to rain, and I found that I must have left my umbrella somewhere. I suppose I was aiming for Paddington, until it occurred to me that there would not be another train that night.

I handed over almost my last notes at rather a low hotel near Marylebone. The bedspread didn't bear examination, but I climbed on to it and fell instantly into a long sleep.

I woke in the morning, to the humiliation of my crumpled skirt, my smelly blouse, and a deep hunger. Mrs Smith and Flora Myers and Edward's grubby housekeeper at the door of his dingy lodgings were tangling together in my mind. I felt foolish in the daylight. That I had run away like that, when his visit to Miss Myers – Mrs Sewell, I corrected myself – might be perfectly innocent. Why shouldn't a widow and a widower comfort one another in friendship? And as to his account at the club – well, many found themselves, now the war was over, in altered circumstances.

But I couldn't go back that morning, face that housekeeper

again, nor Edward, in my current state. Neither could I afford the train home; I must get money, somehow. And so I took the Hampstead tube, descended to the rattling darkness, and emerged some time later at the foot of the heath.

It was freezing. The people on the pavement were less hurried. I stood still at a narrow place for a brewery dray to go slowly by. And then, all at once, it was grass under my feet, and a steep slope. I climbed, past lines of washing, the crack of it in the breeze under the cold grey sky. I climbed until I was warm enough to sit on a bench.

I could see the upward smoke of the city. One or two of the ways in which I had been a fool. I had three shillings left in my purse.

At a decent hour, I walked stiffly down to Edith's street. It was only on the step, beside the pots of dormant geraniums, that it occurred to me that she too might be out. But she was not out – they were just finishing their morning tea – two of her girls visiting, and all their children. Over the slamming of doors and running feet, Edith twittered around me.

In the corner of the drawing room was the most enormous Christmas tree.

'No, truly, no emergency,' I said. 'I was simply passing, and I . . .'

Beside Edith and her daughters, all exquisitely turned out, I felt a fright, and spent the hour until luncheon petrified that my stomach would make some terrible sound, and betray me.

The children had quoits, out in the garden. We watched them through the glass, bundled up in their coats like puddings, while Edith's girls discussed their accomplishments and ailments, and Edith kept throwing me curious glances, which I was careful to avoid.

The eldest was a lad about ten. Something about him, the particular flush of his cheek, reminded me of William Tremain. Who would have caught the war, I thought, if he'd lived. He might have grown, had children of his own, and died this last summer. Or survived. Everything might have been otherwise.

Luncheon restored me somewhat, the children diverting Edith

into various lessons in manners, and at length they all went, and we were left alone. I had missed the afternoon train.

'Catherine seems well,' I said.

Edith smiled. 'Yes. She's pregnant again. No sickness, this time . . .' She paused. 'You're staying for dinner?'

I looked at her. 'The night, if I may.'

She went off to speak to her cook, and then came back, shutting the door behind her. 'John's at a meeting, he'll be back at seven,' she said, fussing with the sofa cushions. 'If you'd wired, you know, I'd have put the girls off.'

'No, no,' I said. 'It was so pleasant to see them.' I hesitated. 'Actually, would you mind awfully wiring to Mrs Fossett? Just say that I'm in London, and I'm coming home tomorrow.'

Edith's eyebrows lifted, but she went off again, to send a boy.

She came back as the clock was chiming, a pinging, overwrought sound. Edith perched herself on the sofa and looked at me seriously.

'Now. How on earth did you come to be *passing*?'

I looked at my hands. The trouble was that I had never told her any of it. She knew, of course, about William Tremain's death, the scandal of Old Tremain and Agnes Draper. But I had never confessed to her my full part. When I had enquired, over the years, whether she had heard any gossip of Edward, I suppose she took it for idle curiosity concerning a man about whom I had been briefly foolish as a girl.

Even were I to tell her about the Polneath business now, I thought, facing her expectant stare: did I expect sympathy for having turned up yesterday at Edward's house, to be told he was out dining with a wealthy woman in Mayfair, and my husband still breathing his last at home?

'I wanted to see you,' I said. 'That is, Richard –'

'I *knew* something was amiss,' Edith said.

I looked at my hands again. 'He is rather worse. It's so difficult with his chest when he's confined to his bed . . .'

She came to sit beside me, and spoke of another friend whose husband had suffered an apoplexy, and could not even speak. 'Oh,

Ivy. And you stuck down there. Of course you need a rest. A change of air –'

'It's not only that,' I said. 'Of course, I've had to do more. With the estate, and so on.'

Edith nodded.

'I looked at the accounts. It seems he's been paying a – a Mrs Smith. A modest living, as long as we've been married. And his will leaves the Polneath woods, to – I can only assume it's her son.'

'Oh dear,' Edith said.

She asked whether I had suspected, I said I hadn't. She rang for the maid, who brought sherry. I couldn't drink mine, but Edith sipped steadily. Edith told me she thought John had visited someone, soon after their younger girl was born. Only for a year or two.

'They aren't like us,' she said.

I thought about all the men I knew. Richard and Jake. But were women so different? What I had been doing, with Edward – was that different? I tilted my sherry glass, but didn't drink.

'Why the Polneath woods, though?' Edith said. She put her glass down. 'That's queer.'

We stared at the fire.

'Did she ever make a claim on him?' I asked. 'The girl John was visiting?'

'I don't even know that he was,' Edith said, in a lower voice. 'And if he ever paid out anything, I never knew about it.'

She turned the talk to St Rumon's. I told her about the new doctor, the new vicar.

'Of course, they seem like children.'

'And how's Jake Feltham?' Edith said, suddenly.

'Well. He's well.' I swallowed. 'He does our garden, now.'

'Does he?' Edith said, more animatedly.

We talked about the difficulty of finding anyone with experience, even now that the war was over.

'I should come for a proper visit,' Edith said, after a while. 'I couldn't have stayed, of course, in the spring. But I ought to see St Rumon's again.'

'You ought,' I said. I wondered whether she ever would. Suddenly, I felt terribly lonely. 'Have you ever met a Mrs Flora Sewell, of Mayfair?' I said.

'No,' said Edith. 'Why?'

'It doesn't matter,' I replied.

The hands of the clock had crawled through half past five.

'Do you ever wonder how it would have been,' Edith said, distantly, 'to have done it all differently? Married someone different?'

I shifted uncomfortably in my seat, frightened for a moment that she had guessed. But when I saw her face, flushed from the sherry, I realized that it was only idle talk. 'I suppose everyone does.'

'And Jake Feltham is looking after your garden,' Edith said. She smiled, shook her head. 'Do you know, he was quite gone on you, when we were young.'

I looked at her. 'What do you mean?'

Edith grinned. 'He told me once. At one of those summer teas at the mills. I suspect he'd taken a drink. Asked me if I thought you'd ever think of him.' She gave a little laugh. 'Isn't it delicious?'

And, at that, I burst into tears.

Edith left me alone, after that. She was beautifully kind. She cleaned me up, and lent me something of hers to change for dinner. She kept asking me to forgive her, and telling me that I was clearly overwrought.

The meal passed easily in John's slow, dull talk.

So it was that I found myself in one of Edith's nightgowns, in the pink light of a guest bedroom, before nine o'clock had struck. I did feel exhausted, but I didn't yet feel ready to sleep. The pink room unsettled me. It must have been below the children's, and the dim light was alive with whispering and scuffling.

I thought about Mr James Smith. About the Polneath woods. It *was* strange. Why not simply money? The woods would have been worth more when Richard first made his will, I thought, than they would be worth now. Even with the damage, there had been interest, at first, from more than one quarter in reopening the mills, or refitting them to make the new explosives. But the damage was bad, and there was the steepness of the site – difficult to expand, they said – and so it had come to nothing. Now it was simply woods and ruins.

Mr James Smith. The Polneath woods.

And like that, the ghost of the knowledge came to me, of why Richard had included them in his will. I remembered something, something that had been said, long ago, that day William Tremain's inquest hearing was finished.

Tomorrow, I decided, I would be up early. I would beg my train fare and a packet of sandwiches from Edith. At Paddington, I would buy a ticket to Truro, and, when I boarded the train, I would ask the guard if I might break my journey at Plymouth.

22.

1888

When I came downstairs at Polneath, the morning William's inquest was to be reconvened, I paused on the first floor, and then pushed the door cautiously, put my head into the corridor.

Tremain's bedroom door stood wide. The key was there, in the outside of the door. Edward must have let him out. I moved towards the door, gingerly, sore from the night in a way which felt coarse and unromantic. The window was open, as usual, and a cold draught was moving the fringes of the drapes. The room was knocked about, shattered glass across the coffee table and the bed unmade. Upon the wall, a mirror sat askew. On a little shelf were three fancy cut-glass jars, which contained, I saw now, powdered brimstone, charcoal, saltpetre.

It was hard to believe that Tremain's downfall might really have come – that Agnes would be free of him, as would Edward.

In the kitchen, in her Sunday best, Mrs Bly looked pale. But she met my eyes as she handed over the tray of porridge and tea. The kitchen was spotless. Everything put away, every jar in perfect alignment, every surface scraped clean.

At Agnes's door, I had to manage the tray while I unlocked it, one last time. She was sitting up in bed as I went in. She, too, looked as though she had passed a sleepless night. I poured out the tea, and put in three sugars.

Some of her colour had come back by the time I took the altered dress in. 'Ready?' I asked.

She patted her hair. 'Down, or up?'

'Down,' I said. It mattered still, what the jury thought of her. 'One plait. Like a child. And here.' I gave her the key to the room which had held her those past days. 'Take it with you,' I said, 'and fling it in the sea, eh?'

A look passed over her face which was almost like pain. 'Thank you, Miss Cardew,' she said.

I went back to William's room, to pack my own bag. I would leave it here, and tomorrow morning go back for it, tell Father I had forgotten. Edward would be waiting.

Checking my hair in the mirror, I wondered again when and where we would manage to be married. In a week? In a month? When it was done, I had decided, I would tell Father. It would hurt him, but there was no other way. I would go, first, with Edward. Then I would write.

Casting around for anything I might have neglected to pack, I remembered the yellow nightshirt, William's small yellow night-shirt, bundled up in the bottom of the wardrobe. I took it out, and held it up to the light. I would not take it with me. But I made a promise, as I replaced it in the wardrobe.

'I'll make him pay,' I said to the air. In the quiet, my voice sounded strange.

I walked behind Agnes down the stairs. Boscawen's gig waited on the sweep, the carriage from the King's Arms having come half an hour before for Edward, Mrs Bly and Tremain.

As we bumped down through the trees, Agnes said, 'You're running away, aren't you? With Mr Edward.'

I was silent for a moment, as the carriage jolted.

Then I said, 'You mustn't tell.'

She turned to me. 'Are you certain that you know what you're about?'

I smiled gently, a reassuring smile. 'You worry about yourself, Agnes. Don't worry about me.'

At the King's Arms, we went swiftly inside. No chatter from Mrs Mason this morning, and the noise in the back room dropped directly we entered. Boscawen, from the same chair he had taken before, looked me in the eye, and nodded. The jury were all seated to his right; to his left, Edward and Tremain.

Tremain looked bad, every past drink written in his face, the small veins of his cheeks and nose merging in the unkind daylight. Edward looked poorly slept, and nervous. He gave me a brief smile, and looked away quickly, but I felt myself turning red nevertheless as Agnes and I made our way towards the same bench as before, by the window.

We sat down. In the corner by the storeroom sat Mrs Bly, with Father standing beside her. He gave me an encouraging smile. The room was too warm, too full. People were coughing. Every local man with even a guinea invested in the mills was there; the constable was there, his hand free now of its sling.

By the door stood Jake. People glanced at him, whispering, while he studied a spot on the flagstone floor. It gave me a twist of pain to see him.

Boscawen got much more briskly through the swearing, this time. He had a stack of notes, and looked as though he knew their exact order. I sensed there would be no shuffling, today.

'We are here to continue the proceedings of the inquest into the death of William Tremain, on the twenty-third instant. The viewing of the body has already taken place. Should any further viewing be necessary, I will proceed with the jury to where the body is lying. For appreciable reasons.' Boscawen looked at the jury, and they looked at one another in their turn.

He meant the smell. It was dreadful to think of, that little boy, who a week ago had been fidgeting in his pew through a long sermon.

'You gentlemen might recall,' Boscawen said, his voice irreproachably steady, 'that paint was discovered, under the boy's fingernails. That it was deduced thereby that the room in which he died had been locked, and unlocked again. Mr Thomas Tremain suggested –' he glanced at his notes – 'that Miss Draper had started the fire, and locked William in, intending to hurt him. That she might have poisoned the boy. That she is mad.'

'That's right,' Tremain said. He had not stood, but remained sitting, his hands planted on his thighs.

Boscawen glanced at Tremain. There was quiet in the room. 'Mr Tremain suggested that the key to the room in which

William died – to Miss Draper's room – might be found amongst her things.' Boscawen reached under his notes, produced the key, and held it up. 'And so it proved – under her bolster.'

There was a rush of murmuring, and, for a moment, I doubted Boscawen. From the looks the jury cast at Agnes, it was clear enough that every man there thought her guilty. My stomach felt tight.

'Sir,' Boscawen said, 'I am led to believe that there have been – unsavoury happenings, in your house, these last days.' Boscawen read from his notes. 'A figure of the dead boy, appearing upon the table on which he was laid out, while Miss Draper laundered in the room next door. Saltpetre in her dinner . . .' Boscawen paused. 'Miss Draper was, I understand, distressed after each of these occurrences.'

Tremain lurched to his feet. 'She did all that herself,' he said, impatience in his voice now. 'Like the nightshirt. It's as I said. She's mad.' He seemed to look at Edward, for support.

But Edward was looking at the floor.

'Mad, yes,' Boscawen said, implacable, glancing at his papers.

Suddenly, I trusted him again; realized that he knew, precisely, what he was about.

'Dr Cardew, if we might turn to you next. I know you have examined Miss Draper, and I shall ask you in a moment to comment upon that – but, since Mr Tremain also suggested that William may have been, ah, drugged or poisoned, I will ask you first to relate to us the results of the post-mortem.'

Tremain shifted in his seat.

'You have completed your internal examination of William's body?' Boscawen said.

Father stepped forward. Steady, today, thank God. 'I have.'

'Very well. Please describe for the jury any conclusions you were able to draw, as a result of your work.'

Father nodded again, and looked at the floor. An image came to me, of the small bare foot which had escaped the sheet, glimpsed through the window of Father's consulting room.

Father lifted his head. 'There were no abnormalities. Each of the organs was entirely normal. Death was, as we suspected, by asphyxiation, with no sign of compression or smothering. It was the smoke.'

Boscawen nodded. 'Any signs of poisoning?'

'None,' Father said. 'Nor rough treatment of any variety. Other than the aforementioned paint under the nails. The bruising to the hands.'

'Very well. Dr Graves, you observed the conduct of the examination?'

Another man stood, and inclined his head. Dimly, I recognized him.

'And your conclusions agree with Dr Cardew's?'

'They do.'

'Thank you,' Boscawen said.

Graves sat down. The jury were looking at one another.

Boscawen turned back to Father. 'Now, Dr Cardew, as regards Miss Draper. You have had occasion to examine her in the last week?'

Father's eyes moved. 'Twice.'

'And did you detect any sign of madness in her?'

'Not madness,' he said. He swallowed. 'She is shocked, grief-stricken –'

'As well she might be,' Boscawen said. 'Given what has taken place.'

'But not mad, no.' Father sounded firm.

I had turned to watch him speak, and now his eyes met mine, just briefly, before returning to Boscawen.

'She is emotional. Entirely in keeping with her being with child.'

It was unlike the last time, with the uproar, the competing questions; this time, after Father spoke, there was silence. A painful silence, as though everyone in the room might be holding their breath. Edward had his head in his hands, and Tremain was watching him. The whole of the jury was looking at Jake.

'Mr Feltham,' Boscawen said.

Jake looked at him. 'Yes, sir?'

But Boscawen didn't ask him to deny anything: instead, he took him back over everything he had seen and heard, from the moment Mrs Bly had shrieked 'fire' that night, down on the terrace.

'And when you finally beat back the blaze – which you fought, alongside Mr Tremain – who reached the door of Miss Draper's room first?'

'Mr Tremain did, sir,' Jake said. 'He asked me to beat out the rest of the sparks on the stairs.'

'And when you joined him at last on the upper passage, the door to Miss Draper's room stood open – and the room was, to your knowledge at the time, entirely empty?'

Jake bit his lips at the memory. 'Yes, sir. William having crawled out of sight.'

'Very well . . .' Boscawen paused. 'May I ask what you were wearing – yourself, and Mr Tremain – as you fought the fire?'

The jury shifted in their seats. Perhaps they took the question as a simple test of Jake's confidence in his memories. But I had guessed now where Boscawen was aiming, and Tremain, for his part, had gone quite still.

Jake frowned. 'Breeches, boots. A shirt –' He stopped. 'The master had on a cravat, and he took it off to wrap about his mouth.'

'Very well. Now, it has been communicated to me that, on the evening William died, you saw Mr Tremain and Miss Draper engaged in an altercation. Is that not so?'

Jake looked at Mrs Bly. 'It is.'

'And he saw you, Mrs Bly. Clearing the dining table, and taking your time over it. Near enough to hear what was said.' Boscawen looked at Mrs Bly, and, without being asked to, she stood. 'Mrs Bly,' Boscawen said. 'Do you know what perjury is?'

She fidgeted. 'I do.'

'I hope you do,' Boscawen said. 'You can be transported for it.' He looked at his notes. 'What was the quarrel about?' Boscawen said.

'It was about money,' Mrs Bly said, in a low, clipped voice. 'She gave him her notice, and she wanted two hundred pounds.'

'Two hundred pounds?'

'Not to tell.' She looked at Agnes – her face showing, just for a moment, a flash of hatred. Carefully, she did not look anywhere near Tremain.

'Very well. That will do, Mrs Bly.' Now he looked at Agnes.

A new hush fell.

'Well then, Miss Draper. You were not in your bedroom, the night of the fire. Perhaps you might now tell us where you were.'

'I was in Mr Tremain's room,' she said. 'I was waiting for him.'

And that was when the uproar came, men shouting questions and objections, and the silent people in the room standing out like islands: Jake, Father, Edward with his grey face.

When Boscawen got quiet, he took Agnes through all of it – the quarrel, and how she had waited for Tremain after, but he had stayed outside, smoking into the late hours. Eventually, Agnes admitted, she had fallen asleep on his bed, her own room empty.

'And so I submit,' Boscawen said, above the murmurs in the room, 'that Mr Tremain returned to his office. He heard steps above him, and, taking them for Miss Draper's, set the fire and locked her door. Unlocked it later. Killed, in error, his grandson.'

Tremain, who had listened in silence, looking ever more wildly to Edward, realized now that his son was not going to return his gaze. Spluttering, he stood. 'This,' he said, 'is the most egregious – my son will –'

'But are we to accept this, Boscawen?' the foreman of the jury broke in. 'On the word of one girl, who has allowed herself to be – well, by someone.' The verger had coloured up.

'Just so,' Tremain said. He was looking at Edward for support. 'It's –'

'*Sir*,' Boscawen snapped. 'Hold your tongue.'

There was a shocked silence from the jury; but, when Boscawen said what he said next, I had guessed it was coming.

'Miss Cardew,' he said.

I stood. Every eye in the room was upon me.

'You attended at Polneath, with your father, on the night of the fire. I came to fetch you myself. As you arrived, I believe, Mr Tremain and some others were finishing extinguishing any remaining sparks.'

I looked only at Boscawen, tried to ignore all others. 'Yes.'

'Can you describe what Mr Tremain was wearing, when first you saw him?'

'A nightshirt,' I said. 'He was wearing a nightshirt.'

A noise rose amongst the jury, as they realized what Boscawen meant; that Tremain had gone up to change, before the fire was fully out. As soon as he knew what his false story must be, and how his clothing contradicted it. He had changed his clothes for his nightshirt, to make it look as though he had been roused from his bed.

Tremain was shaking his head, swaying. 'Edward,' he said. 'Tell them. Tell them it was her.'

But Edward looked at him. 'Father,' he said. 'I can't.'

'No,' Tremain was saying, 'no, *no*.'

There was a pause.

And then Tremain launched himself out of his seat, flying at Agnes. At me.

'*Sir!*' Boscawen bellowed.

The constable leapt forward, and one or two others to help him. I had felt myself move as Tremain pounced, but Jake had crossed the room in a flash and pulled me back, so I was forced to watch as the constable prised Tremain's fingers, one by one, from Agnes's neck.

'Take him out,' Boscawen said, and the constable handled Tremain out of the door.

Agnes was breathing hard. I touched her shoulder, and she lifted her hand to show she was well.

Edward looked stunned, strange, newly shocked, as though he had only just been told of William's death. Boscawen, too, looked shocked. But determined.

He allowed a minute, two minutes of racket. Mrs Bly was weeping. Edward sat, clutching his knees, the chair beside him empty, while the jury argued amongst themselves about murder and manslaughter.

At last, Boscawen stood up. 'You will need time, to consider,' he said. 'But I believe it might be a kindness, at this point, to dismiss some of the witnesses.'

Agnes stood up. The jury fell quiet, watching her.

'Might I go?' she asked.

'Of course you might, Miss Draper,' Boscawen said.

Agnes took my arm, and I was forced to lead her away from Edward, away from the packed, hot room, through the front of the inn. Tremain was sitting at a table in the corner; he did not look up, but the constable nodded to us. We gained the fresh air. Father, the Reverend Green, Jake and several more followed us out.

Then Boscawen appeared. 'I've given them half an hour,' he said. He looked satisfied, as though he had played a well-contested game of dominoes.

I wanted nothing more than to go to Edward, but Father had come up to take my arm. Agnes wandered away from the men, across the lane to the church lychgate, and I watched her go.

Boscawen was saying something about the cells at Falmouth being full; that Tremain, being known in the district, would likely be permitted to go home, and they would come for him that afternoon, or the next morning.

He looked at Father and myself. 'Mrs Bly will stay at the King's Arms. I shan't pursue her for having lied, when the inquest opened – she's been helpful enough now, and she lived in fear of him, I suppose . . .' He paused. 'My housekeeper is waiting with your Mrs Humphrey, to take Miss Draper back with us.'

It must have showered, while we had been inside. There were fresh puddles on the ground.

The Reverend Green began to commiserate with Jake, quietly and in a mortified tone, as though the awkward scandal of what he had heard had sent him temporarily unhinged.

'I'm dreadfully sorry for how you have been impugned,' the vicar was saying. And, 'People have always known Tremain for a bad apple, and I myself . . .'

It was clear that Jake wanted to get away.

At length, Boscawen said, 'I must go back in, to help them with the formal verdict.'

The vicar turned to him. 'I hear I am to congratulate you, sir.' The vicar swallowed, glancing from me to Boscawen, then to Father. 'Not the proper moment, of course, but. Yes. A most gratifying conclusion.'

Boscawen wouldn't quite meet my eye, as he turned back towards the inn, and the vicar followed him.

All at once, Agnes was beside me, asking whether I was quite well, as I watched them enter.

'Quite well. Quite well,' I said. I asked her whether she had everything she needed, whether she had thought yet where she would go, after Mr Boscawen's house.

'You've an aunt, that's right, isn't it?' I said. 'Where is she, again?'

'Plymouth,' Agnes replied.

'Plymouth,' I repeated, absently.

Watching Boscawen stoop under the inn door's lintel, I barely listened. Despite that, I must still have heard.

23.

1919

I am sitting in the kitchen, watching the rain track down the windows. My hand is light, and colours seem too bright, too sharp, my thoughts too numerous for the page. I have been sleeping soundly, you see, these last weeks. For the first time in a long time, my sleep has been dreamless.

The table is littered with my post. Incoming, outgoing. There is a note from the vicar, with a sketch of the memorial, which is to go up shortly on St Rumon's green. There is a little note offering a christening present for Theo Stainforth's baby, and an undertaker's bill that needs my attention. There is a postcard I picked up in Plymouth, which shows the great bridge, and on the reverse a message, written in a large, rough hand.

I keep picking things up and putting them down, as though I have misplaced something. The slight furring of ink where it bleeds into paper. The postcard writer's firm hand and the undertaker's florid one. But I haven't misplaced anything. The two buff inquest files sit before me, side by side, but I have no need to open them, now.

I know too well what they contain.

What they omit.

I have Tim's last letter here, addressed to Richard. I only found it today; I see from the postmark that it would have arrived after the news of his death, so perhaps Richard forgot about it, or didn't wish to upset me.

Tim had got wind that he might have some leave coming up. There had been a blackbird knocking around their section, singing its heart out. He missed the blackbirds in the garden at home. He thought he might come back this time, after all, to St Rumon's, and bring with him his batman, Davies, whose friendship had been the only bright spot in all this.

He came to see me, the batman, about a fortnight ago. Late January. I answered the door myself, rather covered in flour. I had been attempting bread. It took me a moment to understand who he was, through his rather stumbling explanation, with its Bristol consonants.

He would have sought me out sooner, but he had only recently been discharged from the hospital. He had walked down from the Truro road. His name was Davies.

'Of course,' I said. 'Please . . .'

I held open the door for him.

I had written to him, to several others who had served with Tim, from a regimental list which Richard had turned up. There had been no answers, but now here Davies was. He stood clutching his hat with frozen hands, his dark hair and his thin, intelligent face exposed to the air. His eyes never rested long in one place.

I invited him through to the kitchen. Jake had gone out for the afternoon.

Davies insisted on taking off his boots; insisted, though it was only a bit of mud. Tim had been the same, on his last visit home. I suppose it came of knowing what worse things he had trodden in.

The kitchen was the only warm room. I offered him tea, or a stronger drink, and he accepted a whisky and lemon when I said I was having one, too. The bread stood expanding gently in its covered bowl between us.

'You ought to have written,' I said, with nervous brightness. 'I'd have sent Jake for you, in the motor.'

'Oh, I like walking,' the boy said. 'Being outside.' He was clutching his mug, and his stockinged feet had crept closer to the range.

'Tim was the same,' I said.

He was young, younger than Tim, though it couldn't have been by much. He had large, gentle eyes.

'I gather from Tim's letters that you were very great friends.'

He seemed almost to flinch.

I averted my eyes, went on, 'He didn't write to me much, but he wrote to his father.'

'Did he? He didn't speak of his father,' the boy said. 'He spoke of you a lot. Made me jealous. My mother died when I was little. Fitted me to the job, though. I'm used to cooking, and that. Trying to get things dry.' He was looking into his cup, lost in thought. 'If I wasn't, I might never have met him.'

I had been watching him, as he spoke. He hadn't said what his wound had been. He had no limp or awkward arm, no rasp or sore blink of a gas victim.

His gaze strayed to the rising loaf, and then to the memorial sketch, which I had been studying, trying to imagine that prong of stone.

'What do you think?' I said, pushed it gently towards him.

He brought the paper near to his face. 'Is it for a grave?'

The page said 'St Rumon's Memorial' across the top, in large letters. He looked up at me.

He could not read.

Smoothly, I explained it to him, how it would have their names alphabetically on all its sides.

'That's well. They can't deny how many, if they're all spelled out.' The boy looked down. 'Mrs Boscawen, I've to ask your forgiveness.'

'What on earth do you mean?' I said gently, frowning.

'It's my fault Captain Boscawen died.'

'Of course it isn't –' I said, but stopped as he met my eyes, and then looked down.

'There were a pair of Jerry,' he said. 'Patrolling. God knows why. The dawn caught them. They were close to our wire.'

'I know,' I said. 'An old pal of Tim's was –'

'Listen, madam,' the boy said, rather fiercely, and then looked into his lap again. 'One of ours picked them off, but . . . it wasn't clean.' He swallowed. 'We talked of waiting till dark and bringing them in. But the CO forbade it. All day, we could hear them crying. I could hear them.' He looked at me. 'The fact is, Mrs

Boscawen, my nerves weren't –' He swallowed, and took a breath. 'Captain Boscawen saw me weeping over it. It was going to be dark, soon, there'd have been no chance of hitting them in the dark. They were going to cry all night. So he . . .' He broke off.

'I see,' I said. 'I see.'

He'd taken a chance, and tried to end their suffering.

'Then he didn't mean to –'

Davies looked up at me. 'No.'

I told him that there was nothing to forgive. I insisted that he must be hungry. I fetched a cold pie, and let him cut his own slice from it, and his stomach made a sound, and I smiled, even though his face was wet. He was hesitant with the knife.

'I'm mightily sorry, Mrs Boscawen,' the boy said, again, when he had finished eating. He sounded steadier, now. 'I know it's been dreadful for you.'

I touched his hand, and he seemed rather shocked. 'It's been dreadful for both of us,' I replied.

But I felt elated. Tim had not wanted to die.

I pressed and pressed Davies to stay the night – or to wait for Jake, at least, and have a lift back into Truro. But he wouldn't, he wanted to be off. I asked him how he would be set up, now that it was all over. He said his father was a tailor: he would be taking on the shop himself. He had all his brothers, still, to help him. The eldest would soon be seventeen.

As he took his leave, I said, 'I wish my husband could have had the pleasure of meeting you.'

I watched him away up the lane, and then, Jake not being back, I went to get some wood in. I grew hot, fetching the wood, with a fierce joy. One always thinks one would like never to struggle again. Only lately have I come to see how essential it is.

I washed up Davies's cup, his plate with its few crumbs, and began to peel potatoes for our supper.

Theo Stainforth had not lied. He had told it as faithfully as he could, but he had been too far away from the wounded Germans. Could not hear them; nor see Davies's tear-streaked face as he'd tried to ready that evening's mess. His face, as Tim had seen it, and then tried to do, without hesitation, what he had done. Kind, in the end, as he had always been.

My son had been kind. I had brought him up to be kind.

I put down a potato, half done, and sobbed, clutching the table with my cold, red hands.

I have never in my life cried like that, before or since.

24.

But I believe I left myself on the train back west from London. Only a few days until Christmas. Edith's sandwiches in my lap, my hands very still inside the sleeves of my coat. Having the compartment to myself, I kept the window open, for the freezing air on my face, and tried for calm by watching for glimpses of the sea.

For when I arrived at 12 Rope Walk, I knew exactly who would answer my bell. But I did not believe, I could not believe, that Richard had made her his mistress. Surely the leaving of the Polneath woods to her son in his will was only what Richard had felt to be fitting. Surely his payments were prompted only by pity . . . And yet I could not forget what he had said in his study, all those years ago. About girls of her station, who sometimes made arrangements. And there was nowhere to hide from my horrible doubt, as I watched the fields rush by.

For it seemed Edward did not trust me, after all – had not thought us dear enough to one another for me to overlook his reduced circumstances. Or perhaps I had mistaken his intentions entirely, and he meant to have Mrs Flora Sewell, instead, as he almost had, once before, all those years ago, when her name was Myers . . .

I got up just before Plymouth to go to the lavatory, half distracted. It was only as I was coming back down the train that the carriage gave a lurch, and I put my hand hard and flat against the glass of one of the other compartments. There was a man inside, gazing out of the window.

It was Edward.

The sound of my palm against the glass made him stir, but, just as he turned his head, I managed to get out of sight. Within moments, I was back in my own compartment. But had he seen me? I could not say. Perhaps he had followed me – but I could not bear to talk to him now, looking as I did, and we were pulling into

Plymouth. I picked up my coat, and swayed and lurched the length of the train, to the third-class carriage, glancing behind me all the way, but no one followed. I alighted from third, and hid behind a coal bunker while they shunted those carriages going on to Penzance. I saw Edward's face, a brief smudge in the window of the first-class carriage. His housekeeper must have told him of my coming, I realized. He'd have assumed I'd be home again by now, and he was on his way to explain that it was nothing, between him and Flora Sewell, to reassure me of his love . . .

Watching the train pull away, I thought I saw the white scrap of his face turn more fully towards me, where I crouched behind the bunker. But I might have been mistaken. My face was red at the thought of his turning up at the house. Mrs Fossett answering his knock. But it couldn't be helped, now; there were three hours until the next train. And even if . . . even if all would be well with Edward, after all, I still wanted to be certain. I still wanted to know what my marriage had truly been.

I had to ask two people the way, before I found Rope Walk. It was a row, not genteel, perhaps, but clean. The houses had three floors, and were peeling white where salt on the wind had robbed the paint of its fortitude. The lamplighter had been round already, and I stood for a moment out of the pool cast by the nearest illumination to number 12.

I was contemplating pulling the bell when a man emerged from the house, and I jumped like a fool. He paused on the step, looked at the failing afternoon, putting the finishing touches to a pipe. Then he saw me, and I made a show of looking at my watch, as though I were waiting for someone.

At length, the man walked past me, and away down the street, behind him a sweet tobacco scent. I knew it was James Smith. He had just her hair.

I climbed the steps. The door had glass panels, with a curtain drawn behind, and a light burning beyond them. I pulled the bell, and that set off an excited barking, which drew nearer. The curtain moved. The door opened, and I had first to crouch to the dog – 'Hello there –'

And then I straightened, face to face with Agnes Draper. It was clear that she recognized me; I didn't have to introduce myself, or anything idiotic of that kind.

She had changed, of course. Her face had thinned and lined. The proud lift of the chin was the same, but there was weariness, too, and humour, dealt out by the thirty intervening winters. She was respectably dressed, in blouse and skirt and apron. Mrs Smith. Bland skirt and blouse, and the blandest name she had been able to think of. She wore no wedding ring.

She didn't speak, and I hardly knew how to begin. So I said, 'Richard is dying.'

She moved the dog with her foot, warily. 'You'd best walk in,' she replied.

She led me through to the back of the house, to a small, warm kitchen. She moved not with a limp, exactly, but gingerly. I wondered what hidden pain was causing it. My mother had moved just like that before she'd died. The dog settled in a basket by the range.

'That was your son, outside.'

'Jim. He's at the docks. Reserved occupation.' She gestured to the chair, and sat down herself in the other. 'You took him, then. Boscawen.'

I looked aside. 'He's ill. I found the payments. A Mrs Smith . . .'

'Ah.'

'But then our agent discovered your address.'

She looked down. Then she said, 'I didn't want to take your money. But my health wasn't what it should have been. After Jim was born.'

That was not what I had meant at all. 'No, of course, only . . .'

She looked at me.

'I wanted to be certain. That Jim is Tremain's child?' That he was not Richard's, I meant; and I suppose I asked it rather desperately.

The Polneath woods were only what Jim would have inherited, had things gone differently, and the boy had his rights. It would have been like Richard.

But now Agnes was looking down.

'Ah,' she said.

My stomach dropped.

'He's not Tremain's,' she said. Looked up. 'But he's not your husband's, either.'

I waited. 'Then whose?'

'I thought you'd fathom it.' She looked away from me, but then straight at me, defiant. 'He's Edward's.'

'Edward's?' I said, stupidly. 'Which Edward?'

She looked at me, and then stood up, wincing, leaned backwards against the range. The dog came over and nosed at the hem of her skirt. She didn't answer.

Edward's. Edward Tremain's.

I said, 'He can't be.' My mind was rearranging everything at speed, or seeing it anew. It was like one of those illusions, with the fair false young woman and the truthful, hideous old one. Then, 'Edward Tremain's child?'

Agnes looked down. 'It had been going on . . . all year, since he'd come back to Polneath, after his wife died. I thought he'd marry me, and then – I found out that the fiancée was coming for Christmas. Miss Myers, you remember her? Mrs Bly told me she was coming – she did it to vex me – she loved Edward, but she hated me. I saw, then, how I'd be left.' She crouched to the dog, and it moved off again, back to its basket. 'I hadn't told Edward yet, about the child. I waited till he retired for the night, packed a bag. And I threatened Tremain. On the terrace. I told him I wanted paying to be on my way, or else I'd stay till the morning, and Miss Myers would know all . . .' She paused. 'I didn't know how little money there was left. If I had, I'd have known the old man would refuse me.' Heavily, she sat down again. 'I knew Edward kept money by his bedside. So when Tremain went back to his office, I crept up to Edward's room . . . said not a word about Miss Myers, made out that I'd come to him, as usual.' She kept her eyes on the floor. 'I was going to wait till he fell asleep, and then go with what I needed. But Edward had hardly finished with me when we heard Mrs Bly shriek fire, from below. We ran up to Will's room, and when he wasn't there, we split up, to try and find him. It wasn't long before I realized where he must be . . .' She tailed off. 'I knew Tremain wanted me out of the way. But I didn't know how bad.'

I swallowed, twice. I could hear the wind outside, the tick of the cooling kettle. 'And then Edward . . . he was going to let you take the blame?'

She met my eyes. 'If it hadn't been for you.' She looked down again. 'That loan got denied, and he must have known he'd get nothing from the old man. You'd taken against his father – and then, when you told him about Jim, I think that was the last straw.' Her voice grew thoughtful. 'Will had always been the only thing in the world he really wished to be tender to. And when he knew there was going to be a child – he came whispering outside my room. Made me promise to run away with him, after the inquest –' She stopped, and seemed to shudder. 'He wanted me then, after all.' A bitter smile. 'Us.' She looked at me. 'I didn't mean it, of course. I wasn't going to turn up. I knew what he was, by then. And the next thing I heard –'

'Polneath was on fire again.'

We sat silent. The only sound was the dog, pattering about the kitchen, the scratching of claw on stone.

She looked at me. 'Tremain got what he deserved.'

He had, I thought, desperately. He had meant to kill her, and instead had let William burn. Surely he had deserved to burn in his turn . . . but I had helped Edward. I had helped him to be rid of his father. When all the time, he was no better.

I had been deceived, all those years ago. For all these years.

'And I? Did I get what I deserved?' I was trying to control my voice.

But she could see my disbelief, and she turned even more defiant, though the shake in her speech betrayed her words. 'I never lied.'

'But Edward wasn't forcing you.'

And then she was scornful once more, dropped her hands, gave a bitter laugh. 'Oh, your sort,' she said, 'you think force must always mean fists –' And she stopped. Perhaps she sensed it.

My rage, barely contained.

I felt cold. Perhaps, even now, Edward was at the house. Mrs Fossett begging his pardon, asking him to repeat his name.

I met Agnes's eyes. 'He's been asking about you. I've been

writing to him,' I said, acidly. 'Edward. And visiting. Since Richard has been ill.'

I saw her face open in dismay. In fear.

'You'd have gone,' she said. 'You'd have gone from Polneath, if I'd told you what he really was. And I would have been alone with them –' She stopped. 'You had sway with Boscawen.'

'I wouldn't have left you,' I said; but I didn't know, as I said it, whether it was true.

Something passed across her face – anger, or guilt – but when she spoke again, her voice was inscrutable. 'All these years,' she said, 'he's never found me. He's even been to Boscawen, asking, but he never told. I've kept safe.' She smoothed the counter with her hand.

I got up, abruptly, startling the dog. I steadied myself on the table. I could not think. Not about Agnes, not now. All I could think about was getting home. I hurried out, down the dark passage to the front door, but I couldn't fathom how to open it.

Agnes was limping after me.

'You needn't keep up the money,' she was saying, though she sounded worried, now. 'I take sewing in. Jim brings in a little . . .'

I stepped out into the night, my coat unbuttoned. The click of my heels echoed in the street. Glancing back, I saw the square of yellow in which Agnes stood. I kept going.

That last afternoon came into my head, after the inquest was concluded. When I had found Edward, on the terrace at Polneath. How he had looked at me: as though, I now realized, he was expecting to see someone else.

There was still more than an hour until the last train. I stepped in at a hotel, and my grey hair and smiling did the trick, and the manager telephoned to Murray to say that I'd be coming off the eight o'clock. Murray said that he'd come for me at the station himself.

I was glad of that. I could not have faced Jake.

I walked down towards the water. All the warships sat out there in the dark; muffled calls and the sound of rigging. A couple occupied a bench, she half inside his coat, and I gave them a wide berth. I took a bench that was further along. It was just about warm enough to keep still.

I knew I should not have frightened Agnes. Saying that Edward had been asking after her. But to be so long, so very long deceived. And she had uttered not one word of remorse.

How eager Edward had been, when I had sent him my condolences, told him Richard was ill. No doubt he was thinking of Richard's money, and his files, too. A fortune, perhaps. A son, at last, to replace the lost ones.

I watched the lights on the water, and thought for a while about how cold it would be. Then I saw a bright square lying in the dirt. I picked it up. It was a postcard, blank, showing the great bridge with its two spans. I had often seen the view before from the train, and thought that the bridge looked very much like how a life feels, marked by incident. How there is everything before, and then there is everything after.

My heart was slowing, my hands were cold. What if Edward *had* gone on to the house? What if he'd seen Richard?

Richard.

All these years he had been helping Agnes, and never said a word. Trying to atone, for that second verdict. Trying to atone for helping me.

Finally, I pulled my eyes from the dark water, and hurried to the station. Not knowing, when I reached home, whom I might find there.

25.

Murray was waiting in the motor at Truro station when I came off the late train. I looked about the station approach, half expecting to see Edward, but there was only Murray. It being my third day in the same stockings, I was wary of getting into the warm closed space with him.

Once he had shut his door, I said, 'Forgive me, Murray, I ought to have asked Feltham, but –'

'Not at all,' he said, quickly. And then, 'Better that Feltham wasn't troubled, he's been for the doctor today already.' He didn't say it reproachfully. Only worry marked his face.

My mouth felt dry. 'Is Richard worse?'

Murray hesitated. 'Mrs Fossett seems to think there's a temperature.'

He made no move to pull away from the kerb. The motor smelled of the good dinner he had probably sat down to, not three hours ago. He shifted his grip on the steering wheel. 'I ought to mention, ah, Mr Edward Tremain was here.'

I kept still in my seat. 'Oh?' I said, carefully.

'He must have taken a cab from the station. I was out with the dogs, he stopped and put out his head. He'd called at your house, I think.'

'I see,' I said, lightly, 'how odd. I wonder what was the matter.'

Murray flicked me a quick glance sideways. 'He said he was looking for you. He seemed in rather a stew. I said I understood from Mrs Fossett that you'd gone up to London. He said quite so, and that he'd seen you there, and that you'd come down again together, but that he thought he'd seen you get off at Plymouth.' Murray kept his eyes carefully away from mine.

Edward had seen me, then?

Murray cleared his throat. 'He said that you seemed rather

upset. He seemed to know about – that is, about Mrs Smith. He seemed worried. And . . . well, the long and short of it is, I'm afraid I gave him the Smiths' address.'

I felt something go cold inside me.

Edward had not come to St Rumon's for me. He must have guessed, when I had first told him, who Mrs Smith might be. Then he had seen me getting off at Plymouth, and put two and two together . . . He had not come to St Rumon's looking for me. It was Agnes he wanted to find. Agnes, and her son.

Murray was saying that he was terribly sorry, he knew it was indiscreet. He'd thought there was another up train, that Mr Tremain could get back to Plymouth tonight, to look for me, although he'd remembered, once they'd parted ways, that they'd changed the timetable so Mr Tremain would be having to wait over to the morning.

'I dare say he took a hotel room,' Murray said. 'And then of course you telephoned, and . . .' He glanced at me again. 'Clearly, I needn't have worried. I know I oughtn't to have, please forgive me, Mrs Boscawen.'

'No,' I said. 'You mustn't apologize, Murray.'

'Would you like me to ask at the station hotel? That's very likely where he's gone – I could tell him you're safe?'

'No,' I said, quickly.

Murray stared rather.

'But I would like to send a wire. To Plymouth. The police station will do it.'

If Murray was shocked, he concealed it well. As he drove the short way, peering through his spectacles to see the dark road, I found an old receipt in my bag; Murray directed me to the glove box for a pencil.

When we pulled up at the police station, I passed him the scrap. 'Say it's for Richard, if there's any bother.'

When he came back, he nodded, and we set off for St Rumon's in silence. Murray drove carefully, hunched over the wheel. I kept my eyes fixed on the lane ahead, illuminated by the white shock of the headlamps for a few feet. Beyond was darkness.

I knew that my message would have left him wondering.

Suddenly, Murray said, 'I feel badly, Mrs Boscawen. I wish there was something I might do, to make it up.'

'You already have,' I said. I swallowed, watching the trees bleached in the light. Then I said, 'Do you remember that business at Polneath, Murray?'

Murray hesitated, nodded in the dark. 'I was William Tremain's age,' he said, lightly, nervously. 'My mother was terribly odd about matches and so on, afterwards.'

I made some vague sound. Suddenly I felt quite exhausted, could not have begun to explain. Did not wish to explain, to comfortable Murray, with his dogs and his pipe and his lovely children.

At the house, he pulled up at the hedge.

I made to get out, and Murray came round to hold the door. 'You'll be alright?'

I nodded. He shut the door, and when he had walked back around to his own side, I said, 'Murray.'

He looked at me.

'It wasn't what we thought,' I said, 'with Mrs Smith.'

I watched him drive off. I let myself in at the front of the house, and Jake came out from the kitchen. The hall was dark.

'Thank God,' he said.

I watched him take in my dishevelment.

'Come in to the fire.'

Low coals settled in the grate. The relief of stepping into the clean, warm, ordered kitchen was beyond anything.

Jake stayed standing. 'Mr Tremain tried to get in to see the master,' he said. 'But Mrs Fossett wasn't having it.'

She appeared in the doorway. 'I think he's out of the woods for tonight,' she said to Jake. She wouldn't look at me.

Jake picked up his cap, which was lying on the table. 'I'll come back, first thing.'

To Mrs Fossett, I said, 'Is he asleep?'

'Not yet, madam.' She had gone to fold a dishcloth and hang it straight.

'You did right, this evening,' I said, to her, loud enough for Jake to hear. 'If he ever comes again, we are not at home.'

She looked at me, and gave one small nod.

Upstairs, Richard was subtly changed, as though something heavy had pressed him ever so slightly flatter and more deeply into the mattress. He opened his eyes and blinked heavily. His face was flushed, his breathing ragged.

'I understand you've been frightening everyone,' I said.

'Fuss over nothing,' he said, but then he began to cough.

I went to him and held him while he coughed, felt it subside.

'How was Edith?' he said.

'Well. And all the children are well.' I perched on the side of the bed. 'I'm sorry for rushing off. I had a fancy to go, that's all . . .'

'Don't be sorry,' said Richard. 'It's wretched for you here.' He tried to roll over, and I helped him. His eyelids were dropping with tiredness. 'Mrs Fossett said. There was a visitor. While you were out.'

I swallowed, and told yet another lie. 'Murray came.'

Richard looked at me. 'He's a good man, Murray.'

'Yes.' I smoothed his counterpane. 'I went to look at the Polneath woods, a week or two ago,' I said. 'There've been poachers in.'

'I know,' Richard said. Then he breathed, rested, and went on. 'I walked there. Quite a bit. Most days. When Tim died.' He stopped again to rest. I waited. 'I ought to've . . . done something, with them.'

'I thought you were always in Falmouth,' I said. 'You know. At the club.'

Richard gingerly shook his head. 'I couldn't bear the way they would talk. About the casualties.' He looked at me, then, mimicking a stuffy voice, '"Not too bad this week, eh?"' He shook his head, which made him cough again. When it subsided, he said, 'And even the ones that weren't like that . . . I just couldn't bear to hear. About the casualties. For any longer than I had to.'

I looked at him. 'But you –' I broke off.

He knew what I was thinking of: how he'd had me read them for him, every morning, for so long after Tim.

He looked down at his hands on the counterpane. 'Forgive me, my dear,' he said. 'The print really was too small.' He looked up at me. 'I thought we might find Tim,' he said, quietly. 'You do hear of it. The family get a telegram. The accounts of it are muddled, somehow. A boy turns up wounded, who has already been mourned –' He stopped. 'I suppose, because there was never a body, I couldn't quite . . . but I know it was foolish. He's gone. He took himself off.'

We looked at one another, then, for perhaps a full minute. It was the sort of look that could only ever have belonged to those very last days.

'I'm so sorry, my dear,' I said.

He looked at me. 'Whatever for?'

I looked at my hands. 'I fussed too much. I smothered him, and you were always telling me not to, and it made him –'

But Richard was shaking his head. He set up coughing, recovered himself. 'Boys die,' he said. 'In wars.' Then he reached for his bedside table, for some papers that were lying there. 'I've this to show you,' he said. 'Came yesterday.' He took a painful breath. 'It's a list,' he said. 'His regiment. Addresses . . .'

'Hush,' I said. 'It'll keep. We'll look at it tomorrow, when you're feeling better.'

'Tomorrow,' he said, in a wondering way, like a little child who has no sense of how far off that might be. He closed his eyes for a full minute, and I thought he had fallen asleep. But then he opened them again. Looked me in the eye. 'I would still do the same,' he said. 'If it were all to do again.' Then he commenced coughing.

'Hush,' I said, 'hush.' I held both his hands, and then I told him he should rest. I told him I would stay until he had dropped off.

He closed his eyes. Gradually, I felt his grip relax, felt his tortured breathing deepen.

I thought of my message being tapped out along the wires.

ET WILL COME TOMORROW. COME TO ST RUMON'S AT EARLIEST CONVENIENCE. BRING JIM. TAKE CARE AT STATION. IB.

I thought of Edward, in Truro, near at hand. Gone to ground.

I had always thought that people could be fathomed. I thought their depths could be plumbed by looking into their eyes, by how kind they were to children, dogs, servants. But horses had loved Edward. He had been a doting father.

26.

Agnes turned up the next day – safe, thank God – with her son. It was just after luncheon. I was almost surprised to see them appear at the gate. The lean young man, and the middle-aged woman, out of doors on a biting winter's day in her shapeless coat. I had worried that, after the day before, Agnes would ignore my message.

But here she was.

Jake was off behind the house, dismantling some part of the motor, and Fossett had gone into the village, so it was Mrs Fossett who answered the bell. I came into the hall as she was stepping back to allow Agnes across the mat. It was clear that she recognized her, that lost soul she had taken in here, after the inquest. But she said nothing, only offered tea.

Agnes shook her head. 'No need. I won't stay long.'

I took her into the conservatory. Before she had sat down, I explained about Murray's slip. I watched her as she digested what it meant. All these years of concealment, and now Edward Tremain knew exactly where they lived.

We looked out of the window at her son, smoking by the hedge. He did have the look of Edward, now one thought of it. The unruly hair, that carelessness in the limbs. Clever hands. I had been relieved when she hadn't brought him in.

'*He* doesn't know,' she said.

I wondered what he thought was going on. He thought Richard was his father, most likely. As I almost had.

'Perhaps a hotel in Falmouth for a few days,' I said. 'Wait out Christmas. I should think Edward will be gone north by now, but you mustn't chance it.'

Agnes raised her eyebrows.

I took an envelope out of my pocket, and pushed it across the table towards her. The Polneath woods wouldn't be worth, now, what they once had been; since the war, there was too much land, and not enough people. So I had invented another, better sum with Murray, early that morning. I had explained to him, explained it properly, as I had failed to do the night before.

He had been shocked, of course. But I knew I could trust him to be discreet.

In the envelope was a banker's draft. Not made out to James, but to Agnes. If the will had been Richard's notion of justice, then this, now, was mine.

Agnes looked at the draft, and swallowed, twice. At last she put it away, and looked at me. 'I still think of William,' she said.

I smiled. 'His room,' I said. 'All the little books. That bear with the white eye.'

'I changed that eye,' she said. 'One fell out, and I let him pick a new one.' She touched the pocket where she had tucked the banker's draft. 'Sometimes I think, if only I hadn't moved bedrooms,' she said. Looked at me. 'It was I insisted on that. I didn't want Will knowing. Worrying. Though I think he caught wind that something was wrong, in any case –' She stopped. 'I never meant you harm, you know. But he was clever, Edward. The yellow nightshirt, the shape in the gun room, that stuff in my food. That was never his father. It was all him. Mrs Bly cleaning up after him, I'd wager. He wanted people to think me mad . . .' She paused. 'Nearly managed it, too. And every night I knew it was only that locked door between me and him. Well. The door, and you.'

I looked out through the glass. At the end of the path, Jim was treading on a cigarette end, and then he looked around, picked it up, and pocketed it. He looked nervous of the neat garden.

'I thought you might try somewhere else,' I said.

She looked down. 'Jim has friends gone to Liverpool.'

I said that sounded suitable. Then I pulled out my postcard, the one of the Plymouth bridge, and explained my scheme. Pushed a pencil across to her. When she had finished writing, I stood up.

'I ought to thank him,' she said, and nodded at the ceiling.

'He's asleep,' I replied, and then, 'I'll tell him.'

She nodded. She was looking at me, looking for something in

my face. I can only think she did not find it, for her own grew hard, as it had when I'd turned up at her house.

'I never meant you harm,' she said, again. She began to button her coat. 'I only gave you the story you wanted. I gave you the story that would make you stay.'

Out of the window, Jake appeared, holding an oily rag. He saw the man by the gate first, and stopped. Then he saw Agnes and me.

He looked at her, through the glass. Raised one black-fingered hand.

I sat in the conservatory for a time after they went, feeling the ghost of the sun on my face.

I was thinking of William Tremain. A worried little boy. Afraid of his grandfather's drinking, his rages; trying to protect Agnes. Trying to protect Edward, who ought to have been protecting him.

Down through the house in the dark. Finding Agnes's room empty, and sitting on the bed, perhaps, to wait. Hearing his grandfather below, and then those boots on the stairs. Hiding, under the bed, but then hearing not the creak of a hinge but that click of the turning key, the boots retreating, and perhaps only a moment later smelling smoke in the room. Thickening. He had yelled, at some point, beaten and caught at the door with his nails, but Mrs Bly was still heavily asleep, and Tremain retreated, to let the blaze catch a bit. Flames had followed smoke, and Will had crept beneath the bed . . .

I thought of Richard: the delicacy, the precision, the flare with which he had concluded William's inquest. He has always said that it matters, how you tell things. The order in which you tell them.

Now I must tell myself that Tremain may not have meant to kill William, but he meant to kill, and kill he did.

That is all I have left, now, to defend what I did in my turn.

27.

1888

I could not believe that the vicar had congratulated us. Us: myself and Boscawen. Who, frowning, had gone off to have a word with the constable, and see about hearing from the jury and pronouncing the verdict. The Reverend Green had gone with him, while Father had installed himself on the bench beneath the consulting room window, leaving the garden gate open for Agnes and me. There was a rushing sound in my ears, like the tide going out, like a sudden wind dying in a mass of branches.

I turned to Agnes. 'Mr Boscawen will write to your aunt,' I said. And then, 'Come. We mustn't keep Mrs Fossett waiting.'

Boscawen's housekeeper was in the kitchen with Mrs Humphrey, and we were overtaken then by their questions and Agnes's low answers. No, she was not cold. No, she was not hungry. Yes, she was very tired.

Soon, I went back out to Father, and we watched Agnes and the housekeeper set out on the short, steep walk to Boscawen's house. The gate swinging shut behind them, the roses looking like twigs stuck upright in the mud. Men were coming already out of the inn, a flood of them: including Edward, steering Tremain by the elbow. The constable helped Tremain up into the gig, and then spoke to Edward. I willed Edward to look in my direction, but he did not. Then he was climbing up into the gig, and it was pulling away.

'You ought to be indoors,' I said to Father.

In the parlour, Father sat by the fire with a blanket tucked around his knees, me by the window. I wanted to put my face against the panes, but refrained.

That was everything done. Tremain finished, the mills finished. My new life, about to begin.

'I must confess,' Father said, 'I'm mightily relieved. Though it was indiscreet of the Reverend to refer to it so publicly. Still, I suppose, no harm.'

I looked out of the window for a moment, at the sleeping garden, at Mrs Mason flopping a dishcloth out of the door of the inn, and felt a rush of anger.

'He really is a good fellow, Ivy.'

'I should think he's very pleased,' I replied, 'with what he thinks he's bought.'

'Ivy!' Father was blinking frailly. He hesitated. 'I wouldn't wish for you to agree to anything which was quite against your wishes,' he said, the tendons of his neck stretching as he swallowed. For a moment he looked like nothing so much as a baby bird I had found once, which had fallen from its nest into the lane, so that all one could make out was a mess of feathers. A wide, hungry mouth.

I ran upstairs. I sat on my bed, which creaked in that old way, that same counterpane with the blue flowers. The bed ought to have seemed large, after four nights in William's, but in fact it felt narrow, girlish.

I oughtn't to have upset Father. I wouldn't have, had I not felt so guilty. About my plan.

Now I had to keep still, somehow, until morning. But the old tasks I had found before – sewing, preserving, helping Mrs Humphrey tidy out a cupboard – seemed invented, suddenly. I thought of Tremain, lunging for Agnes. Would he go to prison? Would he hang? Edward would not shelter him, at least. But I knew that the outcome would be different for Tremain than it might have been for Agnes. Some old acquaintance would take pity on him, and he would have a sunny bench, a pint of small beer, to aid his sinking into regret.

He would be allowed to live. Not like William, pinched out like any small light.

I read something for an hour, some novel Edith had lent me, which I had been in two minds about going on with. At length I found that I was reading a paragraph and, the sense escaping me, reading it again. I put it aside.

Below, in the kitchen, I could hear Mrs Humphrey, moving things about. I thought of how she would be, faced with a wedding. The delighted grumbling, the lists, the long conversations about how on earth one could go about keeping that quantity of strawberries cool.

I would not bear it.

I got up from the chair. I still had my boots on. My coat was hanging in the hall by the kitchen, but I could go out at the front. I tried to keep my boots quiet on the stairs, but Mrs Humphrey came out, drying her hands.

'Going out?'

'I ought to fetch my things.'

'Shouldn't you leave them to themselves?' she said. And then, 'Couldn't Jake go?'

She was working the cloth between her fingers, looking at me shrewdly. 'We saw Mr Edward's fiancée come through, Christmas afternoon,' she said. 'Yellow hair. That's who Mrs Mason said it was.'

But I was already out of the door, mumbling something about not being long.

'Coat!' Mrs Humphrey said.

I was halfway up the garden path. I didn't turn back, though I half expected Mrs Humphrey to follow me, or Father. I walked too quickly, sent my breath ragged.

But when I glanced back at the turn of the lane, there was nobody behind me. And that was when the cold struck me, very suddenly through the thin sleeves of my blouse. Out on the estuary, the rust-headed ducks took fright at something and lifted, wings whirring, the mass of them moving and settling. I stopped at the jetty. My blouse was a yellow one. In the dark water, I made a pale ghost.

What was I doing? The morning was what we had agreed, I ought to wait until then. After today, how could Edward think of love? But I couldn't help but go, my feet and legs were taking me, for with him now was where I ought to be. And it was not only that, not quite. It was a feeling. A bad feeling. As though, if I did not go to Polneath, something terrible was going to happen.

It was windy, another windy day. I had no hat on. I half ran up through the woods, my chest tight, jumped as a pigeon clattered from the rhododendrons, but it was not until I had reached the blast wall that I saw the smoke. Owls were calling. I had never heard them call so loud. The black wall in front of me, and a glimpse above it of the Polneath rooftop, and above that, smoke. Not from the chimneys. Then I smelled it, here and then gone.

Burning.

At the gap in the blast wall, I saw that one of the upper windows, Tremain's bedroom window, was an orange mass. The window was open, as he always left it, and flames licked out of the gaping casement.

And someone, some dark figure was crouched on the gravel of the terrace below. Edward.

My first feeling was the rush of relief, that he was out. There was flickering light in the windows above Tremain's. Soon it would be in the roof.

I did not call out to Edward. I had a feeling that he shouldn't be startled. But I ran around the pond. Mrs Bly was back at the King's Arms. There was no one else but Edward, and Tremain . . .

When Edward heard the crunch of gravel, he straightened, and saw me. Looked at me strangely. Then, his face crumpling, tears came.

That was when I knew for certain that Tremain was still inside. 'What happened?' I said.

How soon would someone else see the smoke? How soon would someone come?

'He must have knocked his candle,' Edward gulped, and swayed towards me. 'He'd bolted a bottle of whisky. We quarrelled,' he said. 'I had to lock him in.'

I swallowed, and swallowed again.

Edward's face was white, his eyes like dark marbles on linen.

'I'll have to go in,' I said. 'One of us must . . . they mustn't find the key.'

But he opened his hand, and there it was. The large crude Polneath key, which William had hidden away.

I looked up at the window.

Smoke was churning out. I wondered whether I could hear shouting. I decided that I could not. My mind was spinning and spinning and working.

'Edward,' I said. 'Edward, people will be coming. They'll see the smoke. I'll have to run down to the lodge.'

He looked quite lost, like a child. He was waiting to see what I would do. I could have run to the lodge, could have run to the lodge then, and left him there, the key in his hand.

But I did not.

I took the key from him, and looked up at Tremain's window to judge the place. I dropped the key in the gravel a few feet from the wall. Then I took Edward's hand, pulled him towards the north wing. I opened the door, and almost thought I heard the distant stir of the fire as it enjoyed the new draught.

Mrs Bly had cleaned most of the house in the days since William's death, but Tremain's office was still soot and ashes. Carefully I blackened my fingertips, and in the dimness, I dirtied Edward's face, his neck, the white of his shirt. I took his hands and put them on the grey of the desk. He kept quite limp, like a child being dressed. When I led him back outside, I helped him to sit with his back against the wall. Now he looked like someone who had attempted a hopeless rescue.

From inside, there came the sound of timber falling.

By the time I brought the lodge keeper and his son back to find Edward slumped and smudged outside the north wing door, the smoke was coming more thickly above the facade. The boy was sent running up to Boscawen's for more help, though it was clear now that it was hopeless.

'I only came back for my bag,' I said, to no one.

The lodge keeper went in, but was soon out again, coughing. To keep himself occupied, he tried to salvage things, emerged from the French doors with a carriage clock. Having rescued it, he didn't seem to know what to do next. He set it in the gravel, and stood back, to watch the burning.

Soon, other men arrived. There was running, and hopeless calling.

I stood near where Edward sat, a good distance from the key. He did not look at me. He looked as though his mind had vacated his body. If I had spoken to him, I don't believe he would have known me. At least now, I thought, he will be free.

The bright, clean horror of the flames increased. It was strangely pleasant to stand close enough to feel their heat. Though it was early, the day was beginning to fade, and there was a thin early moon, dancing in the smoke.

Then Boscawen was there. He had changed his shirt, as though he came to watch his neighbours' houses burn down every night of the year, and it was important to be well dressed for the occasion. He was very calm, and gave out orders.

He came to where I was standing, and, as though following a direction hissed from offstage, he shrugged himself out of his coat, and helped me on with it. It contained his warmth, and I began to shiver.

'I came back to fetch my bag,' I said.

'Of course,' said Boscawen. Nobody was missing but Tremain, he went on. The other men had gone to damp the rooves of the mills, in case of sparks. But it was a windy night. The risk was great. We ought not to stay much longer.

Boscawen was looking at Edward.

'Father ought to see him,' I said.

'I'll see he's put up at the King's Arms,' Boscawen replied. 'Perhaps your father would care to step over in an hour or so.'

'Sir,' said the lodge keeper. He crunched towards us.

In the house, there was the sound of shattering glass.

'Sir – key, sir –' He opened his palm. 'On the ground, just over there.'

Boscawen put out his hand for it, thanked him. Looked at the key. Looked up at the open window. Looked at me, in the dreadful orange light.

28.

Polneath House was abandoned that day to the flames.

For William's inquest, rather than decide between manslaughter and murder, Richard had returned a narrative verdict. The verdict had contained enough for men to come the next morning from Truro to fetch Tremain. But by the time they arrived, the fire had taken him, and the constables were pressed instead into helping the mill workers to fight the blaze.

The weather had remained dry overnight, with a fair wind, and sparks had soon begun to lift from the roof timbers to float and light upon the flimsy rooves of the mills. The blast wall had been intended to protect the house from the mills – never the other way around. The house burned so fiercely that it had to be left alone for two nights, and men worked in shifts to damp the mill rooves.

Once it was safe to go into the house, bones were discovered in Tremain's locked bedroom, just beside the door.

William's funeral took place on the 30th, when the house had hardly finished smouldering. The church was splendid with white camellias. Everyone was there, except Richard, and Edward of course. Father said he had been summoned to Falmouth, where, the weather having improved, Richard was hearing Tremain's inquest with a fresh jury.

Richard padded it to the better part of a day, as I have said, with the state of the roof timbers, the dead man's drinking. But the salient facts can only have taken minutes, and in any case were generally known: the state of the mills' finances, the scandal of Agnes Draper. The open window, and the key in the gravel below. The verdict returned as suicide, though a rumour got about, that Will's ghost had come back itself and locked his grandfather's door.

After William's funeral, I stayed at home, helping Mrs Humphrey with all the small chores which had fallen behind in the days I had been at Polneath. Under her watchful eye I hoped, every day, that Edward would be coming for me.

On the first day of the new year, I watched from the parlour window as the Reverend Green and Father and Jake gathered at first light to bury Tremain. No Edward. Afterwards, Richard came with Father from the churchyard to our front door. I heard Father going upstairs, and then Mrs Humphrey came in, to say that Mr Boscawen was here to see me. I went out into the hall, and stared at the buttons on his coat while he said some words, felt myself nod.

Edward had gone. Left me, without a word. Now I had to act as would best provide for Father, and for myself.

Richard arranged everything. He arranged for our banns to be read, and for a junior man from Truro to take on some of Father's patients. Tremain was declared bankrupt, and at the spring auction, Richard lifted his hand on Polneath – the burned-out house, the mills amongst which the weeds would soon be starting, the unsold powder packed tight into its magazine amongst the singed trees.

One or two of the mills had caught, though the thick walls of the expense magazine had done their job. But Tremain's old customers did not want the powder. There had never been a question over quality before, but suddenly, no one was keen. It was as though some taint hung over it. The powder sat six months after we were married, until Richard, worried that it would get damp and make a hazard, arranged for some men from the mills on the other side of Truro to come collect it, free of charge. It would be washed through, and remilled, nothing wasted; those components one would have thought would remain mixed forever becoming their separate selves again.

I suppose it might have been reasonable to assume that the powder would go up. Neither an inquest nor a private mind is proof against such easy plots, and both Edward and Agnes, I see now, knew well how to exploit them. Old stories. That a good woman, it follows, is helpless. That a bad one always wants more than she is given. That we deserve the things that happen to us.

Richard mentioned, a year or two ago, that Mrs Bly had taken up residence in the Truro almshouses, so I asked Jake, yesterday, to take me into town. I wanted to see her, now that I know everything; wanted to ask her questions, different questions than I had asked her before.

In town, I despatched Jake for an hour and went to enquire, only to discover that Mrs Bly had died, quite lately, of the influenza that has been so bad this winter.

I found myself out on the street. With time to spare, I strolled down to the docks, when I saw, coming down by the haberdashers, Theo Stainforth. With a lady, and a perambulator. He looked rather uncertain, but greeted me warmly. His wife was sensible-looking, with great blue eyes and a pointed chin, which seemed to have been inherited by their little girl, who was sitting upright on her cushions and babbling as her father made the introductions.

Theo's wife seemed to recognize my name. She thanked me for my generous gift; then she glanced at Theo, and offered me her condolences. I thanked her, and said, 'He was very peaceful, at the end.' I peered into the perambulator. 'What a lovely child.'

After I had asked one or two questions about teething, Theo gave his wife a look; the baby had begun, conveniently, to grizzle.

'I shall walk her on,' his wife said.

'I'll catch you up, my dear.'

In a moment, Theo turned to me and said, 'How are you bearing up, Mrs Boscawen? I felt rather dreadful, springing all that on you, when we last met. Anna says I oughtn't – that is, I think I was still –' He stopped.

'You mustn't worry,' I said. 'In fact, I . . . I had a visit, recently. From his batman. Davies. Did you meet him?'

Theo frowned. 'I don't recall.'

I gestured to the iron railing shielding the water's edge, and together we leaned on it. Theo's wife had settled upon a bench along the quay, and kept glancing in our direction. His hand was shaking slightly, and it made me think of Father.

'The fact is,' I said, 'it wasn't what we thought, with Tim.'

Stainforth looked at me. I reminded him about the pair of Germans, told him that they had been left alive out beyond the wire. Described the desperate compassionate chance Tim had taken.

'So he did not mean to die,' Theo said.

I looked at the water. 'No. Although, the more I have thought about it, the more I think . . . it would have been a terrible pity. But no disgrace.'

Theo looked at me. 'I quite agree.'

I was quiet a moment. There was a boat just getting in. I watched a man on deck throw a rope which was caught on shore.

Stainforth put his hand in his pocket. 'I'm simply relieved that –'

'He was not suffering.'

'Exactly.' Theo Stainforth looked out over the water. 'We were very great friends,' he said. 'In school.'

'I know you were,' I replied.

I took my leave of Theo Stainforth, and watched him walk along to his wife, and them together lift the baby out of the carriage to see the boats.

Richard lived three weeks after Agnes Draper came to see me. He slept a great deal. His breathing was painful to hear. On Christmas Day, he barely woke at all, although when I made him stir to be fed a poached egg, he noticed that I was wearing his ring, and he lifted his eyebrows at that, and smiled.

I saw in the New Year quietly, and then, on Twelfth Night, took down the garlands. There was a gap inside me then which I could not touch, could not look at, where Edward had been.

To have been, my whole life, deceived; to have been close, so close, to evil. I feared he would write, or turn up even; the last sight I'd had of him had been through the window of the train, as I crouched on the platform at Plymouth station. The inscrutable smudge of his face. But there was only silence. I was grateful at least that I had found out, by a hair's breadth, in time.

At the last, Richard rallied.

Every day, I had been reading to him, asleep or awake, until my throat tasted of metal. Until one day, when he seemed alert, I glanced up at the end of a paragraph, and saw that he was looking at me.

'My dear,' he said. 'Might you ask –' he breathed – 'Murray to step round? I ought to –' And he stopped, began to reach and shuffle amongst the small pile of papers at his bedside, which had not been moved.

'Let me do that,' I said. And then, 'But why do you need Murray?'

He looked at me.

I put the bookmark in its place. It was one of those still, cold nights.

At last, he said, 'Do you remember Agnes Draper?'

I looked away from him, and put the book down. 'My dear?' I said.

'Yes?'

'Before Christmas, when I went to see Edith . . .'

His face showed nothing. 'Yes?'

'On the way back, I . . . I broke my journey at Plymouth.'

Now he looked at his hands. 'Ah.' He met my eyes.

'Why didn't you say?' I said.

'Because –' He lost his breath, and tried again, 'You'd *know*.'

And I understood, of course I did. If he had been hiding Agnes Draper, he could only have been hiding her from Edward. We would have had to speak of it all. Everything that Edward had done. Including what I had helped him to do, and Richard had concealed. The only stain on an otherwise spotless career.

'He'd gone,' Richard said. 'I didn't think . . . it mattered.' His hand had crept to mine, across the counterpane. It was freckled from old sun, contained wasted strength.

'But that same day,' I continued, 'when I came home from Plymouth, and a man had called at the house.' I kept my eyes on his hand. 'That wasn't Murray.'

Richard looked at me, stirred in the bed, but I patted his hand.

'It's alright,' I said. 'It's alright. I know now. That's what matters.'

Richard looked at me. 'But Miss Draper. And the boy. Should be,' he said, 'taken care of.'

I smiled. 'I've done it,' I said. 'Murray and I between us.' I told him how we had arrived at the sum, and the rest of the scheme.

Richard's hand, over mine, relaxed.

But then he began to fidget again, amongst those bedside papers. 'This came,' he said. 'Before Christmas. I tried to –'

I took it from him. It was a list.

'Tim's regiment,' he said.

There was Tim's name, a cross beside it, with the date he had died, and our address; Davies's name, and an address in Bristol, no cross of course, nor date. A dozen other names, some marked with crosses. And there was the sergeant, Fred Campbell. An address in Scotland. A cross, and a date, only a few days after Tim's.

Despite all I had learned about Edward, despite all that Agnes Draper had told me, my first thought was that whoever had copied the list must have made a mistake. Because I had met Fred Campbell. Fred Campbell was not dead. He had sat at a table with me at the Grand Hotel, tilted his glass to drain out the last drop of cider.

And then I knew. I knew the last of what Edward had done.

'I thought we could write to some of them together,' Richard was saying. Then he touched my arm. 'Don't cry, my dear.' He took my hand, and folded it up in his own. 'I've always been of the opinion that one can only really try to get more right than one gets wrong.' He dropped his voice, squeezed my hand, and then he said, 'My dear. Thomas Tremain was no loss to the world.'

I stared at him, astonished. We sat, holding hands, until I had recovered myself.

At last, I said, 'Another letter's come, about that memorial. What I thought was, I could read it to you, and then in a day or two I could draft something for your signature.'

He nodded and smiled his thanks. I could see he was tiring.

I went to my room – to Tim's room – and stood at the window; thinking, in a day or two, he will be gone. And I began to remember things.

Things I had forgotten, or chosen to forget.

★

Our banns were not yet read. Richard had come to dine with Father and myself. Father had stepped out for a moment, to look out rather a nice bottle, which he had been saving.

Richard straightened his cutlery, and said, 'It's not too late, you know.'

He looked firm, ready to take a blow, and yet under that – what? Quite soft, flinching. I looked at him a minute. It was impossible to pretend I did not know what he meant.

'Thank you,' I said, 'but it is.'

'The inquest is finished, now. That's over. You ought not to think of it any more.'

The clock on the mantelpiece ticked. I could hear Father clanking bottles in the cellar.

'Where did you put Miss Draper?' I asked.

'Her aunt says she can stay there until the child is born.'

'And then?'

He waved his hand. 'I'm sure she can be found a good position.'

I touched my empty glass. 'And the child?'

'The aunt hasn't room.' Richard looked at me. 'I thought, St Margaret's,' he said.

I could hear Father coming back with his bottle, humming to himself.

'If I am to keep to my side of the bargain,' I said, quietly, 'you might try a little harder to keep to yours.'

And then, we had been married a few months. Richard had counselled Mrs Humphrey through the demands of the wedding breakfast, and he had taken me to Bournemouth and then to London. He was very gentle in Bournemouth, and let me walk on the beach alone as much as I liked; in London, he let the company of others soften the shock of our new state.

We had come back to St Rumon's, and I had concentrated all my will upon settling. I hadn't asked again about Agnes. The truth was, I didn't feel as sorry for her as I did for myself. But I was resolved to settle, I was resolved to be happy, when one day, Edward Tremain came to the house.

It was a Thursday. I only knew he was there because I happened to see the back of his head from the window of Tim's room. It was not yet Tim's room, of course, just a small guest room. I was in there, making a list of what ought to be done to turn it into a serviceable nursery, when I saw the back of Edward's head, foreshortened as he strode away.

Had he come for me? Come for me, at last? I could not restrain myself: I went straight down to Richard's study.

He was quiet, and pacing.

'What did he want?' I said. The words were offhand enough, but my face must have given me away.

'He was asking after Agnes Draper,' Richard snapped. He turned away to fill his pen.

Even then, I didn't see; thought Edward felt only a decent concern for his little half-brother or -sister, for the girl his father had wronged.

'And what did you tell him?'

'That Miss Draper wishes to be left alone.' Richard looked at me. 'As do we all.'

That night, at bedtime, I was cold with Richard.

And then there was the next night, and every night after.

It was an unremarkable day in the middle of January when I woke, and missed the sound of Richard's breath in the house. I had been in to turn down his lamp the night before.

'Need anything?' I asked.

'No.'

'Comfortable?'

'Yes.'

'I've written,' I said, 'to some of the men from your list.'

'Oh?'

'Nothing back yet.' I looked at him, at his eyes, wandering like a child's. 'Goodnight, then.'

'Goodnight, Ivy.'

That struck me, even at the time, for he so seldom called me by my name.

I woke in the chill dark of the next morning, entirely alert, though it was nowhere near my usual hour for tea, and I could hear Mrs Fossett weeping downstairs.

When light came, there was a rare hard frost down. There were comings and goings, but for myself I had an empty, holiday feeling, such as I had only known when Tim was very small, and I would take him to a shingly piece of sea. Richard working, and only the aimless time to fill, with the wind and shore and the tottering, unseeing figure in gum boots and little coat. Myself, with half an eye on the waves.

The first day was like that. I simply went about the house, picking things up and putting them down. A glass ashtray. A pair of spectacles.

Once or twice, I stood at the door of the sickroom, which Mrs Fossett had moved through, leaving behind her a white starched sheet, stretched tight, and fresh flowers in the bedside vase.

29.

I chose to arrange Richard's funeral flowers myself. The day before the service, I walked along to the church. Silently, as always, I raised my eyes to the little carved head above the porch entry, and opened the inner door. The smell was of damp cloth, and the hassocks stuffed with horsehair, and old wax.

Jake had found white camellias from somewhere. That, and a quantity of ivy, and had left it piled on the chancel steps. I separated what I needed for the altar and the lectern. Up in the sacristy would be the basket with twine, scissors, bits of wire. Outside, a blackbird let out one, long phrase of song, and suddenly I was thinking of my wedding day. My frock was not black and winter weight, but white and filmy. I held the flowers in the crook of my elbow, and gooseflesh stood out on my arms. I found myself looking up, at that same angel upon which I had gazed as a girl. Either falling or flying: it had never been possible to tell.

'Ivy?'

I must have been standing stock-still. I turned.

It was Edith, advancing towards me, frowning in concern. I had dropped some of the flowers, and three or four had broken.

'My dear.' She took my cold hands. 'I thought,' she said, 'since you paid *me* a visit unannounced –' She took me in a tight embrace.

And I let myself be looser, and lean on her a little.

Edith stayed, for Richard's funeral. She took over from the Fossetts, and helped with everything. With Jake, she was warm and ordinary. She helped me with my correspondence, took down one to the *Herald*, about the memorial. But there were letters from everybody, as there is, after a death. I was thankful that from Edward there was nothing.

I told Edith all of it; it was a relief to do so. She listened, very quietly. She held my hand.

The morning of the funeral, we went early to the church, and she spoke to Mrs Benson about how exactly the tea should run, and gave polite answers as lady after lady in black came forward to press my arm.

'Yes, thank you,' she said, and, 'thank you, yes.'

At the front of the church was the coffin. Richard would have thought the flowers too showy, but I was proud of them.

Old Mrs Mason came over, made her way tottering with her cane, to tell me I was looking too thin. At last the organ ceased, and everyone subsided into their seats.

I had left everything to the Reverend Benson, so the hymns and psalms were entirely the ordinary ones, the no-nonsense, patriotic ones. Though I walk in the valley of the shadow of death, and so on.

When it was time to go outside, I watched Jake bearing one of the front corners of the coffin. Carefully feeding the ropes into the hole. Wind moved the yews and shook the grass on the hummocked wall. The ropes dislodged little spills of earth over the sides of the hole, which fell away into darkness.

Once everyone had followed the vicar indoors for the final hymn, I stopped in the porch, and asked Edith if I might have a moment. She went in, leaving the door an inch ajar, and I took out my handkerchief.

And there, all at once, on the steps, was Edward.

'You ought at least,' he said, his thin hair billowing and the collar of his shabby coat turned up, 'to let me explain.'

I gazed at him a moment. For a moment I felt that only while I kept silent did I hold any power. I suppose he was hoping that he could persuade me that Agnes had lied, but he must have seen, from my expression, that it was hopeless.

He took a half-step back. His hands were in his pockets, his face twisted with bitterness. For a moment I had the wild thought that he would bring out a knife, but he only shook his head.

'You're so eager to let your heart bleed for her,' he said. 'But she was ready enough, wasn't she, to let you take her fall?' When I did not answer, he looked bitterly at his feet. 'And you needn't act so righteous. It wasn't me who put that key down in the gravel.' He was shaking his head now. 'You think I'm as bad as him. But I'm not.'

Suddenly, I felt exhausted. I pulled my coat more tightly about me, against the whipping wind.

'No,' I said. 'You're worse. At least one could see him coming.'

His face fell. Perhaps it helped to be several steps above him, and, behind me, the full and silent church, who at any moment would be spilling past us.

'Give my regards,' I said, 'won't you? To Fred Campbell.'

Around us, the dead listened, separated from us only by those little stone doors.

Then all at once Edith was there, and Jake, and before long Edward was gone.

Afterwards, while Edith was still dealing with Richard's relations, I saw Jake filling in the grave. He was wearing trousers too good for the task, and his Sunday shoes. I went over.

'Didn't think we'd see him again,' he said. He kept shovelling.

'I should think that was the last time.' I paused. 'It must have been odd, before Christmas, seeing Miss Draper come to the house.'

'It's a long time ago, all that.'

'Didn't you offer to marry her? After it all happened?'

'We were good enough friends, Agnes and I,' Jake said, 'and I didn't like how she was left.' He looked at me. 'Besides, I thought I might as well ask her, since there was no other I wanted, who would have taken me.'

Carefully, I refrained from looking at him. 'You did a wonderful job finding those flowers,' I said. 'Where did you . . . ?' And I looked at him, and understood.

The Polneath glasshouse was still there, and only some of the panels gone. Inside, the abandoned camellias would be entirely out of hand.

Jake paused a moment with his spade. 'There's not much around, this time of year.'

We stood quiet for a moment, watching Mrs Benson directing mourners on to the tea.

Then Jake looked at me.

'And what do you suppose you'll do now?' he said. 'I heard some of the ladies saying you'd likely move to London.'

I looked at the earth, mounded just right so that it would settle flat in six months' time.

'Not London,' I said. 'And not forever. But when it turns a little warmer, I'd like to go away for a while.' I looked at him. 'You'll keep things for me, though, won't you, Jake? While I'm gone –' I stopped. 'And you'll be here, when I come back?'

30.

I let the Fossetts go, as soon as the will was read, and have no inclination to replace them – even were servants in ready supply, which Edith reliably informs me they are not, in this changed country. Mrs Fossett had forgiven me, I think, after my diligence through those last days with Richard. But I wished to be alone; well, almost alone. Jake is still here.

These next months, he will make sure the slates stay on the roof and that the garden doesn't turn monstrous.

I have been sorting through Richard's papers, trying to make a bit of space. Now that I have met Davies, I have put Tim's regimental list on the fire. Though I glanced over it, more than once, trying to replace in my mind that man whom Edward had brought to the Grand. Edward had wanted to confirm me in the belief that Tim had killed himself, that it was my fault. My guilt suited his purposes. I have wondered how much he paid the man, have gazed more than once at Sergeant Fred Campbell's name on the list, his date of death, his Dundee address, and wondered what he was really like. I cannot know.

But I know enough, and it is time to begin to try to live with the limits of my knowledge. What Tim truly thought and felt, in his last moments; and little William Tremain, in his. I do not doubt that he feared his grandfather, but I have found myself wondering whether he feared his father, too. Or if not feared, sensed that there was something amiss with Edward. Something wrong. I find myself remembering William, fretfully instructing me on how to keep my hand very flat and very still. Scared of my being bitten, or of his horse choking. Scared of everything.

And then I think of Tremain, the way he would roar and hit and frighten. I wonder about his last moments, about the quarrel, the candle knocked or pushed. I think of Edward, who, like William, had not been born as he became. Who had, no doubt, his own unhappy childhood. Who some might say is not wholly accountable. Yet I hate the thought of his being able to carry on as he ever has, like a swimmer who need not even break stroke.

Richard always said that there are two inquests: the one which takes place in the appointed room, and the one which takes place outside of it, by the mouths and pens of women, passing and piecing what is remembered and inferred. I used to think Richard meant it disparagingly, but I think now he was simply acknowledging the limits of his powers. I think of the people I might write to; of Mrs Sewell, for whom I might do the same favour over again.

Yesterday, Murray wired to Rope Walk, and there was no answer, which I take to be a good sign. And I am bound for my own change of air. In a month I will be sitting on a set of steps carved of butter-yellow stone, the sun showing red through my eyelids, and, perhaps, Edith beside me; she says that John will be perfectly content without her. That she need only be back at the end of June, for the birth of Catherine's child.

My suitcase is by the door, and within one of its compartments is the postcard of Plymouth bridge, ready for stamping or franking when we reach some suitable destination. The message, written carefully by Agnes at my conservatory table, says that IB has written it all down; that a lawyer has the envelope. The last part reads, *If I or my son see you ever again, the lawyer will be told to open it.* It is signed only *A*.

When I visited Agnes, in Plymouth, I felt aggrieved at how she had helped to deceive me. But now I see that she has always been simply trying to survive, and with nothing of her own at her disposal. No husband. Money which might be withdrawn at any time. She never intended to harm me, but Edward drew her into the doing of evil, just as he drew me. Though my case is not like Agnes's. I had Richard, and now I have his money.

Sometimes I think how, if Edward had only left the key in the lock that day, it might have parted me from him. The harm would have been his doing, and only his: there would have been no prospect of saving him from exposure. The powder would have gone up, and I would have been thrown clear. But he took the key with him, and showed it to me; and so I cannot help but weary myself in fathoming what he is guilty of, and which parts fall to me. I must open the door of the stove, and poke at the embers. I must judge.

It does weary me. That there will still and forever be sons and blood and untimely death. There will always be guilt and ghosts, and women forever believing in them, trying to talk to them as women do, and men forever busy adding to their ranks. In a month, I will be fifty, and sometimes I feel indescribably weary, at the thought that there could be a whole third act of life still to come. But then I think of Edith, and sunlight, and butter-yellow stone.

What is more, my sleep these days is dreamless, and when I wake, I wake refreshed, with no compulsion whatever to check beneath the bed. Though there may be ghosts, I am mostly able to believe that they don't come back to wait beneath beds, or to meddle with the three ingredients of gunpowder. The ghost at Polneath, I see now, was Edward's all along. I ought to have seen it at the time. For why would Will – why would Tim – stay behind, to chasten those of us still living? The truth is, we use them to chasten ourselves. As for Polneath, I have resolved, eventually, to give it to the parish, but I cannot quite bring myself to do it, yet. Murray says that children still frighten one another with tales of a yellow ghost, but the ghost has a name now, and its name is William.

I listen to Jake whistling in the garden, and I think of Polneath, waiting there behind that crumbling wall, the brambles advancing and the great dark spaces under the rhododendrons.

The mills. The ruined house.

May it belong equally to the birds and the rabbits and the men who come at night to snare them, until I come back again.

Acknowledgements

This book would never have made it into your hands without the support of many wonderful people. First thanks go to my agent, Nelle Andrew: for everything, always. Huge thanks, too, to the ace team at Rachel Mills Literary.

To Lydia Fried, Helen Garnons-Williams, Vikki Moynes and Ellie Smith in editorial at Viking, and to Chloe Davies, Ella Horne, Ellie Hudson, Poppy North, Georgia Taylor and Federica Trogu in communications: I will never not be amazed by what you accomplished in bringing this book together during a pandemic. My biggest thanks for all your kindness, generosity and skill. Particular thanks to Harriet Bourton, who took this book on fully formed, and steered it into the world with an impossible combination of steadiness and flair. I can't wait to see what we do next.

Thanks, too, to copy editor Shân Morley Jones, and to proofreaders Sarah Coward and Elisabeth Merriman. Your patience and thoroughness are hugely appreciated. A big thank you to Julia Connolly for a gorgeous cover design, and to Rachel Fernández-Arias for a cracking author photograph.

My thanks go next to all at the Centre for New Writing at the University of Manchester: my fellow lecturers, who are hugely supportive of each other's work, and my students, who give my life the blessing of a usefulness beyond writing. Particular thanks, as always, go to John McAuliffe, who gave me the permission to give up on this book, but also made me see that, really, I didn't want to.

Huge thanks to Wyl Menmuir, for welcoming me with wine and conversation during my research trips to Cornwall, and for recommending I visit the old Kennall Vale gunpowder works, upon which my Polneath is based.

Thanks and love to Katy Loftus, who waited a long time for this book, and shaped it in so many ways.

I'm endlessly grateful to Susan Barker and Glen James Brown for helpful plot chats, and to Hester Underdown, Polly Checkland Harding, Abi Hynes and Joey Connolly for reading this book in its various drafts. To Abi, for asking why the fire got started in the first place . . . to Hester, for giving me a yes when I needed a yes . . . to Polly, Joey, and Abi (again), for providing detailed, thought-provoking and fun notes on the last proper draft. If this book has made it to the next level, it's down to you.

Massive thanks to all my friends and family, who are always so excited and kind about my work and help it along in all sorts of ways – with a special mention to my dad, for enthusiastic author accounting services. Big love.

To Chris, to whom this book is dedicated, and who delayed the writing of it by about six months (because who cares about novels, when you've got a new boyfriend?). Thank you for making the home in which I was able to finish this. You're my best and largest piece of luck.

Lastly, to Katy Loftus, who waited a long time for this book, and put so much into it when I was done. For finding the title, and insisting on a proper sex scene. For your insight, your time and your friendship: thank you.

Reading Group Questions

1. Ivy is our narrator and window into the world of *The Key in the Lock*. Do you warm to her? How do you feel about the choices she makes?

2. At the book's opening, Ivy admits that she married Richard even though she wasn't in love with him. Was this a selfish or unselfish act? How does her relationship with Edward compare?

3. This book centres around the mysterious death of a child in a fire. But is this child the fire's only victim?

4. In different ways, Agnes and Ivy are both women hemmed in by their circumstances. What's the main difference between them? What do these characters reveal about life as a woman in this time?

5. *The Key in the Lock*'s setting is as important as the book's plot. What images stayed with you from the book? Were they place specific?

6. Who was your favourite character? Why?

7. What did you feel was the most important theme of the book? Did this stay the same throughout the time you were reading, or did it change?

8. Did you guess how things would turn out? When did you start to guess?

9. The book ends with Ivy coming to a place of peace and acceptance, but what do you think that will practically look like for her? What will her life look like after the final chapter ends?

The page-turning Richard and Judy bestseller

The
WITCH
FINDER'S
SISTER

BETH UNDERDOWN

The number of women my brother Matthew killed, so far as I can reckon it, is one hundred and six..'

When Alice Hopkins' husband dies tragically, she returns to the small Essex town of Manningtree, where her brother Matthew still lives.

But home is no longer a place of safety.

Whispers are spreading – of witchcraft, and the terrible fate awaiting the women accused. And at the heart of it all stands just one man...

To what lengths will Matthew's obsession drive him? And what choice will Alice make, when she finds herself at the very heart of his plan?

AVAILABLE NOW

'A compelling debut from a gifted storyteller' Sarah Perry
'Atmospheric and filled with foreboding' *STYLIST*